Praise for Kathe

"The town of Winsome reminds me of Jan Karon's Mitford, with its endearing characters, complex lives, and surprises where you don't expect them. Reay has penned another poignant tale set in Winsome, Illinois, weaving truth, forgiveness, and beauty into a touching, multilayered, yet totally cozy story. You'll root for these characters and will be sad to leave this charming town."

—Lauren Denton, bestselling author of *The Hideaway* and *Glory Road,* for *Of Literature and Lattes*

"In her ode to small towns and second chances, Katherine Reay writes with affection and insight about the finer things in life—from the perfect cup of coffee and the right book at the right time to enduring friendships, the power of community, and the importance of not giving up on your loved ones or yourself. Reay's fictional town of Winsome, Illinois, lives up to its name and will leave more than a few readers wistfully dreaming of moving there themselves."

—Karen Dukess, author of *The Last Book Party,* for *Of Literature and Lattes*

"Like all of Reay's novels, *Of Literature and Lattes* delivers a story with details so vivid you can feel the fabric slipping between your fingers, characters so rich they could slide into the booth across from you, and a message so hopeful and redemptive it will linger in your mind long after you turn the final page. *Of Literature and Lattes* brings the town of Winsome alive again, and I couldn't wait to return and savor a story of forgiveness, of fresh starts, of literary delights, and of love."

—Melissa Ferguson, author of *The Dating Charade*

"I just love it soooo much."

—Annie Downs, author and host of *That Sounds Fun* podcast, for *The Printed Letter Bookshop*

"Reay understands the heartbeat of a bookstore."

—Baker Book House, for *The Printed Letter Bookshop*

"*The Printed Letter Bookshop* is both a powerful story and a dazzling experience. I want to give this book to every woman I know—I adored falling into Reay's world, words, and bookstore. Powerful, enchanting, and spirited, this novel will delight!"

—Patti Callahan, bestselling author of *Becoming Mrs. Lewis*

"*The Printed Letter Bookshop* is a softly elegant and invitingly intricate ode to books and the power of their communal solace. With the charm and insight of Nina George and the sheer reckless book love of Jenny Colgan, *The Printed Letter Bookshop* enfolds the reader in a welcome literary embrace."

—Rachel McMillan, author of *The London Restoration*

"Dripping with period detail but fundamentally a modern story, *The Austen Escape* is a clever, warmhearted homage to Austen and her fans."

—*Shelf Awareness*

"Reay handles . . . scenes with tenderness and a light touch, allowing the drama to come as much from internal conflict as external, rom-com–type misunderstandings . . . Thoughtful escapism."

—*Kirkus* for *The Austen Escape*

"Both cleverly written and nicely layered, Reay's latest proves to be a charming escape!"

—Denise Hunter, bestselling author of *Sweetbriar Cottage* and *Blue Ridge Sunrise*, for *The Austen Escape*

"As amiable as an Austen novelist could be—but with a pen just as witty—Katherine Reay proves she's ready to become Jane to a whole new generation of women."

—Kristy Cambron, bestselling author of *The Lost Castle* and the Hidden Masterpiece series, for *The Austen Escape*

"Reay's sensually evocative descriptions of Italian food and scenery make this a delight for fans of Frances Mayes's *Under the Tuscan Sun*."

—*Library Journal*, starred review, for *A Portrait of Emily Price*

"*A Portrait of Emily Price* is a portrait of grace and love. Reay is carving her name among the literary greats."

—Rachel Hauck, *New York Times* and *USA TODAY* bestselling author of *The Wedding Dress*

"Katherine Reay is a remarkable author who has created her own subgenre, wrapping classic fiction around contemporary stories. Her writing is flawless and smooth, her storytelling meaningful and poignant. You're going to love *The Brontë Plot*."

—Debbie Macomber, #1 *New York Times* bestselling author

"Book lovers will savor the literary references as well as the story's lessons on choices, friendship, and redemption."

—*Booklist* for *The Brontë Plot*

"Reay treats readers to a banquet of flavors, aromas, and textures that foodies will appreciate, and clever references to literature add nuances sure to delight bibliophiles. The relatable, very real characters, however, are what will keep readers clamoring for more from this talented author."

—*Publishers Weekly*, starred review, for *Lizzy & Jane*

"Katherine Reay's *Dear Mr. Knightley* kept me up until 2:00 a.m.; I simply couldn't put it down."

—Eloisa James, *New York Times* bestselling author of *Once Upon a Tower*

"Book nerds, rejoice! *Dear Mr. Knightley* is a stunning debut—a first-water gem with humor and heart. I can hardly wait to get my hands on the next novel by this gifted new author!"

—Serena Chase, *USA TODAY*'s *Happy Ever After* blog

Of Literature and Lattes

Also by Katherine Reay

Dear Mr. Knightley

Lizzy & Jane

The Brontë Plot

A Portrait of Emily Price

The Austen Escape

The Printed Letter Bookshop

Nonfiction

Awful Beautiful Life,
with Becky Powell

Of Literature and Lattes

Katherine Reay

Thomas Nelson
Since 1798

Of Literature and Lattes

Published in Nashville, Tennessee, by Thomas Nelson. Thomas Nelson is a registered trademark of HarperCollins Christian Publishing, Inc.

Thomas Nelson titles may be purchased in bulk for educational, business, fund-raising, or sales promotional use. For information, please email SpecialMarkets@ThomasNelson.com.

ISBN 978-0-7852-2205-7 (e-book)
ISBN 978-0-7852-2206-4 (audio download)

Library of Congress Cataloging-in-Publication Data

Names: Reay, Katherine, 1970- author.
Title: Of literature and lattes / Katherine Reay.
Description: Nashville, Tennessee : Thomas Nelson, [2020] | Summary: "In the small town of Winsome, Illinois, two people discover the confusing, complex, and beautiful nature of friendship"-- Provided by publisher.
Identifiers: LCCN 2019058097 (print) | LCCN 2019058098 (ebook) | ISBN 9780785222040 (trade paperback) | ISBN 9780785222057 (epub) | ISBN 9780785222064
Subjects: GSAFD: Love stories. | Christian fiction.
Classification: LCC PS3618.E23 O37 2020 (print) | LCC PS3618.E23 (ebook) | DDC 813/.6--dc23
LC record available at https://lccn.loc.gov/2019058097
LC ebook record available at https://lccn.loc.gov/2019058098

Printed in the United States of America

20 21 22 23 24 LSC 10 9 8 7 6 5 4 3 2 1

For the Coffee Man—

Thank you for the lattes.

In every bit of honest writing in the world there is a base theme. Try to understand men, if you understand each other you will be kind to each other. Knowing a man well never leads to hate and nearly always leads to love. There are shorter means, many of them. There is writing promoting social change, writing punishing injustice, writing in celebration of heroism, but always that base theme. Try to understand each other.

—John Steinbeck, journal entry, 1938

It finally happened.

Spring arrived in Winsome, Illinois. It took until the first days in June, but after four consecutive days in which temperatures topped seventy degrees, people grumbled less and smiled more, flowers opened to the sun—and stayed open.

Memories of the winter with its record-breaking lows, unprecedented snow, and ubiquitous clouds dissipated in the warmth, then blew away altogether on a soft east breeze wafting across Lake Michigan. The only price yet to pay was the five snow days that extended the school year deep into the month, making parents scramble to reorganize vacations, camp plans, and dental appointments.

Eve Parker of Olive and Eve Designs stood outside her open shop door and inhaled deeply. She had learned this new type of breathing in her first yoga class three weeks ago and believed she was finally getting the hang of it. She took an eight-count breath to exhale winter, another to combat the day's stress, and one more to endure the store's monthly accounting.

She held that final breath, fearing the monthly books and what they might tell her. Sales had been sluggish all spring, and with the cold not relenting throughout May, the new summer stock hadn't moved. She drew her inhalation deeper yet and catalogued the smells surrounding her: cedar mulch, a slight fish scent off the lake, cinnamon from the Sweet Shoppe . . .

Eve's shop joined ten others to form a horseshoe around Winsome's town square. It was a small plot of land, no more than a good-sized backyard really, with four brick paths dividing it into quarters and meeting in the middle at the town's WWII memorial. Three tiers tall, featuring an unending cascade of water, it was the town's focal point in both geography and spirit.

Today a bird flitted in its lowest basin while two others fought for a worm at its base. Eve lifted her gaze.

"Janet!" She waved across the street to one of the Printed Letter Bookshop's employees.

"Hey, Eve! You're in early."

"May's gone. I've got the end-of-the-month books today."

"Better you than me." Janet Harrison waved again and turned back to face the bookshop's bay windows. She examined them with a proprietary eye before pushing through the front door. A bell chimed, and its clear notes bounced off all the hard surfaces—floor, walls, ceiling, and books—before fading away in the dim light.

Janet heard nothing. Lost in a creative headspace, she grabbed a stack of books, climbed into the bay window—with a confident balance that would have turned Eve green with envy if she'd seen it—and spread them across the small gardening table she'd positioned in the center. She then dropped a set of canvas gardening gloves onto the floor and tilted her head to examine the effect. A satisfied smile played on her lips.

The window's green backdrop provided an opulent base, like a swath of fresh grass, and with the books she'd created a garden utopia. Bright book jackets became flowers spilling from huge earthenware pots. In one corner she stacked the books high and added a trailing vine. Jack's beanstalk never looked better. It invited readers into spring, into a wonderland, and into the shop.

Janet was so focused on her creation she didn't notice David Drummond watching her from across the square. He lifted his hand to wave as she twisted his direction, but lowered it just as fast. He didn't want to intrude. After all, the Bookshop Ladies, as he liked to think of them, were kind enough to let him volunteer any afternoon he wandered in. And he wasn't naive—he knew it helped him more than it helped them. Oftentimes he would recommend a book then not know where to find it, and one of them had to guide both him and the customer. Only last week he'd attempted to shelve stock, and while he had gotten the alphabetical order right, nothing ended up in the right section. Turns out Enneagram numbers had nothing to do with math and everything to do with Emotional Intelligence and Self-Help.

Best not be omnipresent, he told himself as he continued his daily walk, working to loosen what was tight within him. At seventy-six, he thought ruefully, that was just about everything. As he stretched his neck side to side, a periphery motion caught his attention.

"George? What are you doing out so early?" He crossed the street and walked the few steps to the benches circling the fountain. Without another word, he lowered himself next to his friend. Dew from the cool iron seeped into his khaki pants.

"Margery's worn out, but not sleeping real well. I went to fill a new medication for her. Did you know the pharmacy opens at seven? I didn't know anything other than the coffee shop opened so early. But Margery knew . . . I think she wanted me out of the house." He lifted a small white paper bag. Pills rattled within a plastic bottle.

"How is Margery?" David's question carried an affectionate lilt.

He watched George's eyes light up as they both felt the gentle tug of memory to better days.

George shook free first. "She's tired." He kept his focus on the fountain memorial. "We got used to living without them, didn't we? We were too young when our brothers left . . . Didn't know anything else. But this I don't think I'll get used to."

David laid a hand on George's shoulder. "You don't get used to it—and hard as it is, I don't want to."

George nodded and stood. David, holding to the back of the bench for support, did the same. The two men faced each other.

"Coffee before you go? I've missed sparring with you these past couple weeks." David, several inches taller and several pounds thinner, pointed to the coffee shop. "Its grand opening is today."

George nodded and lifted the bag. "Give me a couple hours. I want to get home to Margery, for these, and she's usually best in the early mornings."

"I'll meet you here at nine."

David watched his friend go. He should have mentioned the fountain—how it had been good of George, when he was mayor, to install that heater years ago. He should have reminded his friend that he wasn't alone—that joyful bubbling, in a fountain and in a life, can still happen, even amid the harshest winters.

"Mr. Drummond?"

Jill Pennet stood in the doorway of the Sweet Shoppe, leaning on her broom. "Come try a new recipe."

David patted his flat stomach and shook his head.

Jill laughed and whisked his refusal away with a single swipe of her hand. "You are not watching your weight. Come on in."

David stepped inside the shop and grinned. Dew, sunshine, and a breeze off the lake were good, but nothing beat cinnamon, sugar, and the warm yeast smell of rising bread. Betty had baked every Saturday morning of their fifty-year marriage. Yes, some memories you held tight even if they carried a little sting.

"How's your mother doing?"

Jill's expression clouded. "She's okay. Good days and bad days. It's hardest when she doesn't recognize me—I keep thinking of my own kids. To be honest, it scares me. It scares her too."

David waited. Jill's lips stayed parted an inch as if there was more to say.

But she seemed to blink the thought away, so he stepped into the silence. "I understand that, and I'm sorry . . . She and Margery Williams were on the prom court together back in high school. George just said Margery is struggling too."

"I heard that."

David smiled and changed the topic. "What's that wonderful smell?"

"Try it." Jill handed him a slice of coffee cake resting on parchment paper. It was still warm to the touch. "I'm using a different cinnamon, and I've added almond extract to the batter. Also rosemary. Tell me if it's too much . . . I'm trying out some new ideas."

"Does the new coffee shop have you nervous?"

Jill looked past him out the window. "The Daily Brew didn't compete too much with us, but I don't know what baked goods Andante plans to sell. And the Sweet Shoppe could use something new, don't you think? Mom held on to some of our recipes since I was born."

"Good baking is timeless."

Jill shrugged. "But I need to make something new, do something different. You don't grow any other way, do you? You don't stay sharp. I mean, things change whether we want them to or not."

David nodded. He heard fear in her voice and couldn't blame her. Losing her mother bit by bit, memory by memory, was a terrifying thing. Losing your sense of home was hard too.

Jill cast her gaze back out the window toward Andante. "I should've gone over to introduce myself during those couple months before he closed for renovations, but"—she shook her head—"it was a rough spring." Her eyes filled.

"Jill?"

She snuffled. "Don't worry about me, Mr. Drummond. I'm just tired today."

"You could probably start calling me David, don't you think?"

She laughed. "Wouldn't that horrify Mom? No . . . I don't think I could get used to that."

"I understand. I hope you get some rest soon." He raised the square of coffee cake in thanks and turned to walk out the door.

David took a few steps down the sidewalk, then stopped and stared at the new coffee shop across the square. It felt strange not seeing the old hand-printed Daily Brew sign with its red poppy border mounted above the door. It had hung there since 1977, the very summer he and Betty moved to Winsome.

He chuckled softly. The only stable thing in life is change, he thought, and no, you don't get used to it.

Chapter 1

"You're free to move; we can run your interview out of the Chicago office. We'll be in touch."

Alyssa threw another Tums in her mouth and cracked down on chalky grape. She played the message again, for the fourteenth time in three days, and while the words gave her no new hope, this time she focused on tone. Was there a lightness in Special Agent Denek's voice? Did he sound relaxed? Optimistic?

Once determined to make the call, unable to avoid it for another day, Alyssa had rehearsed what to say countless times, written out two different conversational scenarios, and hadn't drawn a real breath during her fifty-eight-second message—and power-chewed six Tums afterward.

Denek's reply had taken seven seconds.

Alyssa scanned her apartment. Three years. In a whirlwind, she'd moved from Chicago to Palo Alto, started a new job, signed a lease with a new colleague, and moved into this now-empty space. Well, the space downstairs. This one they moved into only eight months before on the promise of a huge raise—a raise that never came. Yet despite that, she and Meera thought they had arrived—even while working fifteen-hour days more often than not.

After all, they had two bedrooms with a living room and a small balcony in a three-story walk-up just blocks off Stanford's campus. They stood in line at chic coffeehouses bumping shoulders with Nobel Laureates and Silicon Valley legends, not to mention the up-and-comers—who could be anybody from the slick Euro-dressed woman in the pencil skirt or the jean-clad skateboarder who hung his board off his forearm as he ordered an oregano-infused Ethiopian pour-over. They paid twenty dollars for an arugula salad with beets and goat cheese and convinced themselves they weren't still hungry.

And they'd held their heads high too. She and Meera knew they were mere worker bees, but they worked for "the" company—the newest and, some said, the greatest of the unicorns. The one that was not only going to make the Uber and Twitter IPOs look like chump change, but the one that saved lives, whole generations, from the chronic illness epidemic that was "engulfing the modern world."

Now there was nothing left.

Like many Vita XGC employees, Meera made the call to the special agent in charge of her division months ago and moved back to New Jersey as fast as she could load the U-Haul. She had taken most of her furniture with her—including their bulletin board with Alyssa's spare car keys hanging from a peg.

For six months Alyssa had been left with only her bedroom furniture, a few plates, an armchair, and the unrealistic hope that the scandal would soon blow over. The furniture she'd sold that morning. The plates she packed into the last box that rested on her counter. And her hope, along with the last of her savings, had fizzled out at new job interview number seventeen.

Sliding the box onto her hip, she grabbed her keys and headed down the tiled stairs. The building felt empty. It *was* empty. Everyone else was at work.

She scrawled her manager a short thank-you note. He had let her out of the lease four months early. It was a gift she hadn't expected and one she desperately needed.

The parking lot was empty too. There was no one to see her off or say good-bye—of her friends from Vita XGC, there was no one left. Period.

Three years in California, and the end of the dream came with a seven-second message from an FBI agent and her key plinking to the bottom of a metal drop box.

When federal agents had escorted every Vita XGC employee from the six-story, state-of-the-art, glass glory of an office building six months ago, just days before Christmas, most thought it was a joke. There was even some jostling in the parking lot that led to handcuffs and stern words. But as the sun set that afternoon, the mood changed. The manic chase for fun that had dominated company events outside the office twisted into the competitive paranoia that had reigned within. Sunset started with whispers, speculation, and glares. Darkness descended in silence with the FBI releasing anxious employees by department late into the night.

Though unstated, Alyssa assumed a "Don't leave town" was implied that night. After all, they'd shut the doors, taken away the CEO, and set up interviews for the executives, who lawyered up right on the spot. And the rest of them followed suit, hiring lawyers within the next two days. Yet to Alyssa's surprise, her lawyer, a young gunner at Perkins and Coie costing $250 an hour, told her that within those two days a lot of XGC employees fled town.

"As long as the FBI knows where to find you, it shouldn't be a problem. You need work, and in a post-Theranos Silicon Valley, no company will want the liability of an XGC hire."

Alyssa dismissed his counsel that day, certain he was wrong. She *needed* him to be wrong—going home wasn't an option. But after sending forty resumes across the country with no reply, and sitting through seventeen failed interviews locally, home was now her only option.

As she shoved the box into her car, her mind cast back to her last-ditch effort, only days before, to remain in Palo Alto.

Interview seventeen began like all the others . . .

"You have an impressive resume. Other than the hiccup at Vita XGC." The older woman's voice arced as she peered over her bright red readers.

Alyssa knew it was a question. She knew what the woman was after. It was the story everyone wanted and, Alyssa suspected, the only reason she'd been granted her seventeen interviews in the first place. She sat silent. She had quit trying to profess ignorance to XGC's perfidy at interview six and her innocence halfway through interview nine.

The woman tried a fresh tack. She offered a smile that only curled up on one edge as she leaned forward, inviting Alyssa into her confidence. "What do the letters stand for, anyway? XGC. I've always wondered."

That was a question Alyssa could answer. "The X was for next gen and GC are Tag's initials. His real name is Gabriel. Vita, vital good health, next gen Gabriel Connelly."

"You've got to be kidding me." The woman guffawed. "The great Tag, the great humanitarian, Architect of Predictive Medicine, Preserver of the People, named his company after himself. Called himself next gen and vital. That should have told us all something."

Alyssa clamped her mouth shut, embarrassed she hadn't peeled back more of the subtext on that one herself. Three years ago, when she had been flown out to Palo Alto and housed at the Four Seasons Hotel by that very Tag, she'd bought his whole story.

My mom died early of Korsakoff syndrome, a form of dementia, and that shouldn't happen. We can know what's in our genes, and that means what might be in our futures. But now we can and will make our futures better. I will never stop loving my mom or feeling fury at her loss, and I will give everything I have to stop this epidemic of chronic disease and illness from engulfing generations.

He had spun heartwarming stories of reading, fishing, building forts, and hiking with this gorgeous, almost mythical-sounding mother. By the end Alyssa had wanted to trade her mom for his, despite her early death.

And that's what bothered Alyssa the most. She hadn't done her due diligence—fleeing Chicago and joining Vita XGC had been a hasty and emotional decision.

Homes and moms were very emotional topics.

The woman finally stopped chortling and scrolled across her tablet to resume the interview. "Let's track back through your experience. You left 'XGC'"—she made air quotes with her free hand—"in December last year."

"Yes." Alyssa didn't add that everyone left XGC that day, under federal escort.

"Describe your responsibilities there."

"I worked on a team of eight that built the company's predictive algorithms."

"You managed the data?"

"No. We worked with scrubbed data. All departments worked that way because the amount of information made the data incredibly powerful. They were very protective about that."

"Sure they were," the woman scoffed. "So basically, you were responsible for all those people thinking they were headed to Alzheimer's, lupus, MS, diabetes, or whatever else was going to kill them. Tomorrow. How convenient—can't get sued for something that *might* happen."

That sentence wasn't a question, but the woman's sneer demanded an answer.

"So it seems." Alyssa tried to bank her bitterness, which had crept in at interview number ten. While she knew it was off-putting and unlikely to land her a job, she found that her anger—at the company, at the lies, even at herself—kept her from crying, which was how she'd answered that line of questioning during interviews one, two, and three. Because it always came up.

During interview number four, she'd tried for honesty . . .

"Everything that happened is being unraveled, and it was horrible. But I do think my team's algorithms worked. Through three testing rounds we matched perfectly the reconstructed data sets . . . I don't know what went wrong, and if our work unwittingly harmed someone, my hope is they can be notified. Some customers . . . I can't imagine their questions and concerns. It was big stuff we were looking toward, but it was always years ahead. People can be notified, and the worry can stop. It was all predictive, not diagnostic—"

"Stop!" the interviewer had shot back. "Stop justifying yourself. No one had anything! You were playing God, for profit, and you have no idea what that lie could do to someone, to whole families." He escorted her out of his office within thirty seconds, and she stood throwing up in the parking lot within sixty.

The underlying questions in each interview had boiled down to a caustic mix of *How could you be so stupid?* and *Are you really that greedy and cruel?* One interviewer actually used those words, and Alyssa couldn't blame him. They were the million-dollar questions. Or in XGC's case—the 1.2-billion-dollar questions. Everyone in Silicon Valley wanted the answers, as did the federal agents working the case. And those questions were the reason why Alyssa, and everyone else involved, remained the subject of multiple investigations, gossip, and speculation—and unhirable until answers were found.

The questions haunted Alyssa in her quieter moments as well. She tossed and turned most nights, stomach on fire with the ulcers that simmered during her final months at XGC and flamed higher during the last six unemployed.

Looking back, she could see last fall more clearly now. Tag had taken XGC's frenzy to a whole new level.

Always cavalier and charismatic, he showed signs of cracking. At the time she believed him—it was because they were close. Now she knew the truth . . .

We are at the end. All our hard work is paying off, and testing shows that we did it. We have rolled out results from our first live test. That's thirty thousand clients, and another boy won't lose his mom to dementia because she'll know in her teens how to stay healthy. A young girl, knowing MS is thirty years down the road, will take proper care of her health and happily hold her grandchildren someday. But we've got to push harder. The establishment doesn't want to put healthcare and vitality in the hands of the everyday common person, so we've got to get out there before it can stop us. This is all hands on deck. We're fighting for the future.

Even now, remembering that day, Alyssa felt the flush of energy that had filled her that afternoon. It was consuming and invigorating to be pursuing something pure and true and honest. And, from Alyssa's perspective, it was the first true and honest thing she had known. The light after her own lie.

Then it all came crashing down.

That's wrong, Alyssa reminded herself in the still darkness every night and now as she slammed the back door of her blue CRV. It never existed in the first place. In fact, if the rumors proved true, the only real business that had occurred at XGC came from Tag selling their data to pharmaceutical companies overseas.

Alyssa dropped into the driver's seat. It was hot enough to instantly stick her T-shirt to her back and melt the tension in her shoulders. She closed her eyes in the warm quiet—until her thoughts crowded in again.

She tapped a button on her navigation system to head to the last place on earth she wanted to go, and the only option she had left.

2,175 miles away . . . Winsome, Illinois.

Home.

Chapter 2

"What does Andante even mean?"

Jeremy blinked. Those were not words he expected to hear at his grand opening.

The older man looked around the store, his face pursed as if Jeremy's beans had burned or pulled sour and were stinking up the place. "What was wrong with the Daily Brew? I liked it just fine. What have they done to the place? It doesn't feel like home anymore."

Jeremy looked around the coffee shop, frantic to find something good to counteract the clench in his chest. He'd studied, dreamed, and planned for this moment for twenty years. Five minutes ago he'd been fired up, still nervous enough to throw up in the tiny back bathroom, but satisfied with the remodel and confident in his decision to move across the country to Winsome and open it. He then thought about all that came with both the shop and the move. He now lived near his daughter. She knew his name and his face. She called him "Daddy." He had an apartment she could stay in, one with two bedrooms and a view of Winsome's Centennial Park. No . . . no way could he have afforded any of this in Seattle. This was the life and the home he wanted and there was no room for regret, doubt, or naysayers. It worked. It all worked. Yet even as he cycled through all the good to reassure himself, he watched the man move through the line, eager for confirmation.

When Jeremy had unlocked the coffee shop's alley door at four o'clock that morning, it was because he was too excited to stay in that apartment-with-a-view a single minute longer. 4:02 found him reorganizing the baked goods he and his assistant, Ryan, had made into the wee hours of the morning, whipping up batch after batch of blueberry muffins—hoping no one would suspect they came from a mix. At 5:15 he was rubbing a final coat of oil into the wood counters and every table in the seating area until they felt like velvet. He had then flipped on the lights at 6:25 and stood marveling at his own shop for a full five minutes before he twisted the front door's deadbolt at precisely 6:30 and flipped the custom-painted sign. *Open for Business.*

Now Jeremy's gaze trailed the old man's movements as he turned his head this way and that, taking in every detail. He wondered what the man saw and how it could possibly displease him. It was a little coffee shop bathed in the warm light of vintage bulbs. It featured thick unfinished wood tables with every chair tucked perfectly beneath. It boasted exposed brick walls interlaced with plastered sections just waiting to display good art. And the showpiece—a glass-encased gas fireplace—sat situated between two buttery leather armchairs. How could anyone not love this place?

Jeremy looked to each customer standing in line for approval. No one held that look of awe-tipped admiration he'd anticipated. In fact, in the few hours since he'd opened, he noticed more than a few people looking sour, questioning, and discontent. And far fewer customers than expected had wandered through the doors.

In the two months after he bought the place, right before he closed it for renovations, he'd experienced a greater draw than this. The previous owner certainly had. He'd checked her numbers again and again, and once he took over, his observations and daily take mirrored her reports. Eighty percent of the day's revenue came in from 6:30 to 10:00 a.m., caffeinating the commuter crowd on their way to the train station across the street. And that 80 percent alone brought in enough revenue to keep the shop healthy and vibrant. That's how he knew he had a little leverage for the renovations. The math was in his favor—especially as he planned to bolster the numbers a little later in the day by drawing people back to sip his organic single-origin loose teas and munch on a shortbread cookie with their friends in the afternoon.

He looked at his watch: 9:00 a.m. Where was the commuter crowd this morning? He quickly walked the L from the side counter to the back one and the register, next to Ryan, as the older man and his friend shuffled forward to order.

Jeremy felt his smile waver before he set it fully. "*Andante* is a musical term. It means 'a walking pace.' I wanted to convey that the coffee shop is a part of life as you walk through your day."

"Didn't a shop named the Daily Brew imply the same thing? And besides, where are we supposed to sit? I sat in the corner of my couch for over thirty years, right by that window. You don't even have a couch anymore." The man pointed a gnarled finger, the middle one—perhaps only because his pointer didn't straighten?—toward the corner featuring the fireplace and two armchairs. He gasped. "The pillows . . . What have you done with our pillows?"

The man's friend put a steadying hand on his forearm. "George."

George didn't shrug from the touch or snap back. Instead he gave an almost imperceptible sigh and looked up to the chalk menu board.

Jeremy tapped Ryan's shoulder to bring his attention to their conversation. "While Ryan takes your order, let me go save the two armchairs by the fire for you. I'll put magazines in them so you'll know."

George's friend nodded thanks. George stared straight ahead.

The Daily Brew. Jeremy chewed on the name and the comment as he crossed the room. He had never considered the name in that light, or given it any thought at all. He'd only seen what the space could become, not what it was . . .

What it was was a mess, he reminded himself. It was, to use an expression favored by one foster mom, "used hard and hung up wet." It was a worn linoleum floor, mismatched chairs, antique espresso machines that produced one good shot in three, and over a hundred shabby pillows strewn over every horizontal surface. And the smell—a mixture of lard, dust, burnt coffee, and Pledge.

Jeremy grabbed two of his precisely positioned cutting-edge magazines, *Cereal* and *Mood*, and dropped them into the chairs. Even these early days of June held a morning chill. He turned the knob on the fire to raise the blue flames another inch.

Without willing it, his gaze then landed on Ryan, who stood pulling shots from the temperamental espresso machines. He had been the one to voice caution. "Let's get to know the town first, settle in. We should renovate after we understand the feel of it all and build up more capital."

It was the *we* that had chafed from the get-go. Ryan wasn't a part owner, he was an employee. Ryan hadn't imagined this shop or the ideal life that came with the dream since he was fifteen years old. Heck, Ryan had spent from fifteen to twenty-five in a drug-induced haze and was only just clear of that. Sure, he'd moved to Winsome from Seattle to help Jeremy out, but he'd needed a new start just as much as Jeremy had needed the help.

Jeremy checked himself. Stress was making him unfair, ungenerous, and just plain wrong. When Ryan had walked through the doors of Seattle Roasters two years ago, days after his release from a six-month residential program, he'd laid out his full story with hesitancy, yes, but with courage and honesty too. At that moment, sealed with a firm handshake across a counter, Jeremy had sensed that the younger man had character and would keep his word. Not only that, he'd given up a lot to follow Jeremy across the country.

But no one likes to be wrong . . .

Jeremy thought back to the day they'd both walked into the shop for the first time. He'd already agreed to the sale, but had not actually seen it or his new hometown. His eyes widened when he saw Winsome. He hadn't expected the town, sitting just north of Chicago, to feel so small, even insular. As for the shop, his jaw dropped. He hated every threadbare inch of it. It was everything he wanted to leave behind, and nothing he ever wanted to come home to.

Ryan, however, had walked into the Daily Brew, dropped onto that same brown couch George mentioned and grieved, bounced on its squeaky springs, and declared, "This is it, man. It's perfect."

It chafed that his assistant might have been right after all, had known something instinctively that Jeremy failed to recognize.

"Jeremy?"

He shook himself into the present. Janet Harrison, one of the women from the bookshop three stores down, had materialized in front of him. "Sorry. I was just thinking."

"I called your name twice." She laughed. "You were daydreaming." She shifted her gaze from him to the fireplace, then across the walls and back to the counter. "Stay awake today. This is really something."

Jeremy pressed his lips together to savor her compliment and the note of wonder in her voice. That's it, he thought. "It is, isn't it? It cost a lot, but don't you think it'll be a hit?" He pressed his lips tight again, this time to keep himself from saying more. He hoped she hadn't heard that last lift of eagerness, that plea for approval, in his voice. He cleared his throat, dropping his voice at least five notes. "I mean, all the elements are in place."

"I feel like I'm in Streeterville or Bucktown, someplace far more hip than Winsome."

"The coffee is as good too." Jeremy glanced to the counter and landed on the two ancient machines. "Or it soon will be. I've got a replacement for those two on the way. But even until then, you won't find a better cup."

"I should go try it out then. Congratulations."

He stepped in front of her. "Janet . . . can you tell me who the older man in the blue windbreaker is? The one waiting at the side counter?"

Janet leaned around him and narrowed her eyes to focus. "George Williams? You haven't met him? You'll love him. He's got like six kids, some still live in town, and he used to be mayor back in the eighties. He's standing with David Drummond, who helps us out at the bookshop." She tugged at his elbow. "Come meet them both."

Jeremy lifted a hand. "Not right now. Let me get your coffees. The usuals?"

"You remember?"

"We weren't closed that long. Three lattes. One coconut milk, one almond, and one regular."

"Please." Janet smiled.

Jeremy circled the counter and moved to the second espresso machine. From the corner of his eye he watched George and David collect their drinks, vacillate a minute, then head to the two chairs. He sighed, sure that given another second they'd have left Andante—for good.

Ryan turned from the machine next to him and offered a cappuccino to a waiting customer.

Even with so few customers, he needed more help. The old machines took too long, and customers stood unattended. He needed to hire someone else . . . He had to check the tables . . . He hadn't thought about the need to constantly wipe them down, clear them during the morning rush . . . And what about—

Jeremy pulled the basket from the grinder and felt his breath synchronize with his actions. The cacophony within his mind calmed. This was what worked. No matter where, when, or what was imploding in or around his life, he understood this movement and this rhythm—the science, and the art, behind a perfect shot. The rest would work itself out.

He counted the seconds as the shot pulled. Too few. He huffed. The beans were fresh, the tamp felt firm but not tight, yet the machine pulled forty-four grams in twenty-five seconds. While some baristas believed in a one gram to one second ratio, Jeremy was a devotee of forty grams to twenty-five seconds. It produced, in his mind, an optimally balanced shot. A slow pull goes bitter. A fast one sours. Most palates couldn't taste a four-gram deviation from ideal, but Jeremy refused to serve it. He sank the shot, tapping it out into the knock box, and began again.

Three drinks in hand, Jeremy circled the counter to find Janet. "Sorry. Perfection took a little time this morning."

"No worries." Janet stood scrolling through pictures on her phone. "Look how cute she is." She tilted the phone to Jeremy and sped through well over twenty pictures of her granddaughter dressed in varying shades of pink.

"Krista used to do that too—dress our daughter in so much

pink she looked more like a puff of cotton candy than a kid. She basically grew up, in pink, on Instagram."

"This one will too. My daughter-in-law set up a dedicated account for Rosie." She pressed the phone to her chest. "She's pretty perfect, isn't she?"

Jeremy banked his chuckle too late. "Absolutely."

Janet snatched the carrying tray of coffees from him, laughing at herself now. "I'm fully aware I've become a total cliché."

"You could pick worse clichés."

"So true." Janet rolled her eyes. "Doting grandmother is an upgrade from bitter divorcée."

"Always."

Janet left with a wave and Jeremy followed her departure with a lingering smile. He'd heard rumors about her. Something about that bitter divorcée she spoke of and a wicked temper to go with it, though he'd never witnessed it. From what he'd also heard, he had arrived a month too late and might not ever meet that Janet. Something had happened in February to turn the lion to a lamb.

All Jeremy could say for certain was that from day one she'd supported his shop and welcomed him to Winsome. And today she'd given him his first congratulations and had been the only person to show genuine enthusiasm for Andante.

Turning back into the store, he noted the line had grown a few customers longer. It wasn't the grand party he had expected, but it wasn't nothing. And a steady stream of customers kept filing in. Some clearly pleased. Some discomfited. But customers nonetheless.

He glanced around the shop and considered every aspect of his venture. This could work. He knew coffee, he knew what he wanted, and he knew the way forward.

It would just take a little time.

Chapter 3

"This card's been refused. Do you have another?"

Alyssa thought the pump's screen read *See Attendant* because *it* was faulty—not because she was. Her eyes stung and she blinked, unsure if it was actually tears or exhaustion. She suspected exhaustion, as Wyoming and Nebraska had absorbed all the tears.

She dug in her wallet and flipped past her Saks Fifth Avenue card, a priority black card for Marriott, and her platinum XGC American Express. A derisive chuckle escaped. No need, or money, for any of those anymore. She pulled out an old Capital One Visa—the first card she got when she left home for college.

Back to the beginning. Thirteen years later.

"Try this one."

The gas attendant swiped it. "Forty on pump three?"

Alyssa shook her head. "Better make it twenty."

He raised a brow but didn't comment, only offering a "Have a nice day" as he passed back the card.

She nodded and turned away, sure the tears were about to start. Again.

After filling the tank with twenty dollars, Alyssa dropped into her car and tossed her purse onto the passenger seat. The police report crinkled under the pressure.

It was hour forty and she was wrecked.

Hour one had been consumed with recriminations. How did I not see? Was I stupid? Gullible? Greedy?

She had asked herself the same questions every interviewer either asked or implied and, in doing so over six months, could admit to a few answers. She recognized that, at the start, she'd been running *from* something rather than running toward—and hadn't asked nearly enough questions or done a fraction of the due diligence she should have. She groaned at how cliché that answer sounded. Blame someone else. But she knew exactly who, and that was another problem.

There was no way to avoid her mom in Winsome.

That thought naturally stretched into hour three with a trip down Memory Lane to her last real day at home. Three years ago she drove up from Chicago to shove some boxes into her childhood closet on her way out of town. Her mom had just taken a job at the local bookshop and shouldn't have been home.

But she was.

"Why are you moving? You always said you wanted to live here. Get married and move back from the city. That was the plan. It was perfect."

Perfect. Oh, how that word had crawled up her spine that day, reached around her throat and almost choked her. It was the first time Alyssa understood the term *silent rage*. She had actually been so angry, and without air for a few heartbeats, that neither a breath nor a sound could escape.

Yet her mom was right. That had always been the plan, and it had been perfect. After all, it was her mom's plan—which meant it was flawless. Zero chance of failure. Her mom's plans never failed, and this one she'd modeled so well.

That was the lie Alyssa had believed.

She had swallowed the Kool-Aid like everyone else: her parents were the ideal life partners, never disagreeing on even minor details, much less wasting time fighting about them. They experienced wedded bliss to the enviable degree that after almost thirty years they still called each other "darling" and "my bride." Their home was perfect; their cars clean; their yard perfectly manicured; her mom's garden varied and impeccable, maintained by herself, of course. But don't worry—despite volunteering around town daily, she would still have dinner on the table on time and at the ideal temperature.

In her impotent anger that afternoon, Alyssa had shoved a box into her closet with such force she'd pulled off an edge of the doorjamb. The rip in the wood tore something within her as well. It brought a sense of release with a wellspring of vitriol.

"Your warped idea of a perfect life doesn't fly with me anymore. You made it look good, I'll give you that, but the emperor hasn't got clothes. Right, Mom? Or should I say *she* took them all off?"

It was a low blow, and even as the words flew from her mouth, Alyssa was surprised at her own courage . . . insolence . . . despair.

The words and the icy blast that carried them clearly shocked her mom. Always one with a firm grip on her demeanor, if not every attitude behind it, her mom, wan and red-eyed, sank onto the corner of Alyssa's bed. "That's not fair. If your dad and I divorce, I'm not the villain. You always believe he can do no wrong, but—"

"Don't even talk about him." Alyssa shoved in the last box before turning on her mom. "I'm done with you. You. Cheated. On. Him. Of course he's going to divorce you, and please consider this a family affair—only I don't have to wait for a judge. I can leave you right now."

"Alyssa." Her mom's bark had morphed into a squeak as Alyssa stormed down the stairs and out the back door.

Revisiting those last moments at home made her stomach turn, so at hour five, Alyssa shifted her memory to the day when the FBI cleared XGC's offices and shut it down. How, once people realized it wasn't a joke, they became scared and wary of each other. After leaving Chicago, Alyssa had wanted family, a connection that felt like home had once upon a time, but one that wasn't based on a lie, one she formed herself. You don't have to be born into a family, she told herself during that initial thirty-six-hour drive, you can create one. And she'd chased it—she'd envisioned a better, truer life, and everyone at work seemed wired the same way.

Yet the illusion didn't withstand a few months at XGC. People she hoped could become close friends became strangers within her first six months, enemies in the last six, and vanished altogether once the company folded. In fact, the first advice her lawyer gave her was "Trust no one."

Hours six, seven, and eight recounted each and every moment of the seventeen failed interviews, including the one time Alyssa had essentially begged for an entry-level number-crunching job. *I'm overqualified for this. You won't have any problems with me, and even though I can't answer these questions, I'm honest and I'll be out of all this someday, and I'm smarter now. You won't find a more dedicated employee.* She'd stopped just short of tears that time, and far from getting hired.

Hour ten questioned the Pulse and how many times the same song could be played within a one-hour period. Hour eleven questioned why she hadn't canceled her Sirius XM account and how much money that might have saved.

Hour thirteen was spent listening to a podcast on best interview practices, which proved singularly unhelpful. Didn't everyone know to look an interviewer in the eye and offer a firm handshake? What about if you're involved in the Scandal of the Century? The one that some pundits quipped made Elizabeth Holmes and Theranos look like amateur hour . . .

Hours sixteen through twenty-three were spent crashed on a lumpy mattress in a Motel Six in Rawlins, Wyoming.

Hours twenty-four through twenty-seven were spent filling out a police report and staring into her empty car.

"You didn't unpack your car, ma'am?" was the officer's first question. "There's no sign of forced entry; did you even lock it?" was his last.

That was when the tears started.

Hour thirty-two was spent in a full-on self-lecture—out loud. "Everyone takes some time off during the summer. This is a summer break. By fall you'll be cleared, back on your feet, back in Silicon Valley if you want, and back to work. You can do anything and go anywhere. You're okay. This will not defeat you. Do not let this defeat you."

Several hours after that were spent pondering the inconsistency between Subway salads as Alyssa found herself unable to focus on anything else.

And after another few hours of fitful sleep at a Comfort Inn, hour fifty found Alyssa, wilted in defeat, at a stop sign and a bed of daffodils at the edge of Winsome.

She stopped at the intersection and pondered the conundrum that was Winsome. None of the affluent suburbs stacked upon Chicago's North Shore had stopped the city's traffic, busyness, and development from creeping through them on the city's ever-outward expansion. But little Winsome—not affluent or optimally situated—had. It sat just out of reach of those nineteenth-century carriages carrying summer residents to their holiday homes and remained a little too far north for twenty-first-century commuter comfort now.

In high school they all called it "Lose-some," but today her heart lifted at the sight of the stop sign at North and Westover. She felt hungry for Winsome's stability and familiarity. Nothing ever changed in Winsome. Not the stores. Not the traditions. Not the people.

She could find her footing here. She could live with her dad at his apartment, get a job, perhaps waiting tables at her best friend's restaurant, and build up a cushion while looking for work. She shook her head, wondering why she'd waited so long to come home. It was perfect—an unchanging, welcoming, soft landing spot.

The plot of grass surrounding the fountain, still flowing strong, looked lush and green. To the left, the Printed Letter Bookshop, J. Barlow Antiques, Winsome Bank, Olive and Eve Designs. Even Jameson Sports, where every high school team purchased their gear at a 15 percent discount, stood in its usual place.

Then an incongruence caught her attention. She pressed a fist to her stomach. The Daily Brew's hand-painted sign with its red poppy border had been replaced with burnished wood and black lettering. Andante.

Alyssa slowed and found a parking spot. She got out, stretched, and glanced toward the bookshop. Her mom still worked there, and Alyssa wasn't ready to see her. But coffee? That she needed.

She pushed open the glass door and stalled. The interior knocked her off balance. Gone was the kitschy, comfortable world of the Daily Brew. The sights, smells, sounds, and even the tastes of honey and walnuts from Mrs. Pavlis's baklava that filled the air and enveloped you upon entering had been scrubbed away by orange-scented cleaning oil. She wondered how Winsome was handling a coffee shop that rivaled any in San Francisco—and one without a pillow in sight. She wondered how she would handle it.

She let her eyes trail from the scored cement floor to the exposed beam ceiling and back again, hovering midway. Gone were the family photos and the big bulletin board where Mrs. Pavlis pinned Polaroids of customers. When the shop was packed and no one waited at the counter, she would weave her way through the tables, camera in hand. Customers clustered and grinned, then pored over themselves, laughing, as they stood in line ordering their coffees the next day.

Now the walls stood bare, except for a series of several small portraits near the front plate-glass window. Their broad strokes and abstract design gave just enough definition to hint at character and physicality, but not identity. They reminded Alyssa of Picasso's Cubism works and her favorite class in college.

She tilted her head, staring at one with the sense that if she gazed hard enough, long enough, she'd recognize the subject.

"May I help you?"

Alyssa startled to find herself at the front of the line. "A medium drip coffee, please."

She tipped her head back, noting how odd the motion felt. At five eleven, she rarely needed a full head tilt to see eye to eye with anyone.

"I've got the San Roque from Colombia or the Yirgz from Ethiopia. Which would you like?" The man's voice was all eager friendliness, which somehow pulled Alyssa's already frayed nerves.

"Your house favorite."

While a valid question in San Francisco or Palo Alto, where coffee was bathed in unicorn tears and roasted on coals from Pompeii, it didn't fit in Winsome. Alyssa let her tone tell him that.

"The house doesn't have a favorite." The man batted the tone back with a stiff smile. "Do you prefer clementines and cherry cola or lemon zest and vanilla?"

"You're teasing." Alyssa floated a quick smile to smooth his ruffled feathers.

He didn't accept her smile, and his disappeared. "Not today."

"Lemon zest."

"Yirgz it is. Grab a seat and I'll bring it over."

"To go, please."

Alyssa slid her card in the reader resting in front of her, then perched against the side counter to wait. There was now a fireplace! Although part of her wanted to scoff, she had to admit, even in June, the effect was appealing. It almost made her want to run three stores down and buy a book to curl up with. Almost.

The man set her coffee on the high wood counter next to her.

"This is nothing like what I remember."

"I bought it a few months back, closed it for renovations, and reopened two days ago." He lifted his gaze across the shop. "The style is a little different, but I hope it still feels welcoming."

Alyssa noted how his voice lifted. Everything in her that chafed before melted in empathy. Not sympathy, as if she understood or pitied him, but true empathy—she identified with him. To try to make a home in the world, a spot that's truly yours, yet still yearn for approval and acceptance, was tough stuff.

Yet his home had changed hers—and left her unsettled.

"It's Winsome. You hardly needed to go to this much effort. You could pour swill and this town would come running, because there aren't other options."

He studied her, eyes widening.

"No, I mean . . . I grew up here, and this place was always packed, despite the fact that Mrs. Pavlis's coffee wasn't— Never mind." She glanced around. Andante was decidedly not packed. "It may just take time."

Embarrassed to linger longer, she grabbed her cup and fled the shop. She'd been rude—beyond rude. But she'd been surprised too. Sure, there were a few obstacles to a summer of relaxed bliss—no money, no job, and who knew what her dad would say when she landed on his doorstep? But even with all that, she had convinced herself she could make it. She could find sanctuary here.

But something about Andante had undone her carefully fabricated lie.

Chapter 4

Dropping back into her car, Alyssa watched customers come and go at the Printed Letter Bookshop. Her dad had taken her and her brother, Chase, there almost every Saturday when they were young to buy a book from Mrs. Carter, the owner.

Charlotte's Web. The Lion, the Witch and the Wardrobe. Charlie and the Chocolate Factory. Pippi Longstocking. The Phantom Tollbooth . . . She grinned, remembering them all, especially *The Phantom Tollbooth* and Milo. The literature of math, she thought with a sigh as she started her car.

At North and Chestnut she turned west, away from town and away from the lake. A Pilates studio still stood next to Winsome Realty, and a new yoga place resided two storefronts away, beside the hardware store. After another right turn at the Presbyterian Church and a row of Craftsman-style houses, Alyssa pulled into the parking lot of a large redbrick apartment building.

There was no buzzer, no lock, just two quick flights of stairs opening from the lobby. Within minutes she stood outside 3E. She knocked. She waited. She knocked again before the door opened.

"Hello?!" Seth Harrison's voice lifted and arced as he stared at his daughter. It was 10:00 a.m. on a Sunday morning and he looked as if he'd already run, read the paper, and probably cleaned his small apartment. He also looked as if caught between an exclamation and a question, but something in her eyes must have stopped him from saying more.

He stood silent for a beat, then lifted his hand. "Honey?" he whispered.

Alyssa bit her lip. She'd been wrong. The tears weren't all gone. She stepped into his arms and got out only one word as they started again.

"Dad."

"YOU CAN'T STAY HERE."

Of all the words Alyssa thought her dad might say, after hearing about all she'd been through, those four never occurred to her.

Seth Harrison had hugged his daughter, welcomed her inside, poured her another cup of coffee, and then settled into his one armchair to face her as she curled into the corner of his couch and relaxed for the first time in months.

"It wasn't supposed to be like this." She tucked a foot beneath her.

"Nothing ever turns out quite like we anticipate."

Alyssa expected her dad's voice to carry the same sad derision she'd heard for three years. She expected to find a fellow soul wallowing at the bottom, had imagined the two of them spending the summer commiserating over old-fashioneds, ice cream, and Cubs games. But something in his voice told her that reality was as altered as the Daily Brew to Andante. There was a resilience and an energy, a note of excited anticipation that, for the second time that morning, left her both surprised and unsettled.

Seth continued. "You believed in the mission and it was a good one, and while a lot went wrong, this will pass and you'll be fine. When is your interview?"

She knew he wasn't referring to any of the seventeen job interviews. Nor was he talking about the latest three resumes she'd sent to companies in Atlanta, Charlotte, and Minneapolis. He was talking about the only interview, in the end, that mattered. The one with the Federal Bureau of Investigation.

"The message didn't say anything, just that they can interview me out of the Chicago office. They have all my emails. Heck, they have every keystroke ever made at XGC, so they have to know I knew nothing . . . But what if I really am to blame?"

"You're not to blame."

"You don't know that. I don't know that. Because no one will tell me anything. Even my lawyer doesn't know what they're up to . . . Do you know they've interviewed every other department? He told me that. Even members of my team. But not me. Nothing. Silence."

"It might be clear you're innocent."

"But I'm not . . . My team created that code, made those predictive algorithms. If someone got told they were headed toward ALS, it's because we told them so. Then all that data was sold. Did you hear that? That's what they're saying. Fox News and CNN reported it, and if they both agree, it must be true. Who knows what kind of marketing these people have gotten. Can you imagine? Your most horrid fears showing up as ads in the sidebars of your Google searches? I'm going—" Alyssa couldn't pull in air. It felt as if her heart was thumping up and out of her chest and closing off her windpipe.

"Enough." Seth leaned over and clamped a hand on her knee. His grip was so tight she gasped as the pain shifted her attention. He released her knee and sat back again. "My college soccer coach used to do that. Worked every time."

"Oddly it does." She rubbed her knee.

"Sweetheart." He waited until she met his eyes. "Looking to the past, especially when you don't know the whole story, won't get you anywhere. Take it from me—and I don't mean just about work. I mean life. You'll make assumptions."

He paused so long Alyssa sensed he was talking about more than XGC.

"You will make mistakes," he continued without prompting. "Focus on here and now, and your next first step. Only that . . . And I'm glad you're home."

"Thanks, Dad." Alyssa felt her pulse slow. She knew he was trying to encourage her, and no matter how hopeless it all felt, she appreciated it. But she also feared he was skirting close to talking about her mom. She didn't want to—no, she couldn't—go there, not today.

She looked around her dad's small apartment, the most visible and tangible reminder of their divorce. While it wasn't what she imagined for him, it did look like him. She envied the cozy, comfortable space he'd created for himself. Fly fishing photos from his trip to South America displayed on his bookshelves, Cubs tickets pinned to the small bulletin board outside his kitchen, the pillow she'd made for him in eighth-grade home economics class tucked behind him into the corner of his one armchair.

She looked toward the outer wall. Two French doors opened onto a tiny balcony. The eighteen inches didn't even allow for a chair, but double doors gave the room a sense of space and filled it with clear morning light. It was an apartment she could envision for herself. She could rest here.

The realization that she could, in fact, rest instantly heightened her exhaustion. Her stomach started a slow burn, but she couldn't bring herself to cross the living room for her handbag and Tums by the front door.

"Can I crash in your spare room while I find a job and build up some savings? I'll be gone by Labor Day. I'm giving myself the summer to get a cushion under me. I'll work anywhere. Maybe Lexi will let me wait tables at Mirabella."

She mustered up bright expectation and was a little confused by his steady stare back.

Then it came . . .

"You can't stay here."

Four words and nothing more.

Alyssa blinked. Her dad now held her gaze—without blinking. She felt her mouth drop open, but no words came.

He leaned forward and tapped her knee. This time it was gentle. It was the kind of tap you give a five-year-old soccer player rather than one falling apart on the field in college. "It's not that I don't want to help, Alyssa, but it's not what's best. I have only that pullout chair in the other room and . . . You need to stay with Mom. She's got that whole house and . . . That's it. You need to stay at home."

Alyssa smashed the heels of both hands into her eyes. If she rubbed hard enough, maybe the exhaustion, the conversation, or best yet, both, would disappear. When the stars dimmed in her dark blue inside-eyelid sky, she opened them. "It's true then, isn't it? Chase said you two are dating."

Seth's ears tipped red. "I never thought my children would gossip about my love life, but yes, and if you had been willing to talk about it, I'd have told you directly."

"Mom tried."

"You talked to your mother?" Seth's voice lifted in approval.

Alyssa bit her lip and shook her head. "She left a couple messages."

"I see. Then this will be good for you both."

"How is this happening? She cheated on you. You divorced

her. How can you just forget that?" Alyssa pressed her lips shut. She sounded like that five-year-old.

Seth moved his head in a slow nod. "While true, that's too simplistic. Don't make her the bad guy and let me off the hook. And I haven't forgotten. I've forgiven her and she me."

"What'd she have to forgive you for? You weren't the one playing Hide the Paintbrush with the art teacher." Alyssa gasped. Sharp, snarky comments usually resided in her head. If there was one thing her mom had drilled in deep, it was to never let them out, to never give less than a perfect impression of herself.

And besides all that—had she really just said that? To her dad? "I'm sorry. I didn't mean to say that. That was horrible." She held up her hand, fully expecting her dad to deliver a well-deserved lecture on rudeness and respect to his thirty-one-year-old daughter.

Instead he chuckled. "I can see you and Mom are going to have a wonderful time together."

"You can't be serious."

Seth stood, and that was lecture enough. Alyssa knew the conversation was over.

She looked up at him. "Can I have a day? Can you let me crash here, then I'll head home tomorrow morning?" She offered a shaky smile. "Sometimes we don't say things the right way when we're tired, and Mom and me, we're not . . ."

He raised a brow.

"Again, I am sorry I said that, Dad. I promise I will go tomorrow."

"Of course." Seth sighed and moved toward his front door. "Before you sleep, let's get your bags inside and make up that pull-out."

"I've only got my purse . . . Everything else got stolen on the way back here."

He turned around. "You have had it rough."

Alyssa managed a weak nod. Anything more would have brought the tears again and the only four words she wanted to say.

Don't make me go.

Chapter 5

Andante eased into an afternoon lull at one thirty. The morning wasn't as busy as Jeremy had hoped, but it wasn't dangerously quiet either. He consoled himself with the thought that Winsome was a slow burn kind of town and that any grand opening might naturally take on a more *adagietto* pace, and certainly never an *allegro*. It would all be okay . . . He was only a week in. There was no need to panic. More than that, he could make it great.

With that pep talk, he looked to the counter where his new hire, Brendon, stood chatting with a customer. Perhaps he was taking a little long, considering a few more waited to order, but wasn't that what Jeremy wanted? An employee who knew the town? Brendon flicked his head, and his long bangs swept out of his eyes. Tall, clean-cut, and captain of the high school lacrosse team, he possessed an easy charm and confidence—and a hair flip—Jeremy envied.

Ryan had resisted hiring Brendon, but that felt like nothing new. Lately everything Jeremy suggested, Ryan protested.

"We don't need more help. Give me more hours, more responsibility; I can handle it."

"Forget it. There's a lot riding on this, and I'm already working fourteen-hour days."

"But I'm not."

Jeremy turned away. He had not wanted to point out that Ryan cost twice what a high school kid cost and that he didn't engage customers any better than Jeremy did. Neither of them gave off that "favorite son" vibe Brendon exuded.

On some level, after the shop was closed and Jeremy stood alone wiping down those multithousand-dollar wood counter tops, he feared that he was in over his head. And if he felt that way, surely Ryan must too. After all, Ryan had made amazing strides, but moving was stressful, starting a new job was stressful, life was stressful . . . Bottom line, Ryan was only a couple years out of rehab. And Jeremy, with so much on the line, not only couldn't afford any mistakes, but felt like he was jumping out of his skin with the weight of each decision, each moment, and each sunk shot from those ancient machines.

He could feel the tension right then, making his skin heat and his words rush out faster than his brain could make them kind or polite or even cogent. He pushed them out of his mouth at a rapid-fire pace.

"Why don't you take over the baking? It's all mixes. Super-easy stuff and, if you add some variety, maybe we'll sell more. Food has a higher margin."

"Fine." The younger man stared at him for a beat or two. "Also, why don't you let me look at the books? Back in Seattle, you were prepping me to cover those. I'd like to take them on here. I think we've got some waste. Our first couple months we ordered so often I think we overpaid in shipping."

"Let's hold off on that. The goal is to keep things fresh, so there's bound to be a little loss as I get the business dialed in." He shrugged away Ryan's request and his concerns.

Yet as each and every assurance raced past his tongue, questions, doubts, and fears grew behind them. "I'll go over the ordering again . . . Besides, if you did all that, how would I spend my evenings?"

"With your daughter?"

Jeremy looked away again and busied himself wiping down one of the espresso machines. He didn't have an easy answer for that one, or for why he was keeping work from Ryan. It was a strange feeling, to be so close to what he wanted and yet so afraid it was slipping away. It felt as though if he didn't grab hard and fast, keep focused on the end prize, and crank that death grip tighter yet, it would all slide though his fingers.

He felt the same about Becca. Moving to Winsome, purchasing Andante—it had all started with his need to spend time with his seven-year-old daughter. And if he were to believe his ex-wife's Instagram feed, that was happening. Daily Krista posted pictures of him with Becca, edited with sepia tones and soft lighting. Only if one looked carefully would one see their outfits were the same on three or four different "outings." Heck, he almost believed Krista's skilled storytelling himself—the idea of their "conscious uncoupling," as she called it, their amicable agreement on every parenting decision, the "generous" time and effort they both put into their relationship and communication skills for their daughter's sake. It sounded perfect. It looked perfect.

But it wasn't perfect. Despite his moving across the country to be near Becca, Krista still kept him a good distance from their daughter and was wary of the time he spent with her.

Jeremy watched as Brendon handed a customer a blueberry muffin with a winning smile. Yes, hiring that boy was a smart decision, he told himself. A good coffee shop was an extension of your home, your own living room, of *my* living room, Jeremy thought, where everyone was welcome and felt comfortable. And who better to welcome the town than a treasured one of their own, a rising star?

Jeremy felt his breath even out. All the pieces were dropping into place. The shop looked great, the staff now gave the right image, and soon his new state-of-the-art espresso machine would arrive and it'd be smooth sailing . . . And this was only week one.

He turned back to the two ancient machines he needed to nurse through another couple weeks. They might be old, impossible to calibrate, and on their way out the door, but they were still gorgeous. The previous owner, Georgia Pavlis, had treated them well over the years, and their stainless-steel casings shone like mirrors. Not a scratch on either one.

Wiping them down, he puzzled over the incongruence between the care Georgia had given these machines and the chaotic mayhem of her shop. There was a disconnect he couldn't understand.

A breeze from the front door reached him, and he twisted toward it to call out a cheerful hello. He stopped upon seeing Janet. "Hey there . . . I don't usually see you in the afternoons."

"It's quiet in here." She smiled.

"Coffee shops often are in the early afternoon." He cringed at his perky voice. He was certainly working hard to convince someone.

She flicked a finger behind him. "You can almost see your reflection in those."

"They need to hold out another couple weeks until my new machine arrives. None of this came cheap." He gestured into the shop.

"We're facing the same issues. The bookshop's remodel hit us hard. We'll both hit our stride soon."

"I hope so." Jeremy clasped his hands behind his back and stretched his chest. "What can I get for you?"

"I came to invite you to the business collective meeting tonight. You said you were too busy a few months ago, and last month you closed to renovate, so tonight it is." She winked.

"Is that the Chamber of Commerce thing?"

"No . . . Until they find a new executive director, that's at a standstill. This is a group Claire started, and it'll be good for you. We share what we're up to, what help we need, chat, often gossip, and it builds friendships, promotes goodwill, and champions buying local."

Jeremy opened his mouth to say yes and sighed instead. "I've got my daughter tonight."

"Bring Becca along."

Jeremy chuffed, but felt reluctant to miss an opportunity. Even accounting for an afternoon lull, Andante was too quiet. He needed customers. "That wouldn't work, but I'm sure I can pick her up afterward. Count me in."

"Excellent." Janet clapped her hands together, and Jeremy noted purple paint on the tips of her fingers. "Come to Winsome Realty at seven and bring some coffee. Two of those cardboard carrying things should do it. Your coffee really is much better than anything around, and it's time everyone knew it."

JEREMY STALLED OUTSIDE THE realty office. He stepped back, forward, and back again. He felt like the new kid once more, the one everyone knew had lost his parents and got thrown into foster care, but rather than say it to his face or even welcome him, they talked behind his back.

He placed the bags on the sidewalk, straightened his spine, tucked his shirt into his jeans, again, and steadied himself. Only his death grip on the bags as he picked them up, crinkling the paper handles, belied his calm façade as he pushed open the door.

The smell hit him first. Burnt coffee. Old, stale coffee. I can fix that, he thought.

Janet spotted him as he entered the back conference room and beelined his direction. "Am I glad to see you." She led him to two tables pushed against the side wall and cleared him a space between flyers and an old stainless steel coffee urn.

A few heads turned to watch them.

"Set up right here. I was so afraid you weren't going to come. When I asked, you looked like I was force-feeding you Folgers. Dry."

"Hey—" Jeremy laughed. While he couldn't tell her he'd been so nervous he'd changed his shirt three times, he was glad she made a joke about it. Somehow calling it out made it easier to handle.

Janet lifted one of the coffee containers from the bag. "I really appreciate this." She stepped closer. "Hang around afterward and I'll introduce you to everyone one-on-one. Claire's already jumpy about running late, so I can't now. You won't run off, will you?"

Jeremy set a decanter of cream on the table. "I won't."

She nodded, crossed to the front of the room to where her co-worker, and one of the Printed Letter Bookshop's owners, Claire Durand, sat, and clapped her hands. "Everyone, attention please. Before Claire begins, go grab a coffee if you want one, generously donated by Jeremy Miller of the Daily—excuse me, Andante." Janet widened her eyes with her mistake, then gestured to the room, palms out. "Sorry about that. Andante provided tonight's coffee."

Jeremy sat as Claire stood to welcome everyone. At her first word, his cell phone rang, and all heads again turned his direction. "I'm sorry. I thought I silenced this."

Noting his daughter's smiling face on the screen, he swiped Accept and walked out of the room.

"Jeremy? Jeremy? Are you there?" Krista's tiny voice squeaked at him from a distance.

He crossed through the real estate company's outer office and hit the pavement outside. "Sorry. I was in a meeting. I left you a message about it."

His ex-wife was silent a beat. "I got the message, but I also have plans tonight. I need you to get Becca when you agreed, as you agreed."

"This is important. It's for my business, Krista."

"So is this, Jeremy. We've got an event tonight and we're already short-staffed."

"We?" he scoffed. "You're an employee, Krista. I own this shop."

"You did not just say that to me."

Jeremy closed his eyes and leaned against the brick building. Despite the day's warm sunshine, the bricks had cooled with the evening. "No. I didn't. Can you get your parents to help? Just this once?"

"If they were in town. But they're not."

"Get a babysitter. I'll cover the cost and get Becca first thing tomorrow, and keep her all weekend."

"Forget it, Jeremy. I'll talk to you later."

"No, wait!" He pushed off the bricks.

"No. You wait. I didn't ask you to move out here. I never asked you to be a part of Becca's life. We had it all worked out, but you changed everything and now she believes you're in her life, that you're her dad—"

"I am her dad."

"Then act like one. Be where you say you'll be, when you say you'll be there. I won't play these games with you."

"That's rich, coming from you." Jeremy winced at his words, at his tone. It wasn't that they sounded angry—though they did. It was worse than that. They sounded broken, hurt, and he wondered if that feeling, that emptiness, was ever going to go away.

When Georgia Pavlis said *Buy my shop*, the Seattle roasting house owners said *You've done good work* and rewarded him for it, Ryan offered to move with him and be his right-hand man, and Krista didn't kick up a fight, he thought he had found it—that place where he belonged and could call "home" had finally materialized.

Standing alone on the sidewalk, nothing felt like he'd expected.

Krista held the silence a few beats before moaning, "I'm not doing this anymore. Go back to Seattle, Jeremy."

"I'm trying here, Krista . . . Don't . . . Please don't cut me out . . . Just hang on. I'm coming to get her." Jeremy crossed the street, pulled his keys from his pocket, and tapped open his car door. "I'll be there in a half hour."

Chapter 6

Janet pushed open the alley door to the bookshop. Peace filled her like oxygen. She took another breath to make sure it was real, and hoped it would last. Sleep had abandoned her the past two nights with her ex-husband's call—or was he her boyfriend now? Their daughter was home. Alyssa had slept at Seth's apartment upon her arrival Sunday night, but then again last night too, as Seth had worked late and hadn't realized Alyssa was still in his spare room. But she was coming to Janet sometime today. Today. Janet breathed deep.

And while it hurt that seeing her daughter required a paternal ultimatum, after three years of virtual silence, she'd take what she could get. Three years . . .

The memory of that day was still sharp, vivid. Alyssa had cleared out her Chicago apartment, driven to Winsome to dump some boxes in her old bedroom, spewed a gale-force storm of venom at her, and headed west. Within two weeks of finding out about Janet's affair, Alyssa, as far as Janet could determine, had blown up her life. According to Chase, who had relayed the events to his sister, she hung up on him, walked straight into her boss's office, and quit. A quick flight to California for a couple interviews a day later, and she was heading west before Janet had even caught her on the phone.

She had lost more than her husband on that night three years ago. She had lost her daughter.

But now . . .

Everything was different. You've learned to look back, accept what has come before, and ask forgiveness, she reminded herself. Some days all the work left her defeated, tired, and back at the beginning with too much hill to climb. But she also knew everything was being made new, and that took time, patience, grace, and a good dollop of mercy. There was no way it couldn't include her relationship with Alyssa.

The bookshop's windowless office was so dark she moved by memory rather than by sight as she dropped her bag on her desk and pushed open the door to the storage room Madeline and Claire, the shop's owners, had allowed her to convert into an art studio. It was her favorite place.

Right in the mix of books and story, with her two best friends beside her, she got to create art—and through art she found herself. That was new too, as well as exhilarating and a little frightening. Sometimes she wondered how different her story might have been, how different *all* their stories might have been, if she hadn't denied what was real and vital to her well-being for some unnamed and unreachable ideal—if she had followed what *was* right rather than what *looked* right.

She flipped the light switch and discovered the bookstore cat, Chesterton, curled on her high table, burrowed in her favorite sweater.

"Oh, no you don't." She swept him up with one hand under his belly. He draped over her arm like a warm heating pad as she pulled him closer. Then, as if recognizing who held him, he stiffened and leapt to the floor.

"I've apologized, you know, and it's not nice to hold a grudge."

Offering an apology didn't mean it was accepted—and Alyssa

held grudges well. Her daughter's stubbornness had been adorable at two, formidable at twelve, pummeling at eighteen, and arctic at twenty-eight. Now, after three years held hostage in the cold dark, Janet found nothing "adorable" about blazing eyes and an unyielding spirit. They terrified her. They reminded her of herself.

She sank onto a stool and heard Chesterton purr at the alley door. She sighed and crossed the dark office again to open it for him. "Be back by lunch or they'll think I was mean to you again . . . You'll get me in trouble." She called the last part, but the cat didn't look back. He had slinked through the door's first crack of light and had already rounded the corner, probably heading to Olive and Eve Designs.

Olive and Eve had opened their women's clothing shop in April 2005. Actually, Olive opened it. High end, but with little markup; edgy, but not so on-point that the more conservative Winsome women didn't embrace it; and varied enough to keep her clientele coming back almost weekly. But while her customers didn't break the bank shopping there, Olive almost did, keeping it open. Six months in, Eve came on board. She ran the books, managed the inventory, and kept Olive's sartorial dreams in check.

And gave Chesterton a bowl of cream each morning.

"You're late." Eve sat at her desk, the alley door propped open next to her with a brick. She bent down as the cat pounced into her lap. "You'd think I have nothing better to do than pamper you." She pushed her computer keyboard across her desk as if distancing herself from something unpleasant. "We're in a little trouble, Chesterton. Please tell me you've got some ideas."

Chesterton purred and wiggled out of her arms. He dropped to the floor and slowly, with his back arched high, padded to his breakfast. Eve watched him until, bowl empty, he slid back through the alley door without a backward glance.

"If you don't bother with a thanks, I might stop, you know."

Chesterton didn't pause. Eve suspected it was because he knew she was bluffing. The cream would be there tomorrow, and even in the dead of winter she would crack the alley door until he arrived. With kids long gone and moved away, she looked forward to her moment with that spoiled yet soft cat probably as much as he looked forward to his breakfast.

Brendon, on the other hand, did not look forward to seeing the cat. For the past four days, it sat perched on the dumpster as he took out the trash. His first two days, suspecting someone might hear, he'd shooed the cat away with a low voice. Yesterday he'd had a little more fun and launched the trash bag to the dumpster from across the alley. "Almost got you," he'd jeered at the cat.

Today, his aim was even better. The bag skimmed Chesterton so closely it created a vacuum between him and the dumpster's chasm as it sailed by. Brendon watched as the cat twisted in midair and arched away from the pull into the dumpster.

"Get out of here." He crossed the alley and stomped near the cat's landing spot. "You dirty old—" Movement caught his eye. He looked up. "You guys are early. Wait here."

As Brendon opened Andante's back alley door, Chesterton bolted through the back door of the Printed Letter Bookshop. Within seconds, he glided over a pair of feet and dived into the small space under his favorite desk, next to his favorite person.

"What's up with him?" Claire remarked.

Chapter 7

Ping.

Light, but not bright midmorning light, crept through the crack in Jeremy's shades. He rolled over and grabbed his phone as the text pinged again.

I need Becca back here by 10

He punched his pillow before tapping Krista's number. This time he skipped the preliminaries. "You said I have her through the weekend."

"We got into Dr. Benson's practice. They just called."

Jeremy sat up straight. "That's great."

"Save it. She doesn't need this, but the school will get the report so we have to go."

Jeremy closed his eyes. Becca's school had been at Krista for two years about the reading issues. In fact, if Jeremy hadn't moved closer, he doubted he ever would have heard about them.

"If they insisted on a doctor's assessment, Krista, then she needs it."

If he'd unraveled the story correctly, the questions from Becca's teachers had started when she was in kindergarten. The school got officially involved halfway through first grade, and bandied about words like *phonetics*, *comprehension*, and *developmental milestones*. Krista had ignored it all. But now, entering second grade, Becca faced terms like *consolidation*, *cognitive assessments*, and *dyslexia*.

"I'll get her back. See you soon."

Krista clicked off without another word.

Jeremy pulled on a sweatshirt, shuffled to the kitchen, and pulled an espresso shot. He had restored an old La Pavoni machine during the evenings last month and had finally calibrated it the day before. It was never going to pull a shot the quality of the La Marzocco that was coming to Andante in a couple weeks, but its temperamental nature and the constant fine-tuning it required made each shot a fun adventure.

He'd only been a few minutes tardy to Krista's house the night before. Yet he'd still gotten an Anna and Elsa duffel bag launched at his chest.

"I'm late now." She strode out the front door with Becca in tow.

"I came right when you called." He backed up.

Krista, though ten inches shorter and eighty pounds lighter, was fierce when angry. "Forget it, Jeremy. It just makes me look bad. Why should that bother you?"

The derision in her voice cut, as did the question. Fights were never simple with Krista. Each dug into every argument before, stirring them up and turning them into the light, and each ended with a question, letting him know he wasn't enough—not aware, not thoughtful, and, last night, not on time.

"There was traffic."

"You moved here to be a help. Don't become a complication."

As Becca emerged from behind her mom, Jeremy shifted his attention. "Ready, Ladybug?"

Expecting a huge grin, Jeremy deflated at his daughter's nod.

Her mood appeared to match his. She didn't reply, nor did she smile—and none of that changed for their entire thirty-minute ride to Winsome or throughout a dinner of pasta and his "famous" Bolognese sauce. He even fell flat on her favorite vegetable.

Becca had scrunched up her face at the broccoli. "It's not my favorite."

"Tell me a green vegetable you like better."

"I like avocados."

"They're a fruit. Try again."

"Peas."

"Okay, you got me." Jeremy leaned against the counter. "But this is great stuff. I thought you liked broccoli."

"I do."

"Then what are you complaining about?" He tried to keep his voice light, but he could hear Krista in his daughter's whine—her insistence that everything look and be just so, and on her terms.

"It's just not my *favorite*. You didn't ask if I liked it."

He felt his body flood with delight at her logical innocence. "Good point. I'll remember that next time." As he cut the broccoli, he brought up Krista again, wondering if that was why his daughter was quiet. Perhaps their quarreling had upset her, and if he said Krista's name and made it sound like all was right between them, Becca might feel safe. "You're going to love the crispy bits. Does Mommy ever cook it like this?"

Nothing.

Next he suggested they read *Alexander and the Terrible, Horrible, No Good, Very Bad Day*, thinking she could relate. Still nothing.

But he'd probably gone about that wrong too. Rather than simply read to her and let her enjoy the story, he'd peppered her with challenges. By the end of the story even he knew he'd crossed a line.

Why don't you read this page?

What does Alexander say here?

Can you believe he said that? Read this section.

He had closed the book feeling as shredded as his daughter. Looking at her tight face and watery eyes, he couldn't tell who was worse off. Her for knowing she couldn't do what was expected, or him for being the misguided dad, sure if he pushed just the right amount and in just the right ways, she'd feel confident and secure—and read like a champ. Whatever that even looked like.

He'd almost given up and suggested bedtime, just to end the whole night, when she noticed a large red box sitting on his living room coffee table.

"That? Go look." He lifted her off his lap. "There's a bookshop a few doors down from the coffee shop, and one of the women brought me that last week. She said you might like those."

Becca crossed the room and dropped to the floor at the table, moving with a weary wariness. Then inside the box, his daughter discovered eighty-six rubbery Smurfs and two odd mushroom-looking houses, and her first smile broke free.

Within minutes, they set out the houses and discovered there weren't nearly enough for all the Smurfs. They needed a whole village.

"What about Tupperware or books?" Jeremy suggested. "We have lots of books. Go grab some from your room too and we'll build a book village."

Becca ran down the short hallway, and Jeremy noted that her flip-flops slapped the hardwood floor in tiny raps rather than the heavy thwapping sound they'd made when she shuffled in his door at the beginning of the evening. His heart lifted in victory.

And the evening only got better from there.

He smiled as he ground the beans for his coffee, remembering how poor Kurt Vonnegut's *Slaughterhouse-Five* almost became a residence for Smurfs. As Becca searched her room for books, he scoured his own shelves, bypassing his Stephen Kings and true crime in favor of Tom Clancy and Robert Ludlum. *The Hunt for Red October*, *Rainbow Six*, and *The Road to Omaha* were titles more appropriate-sounding for a seven-year-old building houses. And they were all hardbacks—much better construction material.

"I've got some, Daddy," Becca called from behind a stack of books. Jeremy could only see her eyes above the pile.

"You found all your old board books." He straightened *Good Night, Gorilla*; *Barnyard Dance!*; *The Very Hungry Caterpillar*; and *Green Eggs and Ham*.

"They were in the cabinet, but I don't read them anymore."

"You're a little beyond them, aren't you?" He propped *Dear Zoo* open and upright to form two walls for a house.

The look of panic that washed over her expression caught his attention, and his heart sank again. "Those are some of my favorites, though. Do you want to read or build houses?"

"Houses."

Yet once the village of book houses covered his living room floor, Becca's questioning eyes returned to the books.

"Do you want to read any of those?"

"I can't." She pursed her lips and her eyes held a sheen of tears that cracked Jeremy's heart. "There's something wrong with me."

"No . . . Ladybug. Who said that?"

Becca shook her head.

Knowing the answer could be as obvious as classmates' taunts on the playground or as subtle as unspoken gestures—even ones given unwittingly by him—he lifted Becca into his lap and tucked them both into a corner of the couch. "I'll start."

He opened *Green Eggs and Ham* first and *Guess How Much I Love You* second.

Then, without noticing the shift, Becca read the book he had settled in her lap. *The Snowy Day*.

Yes, they were board books others might deem too young, he conceded, but Becca finally enjoyed their time together. She read slowly, sounding out each word as if it was new, and hard to chew and swallow. But listening, Jeremy sensed his daughter loved to read. She kept at it with diligence as if a treasure awaited her on each page. That was all that mattered.

Jeremy couldn't remember the years when he was Becca's age. In fact, he remembered nothing before the age of ten, but he certainly remembered everything after that. There wasn't a time his own insufficiencies, real or imagined, hadn't embarrassed him, so to watch his daughter openly struggle, with no fear, nestled next to him, broke his heart and lifted it at the same time.

They had ended the evening with one of Becca's favorites, Mo Willem's *My Friend Is Sad*. She read the entire book herself and giggled as Elephant told Piggy about all the wonderful things he'd seen, completely unaware it had been Piggy in disguise each time trying to cheer him up.

Becca had gone to bed pleased and at ease. Jeremy, on the other hand, tossed and turned all night. Becca needed help, and that meant going up against Krista. But it was more than that. He had felt struck anew, despite reading the story countless times before, that Elephant had never seen Piggy clearly, that he never understood what he missed, what was right before him all along. That thought—what was he missing?—led to the uncomfortable questions that always spoke in the still, dark night.

Now he carried his cup into Becca's room and sat on the edge of her bed.

"Hey, sleepyhead. I gotta get you back to Mom this morning. She said you have a doctor's appointment."

"For dyspexa." Becca's eyes clouded.

"Dyslexia. And it's going to be fine, Bug." He watched her a moment, trying to listen to what wasn't said. "How do you feel?"

Jeremy winced. Endless social workers and lawyers asked him that same question after his parents died. How at ten, fifteen, or even seventeen could he tell them how he "felt"? He'd had no way to articulate the swirling pressures, colors, emotions, and forces he couldn't separate and understand, much less name.

Becca gave the answer he expected. The same one he gave all those years ago. She shrugged. Then she pushed herself up against the headboard. She wore her latest Christmas ladybug pj's, already too small.

"You need new pajamas. I might not be able to wait till next Christmas." He plucked at the sleeve that, six months before, circled her wrist rather than her forearm.

"Mommy says I grow too much."

"Sorry, Ladybug. That's my fault." He laughed, stood to his full six five, and patted his head.

Becca giggled. "I like it. I'm tallest in my class, taller than the boys too."

"That's a good thing. It keeps them in line." He bent, kissed her forehead, and lifted his coffee cup under her nose. "Smell this."

Becca inhaled, eyes closed, just like her dad. "Chocolate and cinnamon. It smells sharp, Daddy."

"You are getting so good. It's an Ethiopian bean . . . And you're right. It pulled too fast today. I underestimated how much beans can dry in a single day. It was perfect yesterday . . . So what happened?"

"Today the water went through the dry beans too fast to pull the mellow flavors. It's going to be sour."

"That's my girl." He ruffled her hair. He'd done the same thing last night and had pulled at her ponytail. This time, with her hair long and loose, he made a complete mess and covered her face with a curtain of thick hair—exactly his intention.

"Daddy!"

Jeremy laughed his way out of the room and began breakfast. Becca emerged a few minutes later with an Amelia Bedelia book tucked under her arm.

"Do you want to take that one with you?"

She nodded.

After a quick breakfast and a drive with no traffic, they pulled up to Krista's with ten minutes to spare. Nevertheless, she was already waiting on the front stoop.

Krista hugged Becca, then tapped her shoulder. "Go inside, honey. I'll be right in."

As their daughter turned to go, Jeremy bent down. "Remember that I love you just the way you are—to the moon and back again."

Becca wrapped her arms around his neck and hugged. He closed his eyes and truly believed he could stay in that moment, quads burning from the squat, forever.

As Becca walked inside, Krista turned back to Jeremy. "Look, I want to take this at my own pace. No jumping ahead here. I'm her mother and I'll decide what help she needs."

"Life doesn't follow clear lines, Krista."

"I never said it did."

"But you want it to. You want it glossy and neat. If Becca needs special classes, attention, then that's what she needs. We read together last night and—"

"I told you. I'm handling it."

Jeremy shifted his gaze above Krista's head toward the house. "She's nervous and she feels that she's not measuring up. She brought Amelia Bedelia with her." At Krista's perplexed expression, he continued. "No one does things more differently or is less understood at the beginning than Amelia Bedelia."

"It's a kids' book."

"You know what Madeleine L'Engle said . . . If the book's too difficult for adults, write it for children. Kids' books are important."

Krista scoffed.

"I'm serious, Krista. This isn't about you, or me. You may be her mom, but I'm her dad."

Krista's face hardened.

He stepped back to his car in hopes a physical retreat would signal an emotional one. "I'll come back in a couple hours. I'd still like to spend the weekend with her."

"No. I don't—"

Jeremy raised a hand. "Please. I don't get a ton of time with her. And I didn't mean to push."

He noted the instant Krista relented. Her eyes softened. In those moments, although few and far between, he remembered why he had loved her and why he had married her. When she forgot to push and strive, there was vulnerability, softness, and a light that enthralled him. When they'd met, she'd just finished her sophomore year of college, had had a rough time with some boyfriend, had struggled in school, had fought with her parents . . . It wasn't an ideal time to start something new, but she had also needed someplace safe to land, and that someplace and someone had been him. The ability to hold her, love her, and even help her heal had formed the greatest six months of his life.

She stepped forward. "I need to tell you something else." She too glanced back to the house. "We're moving, Jeremy."

"Closer to me?"

"North Carolina. The company's expanding, and I've been asked to run point in Charlotte. No more supervising parties. I'll set up the whole operation." She held up a hand to stop him from speaking. "I've already done the research. The office is in a great area with an excellent school system—smaller classes, individual attention, special programs. It's everything you want for her."

"You can't . . . Is this what you planned all along? To get me to push, then spring your already pat answer on me?"

"That's not fair."

"You can't do this, Krista. I just moved here. I have everything invested here. I can't get out. I can't—"

"As you said, this isn't about you."

"That's not what I was talking about and you know it. You never asked me to move here, I get that, but I came. You can't just leave. Don't act like you're doing this for Becca—they have all those classes here. And what about your parents? They love having her here."

"I'm not twenty anymore. I need out . . . And this is good for her. Great for me. You can't be against this." Krista slid her phone from her back pocket. "I've got to go. We can talk later, but this is happening, Jeremy. It's exactly what I've been working for."

"It isn't. You've always wanted to do layout and design, not manage infrastructure."

One of Krista's more recent social media campaigns flashed in Jeremy's memory. She'd created a series of pictures of different foods the catering company sold. Beautiful croissants, bright green salads, savory tarts. But when he'd replied to ask the cost for Andante and if it was all as good as it looked, she'd replied, *I have no idea. After the pictures, I throw it all away.*

"That's what they're offering me, Jeremy."

"We have to talk about this."

"Later." She spun toward the door. "I have a doctor's appointment to get to."

As he drove away, a prayer floated into his consciousness. He quirked a small smile because, unbidden, it always arrived when needed and brought a sliver of peace each time.

God, grant us the serenity to accept the things we cannot change, the courage to change the things we can, and the wisdom to know the difference.

He had heard it for the first time at one of Ryan's AA meetings back in Seattle and liked it so much he'd grabbed a small printed card of it on his way out the door. He knew he should pay attention to the first clause. It pricked his conscience like a small, calm voice every time he raced over it to get to the middle part. Yet he never did the accepting. He rushed on, like a parched man to water, certain that with hard work and perseverance he could create the outcome he wanted and be sated.

The courage to change the things we can . . .

He just needed to work a little harder.

Chapter 8

A half hour spent nursing a now cold coffee at Andante didn't alter what needed to be done. Alyssa checked her email accounts twice in an attempt to look like everyone else in the shop, glued to their phones, but none of the three companies to which she'd submitted resumes had replied. In fact, a new email, not spam, hadn't landed in her three in-boxes in four days.

As for social media, she'd closed her accounts months ago. She couldn't post as her life fell apart, and she had felt like a voyeur peeking into the PicMonkeyed and Facetuned lives of her friends, celebrating marriages, births, promotions, and exotic vacations. Everyone was always out doing something, moving forward.

Going back is the quickest way on.

The thought drifted in and through before she could grasp it. She'd read it somewhere—something about the fact that, after taking a wrong turn, traveling farther down the road doesn't get you any closer to your destination. You have to go back in order to go on. There was truth and logic to it, and she remembered it striking her at the time, but she remembered sneering at it too. There was no way she'd ever go back, she had thought. Every memory's glossy veneer had been blasted away in a single revelation.

Yet three years later, the short phrase struck her anew—she was back at the beginning, and perhaps, the saying didn't deserve a sneer after all. Perhaps it was true.

Alyssa threw the last of her cold coffee down her throat and stood.

It was time to go home.

She stepped outside and looked toward the Printed Letter Bookshop. Its window was a gorgeous and opulent display of life through literature—nothing like the unimaginative row of books that had lined the bay window's floor, and the empty armchair that had commanded the window's focal point for years. Mrs. Carter always said that if you sat in the armchair and read in her window for all Winsome to see, and stayed there for at least an hour, you could keep any book you wanted. Alyssa didn't recall that anyone had ever taken her up on it.

The sun ducked behind a cloud and, rather than bounce off the window, shot through it and illuminated the shop within. There stood Alyssa's mom a mere ten feet away, conversing with a tall man. Not Andante tall, but still a few inches taller than Janet. As she spoke, her hands waved through the air. It looked like she was telling the best story Alyssa had never heard.

Unable to step forward, she turned back to her car and, within a matter of minutes, pulled into the driveway of her childhood home and parked in the small space between the backyard and the garage. The bushes were taller, scruffier—not pruned into the neat, tight configurations of yesteryear.

She stepped out of her car and looked around. Everything looked a little off, as if time had worn away that veneer here too and let a glimpse of true life escape. It must drive Mom nuts, Alyssa thought as she fingered through her keys.

She unlocked the back door and stepped into the kitchen. It looked the same—the same clock on the wall, the same stove, refrigerator, and appliances on the counters. But it felt quieter, as if no one cooked in here anymore. It had always been a place of emotion—laughter and banter, sobs and frustration. It was where she found her mom, the "control center" from where her mom ran the house and their lives.

Janet loved to cook. She always made dinner, cookies for Alyssa's friends most afternoons, and extravagant egg-sausage casseroles on the weekends. She brought dishes to every school event, potluck, and bake sale; she organized church meals for babies, moves, and funerals. The kitchen was the lifeblood of their seemingly idyllic family.

Alyssa passed through the kitchen toward the stairs, noting her dad's old study to her right. Many of the pictures still hung on the walls as if he still worked there. She paused and looked closer. His blotter, pen holder, and even his computer monitor still sat on his desk. In fact, nothing signaled that he had ever left. Not a picture missing. Not a book out of place. His study, the living room, the small sitting room to the left—it was as if the house had frozen in time three years ago when her dad walked out the door.

She cast back to his apartment. Other than the pillow she'd made him all those years ago, everything was new. How had it taken her so long to recognize that?

She thought about the last time she'd entered the house. Two and a half years ago, at Christmas. How had she not seen it then?

Her dad had moved out in September, and Alyssa had fled to California the following week. But they'd all agreed to try to come together as a family at Christmas. She had flown home, crashed on Dad's pullout armchair, and driven over with him Christmas morning. He had been silent and taciturn in the car, and Alyssa wondered why they were bothering at all. But her mom had insisted, still clinging to the standard she'd created.

Chase arrived at the same time they did, having driven up from the city with his wife, Laura. And all four of them had stood on the front doorstep, stymied as to what came next. After a few awkward glances, Alyssa reached forward and rang the doorbell. It sounded loud and discordant, and she suspected none of them, including Laura, had ever rung it before.

"What are you all doing out here?" Janet had been beyond perky that morning, wound into a tight knot, and the house had been decorated to the nines. Garlands followed the bannister down the stairs, poinsettias flanked the fireplace, stockings hung in a row. Warm smells of hot apple cider, coffee, and one of her signature egg-sausage casseroles wafted on the air, which was buzzing with the soft notes of Christmas carols.

The fantasy lasted mere moments, and the morning, not ten minutes old, ended with Janet screaming at Seth in the driveway. Alyssa had been up in her room and had gotten left behind as her dad sped away. Without a word, she walked down the stairs and out the front door, getting an equally good berating as she walked down the driveway. In fact, she suspected her mom continued to yell well beyond earshot. Janet never gave up.

Alyssa took a deep breath and looked up. Her favorite painting still hung at the top of the stairs, a huge modernist piece that hung crown molding to baseboard and stretched at least four feet wide. It always made her feel as if she were climbing to space and part of a larger story. Its portrayal of a midnight sky had been created with a palette knife. Deep curls of midnight blues, flashes of silver, white, yellow, and gray. It was three-dimensional, textural, and spoke of vast, immutable realities. It comforted her, giving her a sense of place and possibility. Over the years Alyssa had even worn smooth a ridge of oil on the left edge by touching it each time she climbed the stairs.

Seeing it brought back another memory too—an older one, yet still poignant. One afternoon her mom had found her staring at the painting. Janet had curled her lip at it and slid her hand along its right edge, as if trying to lift it from the wall. "This ugly thing belongs in the trash. I can't look at it anymore."

"No, stop." Alyssa had swiped at her hand.

Janet turned. Her face was full of something Alyssa had never seen before. It wasn't anger, despite her words. It looked and felt like agony.

"Please don't." Instinctively Alyssa knew to stay away from the painting. She looked up at the crown molding instead. "You'll bring it crashing down and ruin the wall."

Janet shrugged. "Fine. I'll get someone to handle it later."

Alyssa never mentioned or touched the painting again. Deep inside, she believed if she ignored it her mom might forget and leave it hanging. By loving it, she sensed she had created a problem. And perhaps, she thought as she now climbed the stairs, she had been right. With Alyssa not calling attention to it ever again, her mom had never removed it.

She stalled before it and touched the smoothed bump of blue at its edge. Home. Yellow light caught her eye. The sun was back out, and beams of liquid sunshine spilled into the hallway. She'd forgotten how much yellow her room cast in the sunshine. Although the rug was white, the bedcovers white, the trim white, and the roman shades a blue floral print, the yellow walls bathed everything in a warm glow. It was a happy room, a sanctuary.

She crossed the white carpet, noting that nothing new had stained it in fifteen years. The only mark was the faint smudge from a blue pen that had exploded in ninth grade. Glancing around, her eyes struck upon memories—so many good. Most good, in fact. Pictures of friends. Makeup in dishes still sat on her dresser, dried now, but oh-so-important back then, especially the colored mascara. Lexi's cheerleading poms were still tucked behind the corners of her bulletin board. Alyssa had taken them one night from her best friend and never returned them. She pulled them down now and liked how their soft rustle filled her silent room. Pens on her desk. Three Mason jars full. She'd forgotten how many she owned and how she'd written her notes in a rainbow of colors throughout high school and college. Red for lectures, green for readings, blue for original thoughts, purple for connections and correlations, black for the answer to any problem—in English, math, science, or history.

She pulled open her dresser drawer and cringed at the graphic T-shirts and prairie tops she found there. The next drawer held jeans and a couple pairs of cargo pants, one with a pink camo pattern. The early 2000s had been an odd time for fashion, she thought. Yet as she looked down at her own clothes—ones she'd been wearing since everything in her car was stolen in Rawlins—she decided she'd had enough. Odd or not, she pulled out the camo pants and a tight white cropped T-shirt with capped sleeves, pleased she could still fit into them. She looked in the mirror and, noting the dish of tiny hair clips, piled her hair into her signature high school style, a high ponytail with clips pulling back the bangs and sides.

"You look good."

Alyssa spun with a yelp. "What are you doing here? You scared me."

Janet's eyes were bright and clear and danced with laughter. The look startled Alyssa more than the interruption. Was it size? Shape? Color? Alyssa dismissed each as she questioned. Nothing was different. Yet she hardly recognized her mom's eyes. Something new was igniting them from within.

But whatever it was, it was gone in the flash it took for her mom's gaze to lock on hers. Her expression changed, and the light vanished. "I'm sorry. I assumed you heard me come up the stairs."

Alyssa thought she heard a note of contrition, but that didn't fit. Janet had never been one to show embarrassment, regret, or self-reproach. As far as her mother was concerned, Alyssa firmly believed, a good offense made for the only defense.

And Alyssa was her mother's daughter.

"I didn't," she snapped. She hadn't intended her words to carry such aggression, but rather than pull back, she let her harsh notes drift between them. She felt her pulse pick up its pace to prepare for battle as words—most unkind and rude—filled her head.

Yet even as the words flooded her brain, she also felt a skipped beat in her heart. The longing that she'd felt leaning into her dad's hug, the sense of camaraderie she'd felt staring up at Andante's tall owner, overwhelmed her with the undeniable truth that she yearned for such a connection with this person too. Her mom. It was a pulled-inside-out, laid-bare feeling. She glanced down to her twisting hands and tried to still them.

"I came home early because your dad said you were moving in with me today." Janet gestured into the room. "I washed your sheets yesterday to make sure they were fresh, but then when you didn't—"

"He called you?" Alyssa cut her off.

"He calls me every day." Janet spoke softly, slowly, as if trying to share with her something more than mere facts.

"How'd you convince him to forget what you did? How'd you do it?"

"I didn't convince your dad of anything, Alyssa, and he'll never forget. Neither will I."

Janet stepped into the center of the room. Her perfume filled the space. It was rich and floral, the height of spring tipping to summer, filled with jasmine, lily, and sunshine. Then a vanilla note reached Alyssa—the base note that grounded all the others and brought them home. This home. Alyssa stepped forward before she caught herself, and stepped back twice to make up for her lapse.

Janet smiled and gestured to Alyssa's outfit.

Alyssa looked down and could only imagine how silly she looked. She pulled at the T-shirt, trying to create space between herself and it, trying to create distance from the girl she had been to the strong woman she thought she had become.

"Dad also mentioned your car was broken into and that you lost all your stuff. Not that you don't fit into those." Janet smiled again.

"Lucky me." Alyssa plucked harder. "Until I make some money, this is what I've got."

"You can borrow some of mine. Or I'll take you shopping."

"No," Alyssa barked. She looked at her mom's outstretched hand and shook her head at the offered olive branch. "I can't do this . . . I don't know how you manipulated Dad, but I can't pretend everything's okay, Mom. I can't borrow your clothes or take your money. We don't have that kind of relationship. You ruined it."

"But we can. If you let us."

"You think it's that easy? That all of a sudden anything and everything I do is going to be good enough for you? That what you did—because you're the one who did it—should be okay and everyone should just forgive, forget, move on, and get with the program, your program, because you say so? Well, we can't. We are not okay, Mom. I am not okay."

Chapter 9

Alyssa heard her last sentence. It took on a life of its own and filled the room. *I am not okay.*

It was so much more than XGC, more than losing everything and landing back in her old clothes in her old room. It was a new reality she hadn't yet had the courage to face. *I am not okay.* She repeated the words to herself, unable to deny their truth.

She dashed from the room and down the stairs, through the kitchen, and slammed the back door on her way out. When had she last been okay? It was a question she hadn't drawn close to asking. Probably because she instinctively knew there was no answer, no incident or point within her life she could fix upon. Besides, what was the point of asking questions that had no answers? But they do, something deep within her whispered. All questions have answers.

Taking out a few flowers while turning around in the driveway, Alyssa sped onto Little Pine Avenue and headed west. She dug through her handbag, popped three Tums into her mouth at the stop sign, and looked down at her clothes with a groan. She was still dressed in 2004.

Going back is the quickest way on.

She almost laughed because it was the only way on. She literally, figuratively, and all -ivelys in between had nowhere else to go *but* back.

She lowered her forehead to the steering wheel and tapped it as she cycled through her options. Unless her dad relented, and he wasn't going to, home with Mom was all that was on offer. With no money, even crashing with Lexi and her husband was not an option—not that crashing in their tiny two-bedroom ever was. There truly was only back.

Alyssa sat up straight. She could do this—until Labor Day weekend, just as she'd said. She could play the game. After all, she'd learned from the best. Her mom was formidable, always had been, but Alyssa too could be a force—of unblinking obduracy. She needed the summer to get her feet under her, and if ignoring her mom for a few months was what it took, so be it.

She pushed the accelerator and turned the wheel to circle the block and go home.

The car didn't move.

"No . . . no . . . no . . . Not now."

The engine flipped at her first attempt, ground oddly at her second, and after another four tries stopped turning over at all. She gave up and walked the half mile of tree-lined Little Pine Avenue to Cypress Street and on to Jasper's Garage three blocks farther down.

"Mr. Jasper?"

The sun was hot now, and a small rivulet of sweat ran down that too-tight white T-shirt. Alyssa plucked at it again.

"I know you. How are you?" The man grinned, calling forth an answering grin from Alyssa.

He had been giving that line to everyone for years. Alyssa doubted he remembered her at all, but the way he always said it, even when she was a teenager buying Red Vines, made her and everyone else feel seen and welcomed.

"Alyssa Harrison. It's nice to see you, sir."

"Sir?" Jasper rubbed his hands down his uniform shirt. "You call me Jasper. What can I do you for?"

"My car died." Alyssa pointed down the street. "It's a 2010 Honda CRV."

"Did it now?" Jasper followed her gaze down the street. "I got no one here right now. I can call you a tow unless you can get her here."

"The engine stopped turning and—" Alyssa's lips fell open as the consequences of some money-saving moments materialized. She'd dropped the rental, towing, and a few other amenities to her insurance three months before. An eight-dollars-a-month savings was going to cost her hundreds now. "Don't call anyone. I'll get it here," she assured him and headed back to her car.

For the entire walk she chanted, "It'll start," to herself, only to change the mantra to a full lecture upon reaching the car. "You have to start. Do you hear me? You don't have any options, so get the job done."

Five minutes of solid lecturing did not start the car. Two more minutes got it to start and roll through the intersection, but then nothing. Another ten minutes of red-faced berating didn't turn the engine again.

Alyssa shot straight up as someone tapped on her driver's window. He looked familiar, but she couldn't place him.

She stepped out of the car again—even the electric window no longer rolled down.

"Do you need help?" His eyes were warm and welcoming. Then he blinked, and his smile tipped into a grin. "I'm Chris McCullough, and you are clearly Alyssa Harrison." He pumped her hand. "I'm a friend of your mom's. What's the trouble?"

"It won't start, and I need to get it to Jasper's." She pointed down the street, then faced Chris again. "Did . . . did she send you?"

"Was she supposed to?" Chris tilted his head in question.

At Alyssa's head shake, he tapped her car's hood. "Put it in neutral and keep your foot off the brake."

She watched him walk back to his pickup and tried again to place where she'd seen him.

He moved his truck slowly into her car, bumper to bumper.

She quickly climbed into her car, put the engine in neutral, and kept her feet flat on the floorboard. His truck pressed so gently she didn't feel a jolt, just the movement of her car forward. Soon she was turning the wheel and rolling it into Jasper's parking lot.

"Thank you so much. I don't really know what to say."

"You're welcome and it's very nice to meet you, Alyssa. I'd stay, but I need to be at the hospital in ten."

"Oh . . . I'm sorry."

He threw her a quizzical glance. "Don't be . . . Tell your mom I said hi."

She shook his hand through his truck window, and as he drove away, she remembered. It was the guy her mom had been talking to in the bookshop as Alyssa looked through the window. She remembered Janet's animated face, Chris's laughter, and his joy just now at mentioning her mom's name. It matched her mom's light and laughter upon entering her bedroom—and none of it made any sense, like a puzzle with edges that didn't align.

"Ohhh . . . eeee . . ."

Alyssa turned. Jasper was deep under her car's hood.

"Is it bad?"

"Real bad. You've blown your mass airflow sensor and your alternator is shot."

"Will it cost a lot?"

Jasper looked at her, and something in his eyes flickered and softened. "Even if I don't charge you labor, the parts will cost you close to $1,200."

"I don't have that kind of money." She closed her eyes and felt like Alice falling down the rabbit hole. She opened them quickly before she hit a new bottom, and her gaze caught upon a sign.

She pointed to it. "You have a Help Wanted sign in your window. Can I work off the cost of the repairs?"

The older man's eyes widened beyond reason. "You want to work here?"

"I need the money. I need my car. And you need help."

"I do, but I don't think that'll work." He worried a rag between his hands.

Alyssa noted the dark lines of grease following each wrinkle and along his cuticles. She almost agreed with his statement until she remembered hers. She needed the money. More than that, she needed someone to believe in her and let her prove herself on any level. "Please. I need work."

Jasper stared at her. She worked to keep her gaze steady.

"I'll give you a try."

Chapter 10

Best hour of the week." Mike Stowell, dressed and ready for work in his Gramercy Electric uniform shirt, reached across Seth Harrison for a packet of sugar.

"Certainly the one I need the most." Seth chuckled and turned to look around the room.

Over the twenty years they'd gathered, these men had become good friends, trusted friends. In good times they'd watched ball games together, met for Saturday afternoon beers to chat work and life, and shot each other random emails, jokes, and texts to stay connected and encourage each other through the week.

But in bad times—and the last three years had been saturated with those—they had really shined. Mike, showing up with frozen dinners at his apartment right after he'd left Janet. Roger, meeting him for coffee and even switching trains so Seth had a friend to chat with in the mornings on the way to work. Pickup games of basketball or tennis on the weekends. And this group every Thursday morning.

Seth saw Andante's new owner walk in the door . . . Jeremy something or other. He tried to remember what Janet had said about him. She liked the young man, said he was working hard, that he reminded her of herself.

For years people had seen one persona of his wife—confident, charming, adept, pulled together, the consummate hostess. The kids had seen other traits within their mom—controlling, manic, and manipulative. And while he'd reprimanded them when they rolled too far, he had to admit he'd let them vent too often and with too much freedom over the past three years.

It had soothed his ache. It felt good to have all those fingers, those daggers, pointing at Janet and not at him. But all along—even in his lowest moments—he'd known the truth. Janet's control and brave façade covered a bottomless well of doubt. So certain that her substance was virtually nil, she had buffed on the brightest gloss. Only when scratched could one see how thin her top layer really was.

And while that brought some measure of comfort, it also brought his greatest hurt. Yes, Janet had been the one who cheated. In one night she'd betrayed him, their marriage, and their family. She had defied everything he thought they were. But that night also made it painfully clear how for years he'd taken his understanding of his wife for granted; how he had acted as if the image, and not her substance, was the real Janet; how he had left her alone years before she left him. And how, in the end, it wasn't his strength that had ushered in their newfound "good times"; it was her act of humility and courage.

Mike caught sight of Jeremy and pounced. "You own the Daily Brew, don't you?"

"I renamed it, but yes." Jeremy's eyes widened, and a minute step backward revealed he was one handshake from fleeing.

Almost as if Mike sensed it, he clamped a congenial hand on Jeremy's shoulder. The younger man was going nowhere now. "I keep forgetting to call it that . . . Georgia Pavlis is my aunt."

"You're kidding." Jeremy smiled. "She's a good woman. She used to call up personally to buy her beans from a place I worked at out in Seattle. She never ordered online."

"That's Aunt Georgie. A few decades late and always up for a good chat." Mike laughed, and Jeremy visibly relaxed.

Their little group broke up with no more words as the new pastor called them to a circle of chairs.

Seth noted that Pastor Zachary Lennox, only three months at Winsome Presbyterian Church, in whose basement they sat, looked to Father Luke McCullough from St. Francis de Sales Catholic Church for confirmation as he waved the men to order. Once seated, Father Luke gave a tiny confirming nod, and Pastor Zach bowed his head.

"Lord, thank you that so many of us could make it here today. Bless our brothers who couldn't join us and be in our conversations this morning. Also stay close as we leave and travel into the day. Help each man to follow you in every aspect of his life. Amen." He looked up and smiled across the group. "I'm so glad you all are here today. This week I sent out Luke 6:42, and I'll read it quickly to start off our discussion. 'How can you say to your brother, "Brother, let me take the speck out of your eye," when you yourself fail to see the plank in your own eye? You hypocrite, first take the plank out of your eye, and then you will see clearly to remove the speck from your brother's eye.' Any thoughts about that big old plank and the tiny speck?"

"Some reading, Pastor," Mike offered with a laugh. "Sure brought home that I don't see things clearly."

Seth, usually reluctant to chime in, found himself joining Mike. "It was a hard passage for me, actually. Self-reliance fooled me for years. I thought it was a virtue, but I—" He looked around the room and conceded that every man knew him, and his story. "You all know I blamed Janet for"—he shrugged—"a speck—a sharp, painful speck, but still a speck—compared to my own plank."

Pastor Zach nodded. He, of course, didn't know what everyone else did, but by the nods, murmurs, and soft chuffs, he could tell the other men had walked closely with Seth. This group continually surprised him like that. He'd been at four churches in his short decade as a pastor, and never had he witnessed a group of men who shared so openly and spoke with such honesty—and met with such regularity. One hour each and every Thursday morning, without fail.

"Just don't get in our way," one of the members had told him early on. "We want you there to guide us, but don't tell us what to think or how to meet each other where we need to be met."

Zach had swallowed, nodded, and heeded the warning. But it had left him on edge too. He didn't want to detract from their meetings in any way, but wasn't he also supposed to guide and shepherd them? But rather than get the job done, it always left him looking to Father Luke from the Catholic church down the street, the other clergyman who attended the Thursday morning gatherings.

A prolonged silence snagged Zach's attention. Everyone stared at him. He cleared his throat. "I'm sorry . . . Could you repeat that?"

Zach grimaced as a man with "Pete's Plumbing" embroidered on his shirt—what was his name?—repeated his words.

"I said planks also hold things up. A good plank provides support . . . And it got me thinking about stuff I rely on, not unlike what you said, Seth. Stuff that I shouldn't rely on. I can't help anybody if I'm hanging tight to something."

"Good point." Zach leaned forward. "That's a really good point."

He doubled his efforts to engage with enthusiasm, until he

noted a couple men glancing at their watches. He lifted his wrist. "Oh . . . Hey . . . We've run over. I'm sorry, gentlemen. I should set a timer. Any prayer concerns before we go?"

Mike Stowell raised his hand. "I'm sure you all notice George isn't here today. Margery isn't doing well."

Quiet concern filled the room. Zach didn't remember George. He needed to remember their names, their faces, and their concerns. How could he guide them if he didn't even know them? He took a quick silent survey as the men asked Mike about George and Margery, and realized he only knew the names of half of those present.

It didn't matter that he was new. It didn't matter that this was his first assignment as head pastor, of over one thousand congregants, and that his head spun with all the input and the suggestions, the names and the faces. His wife said it would all come together, but he suspected she was just being kind. She knew far more names than he did, and had integrated much better into the life of their church, the schools their kids would attend, and their community. Last week he'd started to have nightmares about the whole thing.

As the questions and conversation faded, all looked to him again to close the morning. He, of course, looked to Father Luke, who smiled back at him, then bowed his head. "Let's close in a quick prayer."

As the men left, Zach busied himself with replacing the chairs. He needed to stop looking to the other man for advice. Grabbing another chair, he almost bumped into him.

"It's not easy, is it? At least you don't rotate like we do."

"Thank God," Zach exclaimed. "It is truly an answered prayer for me." He looked around the basement room. "If I don't screw this up, I could be here till I retire."

Father Luke chuckled. "I get it. In my twenty-five years, I've had nothing longer than seven years in one parish. Most have been three to four years."

"And St. Francis?"

"I've been here four years. I suspect they'll keep me a full seven, if not a little longer. I'm not getting any younger, but more importantly, the parish is growing and thriving right now—another 'Thank God.'"

Zach laughed. "This one too, if I don't get in God's way . . . I like this town, and my eldest will start school in the fall here." Zach took a deep breath. He needed to address another issue that was causing nightmares. "What would you think of our congregations joining for a Labor Day potluck? They've had one here every year for the past twenty as far as I can tell, but the woman in charge moved away and I'm not sure whom to ask on such short notice."

Father Luke chuckled. "I'm not a fan of potlucks. I got food poisoning from a quiche sitting too long in the sun. What do you say to a real barbecue? I've got a parishioner who is magic on a smoker. Best ribs and brisket you'll ever taste. How about St. Francis will host this year, and you all can be our guests?"

"Thank you." Zach laughed for the first time in three months. "I'd really like that."

Chapter 11

"When it rains, it pours."

Jeremy picked up the Morton Salt with its girl in yellow and tapped it back onto the counter next to his cell phone.

"What's that, Boss?" Brendon paused, then pulled another platter of muffins from the refrigerator.

"You know this started as a proverb, became a brand slogan, got picked up in a country song, and who knows what else . . . Now it's descriptive of my life."

At Brendon's befuddled expression, Jeremy waved his hand to the front. "Never mind."

Brendon nodded and pushed out through the swinging door.

Lucky kid, Jeremy thought. Not a thing in the world to ripple your waters. Good home life. Great town. Most popular kid at school. The full package.

Jeremy rested both elbows on the cool stainless-steel counter and ran his hands through his hair. He had pushed too hard. Again.

"There are some issues. I can see that. She doesn't read, Krista, even the most basic words and sounds, with any comfort." He had meant to start calm and measured in his tone, but as the words landed just as he wanted them to, he toppled over them in his anxiety. "Do you ever read with her? Have you not heard any of this?"

"Yes, I read with her. I'm a good mother, Jeremy," Krista rushed in. "And you have virtually no responsibilities here, so it's easy for you to point the finger at me. It costs you nothing."

"That's not only not fair but it's what I've been asking for the past three months . . . *Give* me responsibilities."

Echoes of his conversations with Ryan and something unspoken but real passed between him and Krista. She shifted away—just as he had done to Ryan. Her voice confirmed it—just as his had—calm and in control, yet teetering on the edge of defensive.

"The doctor's report isn't in yet. I'm not going to make any decisions, and especially not label her in some way, until we know what we're dealing with. Besides, people can get through life without being top-notch readers, Jeremy."

"Of course they can. But this isn't a label either. Teaching her differently, according to how her brain works, will help her in every way."

He thought back to his own middle and high school years, and the classes he'd been required to take, not that he'd ever told Krista, or anyone. It wasn't about learning for him; it was about recording, assessing, tracking. New home placements often came with new schools, and he was questioned, tested, and given special classes to either "come up to speed" or "acclimate more smoothly" each time. He always suspected he could track his school experience far better from his State of Washington files than from his high school yearbooks. If he were completely honest, he couldn't separate the homes from the moves from the classes. The constant moving and endless transitioning were isolating. He feared the same for his daughter.

"You shouldn't move." He ground out the words.

"How'd you get back there?"

"She needs a stable home. You think moving will help, starting her somewhere new, but you're changing everything at once. I'm not there, her grandparents won't be there, you'll be working all the time, and now they're talking maybe a whole different learning track."

Sparks shot through the air. He could feel them torpedo across the line.

"No one has said anything close to that. She's seven. And we are not having this discussion."

Jeremy blanched. He had heard those words and that tone only once before, and he would never forget when and where. They were delivered in a harsh staccato with a cadence unlike anything else Krista had ever said. The exact words she'd hurled at him when she walked, six months pregnant, out of their marriage. *We are not having this discussion.*

And they didn't.

Nothing more was said. She didn't engage. She didn't relent. In fact, the closest he got as she flew home to Illinois was a call from the airport. "There is no shame in an imprudent and quick marriage, Jeremy. Think of this as a conscious uncoupling where two people are mature enough to part ways."

At the time he'd wondered where she'd gotten those words too. But he didn't anymore. They had become part of her lexicon.

Yet this sentence, *We are not having this discussion*, still wielded power.

"We can take it slow. I won't push—"

Krista had hung up.

Jeremy drew himself back to the present and his Morton Salt container, tapping it against the counter. He straightened as Ryan pushed through the swinging door.

"You got Brendon closing tonight?"

"Yeah, I forgot to tell you. I'm trying to take Becca more. I figure if Krista feels more supported, maybe she won't move away." He shook his head, unwilling to confide. "I've got to do something. She's why I moved here, after all." While he tried to make his words sound light, they fell flat.

Ryan spread his fingers on the counter. "This shop is why I moved here. I came to be your assistant. This kid has been here five days. Why wouldn't I close?"

Jeremy pushed back from the counter. "Come on, man. You came 'cause you needed out of Seattle. We both know that."

Ryan looked like he'd been slapped—and figuratively, he had.

"I shouldn't have said that. But you've got enough on your plate, and face it, that kid is more pulled together than both of us on our best days. The luck of birth, right?" Again his quip fell flat. "Look, he said he wanted to stay on through his senior year, so I figured he might as well take on more responsibility from the get-go. We've been working unbelievable days this past week. You should appreciate a break."

"It's your shop, Boss." The words were right, but the tone behind them cut.

That had never been an element of their relationship before. Boss and employee. Passive aggression. From day one they'd found a brother in each other. Jeremy reeling from a childhood in which all choices were made for him; Ryan recovering from a youth in which all the choices he made harmed him. Yet the bond that felt so strong when they'd packed the last of Ryan's boxes into the back of their U-Haul and jumped into Jeremy's Subaru Forester for the thirty-hour drive, during which they talked nothing but coffee, felt a lifetime ago.

Ryan gestured across the kitchen to the small office tucked into the back corner. No walls divided the space; it was delineated only by a change in flooring. The kitchen's concrete gave way to wide plank wood slats.

In the remodel, Jeremy told the contractor not to touch that corner. He loved the small office. It felt grounded and wood warm. In the six-by-eight space, with the two corner walls lined by floor-to-ceiling bookshelves, sat an old heavy oak desk, probably used and left by some accountant in the 1930s. It was beat up, massive, probably weighed more than the eight-burner industrial stove, and it was too big to get out the door. All of which pleased Jeremy. Something about its permanence and utility appealed to him.

The chair tucked under it was equally large, sturdy, and sat on brass balls. The seat also held the only pillow he hadn't removed in the remodel. It was an accountant's green fitted seat cushion, sensible, old, comfortable. It gave the impression that anyone who calculated numbers while sitting on it would always come out in the black.

"We've dipped too far into savings. We won't meet operating expenses soon."

"Impossible." Jeremy sighed. "I set the budget. The bank even reviewed and approved it for the loan."

"We way outspent on the remodel, and for the budget you calculated these first weeks at 80 percent previous revenue. You said that was conservative considering how great we made this place. We're at 50."

"So I was wrong. Is that it?" Jeremy stretched to his full height. The move would have been far more intimidating if Ryan hadn't been only four inches shorter and fifty pounds heavier—and all muscle.

Ryan sighed. "Not wrong. I'm simply trying to tell you what's up."

"Do you think I don't know what's up? Do you think I don't

know I overspent, and that it's actually not 50, that instead the shop's only pulling 43 percent of the Daily Brew's revenues? Do you think I don't know that my 'cushion' isn't so fluffy anymore? Do you think I'm oblivious to all this?"

"No. I—"

"No? No what? You think that for all my planning I can't work out the math behind a simple coffee shop. Revenues have to be higher than expenses, right? It's that simple. Or am I missing something?"

"Nothing." Ryan stared at him. "You've got it all in hand." Without another word, he pushed out the alley door.

"Take the rest of the day off," Jeremy called after him. "That'll save me twenty bucks an hour."

Alone he sank into the chair and dropped his head to the desktop. The pounding in his head backed off to a dull thump, and his heart soon steadied its beat. And a sliver of truth broke in so softly he let it wind its way through his thoughts.

He *hadn't* known.

He knew Andante was in trouble. That was obvious. Only one full week open and nothing looked like what he'd expected. But he'd made up the 43 percent number. He'd made it up and thrown it out there with anger and bitterness because he had overspent and was caught off guard, and was embarrassed, and was ashamed. Bottom line, he was lost.

He lifted his head and caught sight of Ryan's worn paperback resting on the edge of the desk. He'd worked after closing yesterday, not asking for or probably even expecting pay, baking another five batches of those semi-dreadful from-a-box blueberry muffins. He must have forgotten it when he stayed late.

He stayed late.

Jeremy repeated this reality as he bent the thin copy of *Of Mice and Men* in his hands.

And that was how you thanked him, he thought—and dropped his head to the desk again.

Chapter 12

Janet let the cat out the alley door and had just turned to walk back to her studio when a knock echoed through the office. She pushed the door open.

Chesterton scurried across her feet and Alyssa faced her. "He was frantic to get back in."

"Silly thing, I just let him out." Janet poked her head out the alley door. Other than a few teenage boys standing with Jeremy's new hire, Brendon, at the far end of the alley, it was empty.

"What—" Janet stopped. She was about to ask, "What are you doing here?" It was the very question her own mom asked every time she visited her apartment, and it set the hairs on the back of her neck straight on end—not unlike the cat's when Janet used to try to pick him up.

She rolled the question into a quick statement. "What a lovely surprise. I'm so glad to see you. Come in."

Alyssa stepped past her and stood in the center of the dark office. She looked smaller to Janet, less formidable than she had when she stormed out of her bedroom two days before. The whole episode, including the circa 2004 clothing, had reminded Janet so much of Alyssa's high school years that she had spent the rest of that day vacillating between laughter and tears. They'd lasted three minutes in the same room. It did not bode well for the summer or for their relationship.

Now she watched Alyssa look toward the front of the store as if calculating her exit options. Light poured in through the front bay windows, making the books look lit internally, as though their stories were too bright, too colorful, and too alive to remain between their covers. The store glowed. She smiled and glanced to her daughter. Alyssa too held that look of wonder—until she directed her attention back to her mom.

"Remember when you sent me here for my college essays?"

Janet did remember. She remembered all their yelling matches. She remembered every standoff. In the past few months each memory had washed over her anew. And, while revisiting each was painful, the insights gave her hope. What before she had regarded as instances of Alyssa's ingratitude, obstinance, and petulance were recast in light of her own issues of control, manipulation, and anger. The wave of memory should have broken her, if it hadn't also become freeing. And if looking back and accepting the past felt freeing, how much better would forgiveness and resolution feel? Janet struggled to hold herself back. Alyssa wasn't there yet.

"I still have a lot of the books Mrs. Carter gave me."

Janet straightened. Back then one issue was that Alyssa wanted to handle her college applications herself. But Janet had wanted them to be the best. Mrs. Maddie Carter, the retired English teacher who owned the bookshop and tutored out of a storage closet, was their compromise. But she never knew Maddie had given Alyssa books. Granted, she only became friends with Maddie once she herself started working in the shop three years ago, and only two before Maddie died, but still . . . She'd never known.

"What books?" Janet held her breath in anticipation. Maddie

never suggested books without a reason. Her suggestions were personal, indicative, instructive, and life changing. To have such insight into her daughter was both enticing and terrifying.

"*The Catcher in the Rye*, *Bridge to Terabithia*, *Where the Red Fern Grows* . . . I liked that she didn't give me books I 'should know' rather than books I'd enjoy. *From the Mixed-Up Files of Mrs. Basil E. Frankweiler* was one. Kid books, middle-grade books, adult books—age didn't matter. I'll never forget Ramona, Katniss Everdeen, and Antonina Zabinski." Alyssa's voice sounded wistful, as if she had forgotten them and was only now remembering.

"Voice, courage, companionship, place."

Alyssa shot her a glance.

Janet shrugged. She should have kept her mouth shut. "That's what I get from those books and those characters, but it's probably different for everyone."

Alyssa nodded, more in a synthesizing information way than an *I agree* way. "I think I owe you an apology for yesterday."

Janet felt a snarky *You think?* rise within her. Her snappy anger still felt like an old comfortable coat she often longed to wear. It was familiar, almost soothing, and for years, she would have let the comment fly and enjoyed the sting it brought both her and Alyssa. My oh my, she ruefully thought, this changing stuff is hard work. She tilted her head to her studio. "Come in here and we can talk."

Alyssa stepped through the doorway, and Janet watched as a series of emotions played across her face. Alyssa's first flash of awe and delight made her smile. Yet a sharpness lingered last, and Janet felt her face drop into a frown mirroring her daughter's.

She trailed Alyssa's gaze, trying to imagine what she saw, what it said to her, why it irritated her. Janet's heart sank, because her art was the purest expression of her very self. Her creations covered the walls, some in charcoal, some in delicate watercolor, others made from huge swaths of bright acrylic paint. Two new oil paintings were propped along the walls, and a stack of canvases blocked the doorway to the shop's powder room.

Alyssa's eyes drifted up. Janet's followed. A skylight bathed the room in natural light, and through it she caught a glimpse of cerulean blue. It was going to be a beautiful day.

"What—" Alyssa did not finish her question, as the answer arrived with the asking and she was reminded of a verse that had struck her long ago: *For now we see through a glass, darkly . . .*

She was under no illusion that the verse referred to a daughter seeing her mother, but the truth of it still applied. She had "seen through a glass darkly." No, worse than that, she hadn't seen at all.

The reality of the room clarified so much in her life, and her interpretation of it. Even though she'd never seen her mom hold a paintbrush or doodle with a pencil, she recognized her in every brushstroke and line within the room. And they did not reveal a mom she knew or a life she understood and lived, but a world she had somehow missed. One that should have existed, but never did. Her senses were captured by the creative cacophony. Forget the window displays, she thought, this is where someone shot sunshine and infused all with its life and color.

"You're an artist," Alyssa said softly.

She faced her mom and fully absorbed what she'd seen in Chris's eyes as he met her at the side of the road. He had known her by sight, and looking now, it was so clear why he had. In the three years since she'd moved, Alyssa knew her face had thinned—she was perhaps too thin now. Too much work, too much stress, too little sleep . . . But her mom—she looked better than she had in years. It felt as if across time and space their ages had crept closer together rather than running parallel.

This was not the Janet of three years ago—wan, thin, with dark circles and angry eyes pink from perpetual crying. This was not the Janet of Alyssa's high school years either, almost brittle in her own need to manage every moment. She was something entirely new, animate, happy, alive—and completely disconcerting.

The rest of the verse drifted to Alyssa's mind . . . *But then face to face: now I know in part; but then shall I know even as also I am known.* Again, not about a mother and a daughter, nor about revelations here on earth, yet to see someone or something more clearly than ever before, as if seeing their essence, not just their being, felt as revelatory and consequential.

Janet had always had a certain flair, in decorating, in dress, and in a vocabulary she wielded like a weapon. Despite striving with every single breath of every single day, Alyssa had never measured up, never quite felt secure in Janet's love. There was her second-grade self-portrait. They'd been studying Van Gogh and other artists, and Alyssa could still feel the pressure of each word delivered during the parents' tour of their art exhibit. *Proportion*, *dominance*, *realism*, *abstraction*, and *exaggeration.* Somehow she'd missed each one. Then, in fourth grade, they got to pick any subject to paint they wanted. She'd painted their house, hoping it could hang in the kitchen over the light switch. But that attempt brought new and different words. *Shading*, *relief*, *focal point*, *composition*. Some of the words her teacher had taught the class, but clearly Alyssa had again missed in their execution. In response, or maybe retaliation, she had switched to an extra math class in the fifth grade and for her art requirement signed up for choir after school. In fact, her mom never knew about that one art appreciation class she'd taken in college—her only one. Just like Mrs. Carter's books, that class had been her secret and savory delight.

Janet's happy sigh brought her back to the present. "I'm becoming one. Again. Can I show you around the room?"

Alyssa couldn't move a muscle.

Her mom took it as a yes and eagerly pointed to one wall. "This is where it began in February. I call her *The Woman*." She described all the words she'd penned in different fonts, inks, textures, and sizes into a large word cloud of a woman moving forward toward the viewer. And in the center of a large piece of linen paper, Janet had created something extraordinary. Tall and strong, the mass of words didn't cover the woman, they created her. They defined and propelled her.

Alyssa stepped close to untangle them. *Confidence, good, eager hands, food, confers, buys, earnings, plants, vigorously, strong, profitable, open arms, no fear, scarlet, fine, purple, dignity, wisdom, household, blessed, noble, praise.*

"The words come from Proverbs 31. Maddie, Mrs. Carter, gave it to me in a letter."

Alyssa stepped back and took in the room again. "Four months? How is that possible?" She heard the note of sarcasm in her voice and bit her lip against it.

Janet, by her wondrous expression, didn't hear it. "Some nights, early on, it felt like I lived and breathed only this. There was a clarity, creativity, and a hyper-focus I can't explain. Look here. This is a painting I did of you. Do you remember the photo we took of you on the swings in Milan? The street artist painted your face? And this one . . ."

She moved through the room pointing here, there, low, high—Alyssa barely kept up with the color, the light, the commentary, the perspective. She found that the most challenging. The perspective. She didn't recognize her own mom.

Janet must have felt her shift of emotion, because she stopped and stared at her. She reached out as if to touch Alyssa's arm, then pulled back before making contact. "I'm sorry. I've thought about this moment for a long time, and I'm messing it up, not unlike Tuesday. I would've talked to you that night, but your light was off when I got home and then you were gone all day yesterday and . . . I didn't want to wake you this morning."

Alyssa kept her eyes on the walls. Looking at her mom was too hard—like when she tried as a kid to look at the sun and not blink. More had changed than she anticipated, and in that moment, when again the ground gave way beneath her, she struggled in her desperation to find stability.

"Nothing's the same, is it?" The words came out in a whisper and felt more for herself than for her mom.

"I'm not sure what you mean." Janet stepped toward her again.

"I mean you, Dad, home, not home, me . . . this." Alyssa waved her hand around the room. "I thought I could start again. That, in coming home, maybe I could catch my breath, catch up." She twisted her wrist, fingers now pointing toward Janet. "Where was this when we were growing up, Mom? You don't just go from zero to this in four months." She stopped. The back of her throat stung with tears.

"I think I'd been storing it up for years. It kind of exploded out of me. And that was wrong, but I didn't know—I promise I didn't know."

"Didn't know what?"

"That art, expressing myself in this way, was such an integral part of me. I got it wrong. I listened to the wrong voices and was punishing myself, or your father . . . I don't even know anymore, but I ended up punishing you and Chase too. We moved here so fast, then you were born and I wanted to make everything perfect for you. I wanted to be perfect. The perfect wife. Mother. Friend. Neighbor. PTA volunteer. There wasn't any room, at least I didn't see any, for this, for me. I thought I had to leave it behind, that it was selfish and—"

A chime broke across the moment. Janet looked past her into the dark office. At the click of a switch, it filled with light.

"Janet?"

"In here," Janet called before dropping her voice to Alyssa. "Madeline. Maddie Carter was her aunt and left her the shop. She and Claire own it together now."

Alyssa turned, expecting to meet a slightly younger Mrs. Carter, someone near her mom's age. Instead she found a woman exactly her own age—and almost her height. Auburn hair arced up at her forehead, giving her face a heart-shaped appearance, before it curled past her shoulders. Madeline's brown eyes widened upon seeing her and lit with delight.

"Wow. You're Alyssa." She laughed. "Chris was right." Madeline looked between Alyssa and Janet. "Come on, you two. Don't tell me you can't see it? You're twins—well, Janet's got more wrinkles and something concerning waddling just below her chin." Madeline winked at Alyssa.

"Thank you." Janet smirked.

"Don't see what?" Another woman stepped around and in front of Madeline. This one was closer to Janet's age, with darker brown bobbed hair. "Alyssa . . . Oh, it's so good to meet you. Are you here long?" The woman threw a questioning glance to Janet and thrust out her hand. "I'm Claire Durand."

"Claire, as I said, owns the shop with Madeline," Janet added.

"How long are you here?" Madeline pressed past Claire and brought them both spilling into the small room.

"I . . . I have to go." Alyssa swiveled around them and backed through the office toward the storefront. "I really do. It's nice to meet you both, but I didn't realize how late it was." She glanced back to her mom, unable to hold her gaze. "I'm meeting Lexi for coffee."

With that, she bolted out the storefront and onto the sidewalk.

Chapter 13

Hello? Earth to Lys?" Alyssa's best friend waved a hand inches from her face. "I've been calling your name since across the street."

Alyssa grabbed her into a hug.

"Good to see you too," Lexi laughed.

Alyssa almost mentioned the studio, the women, the shop, then realized Lexi already knew. Lexi lived in Winsome, and had stayed since college. None of this was a surprise to her—only Alyssa had been left in the dark. She offered an "I'm so glad to see you" instead and looped her arm through her friend's.

Lexi spun them toward Andante. "I can't believe you didn't tell me about coming home until yesterday. Seriously, you go radio silent for six months and then you're here . . . Why are you here?" Without waiting for an answer, she cinched Alyssa tighter at their interlaced arms and whispered, "Wait till we're seated. I want to hear everything."

As they walked the few steps to the coffee shop, Alyssa took in Winsome—and saw it as if for the first time. What was once poky and provincial now bustled with activity. The town square was crisscrossed with people. New, and more, parking spaces were delineated on the diagonal rather than running along the street parallel. New plaques emblazoned the doors between shops. By the signs, many of the above-store apartments had been converted into offices—an architect, a lawyer, a dentist . . . A medical spa spanned the space above the coffee shop and Olive and Eve Designs. Even Winsome Jewelers, its protruding sign visible down a side street, sported a new logo and graphics as swanky as Andante's.

Lexi held open the coffee shop door as Alyssa focused on the fountain. Despite everything said against it for decades, she liked that the town had installed that fancy heater all those years ago and that the water now flowed all year round. There was something hopeful about that symbolism and its plaque declaring Winsome's "never-ending flow of love and support for those who have gone before us."

"Do you love living here?" she asked Lexi, who directed her toward the counter.

"Of course, you know that."

"Not too small?"

"Things are only as small as you make them. Besides, it's home."

Lexi turned to order, leaving Alyssa to chew on her comment. She thought back to Palo Alto, Silicon Valley, and how she believed that area and that time to be the antithesis of Winsome and all that occurred here. It was a happening place, moving at Mach speed with the flow of new ideas, innovation, and cutting-edge thinking—politics, progress, and a propulsion that defied gravity. Yet some days she'd never felt so small, isolated, and alone. The fact that she knew the moment her dad hugged her that no one had come nearly so close in at least six months stunned and dismayed her. She couldn't deny that even before XGC imploded, the loneliness was creeping in. And once XGC did implode, the emptiness grew more pervasive and consuming. She'd lived her last month prepping for interviews, eating the cheapest food she could buy, and only talking to her lawyer when necessary—which was hardly a legitimate human connection when he charged her $250 per hour for their chats.

Seated, Lexi issued a one-word command. "Spill."

Alyssa sighed and tried to unravel her last six months, and even the two and a half years before that. They took on a new dimension with recent revelations and events. But before she could synthesize her thoughts and create a cohesive trail through the scandal and failed interviews, Lexi shot for the heart of the matter.

"Why wouldn't you call me back? No text. Facebook. Instagram. You disappeared . . . I'm your best friend."

Alyssa snorted, then covered her nose. "Please, with my life, I closed my accounts."

Lexi's face told her that wasn't good enough. She reached across the table and tapped her friend's hand.

"I'm sorry. I was embarrassed. I still am . . . a little ashamed too."

"Ashamed? It's not your fault. You couldn't have known."

Alyssa slumped in her chair. "Yes. I could've. I could have asked more questions. I could have taken more time. I rushed. I raced ahead like I always do." She waved at Lexi. "You say it all the time. But I wanted it to work, Lex; I needed it all to be real. Nothing here was real, and Tag made XGC feel like it was the most real thing that could ever be."

"Life here was real, Lys, and it was yours. It just had more dimension than you thought, and you got rolled. Heck, I felt betrayed, and I'm not a member of your family."

"I love that you call *that* 'dimension.'"

Lexi raised a brow, and Alyssa felt herself sink deeper into her chair and concede the point. To Lexi, who'd been through far worse and survived, it was "dimension"—an aspect of life to come to terms with, accept as far as you can, and forgive the pain as you reach the other side. And Alyssa couldn't fault her. It wasn't an untried Pollyanna approach; Lexi had lived it—and through trials and circumstances that would have done much more than "roll" Alyssa.

Alyssa nodded a *You win* and jumped to her next thought. "You were grafted into the family years ago . . . Have you ever heard of 'confirmation bias'?"

Lexi laughed and shook her head. "I'm sure you'll tell me."

"We work against it running numbers, trying not to let what we want to be real, what would fit our vision of things, affect our interpretation of them—but we do. We let what we want to confirm determine what we choose to see. I needed XGC to be legit, and good, and even successful, because I needed to be those things. I needed to strike out on my own and succeed. But by someone else's standards. As always, I defined myself by another's metrics."

She said "another," but she knew Lexi understood. There was only ever one "someone." Her mom.

"And once again, you've been in your head too long. Everybody wants that, Alyssa. We want our parents to be proud of us, our peers to respect us, our friends to love us. So stop doing that too . . . You take something normal and make it sound like you're the first human to get it wrong."

Alyssa smiled. Unwittingly she had struck upon another long-time debate. This one began fourteen years ago, starting when Alyssa tried her first beer at seventeen, then got in massive trouble with her mom and grounded for three months. Oddly, her mom hadn't even been upset about the beer. *Do you know how it would look if you'd gotten caught? Do you know what that would say about me? About our family?* Alyssa, terrified, barely sipped a drink again until her twenty-first birthday. She also endured four years of Lexi chirping at her to "let yourself off the hook," "chill," and "gain a tiny bit of perspective."

Alyssa shook away the past. "Fine. But nothing about what XGC did was normal, and I was right in the center of it. I can't let myself off that easy."

Lexi sat forward. "Try, because it's over."

"Not for me."

Something in her voice cued Lexi, because she sat straight.

"I could still be in trouble. My lawyer says the FBI has gone division by division, and they've interviewed everyone in mine but me. They've made arrests; he won't say how many or who, but it's crickets where I'm concerned. They haven't reached out at all."

"That could be a good thing."

"Or they could be building a case."

Alyssa felt her breath hitch and knew she needed to change the subject. After "Trust no one," her lawyer's next piece of advice was "Never worry until I tell you to." It was good advice; dwelling on the unknown, the past, and all the questions she couldn't answer would get her nowhere. But it was hard too because—as Lexi said—she was often too deep in her own head.

Alyssa took in her friend, whose eyes now mirrored the panic she felt in her own, and wondered why she'd gone silent for six months. How had she forgotten how much they'd been through? Her withdrawal had diminished their friendship. Alyssa reached out and squeezed Lexi's hand. And from Lexi's smile, she knew nothing more needed to be said.

She also noted that Lexi's hair was dark again, back to her natural auburn. The last time she saw her friend, when she'd come for a Napa wine-tasting weekend the year before, she'd just added blonde highlights. They were now gone, and the dark suited her complexion better. "You look fantastic, by the way."

"I wish I could say the same for you." Lexi delivered the line deadpan, then leaned back, pulling her hand from Alyssa's, and crossed her arms.

Alyssa recalled giving the same reply regarding the highlights. "Touché." She grinned. "Remind me again why we're friends?"

This time it was Lexi who reached across the table and seized her friend's hand. "It's going to work out. Come crash with us. Our new place is in those townhomes they just built near the lake, and I just decorated the spare bedroom. You'll love it."

"Yes . . . I'm sure your husband would love me lurking around your place every morning."

"He would," she protested.

"Liam's fantastic, but I can't. I'm broke, Lex."

"We wouldn't charge you rent."

"You don't understand. I'm broke to the point I can't pay for groceries, gas, anything . . . My lawyer promised his firm wouldn't charge interest on my outstanding fees because I'm running a debt there too. Do you see what I'm wearing? Remember this?" Alyssa grabbed a fistful of her bright cotton skirt, then continued before Lexi could comment. "My checking account has $124 in it, my credit cards are maxed out, my savings are gone, and my car died yesterday. In fact, I gotta get going soon. My shift at Jasper's Garage begins at noon."

"You're kidding." At Alyssa's expression, she shook her head. "You're not kidding."

"I've got to pay for the repairs somehow. I need a car, Lex."

"But your parents—"

Alyssa pulled her hand away. "No way. Don't even go there."

"I'm sorry . . . I didn't know, about any of it."

"Because I couldn't tell you," Alyssa whispered as the full-pressured throb that always preceded tears filled her head. It was an all-too-familiar feeling, and she gave it her standard answer: she widened her eyes and set her jaw. As usual, the pressure dissipated.

Lexi leaned back in her chair. "Okay then . . . I've got a job for you too. And I'll pay you."

"I can wait tables? Jasper's closes at six; I can shower and be to you by six thirty. I'll work every night you'll let me." Alyssa reached for her bag and shook a couple Tums from her bottle.

Lexi raised a brow but didn't comment. She'd commented enough on those during that same Napa visit.

"I need you for something else, if that's okay, but if you're desperate we can talk tables later too. This'll be more money, though . . ." She leaned forward again. "As of last month's payment, Liam and I own 51 percent of Mirabella. The restaurant is killing it, Lys, and now we want to look at how the VC guys have run things. When they bought the place to flip, they set up their own PR, accounting, and suppliers, and while we've taken over the suppliers, they still manage the other stuff. But the spending has bothered me for a while. I don't see any good coming from it. In fact, I think we could throw dollars out an open window and create more buzz. Liam and I are the ones with wheels on the ground, and honestly, those guys are all downtown and have no clue how things run out here . . . But now we own the controlling interest."

"So now you've got a voice."

Lexi grinned. "Isn't that a lovely thing?"

"It is . . . And using your money better, growing faster, means you can buy up percentage points faster too."

"Exactly." Lexi's grin widened. "Can you imagine it? Me? Me owning my own restaurant? Liam too, of course."

Alyssa noted it wasn't the thousand-watt confident smile the world saw. Lexi's grin was the more unguarded *you've been my best friend since I was four* smile. It swamped Alyssa and left her aching about her silence over the preceding six months—Lexi would have been there for her.

As she could be there for Lexi now.

"I absolutely can. You're the hardest worker I know. Liam too, of course." She winked.

Lexi flapped a hand to her. "After you, you mean . . . Isn't that the kind of thing you did at Capital One right after college?"

"Close. I built algorithms to determine what types of spending versus income sources indicated businesses could pay back loans, but it's the same principle. You just need to break down the numbers, see where everything is going, from where everything is coming, and assess if better choices can be made."

"I don't need to. *You* need to. That's what we'll pay you to figure out for us. I interviewed two consulting firms last week, so you're lucky you finally called me and came home."

"You're hiring someone to do this for you?"

"I'm hiring you. I'm serious about this, Alyssa. This isn't friendship; this is my business . . . Both the firms I interviewed charge about five thousand for this kind of job, and you're as qualified as they are. I'd rather hire you."

"Five thousand? I can't take that."

"But you can do the work, right?"

"Yes. Of course." Alyssa tapped her hand on the table between them. "Can you pay me three thousand?" At Lexi's dark expression, she shook her head. "It's enough, and if you're wowed, tip me extra, because I can do this; but you're helping me out here too, and three thousand would be huge for me right now. Huge."

Before Lexi could reply, a shadow fell across their table.

Lexi looked up first. "Jeremy. I have someone for you to meet. Alyssa, Jeremy Miller. Jeremy, Alyssa—"

"Harrison." Jeremy talked over Lexi.

"You've met?" Lexi glanced to Alyssa.

"No," Alyssa offered in concert with Jeremy's "Last week."

Alyssa stared.

Jeremy shrugged. "I took a guess. You look exactly like your mom. You sound like her too."

Alyssa dropped her gaze to Lexi, who nodded and whispered, "You do, but I didn't think you'd want to hear it."

Jeremy pointed to Alyssa's cup. "Do you like the Yirgz? I saw you ordered it again today."

Lexi widened her eyes.

Alyssa pretended not to notice. "I definitely taste that lemon and vanilla this time."

"Really?" Jeremy narrowed his eyes, but a smile hitched on one side. "I told Brendon to give you the San Roque, just to give you a new experience and all. Clementines and cherry cola."

"Oh . . ."

"I'm messing with you. It's the Yirgz." He ran his hands down the half apron tied at his waist. "Can I get you ladies anything else?"

"I think we're good." Lexi's tone carried too much laughter for Alyssa's comfort.

"Say, what do you think of the art?" He gestured to the four small portraits hanging in a vertical line near the window. "I think I finally got the lighting right."

Alyssa straightened. "What?"

"Your mom's paintings . . . I kinda begged her for them. It was a messy moment because she refused to sell them. But then she gave them to Madeline, who gave them to me. I think she still might come steal them one day. But I really liked them and thought the colors set off the muted tones in here well. You must see them all the time, but they really spoke to me. She won't tell me who the subject is." He paused, but when Alyssa didn't reply, he rushed on.

"I had LED bulbs on them, but the beams were too bright. Your mom's work needs a broader, softer light. I got these warmer halogens yesterday."

"They look great." Alyssa nodded. She hadn't processed a word past "your mom's paintings."

"Thank you. I'm hoping they'll start conversations or something. But maybe they'll only make me happy."

Lexi gestured to them and raised a brow to Alyssa. "You know who that is?"

Alyssa nodded, only now recognizing what she should have seen at once.

Jeremy looked between them, then back to the paintings. "Oh . . . Wow . . . I . . . They're of you. I . . ." He stared at her. "I . . ." He repeated the word as if trying to backtrack through all he'd said in order to recant any imprudent words. He stopped, probably with the realization that he was now staring at her, and shook himself free. "They're beautiful."

Alyssa blushed and said nothing to either of them.

Lexi broke the moment. "Enough of art. Jeremy, come join us . . . I have an idea for you." She reached to the empty table next to them and dragged a chair over.

Alyssa widened her eyes.

"Trust me," Lexi whispered to her.

"Sure . . . Give me five? I'm a little shorthanded. My assistant isn't here." Jeremy headed toward the counters.

Lexi tilted her head to the paintings. "You've never seen your mom's work before, have you?"

Alyssa fixed her eyes on Lexi, the one friend who knew everything—every harsh word spoken, every standoff, every angry, bitter thought, and every angst-filled longing. "Have you?"

Lexi nodded. "Only in here and at the bookshop. She did a

series of book cover paintings they sold with a really cool book talk a few weeks ago. And there are the letters now circling the shop's crown molding. Her work's amazing, Alyssa, and I should tell you something else. She's different. I see it in her face; I hear it in comments at the restaurant—it's amazing how people gossip; and it's so obvious in her art. Just . . . Just be careful."

"What's that supposed to mean?"

Lexi shrugged. "As much as you used to say she didn't see you, you never really saw her either. You might attack and later wish you hadn't."

Alyssa narrowed her eyes at Lexi, who tapped the table between them. Her lavender nails made tiny bullet-like clicks on the wood surface.

"Don't give me that look. When you blew out of Chicago, I helped pack your bags. I've always stood by you, but don't ask me to forget what she did for me or lie about what I see now. In a lot of ways, your mom was my mom. It's not the same, I get that, but you know what my house was like, and your mom was always there for me . . . And things are different with her. Don't ask me how or why, because I don't know. She steers clear of me. I used to think it was because she was mad at all of us after your dad left, but I don't think that anymore. I think she was ashamed and scared, and maybe she'd been that way for a really long time." She held up her hand to Alyssa. "Don't scoff; I'm serious. Just keep an open mind, okay?"

"Dad won't let me stay with him. Refused right as I walked in the door. I'm living with her."

"That's why you won't ask him for money." Lexi laughed. "There had to be a reason, because I know he'd do anything for you."

"Now you have it."

"And your mom?"

Alyssa glanced to the door. "I just saw her studio in the back of the bookshop."

"And?"

Alyssa shot forward. "When Dad described Mom's friends, the two in the shop, I pictured three contemporaries sitting around complaining about their aching bones, the dissolution of their marriages, and the travesty of their little failing bookshop with its dusty chair in the window. Did you know Madeline is our age?"

Lexi burst out laughing. "Good to know you haven't changed. At all."

Chapter 14

Jeremy scanned the shop. He couldn't find Brendon even though he'd been told to clear tables. He pushed through the swinging door to the office. Brendon was just coming in from the alley.

"Is Ryan back?" Jeremy asked.

Brendon looked back to the door then back to Jeremy in confusion and a little alarm. "Is he supposed to be out there? I was dumping the trash."

"No. I just thought— Never mind." He gestured to the front. "Come man the register for a few minutes. A customer wants to talk to me."

"Sure thing." Brendon offered that winning smile and followed Jeremy back through the swinging door.

"What's up, Lexi?" Jeremy asked as he reached the table and dropped into the chair Lexi had moved over minutes before.

Lexi sat, arms crossed, like she was about to mastermind some great coup, but Alyssa looked as uncomfortable as he felt. Lexi could be a bulldozer, but she had been the first one to welcome him to town, and for that he'd be forever grateful.

The first day he unlocked the store, with no buzz and no fanfare under the red poppy hand-printed Daily Brew sign, she had walked in aloft four-inch heels with her wavy auburn hair and stretched out her hand.

"I'm Lexi Strahan." Bracelets jangled at her wrist. "I'm your welcoming committee." She looked around the store. "I see you haven't changed anything."

Jeremy shuddered. "I will. As soon as I figure out my plans I'm overhauling the whole space, but right now I'm just trying to keep my head from spinning off. I found out last night that the previous owner didn't tell anyone she was selling. I feel like I'm the thief arriving in the middle of the night."

Lexi had laughed. "Leave it to Mrs. Pavlis to sneak out the alley door. She probably thought it was the only way we wouldn't chain her to the coffee machine. She's pretty beloved around here."

"You know her?"

"Everyone knows her."

Jeremy remembered how his blood cooled at that comment. How suddenly nothing seemed so simple. "I hope this changing of the guard won't be a problem."

But rather than give him easy reassurance, Lexi had studied him for a few moments, then replied, "Only if you let it be. This shop is home to a lot of people in this town."

At least three times a week for those couple months before the renovations, and three times this week alone, she had come in, ordered expensive drinks and a couple of his dense and chewy blueberry muffins, tipped well, and thrown him an encouraging wave and a smile on her way back out the door.

"You happy with business?" Her abrupt question brought him back to the present and his eyes straight to hers. "I'm sure you've noticed it's slow in here."

Jeremy glared at her. He'd mentioned his concerns to her husband, Liam, the night before, seated at Mirabella's bar until the early hours of the morning. Clearly husband and wife had been talking—that's if she hadn't somehow magically overheard his blowup with Ryan that very morning.

"You know I'm not."

Lexi nodded toward Alyssa. "She can help."

"What? How can I help?" Alyssa protested.

"The same way you're helping me." Lexi pushed back from the table. "I'm paying her three thousand dollars for the project she'll tell you about, but the going rate is five. I've done my research, and I promise she'll do a better job for you at a fraction of the price. You two talk."

"And where are you going?"

"I have to go pick up new linens downtown. Our delivery got dumped at the wrong address, and I can't wait for them to sort it out; we've got a huge event tonight." She pointed to Alyssa. "We'll catch up later. I expect you at Mirabella's for dinner tonight."

"You just said you have an event."

"Please . . . I can multitask. Besides, Liam will need a few minutes alone with you to catch up. He has concerns."

Alyssa laughed. Chase, her real brother and three years younger, had nothing on her "new brother," as Liam, three years older, liked to call himself.

Lexi shifted her lavender-tipped finger to Jeremy. "I'm serious. Hire her. You need the help. No one understands numbers better than she does, and she knows this town. Got it?"

Jeremy leaned back and laughed. Typical Lexi. "Got it."

Lexi raised a brow at them both to make sure she was being taken seriously, then, waving her arm above her head with bracelets jingling, she walked out the front door.

"You gotta love her," Alyssa commented.

"Old friend?"

"Best friend." Alyssa sighed. "What's up with this place?"

"I can't hire you."

"You don't need to."

"No, I'd like to. What she said . . . I need all the help I can get, but I'm broke." He looked around. "With things this quiet, I've got until about Labor Day; then it'll be over."

"I've got my own countdown to Labor Day." At his questioning glance, Alyssa waved her hand. "Bottom line is, I've got the time and I owe her. If doing your work for free even brings her a smile, it's worth it to me."

"You must owe her big."

"She's been there for me big, and I haven't been the best of friends lately." Alyssa looked around and took in the empty store. Jeremy watched as she tapped on her phone. She noted the time and shot her eyes to his. "I've been here for almost an hour, and maybe one or two customers at most have come and gone."

"Now you get it." Jeremy sighed.

"But it's early. You must have accounted for a slow start . . . You've been open, what, a week?" She pointed to a small window sign at the base of the door, which he'd forgotten to remove. *Grand Reopening. June 4th.*

"Yes. And yes, I accounted for a slow start, but not this slow. And it's trending down day to day, not up. I need to sell about four hundred coffees a day to break even. Food has higher margins, but I'm barely selling anything there."

"What are you selling?"

They locked eyes on each other. It wasn't a standoff. It was a question, and it was deeper than what was actually said. If he read her right, she was asking for his trust. And when she didn't glance away or talk into the moment, he took the leap. "Less than a hundred, and I only have three months of float max."

"Because that was all the bank required."

"You got it."

Alyssa sat back. "I may not be able to tell you anything you don't already know, especially with such little data, but I'll tell you what I'm doing for Lexi. She'll ask us both anyway."

He chuckled. "True."

Alyssa explained what Lexi wanted and what it meant for Mirabella. Jeremy hung on every word and wished he were in the same position and could capitalize on her help. He suspected she could find the answers to every concern he'd expressed to Liam, every concern Ryan had leveled at him.

"You do this for a living?"

"Not exactly." She wavered. "I did something like it for Capital One a few years ago, but I've spent the last three out in California working for . . . Vita XGC."

The way she said the name, Jeremy knew it was important, but it took a minute to remember just how important. "The predictive medical company? The one that—" He stopped as her face paled. "That's rough. It was big news in Seattle last Christmas. A lot of Amazon and Microsoft higher-ups lost fortunes over that thing. And to get told you'll get Alzheimer's or MS or something horrible, true or not, is pretty rough."

"That's an understatement. And now to find out it was all lies. I can't imagine living like that, wondering if what we told them was true or not."

"Haven't they cleaned it all up? Told folks they aren't dying?"

"Not that I know of." She shrugged. "There's like a black box around the whole thing. Anything the news gets is just gossip. Besides, I have no idea how they'll even determine who received genuine information and who didn't."

"Some people got real information? It wasn't all a hoax?"

Alyssa shook her head. "No. It worked. I created those algorithms, and some of it was true. But, in all our testing, we got too few hits to make it profitable. Then it all went wrong somewhere, and I have no idea where."

"After Theranos, it's surprising it got as far as it did." Jeremy stretched his back.

"I suspect people weren't looking for it. I sure wasn't. It felt like everyone had learned a lesson, and we had no new technology. We didn't take blood; we didn't offer tests. We simply had a new way to synthesize data provided from established labs. It was the perfect foil really, and I fell for it."

"I'm sorry."

"Please, don't." Alyssa shook her head again. "That's my mess to unwind another day. Let's talk about you and your coffee shop."

"Sounds good to me." Jeremy laughed. "Yes, let's talk about my mess."

Alyssa joined him, and Jeremy liked the sound of her soft laugh. While it wasn't happy or joyous, it wasn't derisive either. It was light and melodic. It sounded like it hoped for and still believed in better days. "It's a better subject, for me at least."

"Okay then . . ." Jeremy outlined everything that stymied him, and this time Alyssa hung on his every word. It surprised him how much he revealed, all the fears he couldn't share with Ryan, the things that didn't make sense, even his own deficiencies in solving them. Without realizing it, he went deeper and deeper until he caught words coming from his mouth he hadn't intended to say. "To have that living room, the popular home where people come and feel welcome, and you're the host, that'd be a very special place, don't you think? That's what I've always wanted to create."

He felt a bloom crawl up his neck. It itched a little as heat spread past his collarbone. It always did when he was embarrassed. "You've let me talk way too long."

"I liked it. You'd be shocked at how few people I've actually talked to in the last six months."

Jeremy smiled as red spread all over Alyssa's face too.

She rolled her eyes and pressed her palms against her cheeks. "Back to you."

"Nothing more to say . . . Everything I thought I knew is wrong. I spent way more than I should have on the renovation and I'm still spending more than I thought, in ways I didn't anticipate. Marketing in Seattle was transactional, and here it feels relational, but I don't know what that means, how to be a part of that, and at this rate, in three months I'll declare bankruptcy and none of it will matter anymore."

Alyssa shrugged. "If you're trying to bring Seattle to Winsome, there's a story about that. The guy who endlessly pushes a boulder up a hill?"

"Sisyphus, that's me," Jeremy chuckled. "Laborious and futile."

"Okay then. Let's change that." Alyssa picked her phone up off the table. "Send me everything you've got. Not account numbers—delete those for safety—but all transactional data. Your credit card data, receipts, all inputs, then suppliers and such, rent, payroll, insurance, any and every cost, fixed and variable. Plus everything Mrs. Pavlis gave you from the Daily Brew days so that I can compare them."

"What will all that tell you?"

"Everything. Data tells a story, and by hearing it and acting upon it, we might get that boulder up the hill and keep it there. Basically that's what numbers do if you know how to read them. If you can discover who comes in here and when, and what they order, you know a lot. If you can bring that person back, entice them to purchase something different or more or more often, the story gets better, because there's a lower cost to drawing an existing customer back. Then if you find others like that person, and answer their needs, better still . . . This goes on and on. If you have a strong foundation, you've got a place to stand, and the numbers give you a lever. With those, as Archimedes said, you can move the earth—or at least the needle at one small-town coffee shop."

"Sisyphus and Archimedes on a Thursday morning in Winsome? I think I love you."

"I got a little carried away." Alyssa blushed again. This time her whole face glowed a beautiful rose tipping to a berry tone. "As I said, it's been a long time since I've talked to anyone."

"You've forgotten one small but vital detail."

Alyssa waved her hand. "Pay me in lattes."

"You can't be serious. That's absurd."

"Thank Lexi for that, if you want. Or you can thank Jasper's Garage." At Jeremy's quizzical glance, she continued. "My car broke down and I can't pay for the repairs. He's letting me work to pay them off. As much as I need the money—and I'm super happy Lexi can pay me, don't get me wrong—I need the work."

She leaned forward, and Jeremy got the impression she was about to share a secret. He tipped forward too.

"I don't know if you've ever been there—out of work, unhirable really, but it's horrible. It's . . . it's almost a dirty, hopeless feeling you can't wash away. So yes, I am serious. Pay me in lattes for now, and if we make a difference, and this place soars, do what you want later."

Jeremy watched her a few beats, and once again she didn't look away. "Okay then . . . Thank you."

She pulled out a pen, jotted her email on her napkin, and slid it to him. "Dropbox all the files to this email or text me if you have an

Apple and I'll come back in so you can AirDrop." As he reached for the paper, she pulled it back. "Oh . . . and my cell phone for that, if that's what you want to do." Her face bloomed berry again.

"I definitely need that." He folded the paper into his palm. "I'll pull them together, then text you."

She hiccupped then, still pressing her hand to her cheek. "I'm getting out of here. I've got to go acquire more social skills before we meet again."

Jeremy laughed as she rushed to collect her things and dashed out the door.

And for the first time, he thought things might work out after all.

Chapter 15

Father Luke McCullough locked the sacristy door and ambled down the stairs. There weren't too many opportunities for an amble, with nowhere to go and nothing to do, so he savored each step. A full half hour. He chuckled at the wonder of it and paused to watch a cloud skitter across the blue sky.

At the bottom of the stairs he stopped completely and listened to at least three types of birds chirp, and remembered there was one last slice of the Trager-Howard wedding cake in his rectory refrigerator. But it would still be there in a few minutes, he reminded himself, as he rounded the side of the church and faced the garden. Time to smell the flowers.

He grinned and picked up his pace. His brother sat twenty feet away on his favorite bench. "I didn't expect to see you today."

"I think best here." Chris threw him a sideways glance as Luke plopped next to him. "Must be all that good gardening I did."

Luke slapped him on the back. In doing so, he felt the paternal nature of the gesture and almost lifted his hand. Being fourteen years older than his brother, and a priest, made it all too easy to step into that role. When Chris had left the army after two tours as a doctor in Afghanistan, he needed Luke in that role—to guide, shelter, pray, and even direct. And unable to return to medicine, to such a stressful role, he needed to learn green things could grow and thrive, and that his hand could help make that happen.

But that time was over. Luke smiled. They grow up so fast.

"What's the stupid grin for?" Chris pulled back with a befuddled expression.

"Absolutely nothing. I'm glad to see you."

"You too, man." Chris faced forward again. "I'm going to propose."

Luke nodded. "Are you asking me or telling me?"

Chris chuckled. "I've been trying to figure that out myself. I talked to Madeline's dad already, even our dad, but . . . I've been sitting here for twenty minutes wondering about you."

"I'm your brother. First and foremost."

"The brother who taught me to drive, taught me to tie a tie, pull out a chair and open doors for dates, and probably saved my life last year."

"Stop. I'm blushing," Luke quipped.

The brothers sat quietly for a moment—both lost in the past, remembering the good and the bad.

"You've been a good brother." Chris spoke softly.

"That won't end with your marriage. I'm here, always will be." Luke nudged him. "It's quick, though." Luke used the contraction on purpose. He hoped it made him sound more casual, less authoritative. After all, it was an observation and not a criticism.

"It is, but I'm sure. I want . . . I want everything for Madeline. To be that shoulder she needs to cry on, to support her as she reaches for whatever she wants to reach for. I want to come home to her and download my day, and share everything, and listen as she does the same. She's the best part of my day, the part I strive to get to and do my best for, so that when I'm there, when I get to see her, be with her and hold her, I know the very best of me has come to that moment."

Chris ran his hands through his short hair. In the time since he'd left the military, he'd only let it grow barely past the width of his fingers. "It sounds ridiculous, and I've been cycling through it over and over, because it is fast; I know that. But I've been through a lot and I'm still healing, and in so many ways she is too, and we're healing together and I don't want to wait any longer." He faced his brother. "I love her . . . Does any of that make sense?"

Luke leaned back and smiled. "When will you ask her?"

"You're good with this?"

"I am. I agree with everything you said, and she radiates the same light. Look, if I thought you two were riding some fevered wave of emotion, I'd caution you. But that's not what I see." Luke sat straight and grabbed his brother into a hug. "My little brother's getting married."

"Not so fast. I haven't asked her yet."

"As if she'll say no." Luke pushed him back, but still held him by the shoulders. "What did Essie say?"

"How'd you know I've talked to Essie?"

"Please. Our sister's been collecting proposal ideas since third grade. No Jumbotron, no restaurants, yes sunsets, yes gardens, no trips, yada, yada, yada . . . Of course you've called her, and it's probably all scripted for you."

"She rattled off at least twenty ideas, but I have no clue yet."

"Take your time. The moment will present itself."

"You speak from experience?"

"Ah, you laugh, little brother, but I've ushered over a thousand couples through premarital counseling and counseled twice that many married couples in my twenty years. I could teach you a lot about a good and satisfying marriage."

"I'm not listening." Chris pressed his hands over his ears. "Not listening. Can't hear you."

"Grow up." Luke slugged him in the arm. "I'm not counseling you. No way."

"But you'll be part of the ceremony?"

"In any capacity you both wish." Luke pushed up. "And this is where we part. I have to get over to the hospital for rounds this afternoon and need to eat a piece of cake before I go. Wedding cake, mind you. I'll be thinking of you."

"Care to share?"

"It's coconut cream."

"How did you swing that?" Chris raised his hands. "I get it. Brotherly love only goes so far."

Luke nodded. "You know it. Are you working today?"

Chris stood, stretched, and followed a step behind his brother down the path. "I ended a double early this morning. I'm off for a couple days . . . Hey, you'll never believe who I met last week."

Luke turned and raised a brow.

"Alyssa Harrison. I helped get her car to Jasper's, then Madeline met her a few days ago at the bookshop. She's staying with Janet for a while. You should probably call her."

"Hovering is never good." Luke gripped his brother's shoulder. This time there was nothing patronizing or paternal in the motion. It was simply good to have Chris near. "Janet will reach out if she needs me. I'm glad to hear her daughter's back, though."

Chris left his brother at the rectory door and headed east toward the bookshop. On his way he approached Winsome Jewelers and stalled. He would need to stop in there soon. It was local, and he believed he should support local businesses—especially the bookshop—but the minute he stepped within the jewelry store's door, everyone would know. Winsome's small-town warmth would "heat up" after that.

He picked up his pace, passed the jewelry store in three long strides, and rounded the corner to the bookshop. He pushed through the door with more momentum than expected and almost stumbled over a customer.

"Hey, Chris . . . She's in her office." Claire stood feet away helping another woman in Nonfiction. Janet waved from behind the counter.

Crossing the store, he leaned against the doorjamb to Madeline's "office," really a storage closet with a desk and three chairs tucked tight. Soon after inheriting the shop from her aunt, she'd opened her own pro bono law firm out of the same storage closet her aunt Maddie had used for tutoring.

He tapped on the open door. Nothing. She was so engrossed in something on her computer it took two throat clearings before she looked up.

"That's a serious face."

"It's a serious case." Madeline waved her hand to bring him closer. "But I need a break and you're just the ticket."

"Excellent." Chris dropped a kiss on her lips. "Go for a walk with me?"

"I'd love to. The Sweet Shoppe?"

He laughed. "Has no one fed you today?"

"As I said, you're just the ticket."

A quick wave to Claire with a replying "Grab me one too," and they were out of the shop and headed across the town square.

The sun was shining and Winsome was packed. School had let out earlier that week, and kids seemed to be everywhere—on bikes, walking, hanging all over the fountain, running across the street without looking.

Chris blanched. "I do not want to work today. Does no one look when they cross the street anymore? Do kids act like this all the time?"

Madeline laughed. "Close your eyes, I'll guide you . . . And the kids are having fun and the cars are going really slow."

"Is that your idea of a win-win?"

"If it is, it's my only one today."

Chris pulled her close but didn't ask any more questions. He knew she was referring to a case, and he also knew she couldn't and wouldn't talk about it. She just needed him near—and that felt good.

As they crossed the street, he slid his arm down her back and reached for her hand; she intertwined her fingers within his and squeezed. He pushed open the door to the Sweet Shoppe and took a deep breath of icing sugar and yeast.

Jill stood behind the counter placing cupcakes from a tray into her display case. "Macaron time?"

"You know it." Madeline laughed. "And one for Claire."

"Janet?"

Madeline shook her head. "Something's up there. She says she's giving up sugar in an effort to 'reclaim her figure'—which hasn't been lost, by the way."

"What?" Jill raised a brow.

Madeline raised both brows. "And Seth's been taking her out for dinner more. All very suspect . . . I'll keep you posted."

"Cool it, Counselor," Chris interjected as Jill reached down into her display case and folded two chocolate macarons with pistachio cream in parchment paper.

She handed them across the counter as Chris reached for his wallet.

"Not today." Jill waved at his hand.

"What's up?" He stalled, noticing something in her eyes he should have seen before.

"It's just nice to have you in here."

Something in her voice cued Madeline too. Chris felt her still next to him and watched as she studied Jill.

"What's happened? Are you okay?" Madeline asked each question slowly, with the clear implication she knew full well something had and Jill wasn't.

"Nothing. Of course." Jill offered a hesitant smile and waved them away. She knew neither Chris nor Madeline was fooled, so she dialed it up a notch and added a perky laugh. "You two go enjoy the sunshine. We're supposed to get rain tonight."

They walked out, and Jill's bravado fell. She felt it in her face. Every muscle slacked as if there was no energy or collagen to hold them up. She'd spent an hour that morning with her mother, who not only had not known who she was, but had grown upset at not knowing her. Those had been rare days before but were becoming more common.

She's only sixty-five, Jill told herself. It's too young. But regardless of age, it was happening. On some days a memory would simply evade her mother, like smoke drifting above her. Yet on other days she would catch that smoke—not the memory, but the ephemeral realization that a memory should be enfolded within it. She would chase it with a dogged determination. And then, unable to find it, she became agitated and, this morning, inconsolable. For the first time, a nurse was forced to give her a sedative. That's what shook Jill the most. It marked a watershed moment in her mother's decline. These days will come faster now, she thought.

For me too . . .

How long until she too reached for memories she couldn't grasp? Would it start with a word? An event? A milestone she'd never willfully relinquish? Her wedding day? What about recognizing her own children? Would she ever meet, and remember, grandchildren? Would she too become frantic, almost violent, in her fear?

"Stop!" She yelled the word aloud. Lately she found it the only way to truly halt her cascading fears.

She glanced to her small side desk. A picture of her two kids rested there. Jack was thirteen next week and Carrie, at seventeen, would begin her senior year in September.

They were too young to know, too young to carry that burden.

But it had been months since her Vita XGC results arrived . . . They needed to be told.

Chapter 16

Alyssa watched the car pull away. Inside the slick black BMW sat the third driver that morning who hadn't looked her in the eye, hadn't said please or thank you, and had actually held their credit cards by their fingertips from a cracked window, like she was going to reach in and steal their iced Frappuccinos or give them cooties with her dirty hands. And this particular driver had demanded she clean her windshield three times.

"You've left smudges . . . You're still not doing it right . . . Fine, if that's the best you can do."

Then she peeled out with a glare and a nasty scowl.

"Good riddance," Alyssa muttered and pulled a rag from her back pocket. Grease was everywhere, under her fingernails, in the lines within her palm, and as she tucked her long bangs behind her ear, probably in her hair. She looked down at another winning 2004 outfit—this time capri jeans and a scoop-necked T-shirt—and sighed, "Doesn't get better than this."

She noticed Jasper rounding the corner from the garage bays and set to wiping off the gas pumps. With the rain and the wind from a middle-of-the-night storm, they were already green with pollen despite wiping them down the day before.

"Alyssa?" He nodded to her from a few steps away. "I don't think this is going to work. After you finish that, let's settle up and get you on your way. You can drop off those uniform shirts you never wore whenever you get the chance." He dug his hands into his pockets and rocked back on his heels.

"I'm sorry. They don't fit. But . . . you're firing me? I need to pay for my car."

"We'll figure out something else." Jasper lifted his Cubs cap off his head and swiped at his gray hair. He then nodded like the chat was over. When she didn't move, he bit the corner of his mouth and regarded her more closely. "Maybe you feel this work isn't good enough, or maybe you woke up on the wrong side of your bed every day for a week, but either way I can't have you being rude to my customers."

Without meaning to, Alyssa looked down the road after the BMW and its sour middle-aged occupant. A million excuses and a few defensive retorts came to mind, but as she cycled through them, each sounded worse than the last.

Jasper pushed through her silence. "I'll finish the work on your car, don't you fret. You're smart and you'll get work, and I know you'll pay me too."

"No." Interview six gave the word power.

I'm overqualified for this job. You won't have any problems with me, and even though I can't answer these questions, I'm honest and I'll be out of all this someday, and I'm smarter now. You won't find a more dedicated employee.

She had believed every word when she said that to the interviewer at the financial management start-up, and she believed every word when they came to mind the day she asked Jasper for a job. But it wasn't true . . . She hadn't been willing to do anything, even when offered a chance.

Jasper shook his head. He looked like a grandfather who was

not angry, but sad about a wayward grandchild—the one who never listened, the one who always went astray, yet perhaps the one he loved best. "You tried. I'll give you that, but—"

"Please. If you'll let me stay, you won't regret it. I promise."

"I've owned this corner for forty years, and I like my life here. Some people aren't pleasant, that's for sure, but they're my customers and this is my home. Costco out on Route 10 can charge up to fifty cents less a gallon on premium, but they haven't cut into my business one bit, and that's a miracle." He looked around with a small satisfied smile. "And maybe it's because others feel at home here too. I do good work and most people respect that."

"I'll respect that too."

Her comment drew his gaze to her again. She worked to keep eye contact because she wanted him to see something new in her, something worth believing in. Because he was right. She hadn't respected his work and the joy he brought to it. She had treated it, and him, as if they were beneath her. Her "day job" had already taken a back seat to what she deemed her "real work."

Over the past week she'd stayed up late every night poring over Lexi's and Jeremy's data, wanting to do her best for them. She wanted to wow them and had convinced herself it was because they were taking a chance on her. But Jasper had taken a chance on her first—and when she'd needed it the most. As he studied her now, she got the oddest feeling that he saw through her, and she imagined he saw a small dirty thing, and it had nothing to do with the grime on her hands or the grease under her nails.

"I'm sorry. You deserve and will get better from me."

"One more chance." He held a single finger between them.

"Yes, sir."

"And stop callin' me 'sir.' I work for a living." A smile cut the bite in his words.

"Yes, Jasper."

A car pulled up to the full-service island. The driver tapped the horn to move Alyssa, who was standing in the way.

Jasper stepped forward, but Alyssa held out her hand and moved to the side. "I got this."

"Okay then. I'll get back to that carburetor."

She turned toward the car's driver and froze. Then, with only a minute hitch in her step, she summoned all her courage and walked around the late-model Volvo wagon as the window rolled down.

"What in the blue blazes are you doing here? You're supposed to be setting the world on fire out in Palo Soprano."

"Hey, Grandma. Palo Alto." She leaned in and kissed her grandmother's cheek. "I'm back."

"Back for what?" Her grandmother peered around the gas station. "A summer internship?"

Alyssa leaned down and looked straight through the car's windows. Her grandma's volume and tone, if not her words, had captured Jasper's attention. He had rounded the corner again and stood listening.

Without waiting for an answer, her grandmother continued. "You didn't tell me you were coming home, and she certainly didn't. Never tells me a thing, just manages me without so much as a by-your-leave . . . Never mind, dear, I'm glad to see you. I hope she didn't move you or make you leave what you love."

There was only ever one *she* and *her*. Janet.

Alyssa reached for the pump and pushed the Regular tab. "Not at all, Grandma. This was my idea. I . . . I may go back, but I left my job and had the summer free."

"That's wonderful. What did she say about all that?" Her grandmother leaned out the window.

"I haven't really talked to her yet. She went to Chase's to visit Rosie."

"It takes three years for you to visit, and she leaves to visit a granddaughter she's visited four times last month alone?"

Alyssa felt the past convict her. Every time her mom thwarted what she wanted or came against her in any way, she always found a welcome and often eager ear in her grandmother. And her grandmother, always soft and easy on her, never let Janet off the hook. Alyssa had played into that for years, fully aware of what she was doing, savoring the sense of camaraderie, even victory, as her grandmother took every single one of her complaints and recategorized each as her own daughter's offense.

It would be so easy, Alyssa thought, so tempting to go there again. She would no longer be alone.

She couldn't do it.

Maybe it was that light she saw in her mom's eyes, maybe it was Lexi's comment that she had changed, maybe it was Jasper watching her, or maybe it was what her mom had said when she walked out the door several days before.

"She needed to go, Grandma. She wouldn't have left if it weren't absolutely necessary." Alyssa rushed on to avoid more questions. "Why don't I come by for dinner tonight and we'll catch up? I can tell you about everything then."

"Like why my granddaughter is pumping gas at a service station?" Her grandmother held her credit card out her open window.

Alyssa swiped the card and prayed Jasper couldn't catch the words or the tone. "Yes. Exactly that."

"Fine." Her grandmother stretched her cheek to the window. "I'll make my meat loaf."

Alyssa bent to deliver the card and a kiss, then stepped back. "I'll see you at six thirty."

As the car rolled away, Alyssa's mind returned to that last conversation she'd had with her mom, and she wondered how much, if any of it, she would be pressed to repeat to her grandmother.

Janet had stood in the kitchen, hands clasped together like she was trying to keep herself contained. "I'm going to go help out with Rosie for a few days and give you some space. I know you need to be here, and if you had any other option you'd take it. And this isn't a power play; I'm not trying to make your life hard. Just the opposite."

She then fussed around the kitchen, straightening already folded dish towels and wiping pristine counter tops. Hand-clasping containment wasn't working. "I've stocked the fridge. I made a few of your favorites—those muffins you love and a wonderful chicken stew I just discovered that'll last a few days. I'll stay as long as they'll have me to give you time to settle in and feel comfortable." She gave a sweet self-deprecating smile that Alyssa had never seen and laughed at herself. "If it were the old me, I'd give your brother two or three hours tops before he should kick me out, but last time they put up with me for four days and I thought it was lovely . . . Maybe if I take Rosie on long walks and stay out of their hair, I can stretch that."

"Mom." Alyssa still didn't know what she had planned to say. Only the one word had escaped.

Janet waited, watching, and when Alyssa said nothing more, she opened the back door and paused in the open doorway. "I want to give you everything you need, Alyssa, and the fight is over." She took a deep breath and said it again. "The fight is over. When I get back I hope you can see that, trust that, and we can become something new."

Her mom turned away, and with a blank mind, Alyssa called after her with the only thing she could visualize, her brother. "Tell Chase I said hi."

Remembering it now, it sounded heartless to her own ears. It was an inadequate response to her mom's vulnerable words.

But if Janet felt the same that morning, she didn't let it show. She simply nodded. Then she raised her hand, and Alyssa knew she had meant to step back into the kitchen and give her a hug. She read it in her mom's actions and her expression. She also read the moment her mom caught herself and stopped.

In the end, Janet only nodded once more before walking out the door.

And that's why Alyssa hadn't betrayed her mom just now, and wouldn't at dinner tonight—no matter how Grandma pushed and needled.

She had desperately wanted that hug.

Chapter 17

Alyssa was sitting at her dad's old desk sorting through her notes on Jeremy's data when her mom walked through the back door and into the kitchen.

She stood to welcome her—or at least try—when Janet's voice dropped her back into her seat.

"I didn't know it was a problem. Don't say that. Jasper runs a great business . . . I was giving her some time . . . Yes, perhaps I was wrong . . . I'm sure you're right . . . I'll call again soon. I love you, Mom . . . I—"

At the silence, Alyssa rounded the corner.

Janet sighed and waved her phone. "She hung up on me."

"I'm having dinner with her tonight."

"She said that and that she 'found you' today working at Jasper's gas station." Janet made air quotes with her fingers.

"Is that a problem?"

"It surprised her."

Alyssa leaned against the doorjamb. "It's not like I have choices. I'm sorry to be such a disappointment, but after seventeen interviews and resumes to forty-six companies, Jasper was the only one who would hire me."

"No one said that and I don't think that." Janet pushed two grocery bags onto the kitchen island. "I didn't know you were going out tonight, so I stopped at the grocery on my way back. I wasn't sure how much food you had left."

"She's still mad you moved her out here."

Janet turned, and her whole body seemed to sag. She leaned against the counter top. "What was I to do, Alyssa? The house was overrunning her, and I'm her only family. My dad's been gone twenty-five years. Do you know how dangerous an old house can get in that time? I hoped she'd actually enjoy being close to me, maybe Chase too, and now that you're back . . ."

"I'm not back, Mom."

When Janet didn't reply, Alyssa felt something within her tell her to back away. Something felt different. The air hummed with a different emotional cadence. But she couldn't trust it. For something to be true, it had to be proven true. The warning to back off warred with the compulsion to push, and she recognized that the slow-burning ember inside her only needed a little oxygen to ignite. With its flash, she would know. She would know that years of discord didn't resolve in a few short months and people didn't, couldn't, change in such a short amount of time either. Or perhaps that people could never change at all.

"Did you ever think it wasn't your call to make? That it was her life and her decision?"

"Every time she tells me." Janet placed a head of lettuce on the counter and faced her daughter. "But you weren't there and she couldn't see it. You didn't see how run-down things had gotten. When November hits northern Michigan, you have to be prepared. She wasn't, and that scared me. After my first winter alone here, I finally got it. It's not easy at my age, much less your grandmother's, to shovel the walks, set up the plowing schedule, salt your steps without slipping, get your car winterized . . . Cold is terrifying in many ways. So no, I didn't wait for her to tell me or to fall down her front steps or freeze to death if she slipped on the way to her mailbox. I did what I thought was best. I did what I could to honor her, protect her, and show her I love her."

"So no matter what the rest of us think or want, we're wrong. Glad you got all your virtue back after that blip of yours."

Her mom turned red and Alyssa waited, poised on the edge of the knife. Despite feeling ashamed of her own words and actions, she stood still, unsure which way she wanted the moment to go. Either everything Janet professed was true, or everything was the same old lie. One better, granted, but one consistent and expected—and there was comfort in that too.

When Janet didn't reply, Alyssa doubled down in her own desperation. "So you've gotten Grandma settled, good daughter. You've gotten your husband back, despite your affair, good wife. You never really lost Chase. And now you've got your cute granddaughter to show off on Instagram. Perfect little family for the doting grandmother. But there's still me, the disgraced XGC employee now back living in her old bedroom, wearing her high school wardrobe, and working at the local gas station. Can't take these hands to a dinner party, can you, Mom?" Alyssa held up her hands. Despite scrubbing with the kitchen sink's vegetable brush, grime still trailed each cuticle line.

Janet felt her breath catch and focused on smoothing it out. Rather than face the tornado in front of her, she continued to unpack the grocery bag. Her heart, so full of hope during her drive home, dropped to her stomach with the realization that this was all there might ever be with Alyssa. After all, despite months of prayer and work, it still mirrored her relationship with her own mother. People didn't change just because you had or because you wanted them to. She glanced at Alyssa, who now stood arms akimbo waiting for her answer.

Rather than answer any of Alyssa's questions—they had a certain rude rhetorical flair about them anyway—Janet pointed to something on the far counter and crossed the kitchen. "Did you see these? I took them in for you. I should have shown you before I left, but I forgot." She lifted one of the Jasper's Garage uniform shirts. "You mentioned how horrible they were, but I thought if they fit better . . ." She spread the two shirts on the counter.

Alyssa stepped forward. "He was upset today that I wasn't wearing one."

"I'm sorry. I took them that first night and forgot to tell you they were here. Tell him it was my fault . . . And here, you won't get in trouble for cutting anything." She turned one shirt inside out. "I simply took them in along the seam lines and sewed the fabric down. I can pull it out super easy when or if you hand them back in."

"I'm not going to work there forever, Mom."

Janet didn't reply.

Alyssa shook her head, still focused on the shirts. "You don't need to apologize. It wasn't your fault. Until today I hadn't planned to wear them, but now— How'd you do this?"

"It was easy," Janet laughed. "You probably don't remember this, but I used to sew some of your clothes when you were really young. You had some great little dresses."

"There was one with a clown."

"Your Silly Dress. That's what you called it. It was royal blue with a little white collar, and I embroidered a clown on the front. It took me a whole week to design and create him." She pressed her hand to her chest, right where the clown would have been on the dress. "You loved it. You wore that every day to your two-year-olds class at the church preschool."

"I've seen the pictures." Alyssa held up one of the newly tailored uniform shirts. "Thank you."

"You're welcome."

Alyssa put down the shirt, visibly flustered, and checked her phone. "I'm late for dinner. I've got to go." She headed for the door.

Janet inhaled behind her. She wanted to protect her daughter, and she was also tired of hearing where she'd gone wrong. Yet she wanted Alyssa to spend time with her grandma and enjoy it. "Perhaps don't talk too long about XGC tonight."

Alyssa spun on her, face aflame. "You have got to be kidding me. Fine. I wouldn't want to embarrass you, but when they haul me off to jail, please let her know where I've gone. I doubt you'll be able to sweep that under the rug."

"Stop it. You're not going to jail. I simply meant she's been following it and she's been upset. I was trying to help you, warn you, I don't know . . . She just isn't easy sometimes."

Pressure built in Janet's sinuses, her eyes, her nose. Five minutes home with Alyssa and they were back at square one. Where was all that peace Father Luke talked about? She pinched the bridge of her nose. "I'm sorry I said anything. Forgive me."

She watched Alyssa return to her aggressive cross-armed stance and, for the first time, saw the defensive nature of her posture. Janet wondered if she had misread her daughter and for how long.

"Stop saying you're sorry."

Janet felt her eyes widen and lowered her hand from her nose.

"You never say it for years and now you don't stop. It's fake. I don't believe you, and it makes me feel like I don't know you, like I never did. You always said I was the one overreacting, being too sensitive, and needing to grow up, get a grip, or move on. It was never you. You were never in the wrong. And now you say you're sorry, about everything. I never did anything right, wore anything right, or said anything right. Why apologize now? Why are you changing the rules? You can't just do that, Mom."

"I'm sorry. I mean . . . you're right. You don't know me." Janet reached out as Alyssa stepped back, but she dropped her hand inches from contact. "I didn't know me. Whatever I just said, about XGC, about anything, forget it and give me a chance to explain."

Alyssa didn't say anything, but she didn't run either.

"I couldn't breathe most of your childhood, and it wasn't you or Chase or your father. It was me. I was the one who needed to stop overreacting, being too sensitive, get a grip, and all those things you said. I wanted to be good enough for you. It wasn't that you were never good enough for me, and I'm so sorry I made you feel that way. It was me. Always me. I didn't do, wear, or say anything right—ever. And the things I loved to do . . . They were wrong and frivolous and irresponsible and—"

She stopped herself and swiped a hand against her nose. "I sound so self-centered." She sputtered a wet laugh. "You always did say it was always about me, but not like you think . . . It was never like that."

Alyssa stood in front of her. She still said nothing. Janet wasn't sure what to do with that, but she also knew she had to give up trying to force a "fix" between them. Some things were never meant to be in her control.

"I love you, b—" Janet stopped and swallowed. "*And*. I love you *and* I want you here, but this . . ." She flapped her hand between them. "It's a roller coaster and it isn't going to work. It's not what you need right now, not after all you've been through. I'll buy a mattress and have it delivered to your dad's apartment. He wanted you to live here, for my sake, and for yours too, I think. He believes there is something between us worth saving, but not like this. I'm only causing you pain."

Alyssa shook her head. But Janet didn't take it as disagreement. It looked more like her daughter was clearing away all the discordant words and notes in her head. The cacophony she had put there.

"I've followed you, by the way, as best I could, searching the internet for all that happened with XGC, peppering your dad with questions because you wouldn't talk to me, wondering if you were okay, wondering if you were scared or lonely, or needing help or simply a hug. I didn't know about all the interviews or the companies. I didn't know jail was an option for you. I hope that's not true."

Alyssa didn't reply, so she continued. "But I did know about Jasper's. He's a wonderful man and you can learn a lot from him, maybe even a little about cars too." She smiled.

Alyssa opened her mouth, but Janet raised a hand to cut her off. She wanted to get everything out before another wave of vitriol or something worse hit her.

"And I'm so glad you felt you could come home, even if it wasn't to me." She clasped her hands together to keep them from trembling. "Your dad is thrilled, by the way. He didn't want you to see that. He wanted to respect that you're an adult and, as I said, he was trying to give me time with you, but he's missed you so much. To have his little girl home safe and sound is a big deal. For both of us. I hope someday we can talk, really talk and listen to each other, but until you're ready, it's best you go back to your dad's. After dinner with your grandmother, of course. She's excited to see you too. And don't let her belittle Jasper and your work there, if you don't mind. He really is a good man . . . And for when she starts in on me . . . I'm not so bad, Alyssa. At least not anymore, I hope."

With that, Janet walked out of the kitchen.

Moments later she heard the back door open and shut.

Her daughter was gone.

Chapter 18

Jeremy took a deep breath. He needed to fire Ryan.

Rather than help, in the two weeks since Andante's reopening he found Ryan nipping at his heels, making things worse with his constant complaining and doubts. Jeremy knew the place was a mess, but being reminded of it every single moment wasn't helping. One foster mom used to quip when her kids complained, "Be a problem solver." He'd grown to hate that line—yet he had used it on Ryan just that morning.

An hour earlier, Brendon had been "loitering" in the alley when, according to Ryan, he should have been clearing tables.

"It's hardly a capital offense. You know kids, they move in packs. They just started summer break—it's probably separation anxiety." Jeremy had laughed.

"He's not respectful, and that's not good for business."

"He's a kid and he's fine. Ryan, man, you gotta grow up. You don't need to come to me for this. Be a problem solver. Mention it to him, but coming down on him isn't helpful. He was gone only a few minutes. We've dealt with worse than this."

That was a low blow—one Jeremy regretted the moment the words flew from his mouth.

It was passive aggressive. No, it was worse than that—it was mean. He knew it, yet he couldn't stop himself. Despite his best intentions, he couldn't seem to let go that Ryan had only been weeks out of rehab when they'd started working together, and that Ryan had been a mess back then. And now, rather than feel grace and understanding from him about his own weaknesses, Jeremy felt condemnation. How fair was that?

They used to laugh about their personalities and their pasts. They'd howl at the disaster Ryan was in those early days and what a challenge Jeremy could be on his best day. But ever since Andante opened, everything had changed. Jeremy felt it. With every mistake he made, rightly or wrongly, Ryan let him know it. And, rightly or wrongly, Jeremy held it against the younger man.

Jeremy had then motioned out the back alley door. "They'll give up coming around soon and it'll all be over. It's not that interesting back there."

Before Ryan could reply, Becca had pushed through the swinging door and his face split into a grin. "Becca Boo, how are you?" He scooped her high into his arms as Krista followed her daughter into the kitchen.

Krista took in the sight of Ryan holding Becca, smiled, and turned to Jeremy. "You good for the whole weekend?"

"I am. I've got fun planned and some time off work."

Krista surveyed the space. The kitchen and office combo was small, and a little messy this morning. Jeremy had stayed last night to go over the books and ended up making batches of muffins deep into the early hours when none of the numbers made any sense to him.

He followed Krista's scan of the place, trying to imagine what she saw and thought. He hadn't cleaned well, not that it would have mattered if he had. Nothing he touched ever projected the world

Krista wanted. Heck, Andante, front shop or back office, didn't project the world *he* wanted.

Jeremy shrugged. "She won't spend the weekend here. I promise."

"That's probably best." Krista dropped Becca's Anna and Elsa bag on the floor next to his desk and left without another word.

Jeremy left Becca and Ryan chatting Polly Pockets and books and pushed through the swinging door. In the four months since he and Ryan had moved from Seattle, Jeremy often wondered who had gotten to know his daughter better. On the one hand he understood that Ryan had no parental responsibilities—he could be Becca's friend. On the other hand, their easy friendship pinched at him. The little voice that often whispered his failings chatted up a storm whenever Becca and Ryan were together.

Yes, it was time they parted ways.

Jeremy stalled and counted the customers. Ten. The tiny fissure in his chest cracked wider.

He walked to the register. "What's the take this morning?"

Brendon tapped a few buttons. "It's been a little slow. $410."

"So, what? A hundredish customers?"

Brendon shook his head. "Someone from the bookstore came and bought six muffins and three coffees, so it's not that many individual sales, if that's what you're after."

Jeremy stepped back and ran his hands through his hair.

"I can tell you what everybody ordered if you want." Brendon tapped the tablet.

Jeremy pushed off the counter. "No. Thanks, though." He turned away as a customer approached Brendon. "You get back to work."

In his periphery he noticed Alyssa tucked into a corner table. He pulled an espresso shot, added a little steamed milk, grabbed one of the last muffins from the display case, and crossed the store to slide them onto her table.

"I didn't order anything," she commented without lifting her head.

"I thought you could use a pick-me-up."

That got her head up, straight up. "You're really tall. Did you know that?"

"I've heard it mentioned." He laughed and felt his first moment of ease. "I've noted you're pretty tall yourself."

She stretched her back, nodded to the gifts, and with a thank-you she reached into her bag and shook a few Tums from a large plastic bottle.

"My food isn't that bad."

She laughed. "It's not at all. My last job gave me ulcers and you'd think they'd be gone by now, but this has me in knots." She pointed to her open laptop.

"What are you working on?"

"Your numbers."

"So that's what's bad . . . At least it's not my food." He leaned forward. "How bad is it? You don't look pleased."

Alyssa shrugged. "I'm not *not* pleased and I'm beginning to get a good picture, but there are some questions." She followed her two Tums with a corner of the muffin.

"Such as?"

"Inconsistencies. Let me play around more before we talk, though. I want to follow the trails myself. Anything you say can prejudice what I find."

"It's not a court of law," Jeremy laughed.

"But once you tell me a story, that's the one I'll see. It will influence how I interpret what I find. But do you have any other accounts you didn't give me? Anything at all?"

He shook his head. "I gave you everything." He pointed to one of her spreadsheets. "I hope you noted how much I trust you. I didn't even delete the account numbers."

She smiled. "I deleted them for you. You've got to keep that information secure."

He scrunched his nose. "It seemed like a nice gesture, but you're right."

Alyssa laughed and tapped his forearm. "I caught it. My nice gesture was to delete them."

"Why'd you ask that? About the accounts? What's wrong?" He leaned back and her hand fell away.

"I'm not sure . . . Something." She glanced first at her computer, then at him. "Hey . . . It's going to be okay."

He leaned forward again, his face inches from hers. "I hardly know you, think you're most likely wrong, but I love that you believe that."

For one moment, everything stilled. He vaguely recalled having said something similar to her when they first met and wondered what was up—with him. He opened his mouth to recant, cover, or say something to backtrack, when he looked into her eyes. They were just about the most beautiful blue he'd ever seen.

She leaned back in her chair and studied him. Rather than downplay his words or brush them away with embarrassment, she seemed to absorb them. "I need it to be true too."

He nodded.

She held his gaze a beat longer before she broke eye contact and looked around the coffee shop.

He followed her line of sight and landed on the customer chatting with Brendon. "Do you know George Williams?"

Alyssa twisted around, using the motion to stretch her back again. "Of course, everyone does. One of his kids was in my high school class. Devon, I think."

"He must have been a super-old father."

"Devon and his siblings were adopted long after his own kids graduated. He and Mrs. Williams got all three of them at once. They were in foster care or something and were about to get split up. We were probably in seventh grade then . . . They had grandkids our age too. One was a year or so behind us and used to call Devon 'Uncle' in the hallways."

Jeremy looked at the man more closely. "The first day he came in, he was upset about the pillows, and everything else too." Jeremy rested his arms on the two-top. "In fact, a few customers still grumble about them."

"That's because their kids and grandkids made those pillows." At his expression, Alyssa laughed. "Mrs. Pavlis should have told you. Someone should have. The middle school has an eighth-grade home economics class and you make pillows, or we did back then. A few kids gave theirs to Mrs. Pavlis and it became a thing. I bet at least ten kids gave her their pillows each year. Some got too old to keep, some kids took them back after a while, but there were always at least seventy or so in here."

"One hundred twenty-three."

"No way. That's crazy."

"And it explains a lot." Jeremy sighed. "When we first opened, before the renovations, it was business as usual . . ." He pointed to her computer. "I didn't see a difference between her numbers and ours. But now . . . I doubt I'll make it." He looked around. "All because of some homemade pillows."

"Your changes are amazing. I was pretty rude the first day I was in here."

"Nah . . . You had a point, but not the one you thought you were making. It wasn't about the coffee, was it? People felt at home here, and I took that away." He turned and pointed to the two ancient espresso machines. "See those? I wondered how those could be so gorgeous and the rest of this place such a cluttered mess. I thought Georgia had gone batty, but she knew what she was about. She kept her machines pristine. She respected her business. Her seating area? That was for everyone else. And I destroyed it." He dropped his head and felt a hand, soft and light, on his arm.

"Don't give up the ship yet. You've created something wonderful. Besides, the machines are still here."

"A new machine should be here any day. The last vestige of the Daily Brew gone."

Right as he looked up, she glanced past him and wagged a finger to her right. "Someone's calling you."

That's when the chaos began, and somehow in the following few minutes Alyssa ended up volunteering to take Becca to the park, with a "You can run next door and ask my mom for a reference if you need one." Ryan stepped behind the register because Brendon had gone MIA again, and Jeremy started a verbal showdown with the courier delivering his new espresso machine.

"What do you mean you're loading it back on the truck?"

The man pressed his foot down on the pallet jack. "I shoulda looked before I unloaded, but your check didn't clear."

"Of course it cleared. I sent it last week."

"I got my orders. Call my boss if you want, but it says right here that it's going back." He slid his phone from his pocket and flashed the screen to Jeremy.

"Don't move. Do not move until I talk to your boss." Jeremy dashed back into the office, grabbed his cell phone, yelled, listened, waited—then stood in the alley and watched as the driver reloaded the machine and drove away.

He felt rather than saw Ryan step next to him. "How did this happen?"

"Brendon's back," Ryan replied.

"I don't care about Brendon." Jeremy balked, then lowered his voice. "They took the La Marzocco back—he said the check didn't clear. What's going on here?"

Ryan pulled back. "How should I know? You've called me off giving any real help."

"You know what? I can't do this right now." Jeremy looked into the coffee shop's back office. It looked like a dark hole that was about to swallow him. "I need out of here. I have to go get Becca at the park."

"It's quiet today. Why not take the rest of the day off? Be with Becca?"

"It's quiet every day. Which is exactly why I can't afford a day off."

Chapter 19

Jeremy stood at the edge of the park, scanning the playscape for his daughter. He finally spotted her atop the ladder helping a younger kid prepare to slide. In her bright red T-shirt and ponytail, she looked just like Krista.

While the reminder carried a little sting, the sight of Becca's head thrown back in laughter brought a smile too. Those early days had been good—raw and frantic in many ways, but good. Laughter, walks, holding hands, Seattle sunsets. Falling asleep tangled up in each other and heading out early to watch the sunrise.

Everything felt so heightened he couldn't let go. So sure he'd finally found a home, not a place, but a person, he proposed after only three weeks. And she accepted. They hopped a flight to Vegas and he'd even found them an Elvis chapel. After all, if you were going to be a cliché, you had to go all the way.

Only once did he detect any hesitation. While Krista recited her vows, dressed in a white minidress, she hesitated. Her voice hitched and her eyes flickered away. But even now he couldn't be sure. He thought he saw it, thought he remembered that it had pulled at him, thought it was the first crack in the idyllic façade, but it was smoke. He couldn't catch it and maybe it was revisionist thinking anyway. Maybe she'd been, in that moment, as committed as he was, and things only unraveled later.

But it wasn't the wedding he remembered most, it was their one-month anniversary. The frenzy of their time together had cooled and he hoped they were settling down, finding level ground. Then she told him she was pregnant, and he soared. That wasn't revisionist thinking. He felt the pulse and joy of that moment, even now, watching his daughter laugh in the sunshine.

He had pulled Krista tight and assured her that their baby was everything he hoped for, that everything would be just fine.

Five months later, she was gone.

Becca was helping another kid climb the ladder to the slide. He could imagine her soft, encouraging words. It was the same voice she used on him when they played a game and he didn't understand the rules. And rather than point out to her that he'd never learn the rules if she didn't quit changing them, he would listen as she explained her new and proper way to play school, restaurant, doctor, or Candy Land.

It always astonished him how quickly kids made friends. It'd been only a half hour since Alyssa asked if she could bring Becca to the park, and already his daughter had found another couple kids her age and teamed up with a few younger. He laughed as all six launched from the slide and clambered over the playscape. She'll remember these days, he thought. She'll remember this laughter. And she would remember him.

Jeremy tried to summon a memory of his own childhood. He couldn't. Tragedy will do that, each and every therapist said. But it never helped. Over the years he had worked to push his mind back to his mom, to his dad, to their life together—to recall his mom's hair color, height, smell, or voice; his father's laugh, occupation, hobbies, or height. Did he have a beard? Was he thin or stocky? And every time Jeremy was met with the impenetrable wall formed at their deaths. He thought about the photos and albums he knew his aunt had packed away when she came to clear and sell the house. She came for it, not for him. But he never searched for them, afraid that when looking at them, he'd only find the faces of strangers.

So when a friend commented that he was a stranger to his own daughter, he vowed she would remember him. No matter what it took. He would not become that faceless, voiceless void in her life. Because no matter how involved Krista purported him to be on social media, it wasn't true. He knew marginally more about his daughter, while living in Seattle, than he knew about his parents. But he could change that. Whereas the other, he could only regret.

The kids ran to the swings. Their dash across the wood chips drew his vision left and brought Alyssa in sight. She was sitting directly behind the swings at the edge of the park. He circled the play area. "I didn't see you right away in that sweater."

She looked down as if she'd forgotten what she was wearing. "It was in my bag . . . The sun disappeared again. Do you know I haven't worn this since college? The jeans too. I can't believe I ever wore these. I can hardly hold them up. I hadn't realized I'd gotten so much thinner. Or maybe they were just really baggy back then."

Jeremy dropped onto the bench next to her. "They look normal to me."

"That doesn't necessarily say anything good about the jeans." She laughed and swiped at her eyes. "But since they're all I've got right now, they'll do."

"Are you okay?"

She shrugged and laid her hand on a book sitting in her lap. *Sylvester and the Magic Pebble*. "Have you ever read this?"

"It's my favorite. Did Becca make you read it to her?" He leaned around her and noted a small stack of books on the other side of the bench. "Did she bring them all?"

"I think so. She grabbed them as we walked out the door." Alyssa lifted her head toward the kids on the swing. "We got two pages into this one before she ran off to play." She looked down at the book again. "It's just so sad."

"Sad? Are we talking about the same story?"

She laid her hands on the cover. "Never mind."

"No. What?"

"Sylvester lost so much, everything. He just wanted to be safe. If he'd thought clearly he could've wished to be home, but he didn't and it turned out horrible."

"He went home. He got his family back. You read the end, right?"

"But it doesn't always work like that." Her focus shifted to the kids again. "My car got completely emptied on my way out here. I gather you're supposed to carry your bags into the motel each night."

Lost between conversations, Jeremy grabbed onto the last sentence. "Kind of, at least the valuable stuff."

"Well, despite having nothing valuable, I still got robbed."

"I'm sorry."

"Not your fault, and really it's par for the course lately." Alyssa kept her eyes straight ahead. "I can't seem to find my way home, find a way to make this all okay."

Jeremy shifted to match her posture. Straight forward. "You and me both . . . They just took my machine away. The check didn't clear and I have no idea why."

She twisted toward him. "That's what's been bothering me. You said you have no other accounts, but they don't reconcile. I'm looking into your Square Reader files. Maybe it's a glitch."

"Who knows? I could've set it up wrong. That'd be par for the course for me lately too."

Chapter 20

Mirabella was packed.

Jeremy marveled once again how the restaurant hit every note just right. He'd heard its makeover had been as dramatic as what he had done to the Daily Brew. Local chatter recalled dim lighting, red velvet, gold brocade curtains, and booths that bounced when you scooted into them. It was the epitome of fancy—early 1980s fancy.

But its changes had been embraced with open arms. Now it boasted a black-and-white tile floor, sleek brown leather bounceless booths, and warm vintage Edison bulb lighting. The bar was the real showstopper. Mahogany, lined in copper, with both surfaces buffed to a mirror shine. It was the perfect focal point. Whoever managed this restoration, he thought, sure caught the feel of an authentic Art Deco French bistro, right down to the light notes of gypsy jazz playing over the sound system.

It wasn't as cool and aloof as some downtown spots, but up here that'd be a miss. The color palette, wood, and copper evoked warmth, family, a certain togetherness that would resonate with a more kid-friendly crowd. And the pop of red. That was new—he definitely wanted to steal that idea.

Each white marble table featured a small tight bouquet of red flowers. Poppies on one table, roses on another, tulips on a third, gerbera daisies on another. It gave a shot of light and life, a bold fresh heat, to the room.

He shook his head as reality set in. He couldn't afford bouquets. One flower would have to do. It would set a good tone and give a certain warmth to Andante. He shook his head again. He couldn't afford one flower.

He'd spent hours that morning with Alyssa before her shift at Jasper's, and the story wasn't good. The numbers revealed exactly who once supported the Daily Brew and who now avoided Andante.

"You need to reach out to the community more. You need to remind them you're here for them, not the other way around."

"It can't really be about the pillows, can it? I brought them a coffee shop to rival any, anywhere in the country."

"But did you mean to tell them theirs wasn't good enough?" She had smiled with the delivery, and that had cut the sting—what a smile—but it still set him back.

Her comment reminded him of the book Ryan had left on his desk days before, *Of Mice and Men*. He'd picked it up and read it in one night, staying late to bake the shop's muffins. He'd gotten so engrossed in the story, he burned the last batch. It was the loneliest story he'd ever heard, and he could relate to it. Okay, maybe not Lennie, Curley, and his wife, but he sure knew Candy, a guy so desperately lonely he gloms onto virtual strangers after his dog dies, and appropriates their dream, even offers to fund it, just to not be alone. But the surest way to be alone was to tell everyone around they weren't enough.

"Have I really done that?" he asked her.

"The numbers suggest that most of her regulars, the Daily Brew's bread-and-butter patrons, don't frequent Andante. You've picked up a new cross section of Winsome, but you're missing Mrs. Pavlis's loyal clientele."

He had spent all afternoon pondering her comments. Now he wanted Liam's advice. After all, he and Lexi appeared to have the golden touch. He wove through the crowd to make his way to the bar. There was only one stool left, wedged between two couples. He caught Liam's eye and lifted his chin in greeting. Liam was moving between customers and the waitstaff collecting drinks at the side counter as if he were working Chicago's hottest speakeasy rather than a suburban restaurant catering to families and parents on a rare date night. Jeremy noted the patrons' smiles—Liam knew what he was doing.

Jeremy plopped onto the stool as Liam swiped the pristine wood counter in front of him with an equally pristine white bar towel.

"It's been too long, man," Liam greeted him. "Good to see you."

"It's been a busy couple weeks." Jeremy looked behind Liam to the rows of bottles displayed against an antiqued mirror and stacked five shelves high. In-house fusions of lemons, limes, and who knew what else sat on the first shelf in large Mason jars. "That's new. What have you got in there?" He pointed to a yellow jar on the end.

Liam glanced over his shoulder and lit up. "You gotta try this. I've had it in the freezer for a year and just pulled it out a few days ago. Pineapples soaking in Casamigos tequila. It's sublime."

He poured a tiny sip into a delicate glass snifter only a little larger than a bottle cap.

Jeremy raised a brow and Liam laughed, pouring in a few drops more.

The liquid was clear and thick, and Jeremy tasted the full rich pineapple on the tip of his tongue as it slid by. It was smooth, sweet, and he agreed with Liam, sublime.

"I serve it as an after-dinner drink. Sweet enough to be dessert on its own or as the perfect complement to Chef's olive oil cake."

"I can imagine. I should serve it with my blueberry muffins. Might make them better."

"You gotta get away from the mixes, man. I keep telling you that."

"I can't afford much else right now, or the time to do the research."

"Make time." Liam swiped at the counter again. "Now what'll you have?"

Jeremy stared at him.

"Stretch me a little . . . You for real? . . . Fine. One old-fashioned coming up," Liam droned and shifted away to the next customer.

Jeremy chuckled, wondering how his friend kept everything straight. He reminded Jeremy of one of Becca's favorite characters, that dog from *Up*, who would focus on one thing, then—"Squirrel!"—chase off after another. But while Liam's lack of focus would be a liability in brain surgery, it made him an excellent bartender. He engaged everyone simultaneously, and he forgot nothing—despite his haphazard demeanor.

Jeremy shifted his attention back across the waiting throng and worked to not turn green with envy. Mirabella was an unqualified success.

A familiar face caught his eye. Alyssa had just pushed through the revolving door and stood searching the room. Her blonde hair was long and loose tonight over a plain white T-shirt and another bright skirt. He laughed. He hadn't noticed her clothes before, but since she'd mentioned them at the park a few days before, he couldn't stop noticing. He liked her fitted Jasper's Garage uniform shirt best.

Alyssa saw him and smiled. He waved her over and pushed off

the stool to kiss her cheek when she reached him. Only after the movement, dropping back down onto the stool, did he realize that was the first time he'd kissed her.

"I didn't expect to see you here." Her voice lifted in question.

Jeremy leaned close. "Lexi called as I was closing up. She said I was being a curmudgeon and to get here tonight."

"Did she?" Alyssa blushed. "I got the same message. Except she didn't call me a curmudgeon."

Jeremy laughed and lifted off his stool again, bumping into the couple next to him. "Please take my seat."

"Thank you."

Liam instantly appeared with his ubiquitous white towel and Jeremy's drink. He slid it to him as he tilted his head to Alyssa. "Hey, Beautiful, good to see you." He leaned over the bar and kissed her cheek as well. "Lexi will be right out."

"Thanks, Liam." She pointed to the brown lowball with its orange peel and single ice cube resting in front of Jeremy. "What are you drinking?"

"Old-fashioned. It's really the only drink I like. Drives Liam nuts, as he's truly gifted. Tell him five things about yourself, and he'll make you something spectacular."

"Oh, Liam knows a lot more than five things about me." Before she could say anything more, Liam slid an identical drink across the wood. "Here you go . . . The two of you." He rolled his eyes to Jeremy and walked away.

At Jeremy's bemused expression, Alyssa lifted her glass with a grin. "What can I say? He knows me well."

The couple next to them lifted out of their seats; Jeremy snagged the one behind him and dropped into it, shifting to face Alyssa. Their knees bumped as they re-perched in the small opening.

"I don't want to press, but the books aren't making sense to me.

Have you found that money you mentioned?" The question had consumed every waking moment of Jeremy's past sixty hours.

"I haven't, but that doesn't mean I won't. I have a lead from your credit card reader. Did you know you have that dumping into four different accounts?"

"I kept switching it because of withdrawal rules. It was a savings account first, then . . . It's all a mess." Jeremy shook his head. "I kept my Seattle accounts, opened accounts here, for me and the shop, a sweep account . . . Then when the bills started coming in, who knows where I paid them from? I got a little swamped."

"I know swamped."

Her tone held a derision he'd heard earlier. It felt as if she were fine, even on the edge of enjoying herself, then a dark cloud would cross over her and she'd pull away.

Jeremy bumped her knee with his own. "What's swamped you?" She hesitated, and he bumped her knee again. "Is it XGC? The FBI?"

"I wish it were just one thing. It's everything." She shrugged. "And no, they haven't reached out yet, which is almost worse. I called my lawyer today and he's heard nothing either. I feel like the waiting is actually eating me from the inside . . . Then a few days ago I had a massive fight with my mom. It was my fault. I pushed and I didn't—wouldn't—stop. So she bought a mattress and had it shipped to my dad's apartment so I can crash with him until I earn some money to get on my own again."

"And?" Jeremy nudged her.

"And . . . it's there. Turns out mattresses can arrive same day. But I haven't gone. I can't go, and yet I can't stay either. Dad's angry because I was out of line with my mom. No, don't look like that . . . I don't deserve sympathy—I was horrid. And I don't even know what she's feeling because she hasn't been around. She's in town, but she gets home late and leaves super early, like she's scared."

"Scared? Of you?"

"No." Alyssa shook her head. "That's not it, she's not scared. She's trying to stop a war, and since I won't let her, she's retreating in the face of the enemy. She's basically declaring peace on any terms."

"Really? You're that bad?"

Alyssa pressed her fingertips to her lips as if remembering horrid words that had escaped from them. "You have no idea."

"Well, Alyssa Harrison." Jeremy raised his glass. "To new beginnings."

She laughed and lifted her own. "May the bottom not fall out beneath us."

"Hey, quit that. When I saw you walk through that door, I started feeling positive."

She absorbed his comment with a light in her eyes that intrigued him, but also left him feeling exposed. After all, she was only in town until Labor Day, if that, and was only helping him to repay Lexi.

But maybe he could change that.

"Speaking of positive, did you see the Winsome paper today? There was an ad for the Chamber of Commerce job. Executive Director. It hasn't been filled yet." He lifted his tone in question.

She chuffed. "Please. I'm hardly qualified for that, and I just told you, no one in my family is really happy with me right now."

"Of course you're qualified for that job. The Chamber of Commerce helps local businesses and that's pretty much what you're already doing. And as for your family, just because they're upset doesn't mean they're not happy you're home."

At her skeptical look, he inched his stool closer to hers. "Can I be honest with you?" He took a deep breath and, at her nod, continued. "You're making a mistake. We haven't talked about this, and now is not the time, and we don't know each other well, but I have to say it . . . My parents died when I was ten, Alyssa, and if I could have even one more conversation with them, I'd give anything for those few words. I moved here so my daughter would never say that about me. So that she'd remember my face, my laugh, our fun times together, and our fights. And maybe, mostly for the fights. I think those memories, recognizing our love held past whatever we fought about, will give her security as she grows up."

Alyssa's eyes widened. Her lips parted, but it took a few moments before words escaped. "I'm sorry."

He nodded—and felt a rush of gratitude that Lexi chose that moment to pounce on them.

"You found each other . . . I'm so glad you're here. I've got us a table in the back corner and food is on the way. I need a moment to wrap things up in the kitchen, but we're finally slowing down." She pointed to the back of the restaurant. "Head back to the last booth on the right. You can't miss it."

Jeremy stood and gestured for Alyssa to lead the way. As she stepped in front of him, she reached behind and snagged his hand within her own. She squeezed and didn't let go as she wove through the tables. She wasn't sure how he felt about her, but she knew how she felt: she wasn't alone.

He held on tight.

She stopped suddenly and he bumped into her back. She gestured to the table and watched his eyes light with wonder. The six-top was piled high with food—pasta, meats, salads, calamari, paté . . .

"Isn't it only the four of us?" she asked.

He laughed. "I thought so."

Alyssa touched the bouquet as she scooted around the horseshoe-shaped booth. "She is so good. Lexi never forgets anything . . . Tulips are my favorite flower."

Jeremy dropped into the booth and slid next to her. "They're both like that. Liam will call me up with ideas, reassurance, random stuff about something I mentioned to him or something he just thinks I need to know."

"He does that for me too. Lexi's always done that."

"You two really are close."

Alyssa popped an olive into her mouth. "Family. I think she was the favorite daughter some days." She held up a hand. "I'm not being entirely serious, but she and my mom had a much easier relationship during high school."

Alyssa paused.

"What?"

"After what you said about your parents . . . My 'war'"—she made air quotes, beginning to understand how foolish it all sounded—"has probably hurt Lexi too. More than I was willing to recognize. She lost her second mom the day I threw mine away, and while my brother could do what he wanted, Lexi kinda had to stand by me no matter how she felt."

"It's going to be okay," he whispered.

She leaned closer to him. "I love that you believe that."

There were only a couple inches between them, and she wondered if he'd close it. She felt her gaze drop from his eyes to his lips and knew he caught it too. It brought a little lift to those lips as they descended upon hers. The kiss lasted less than a few heartbeats, but length, she thought as he leaned back and looked into her eyes again, was not the only measure of a first kiss. In fact, she determined, if you measured it by another metric—by the longing it left in its wake—this one blew every other first kiss away.

"What's that smile for?" he whispered.

"Nothing other than I liked that very much."

"Me too."

Alyssa tilted her chin across the table. Lexi and Liam were working their way toward them, stopping for short meet and greets on their way—shaking a hand here, topping off a wineglass there.

"They really do it right, don't they?" Jeremy watched them too.

"That they do."

Within seconds Liam and Lexi had sandwiched them into the booth, ordered more wine and a few more dishes, and started talking over one another about the evening's whos, whats, whens, and wheres.

And they didn't let up for three hours. After a salmon tartare with red onion, egg, and crème fraîche; a stunning foie gras with cognac and cherry jam; a ricotta gnocchi; a pork paillard; a clementine and fennel salad; and an outstanding cassoulet, along with numerous other side dishes, Alyssa thought she was going to be sick.

"No more."

"One more." Liam motioned to one of the waiters, who brought four slices of their famous olive oil cake and four small glasses of his pineapple-infused tequila.

Alyssa reached under the booth for her bag and knocked four Tums into her palm.

"You can't be serious?" Lexi's voice filled with worry.

"You're the one who fed me all this." Alyssa tried to deflect the concern, but Lexi's eyes said she'd failed.

"Good food and friends are supposed to ease your stress, not cause it."

"And they are. It's just going to take time—that and an FBI interview. But I'm getting better, I promise." She gave her friend a half hug and lifted her glass. "To good food and even better friends."

They clinked glasses, and Lexi sighed. She then stood, walked around the horseshoe booth, and gestured for Alyssa, Jeremy, and Liam to scoot over. Alyssa knew she wanted to sit next to her husband. Lexi tucked in next to him as he draped an arm around her. She snuggled back, and he kissed the top of her head.

Alyssa nudged Jeremy. "They do it right."

He nodded.

As Alyssa watched her best friend, something unfurled within her. When Lexi's parents starting fighting, really fighting, in the sixth grade, Alyssa's home became her friend's most weekends. And when Alyssa lost it with her mom, pitched away her life as she knew it, and decided—in a two-week time frame—to go "save the world" with XGC, Lexi had her back. She helped her close down her Chicago apartment, arranged the move, and as far as Alyssa knew, didn't cross the battle lines and speak to Janet again. If her mom was telling the truth and "the fight was over," Lexi needed to be freed too.

And Alyssa thought she should probably begin by giving her best friend both an apology and a thank-you.

Chapter 21

Alyssa unlocked the back door and stood in the dark kitchen. It was as cool and silent as the day she came home almost three weeks before. What saddened her now was not how lifeless and void it felt, but how different it might have been, could be at this very moment, if only she could let it.

She crossed through the kitchen and stood at the bottom of the stairs. In the dim light of the moon shining through the windows, only the bright dots of yellow, silver, and white within her favorite painting could be seen. It felt as if she were looking at an endless night sky, unable to see where the painting stopped and the wall began. She felt small. Insignificant. But rather than upset her, it was a wonderful diminishing. Tonight it made her feel like something bigger existed, and all this would pass away and, as Jeremy said, she'd be okay. That's what the painting had always given her: a place—albeit small—to stand. Tonight it gave her hope. She touched her lips, reliving a little more hope and something even sweeter.

She climbed the stairs and paused outside her mom's bedroom door. It was open, but it was as neat as when Alyssa had left the house that morning. She suspected Janet was staying later at her studio within the bookshop to give her space. Space she wasn't sure she wanted.

Acid burned her stomach, and she turned back down the hall to her own room. She needed more Tums. Lexi had pulled out all the stops tonight but, Alyssa moaned, that didn't mean she should have eaten it all.

She popped a few more Tums, brushed her teeth, and crawled into bed—only to wake what felt like moments later in a cold sweat. At least she thought she was awake. She couldn't clear the fog from her head. It felt like she was thinking through water. Her stomach was on fire and she ached. Her whole body ached, not just her back, but her fingers and her ankles. Even her shoulder felt tender against the pillow. Everything throbbed as she tried to roll over again. She felt herself curl tight with the pain. Then cold shot through her brain.

"Alyssa? Alyssa?"

She pushed against the bed. Her wrists hurt. She tried to gain distance from the cold.

"She has a fever."

Alyssa felt her shoulder shake. The movement reverberated down her spine.

"Honey? Do you hear me?"

"Can they burst?" She spoke through fog, her mouth now full of cotton. She wondered if her lips were cracking with the effort. Her words tasted like a dry biscuit.

"Can what burst?"

"Ulcers."

"She has ulcers?" Janet's voice lifted. Alyssa knew she was talking to someone else and not to her.

"Get her up."

Dad. Alyssa frowned. He sounded upset. He should be, she thought. Mom cheated on him. She wiggled from someone's cold hands. "I want to sleep."

"Hold still." Janet spoke again. "We're taking you to the hospital."

Alyssa fully woke to find her dad pushing her in a wheelchair and her mom walking next to her. White walls, blue industrial carpet. Massive double doors opened as they passed beneath a bright red sign indicating the emergency room.

"We're going straight in. Chris is waiting for us." Her mom surged ahead.

Chris? Ah . . . Alyssa remembered. The green eyes. The man from the store. The man from the pickup truck who took her to Jasper's . . . Madeline's boyfriend . . . One of her mom's best friends . . .

Only he was no longer dressed in jeans and a button-down as he'd been that first and only time she'd met him. Now he wore a white doctor's coat. He reached down and helped her from the wheelchair and onto a bed.

"Ulcers, huh?" He tapped on a tablet.

"I've had them for a couple years. They've gotten worse since Christmas. I lost my job, and the stress . . ." She didn't want to say more and hoped her parents wouldn't. To be in a hospital, yet be part of the pain and scandal XGC caused, was too much. She wondered what any doctor would say and feared it would be far worse than any interview she'd encountered. The vitriol and disdain would be justified. She sank deeper into the bed.

Chris only nodded, then directed his attention back to the tablet. "Let's cover a little ground. Can you tell me where the pain is? Sharp? Stabbing? Throbbing? Can you tell me if it bursts, then recedes? Or does it ramp up? Is it cyclical? Can you tell me . . ."

Alyssa struggled to keep up with Chris's litany of questions as he hooked her up to various monitors. At one point he waved away a nurse and situated the IV in the top of her hand himself.

Finally he rested a hand on her shoulder. "You did great. I'm going to refer you to the GI physician on duty. I expect she'll order an endoscopy to get definitive answers."

"Can they burst though?"

"To be honest . . ." He slid his hand down her arm and squeezed her hand. Her bones felt almost bruised against the slight pressure. "It doesn't sound like we're dealing with ulcers at all, so hold off on that thought. Let me get Dr. Laghari."

He left the room, and Janet grabbed the hand he had held. She held it gently, as if it were infinitely precious to her. Alyssa felt no pain. She looked to their hands and could not tell where her mom's began and her own ended.

"Are you hurting now?" Janet pointed to a series of smiley faces on the wall. Bold words declared them to be the Wong-Baker Pain Rating Scale.

"Seven," Alyssa whispered.

"That's bad." Janet looked to Seth. "That's really bad."

"It's better than eight through ten." Alyssa's hand pulled away as she curled into her side.

"You're tough as nails." Seth sighed. "A seven for you is everybody else's ten."

"I'm not. I just pretend to be," Alyssa whispered.

"That's it. I'll go—"

"Don't." Seth captured Janet's arm. "Chris'll do his best for her, as fast as he can. You know that."

Bad move, Dad. Alyssa thought. She always has to be right.

But Janet didn't move, or argue. Instead she turned into her ex-husband's arms. Seth pulled her close and wrapped her tight. "It'll be okay, J."

Alyssa closed her eyes and, at some level, felt peace.

Some time later Dr. Laghari entered, introduced herself, and launched into another series of questions—far longer and more personal than Chris's. They picked at places within Alyssa she hadn't wanted to face or had even purposely pushed away.

Yes, she did experience some joint pain . . . No, she hadn't been trying to lose weight. She just couldn't seem to gain . . . No, she wasn't the best sleeper. She was awake two to three hours in the middle of every night . . . Feelings of anxiety? Panic? Restlessness? Yes. Yes. And yes. But her job had been incredibly stressful . . . Life had been incredibly stressful.

"It's like pebbles cause gigantic waves within me rather than tiny ripples, but won't that just go away as things calm down?"

Dr. Laghari didn't nod in confirmation. Instead she tilted her tablet to Alyssa and handed her a stylus.

"Time to prep you for an endoscopy. This is a procedure done under general anesthesia and, like all procedures, carries some risks outlined here. Please read, then sign here, here, here, and here."

Dr. Laghari left and a nurse, followed by an orderly, came in with a sedative. She spoke to Janet rather than to Alyssa.

"This will make her sleepy, and Brad here will roll her into the operating room."

Janet squeezed Alyssa's hand, then let it go. She leaned over and kissed Alyssa's forehead. "We'll be right outside in the waiting area until you come back."

"No . . ." Alyssa felt herself growing heavy. Her eyelids dropped. Her head filled with a woolly fuzz. "Don't leave me. Please don't let go."

"I am right here."

She felt her mom kiss her forehead again, and with those four words Alyssa fell asleep.

Chapter 22

One a.m. and the emergency department was still hopping. Nurses and doctors came and went through the glass bays, sliding partitioning curtains and soothing soft cries. A few moans from out-of-sight patients sank deep into Janet, leaving her raw with all nerves firing.

"It's my fault." She and Seth sat in plastic chairs in an enlarged seating area off the main hub of activity.

Seth chuckled. "How do you figure that?"

"I was too hard, too unbending, not fun enough or understanding enough; I pushed. I always pushed, Seth, and I've caused so much pain. You, the kids . . . She absorbed all this, all my years of being . . ." She looked up at her ex-husband. "You know what I was."

"You were and are the woman I love. None of us are perfect. When are you going to realize that?" Seth looped an arm around her shoulders and squeezed. "And we did have some fun. Try to remember that too."

Janet laughed.

"It's time you forgave yourself, J."

Janet dropped her head onto his shoulder. Father Luke had been telling her for months that her problem was no longer asking others for forgiveness, but accepting it herself.

"It's an odd form of pride, you know," he had said over coffee one day. "You decide you know better than God and make your own ruling."

Her dear friend Maddie Carter, Madeline's late aunt, had once warned her of the same thing. So while she wanted to dismiss his assessment—because this anxious anguish felt nothing like pride—she couldn't. *Don't assume God's role or presume you understand his ways,* Maddie told her once with such calm sincerity it stuck. But just because she remembered it didn't mean she followed it—yet.

"But—" Janet glanced up and only caught sight of the edge of Seth's chin. It was a good strong chin.

"No buts. Either you let it go or you live in it forever. *We* live in it forever, J, and that sounds miserable to me. Doesn't it to you?"

We live in it forever. That got her attention. Janet pushed upright. Seth always did have a way of cutting through the drama, and he never spoke carelessly. Forever? "Done."

He raised a brow.

"I promise to try to work to pray to be done. How's that?" Janet smiled. "But she can't come home with me. You're going to have to use that mattress you got all snippy about. She can't heal if she's constantly upset with me."

Seth nodded, and Janet felt simultaneously pleased and dismayed. Pleased to be right, dismayed to be right, and a little hurt Seth agreed so readily. But Father Luke had warned her—that little hiccup of free will he kept trying to explain to her. She could ask for forgiveness, he constantly reminded her, but she couldn't control another's response. Forgiveness may never come and she needed to accept that.

But she couldn't. She simply refused to accept that it was her reality with Alyssa—not yet. But she was ready for a cease-fire. She couldn't avoid her own home all summer.

"No." Seth's nod turned to a slow side-to-side motion. "That ends now too."

Janet felt her heart skip a beat.

He looked down the hall to the Emergency Room entrance. Alyssa wasn't in there any longer, but it was where they'd started. "We don't know what we're facing, J. She'll need you."

"She won't want me."

"Life's not always about what we want."

Janet leaned back. Her plastic chair squeaked on its metal legs. She wasn't sure if he was talking about her daughter or about her.

Seth twisted to face her. "I'm at work downtown every day. You can be home within minutes. I can't cook, I barely clean, and what if she needs help somehow? No woman wants her father that close."

"You're not making a compelling case." Nevertheless, relief flooded her.

"In these past three years, whom have you yearned for most? Besides me, of course." He flashed a quick grin.

Janet shook her head as the sense of relief evaporated as quickly as it had gathered. Peace and unity with Alyssa had always felt fundamental, more so even than Seth's forgiveness, more elusive too. To have peace with one's child felt elemental, as if your own blood ran smooth across the generations. You were whole and tranquil. She felt it now in her relationship with her granddaughter, Rosie. And she knew she was only welcomed into that love because her son and daughter-in-law had invited her there. They trusted her again.

Yes, the "bad" in life bumped down the generations with discord and pain, causing breaks and tumult as well, but it could be healed. It could be made new and, perhaps, made stronger. She thought back to holding Rosie in her lap only days before, pointing at the balloon in *Good Night, Gorilla*. Yes, healing was possible—and worth sacrifice.

"But if she fights me to the point of not healing, we move her to your apartment."

"If World War III breaks out on Little Pine Avenue, we will move her." Seth pulled Janet close again. She could feel his chest move in short silent laughter. "You are so dramatic."

"Another reason you love me." The words came out light and unbidden—and she couldn't snatch them back. She stilled.

In the two short months they'd been back together, Janet had kept a tight rein on her emotions. *Do you still love me? Are you happy with me? Are you upset? What have I done?* These were the questions from her past. Always asking and pressing, for confirmation, for bolstering, for adoration—more, more, more. She had promised herself on that very first day she sought out Seth to apologize, to really apologize for all that came before and all that had ruined their marriage, and to promise that she would try to never do that again. Any insecurity, any anxiety, any need, she would try—she would try to work to pray—to leave it at God's feet and not Seth's. But here, she'd done it.

She pushed against his chest to sit upright. "I'm sorry. I shouldn't have—"

"It is." He cut off her apology and was looking at her. His eyes were the most alluring shade of green she'd seen. "It is one of the reasons I love you so much. Your drama brings color, a little dark sometimes, but color, to my life. Lately more color than I imagined could exist in this world, and I'd miss it if you weren't right here with me. More than you could possibly know."

Janet swallowed.

"Will you marry me, J?"

"What?" The word drifted out on her exhalation.

"Marry me." He looked past her and chuckled. "Not the most romantic location, I'll grant you, but a good one. Right in the mess of our lives."

Janet searched his eyes. They were a softer green now. They did that, changed with emotion. She was reminded how she'd taken this color and this look for granted, only recognizing its absence when she was met with three years of the hard emerald of betrayal and anger.

He clasped her hands and continued without waiting for her to speak. She wasn't sure she could speak anyway.

"When I imagined this moment, I thought about getting down on one knee, but this floor is a little hard. I might not get back up again. Besides, we've been down this road before, and this isn't a new beginning; it's a continuation of our story. We had a hiccup and we got rolled, but we're recovering. Together. So I'm thinking you, me, a pastor, and July fourteenth."

"Our anniversary? That's in three weeks."

"I don't want a new one."

"I . . . I don't know . . ."

"What don't you know?"

Janet studied his eyes more closely and recalled the different shade each emotion brought, and the different shades of emotion she'd brought to their marriage over the years. To be discontented, chafed, irritated, annoyed, she suspected, had been as indelible within her disposition as the changing of colors was within his eyes.

She pulled her hand away and laid her palm against his face. "What if I screw it up again?"

He covered her hand with his own. "I'm present now. We both are."

"You're sure?"

A flicker entered his green. "Aren't you?"

"Yes." She chastised herself for having needed—again—that extra beat of reassurance. She had been sure, certain, thankful, overjoyed in the moment he'd asked, and yet still she had required more. No more, she thought to herself. Trust. Leap.

"I love you," she stated simply.

Seth smiled and moved close to kiss his beautiful ex-wife-turned-fiancée when a man caught his eye. He pulled back. Janet's eyes clouded in confusion before her head turned to follow his line of sight.

"George?" he called down the hallway. He squeezed Janet's hands, both still clasped within his own, and stood.

"Seth." The old man sighed as if he had found safe harbor. "Janet."

Seth noted George's tone carried a little uplift in question with Janet's name. He couldn't blame him. All the members of their men's group had walked beside him during his divorce and its lonely aftermath. And George hadn't been around much in the last couple months to hear the updates.

"What are you doing here? Is Margery okay?"

George looked back down the hallway. "Winsome Pharmacy is closed; the hospital's is the only one open right now. I ran out of my heart pills."

"Couldn't your hospice nurses help you out?"

"I needed something to do. Margery is finally sleeping."

Seth gripped the man's shoulder. George and Margery had been married for sixty-three years, and he couldn't imagine the pain George was enduring. "You need sleep too, my friend. Let us take you home."

"My car is right outside the west door. But you're right. I'm getting tired now." George shook his head. "David Drummond told me about this."

Janet laid a hand on his arm as well. "Told you what?"

Seth noticed George's eyes looked rheumy, red and alone, beyond anything he'd seen in his friend before.

"The night is the darkest time. The kids are home, five of them, and yet in the night I'm empty and alone, deeply alone."

Janet stepped forward and engulfed George in a hug, and Seth loved her for it.

After long minutes, George stepped back. "I'll go now. I expect I'll be able to get a little sleep. Thank you."

Seth rested a hand once again on George's shoulder. "How about I drop by tomorrow?"

"I'd like that." George nodded and walked past them. He stopped and looked back twenty feet later, just as the hospital's sliding doors opened for him. Seth stood with his arms around Janet, who had her forehead resting on his chest.

He smiled and headed out into the parking lot. He had always thought those two would get back together. For years everyone labeled Janet a shrew or worse, but he'd always had a soft spot for her. Just wait, he'd told Margery. Don't give up, he'd told Seth. Seth hadn't seen his wife clearly, and all the fear she carried. But he had—after all, he'd raised Devon, Bella, and Terrell. He knew a wounded soul thrashed as violently as a bitter or broken one. But once soothed and made safe, that soul healed well and was all the more beautiful for the hurt it once carried.

Upon reaching his car, George pulled out the small pad of paper and pen he always carried and made a note to call Devon the next morning. He smiled to himself. It was already morning, but without writing it down he'd still forget.

And that's what he did. After only four hours of sleep, George was wide awake again and had completely forgotten his plan to call his fourth child.

The sun wasn't up yet—which was just how he liked it. He used to love it when the kids would come down for breakfast and find a good meal laid out on the table. He had often made eggs and bacon and always burned the toast a touch. How they would exclaim, as if fairies had left the grub by magic. They knew he did it, of course, but they never realized how much work it required. It took a full hour to make that meal, and by the time they thundered down the stairs before school he'd also already had his quiet time, downed his morning coffee, and read the newspaper. They'd laugh together over breakfast, then head to school and he'd head to the office. It had felt like magic. Maybe it was. He chuckled. Magic for me, he thought, and for them, but poor Margery always got stuck with the dishes.

He put on a cardigan and walked out the front door, greeting the day-shift hospice nurse in the driveway.

"How was the night, Mr. George?"

"She slept well. Deeper, I think."

"She will, and longer now." The slow, compassionate way she said the words signaled to George that this was not a sign of good restorative rest, but the start of the next stage of the journey. "You need rest too, Mr. George. Your coffee will still be there in a few hours."

"Won't be the same, Denise. I'll be back soon."

George walked down Bunting Street, turned left onto Spruce, and within fifteen minutes—it used to take eight, he thought—he crossed the town green to Andante.

The owner pushed the door open just as he reached for the handle.

"George Williams?"

The older man looked up, startled. The young man thrust out his hand. "Jeremy Mitchell. I own the shop. Please come in."

"Thank you." George nodded.

Chapter 23

"This makes no sense." Jeremy slammed his laptop shut as Ryan pushed through the kitchen's swinging door.

"Whoa . . . What makes no sense?"

"Nothing . . . Everything." Jeremy ran his hands through his hair.

Ryan picked up his book from the edge of the desk. Jeremy knew it was more tattered than how Ryan had left it. He had accidentally dropped it and creased the cover, almost to the point of tearing, while devouring it that night.

"Did you read it?" Ryan waved the small paperback at him.

"It's the loneliest, harshest book I've ever read."

"Really? I think Steinbeck gets at the human condition pretty well, and George and Lennie—that's the point—they had each other."

"Until Lennie ruins it killing that woman. Then he loses his life and George loses too. He kills his friend, kills their dream . . . He'll never fully live after that, never get his farm. He's another Candy, alone, with no one and nothing."

Ryan chewed his lip. "You're right."

Jeremy glanced to his laptop and his thinking shifted. "There are lots of ways to betray a friend. I get that Lennie wasn't fully capable of making good choices, at least Steinbeck presents him that way, but we . . . We are responsible for our choices. We know what we're doing and when it's flat wrong."

Ryan watched him but asked nothing, said nothing more. Jeremy slid the laptop back toward himself, and Ryan pushed through the kitchen door to the front of the shop. Jeremy watched the swinging door slow until it stilled . . . He hadn't thought about someone taking the money. He'd only thought he'd misplaced, miscounted it. But what if?

He forced himself to stop and breathe. He was being unfair and beyond unjust. He looked at the clock he'd mounted on the wall above his desk. Alyssa said she'd drop by at ten—she was the perfect person to ask about this.

And, speaking of perfect, that's what last night had been. Not like before, with Krista. That was tempestuous, tense, and uncertain, almost like he was constantly on the verge of the stomach flu. But it had been such a heady experience—easily mistaken for love. While it felt harsh to describe those days with Krista like that now, he thought, time and experience did have a way of recasting one's memories.

But last night . . . He'd reached for Alyssa's hand as they walked to her borrowed car. She'd grown quiet as the evening wound down. Lexi and Liam were clearly exhausted, as he was sure they were every night after closing. Alyssa looked wiped too.

"Am I working you too hard?" he had quipped.

She laughed, but it was tinged with sadness. "I can't tell you how much working for you and Lexi means to me right now . . . There's just a lot going on and . . ."

"What?"

She stopped by a black sedan. "I don't feel like myself. I thought

I would, that once I got here, despite everything that's still a total mess, I'd feel better. I'd be better. And I'm not."

"How can I help?"

"Have a latte waiting for me at ten o'clock tomorrow? We need to talk more about your credit card processing." She lifted up on her toes and pressed a kiss to his lips. Not a peck, he noted right then and there. A real kiss. He almost burst out of his skin as he slid a hand around her back.

"Got it," he whispered against her lips. As she lowered onto her heels again, he gave a final peck at her lips. "And a muffin."

She opened the car door. "You'd better skip the muffin. I always feel a little ill after those. No offense."

"None taken." He chuckled. "I do too."

She dropped into the car. "I've got an idea to change that too. Tomorrow?"

"Looking forward to it. Sleep well."

The conversations, the kisses, the hope and anticipation, all pointing to ten o'clock, had woken him before sunrise and brought him to the shop even earlier than usual. And when he looked out the door at 6:25 a.m. and saw George Williams slowly coming up the sidewalk, he felt emboldened and invited the man in. It felt like the previous night's glow was spilling into the morning and Alyssa had been right all along. Everything would turn out okay.

George had looked surprised at Jeremy's greeting, but thanked him and entered. At the counter he pulled his credit card out of his brown leather wallet and looked up, with a slightly befuddled expression, at the chalkboard sign.

Jeremy waved his card away. "Whatever you like. It's on me."

George dropped his eyes to his credit card and carefully placed it back within its sleeve. He looked back to the menu board. "What do you recommend?"

"How about this? You go sit and I'll bring you something."

George nodded.

Four minutes later, Jeremy dropped into the chair beside him at the fireplace. He put their white china cups on the small table between them and reached to turn on the fire. "It's more for the look than anything in the summer."

"A fire always makes a place homey." George shifted forward in the deep leather chair to reach for his cup.

Jeremy gestured to it. "I heard you order a cappuccino the other day. Today I used a new bean and gave you just a hint of foam, thinking you might like it the way I do, pretty dry. Let me know what you think."

George settled back and closed his eyes with his first sip. "Delicious. I've always liked coffee. It was rationed in the forties, and when it came back it felt like a great luxury. I was a kid then and didn't drink, but I watched my dad." He took another sip. "As soon as he'd let me, it became our ritual. A cup together at our kitchen table every day. Reminds me of him even now."

"I feel that way about it too. I started working for a coffee shop in my neighborhood when I was fifteen. I think my foster mom thought it'd keep me out of trouble, and it did. I loved that place and I understood the beans." Jeremy chuckled. "Odd as it sounds, there's no other way to say it. Smell, touch, taste, when they'd pull dry, when they'd sour; there was an art and chemistry about it, a relationship I understood." He leaned back. "Says something, doesn't it? My best relationship was and probably still is with a coffee bean."

"Ah . . . Foster care . . . I have three kids who started out there. Good kids, good adults now. I wish back then they'd had something as simple and as complex as that—a relationship with a bean."

"They had each other." At George's questioning glance, he held up a hand. "I'm sorry. A friend, Alyssa Harrison, was in your son Devon's high school class. She mentioned him and that he had two siblings."

"He did back then. Now he's got five. But you're right—they started out together, just the three of them against the world. We had some rough early years with that crew." George chuckled with the memories. "They're all coming back now. I . . . I need to call Devon today. He was coming this weekend, but sooner might be better."

"That's wonderful."

Something flickered in George's eyes as he looked to the fireplace. Jeremy got the impression that the homecoming wasn't "wonderful" after all. He searched for a new, and lighter, topic.

"Is it really awful without the pillows?"

George chuckled. "Told you about that too, did she?" He waved away Jeremy's nod. "I was being a grouch that day. I'm finding it hard to let go of stuff these days." He lifted a shoulder and let it drop. "I'm sorry about what I said your first day open." He looked around. "It's a fine-looking place. Not what anybody would expect in poky old Winsome. Kinda puts us on the map, doesn't it?"

"From what I hear, you did that when you were mayor."

"Folks are being nice. We have a good community here, always have, and it's different from all the other towns around Chicago. We're less of a thoroughfare. I tried to build on that sense of home, of community, especially in town here, so that people didn't necessarily need to leave to find work. There's something good and fundamental about living and working in the same community. But things change . . . We can't even fill that Chamber of Commerce position. It's been vacant for almost six months now."

He looked past Jeremy, who turned to follow his gaze.

Outside the window, two people approached the door. George pushed himself up. "They've found me . . . That's Bella and Michael, kids five and two, as I call them. I'm surprised it took them this long to get here."

"Do they want a coffee?"

"No . . . I'd best get going. Thank you."

Jeremy stood. "I hope you'll come back."

With a nod and a wave, George headed out the door to meet his children outside. Michael swung his arm around his father and Bella looped her arm through George's on his other side.

The sight froze Jeremy in place. There was nothing "wonderful" about it. It was heartbreaking and evoked a memory he never knew he held. A crack in the wall. Someone once did that to him. He was shorter, younger, but someone swung an arm around him and someone else, on his other side, had tried to tuck him close. And even though he couldn't recall the exact time or the place, he knew when it had occurred—the day, or soon after, his parents died.

LAST NIGHT'S GLOW AND that chink in his own memories had sustained him all morning—until now. If he was right, and someone was stealing from him, much more was wrong with his shop than he ever anticipated.

Jeremy looked up from his computer. The numbers were swimming before his eyes, and none of them were good. 10:45. Alyssa wasn't coming.

Jeremy pushed his way through the swinging door. Something had to be done. Bottom line: over five thousand dollars was missing, his books were a mess, and Ryan's constant second-guessing and complaining, not to mention the ever-present tension between him and Brendon, was becoming unbearable. It was time for a talk.

Ryan caught his eye from a group of people standing near the front door, and Jeremy motioned toward the office door. But rather than nod and follow, Ryan shook his head as another man stepped between Ryan and Brendon, who seemed to be facing off at the center of the group.

"What the—" Jeremy headed toward the men, noting that every eye in the coffee shop was on them.

"Jeremy Miller?" The man standing next to Ryan motioned to him.

"What's going on?" Jeremy circled the counter to cross toward the front of the store, directly in the middle of its huge plate-glass window. A few pedestrians had stalled on the sidewalk to look in.

Jeremy locked eyes on Ryan. Ryan's eyes widened in return before he glanced away.

"We need you to come with us." One of the three man standing with Ryan and Brendon lifted his chin toward Jeremy. The light glinted off the badge at his waist.

"I don't understand."

"Your employee has been selling Adderall to high school students."

"What? The ADD medication?" Jeremy's eyes trailed to Ryan.

"It's an upper that carries the same high as crystal meth, and he's been selling right outside your back door."

"Add stealing too." Ryan looked at Jeremy rather than the officer. "*He's* stolen almost five thousand dollars from this shop."

Jeremy startled, both at Ryan's emphasis and at his statement. "How—?"

The officer cut him off before he could finish the question. "Is this true?"

"Yes, I mean, I haven't been able to find the money between accounts. I . . ." Jeremy stalled and reddened under Ryan's assessment.

"All right, then . . . We'll discuss that too. Please come with me."

"Me? No. I had nothing to do with this."

"You've got drugs running out the back door of your establishment and money's gone missing." The officer's tone rose in question, as if confused why Jeremy didn't understand the problem. He also widened his stance. "This goes down one of two ways. You come with me now, or I arrest you and you still come with me now." He dropped his hand to his waist and fingered the cuffs hanging there.

"I can answer your questions here." Jeremy looked around. Several customers held raised phones pointed their direction. He felt a panic seize him. "You can't do this here. This is my business."

"That solves one problem." The officer gripped Jeremy's right arm and turned him around. The move was almost gentle, definitely practiced, and Jeremy was in the cuffs before another word could escape.

"You have the right to an attorney. If you—"

"Stop. You're reading me my Miranda rights? Why would you do that?" Jeremy twisted to face the man again. "I'm coming. Of course I'm coming. I was just saying, I was trying to tell you—" Jeremy's jaw dropped as something caught in his periphery.

Three customers had drawn closer, most likely to catch better audio.

Jeremy clamped his mouth shut as the officer now holding Brendon in cuffs led the way out the front door.

He stared at the recording phones, oddly unable to look away. Part of his brain knew he was giving them too much; the other part didn't care.

Andante was finished.

Chapter 24

Nine hours and countless questions later, Jeremy climbed out of Madeline's car in the alley between the Printed Letter and Andante.

"I'm sorry I called you. I didn't understand what was happening."

"They just wanted answers and were following procedure, but it can be unnerving." Madeline reached for her purse in the back seat.

"Can I be charged with anything?"

"If what you said was true, I doubt it. If it's determined that you should have known, there may be more questions, but with no communication on company email, computers, or phones, or drugs sold within the premises or during the execution of any of Brendon's work duties, I can't see this going further."

"You've lost me again." Jeremy rested his hands on the top of Madeline's car.

"Bottom line, I think you're clear, and when they contact you again, just let me know." She turned toward the bookshop.

"When? Not if?" He felt his voice pitch high.

She turned back with a small smile. "Yes, when. You'll be called to testify at the very least, and that's only after all questions regarding you are laid to rest. I can't say there won't be more. They'll probably reach out to Ryan too, if another officer didn't already call him today. Let him know I'm happy to walk him through it too, if he has questions."

"Thank you. What do I owe you? I never asked."

Madeline raised a hand. "Let's talk about that another day."

"Yes, of course, you have to be exhausted." Jeremy looked around and noticed the light. The sun had dipped beyond the buildings, and the alley was draped in evening's gray. He slid his phone from his back pocket. "I took your whole day."

"No worries." She unlocked the door.

Jeremy felt his pulse race again. It'd been going up and up all day. He began to wonder what a normal heartbeat felt like. "But it'll be okay?"

Madeline turned. "Do you have anything to hide?"

"Nothing."

She smiled. It looked worn but genuine. Jeremy felt himself take a full, even, calming breath in response.

"Then I'm not worried, but I will stay on top of it. Now go have a cup of decaf. It's late."

She pushed though the alley door into the bookshop, and Jeremy walked to Andante. He expected the shop to be empty, and was surprised to be met with light.

"You're still here?" He looked around ready to find the kitchen in disarray. If they hoped to recoup the day's disaster, there was work to do. They were now down one employee, and muffins needed to be made, the area prepped for tomorrow, the accounts reviewed from the day—not to mention a long discussion about those accounts. Yet all was quiet. Still. And clean.

"Did you close out the day? Already prep? Was it horrible? I figure you had to give away coffees after all that, right? Keep customers happy? I mean, could that have gotten any worse?"

Questions raced through his brain and out his mouth just as fast, but Ryan answered none of them.

Jeremy asked one more. "Did you know?"

Ryan pressed his lips together so tight they disappeared, and the edge of his jaw worked a full minute before he opened his mouth to speak. "Something was clearly wrong. I tried to tell you."

"You did." Jeremy propped himself against the desk. "And the money?"

"I handled the books through the renovations, remember? I got them a little confused and jumbled, but I also understood them. When you said you were lost, I looked." Ryan mirrored Jeremy's posture and crossed his arms. "You thought it was me. You actually thought I stole from you?"

"No. I thought . . . I . . ." Jeremy stopped prevaricating. "I'm sorry."

Ryan watched him a beat again. "Tell me one thing . . . When did you stop trusting me?"

Jeremy winced. He cycled back through time to give an honest answer. Ryan deserved it. There was nothing left anyway. "When I started failing."

"You trusted some kid because he looked good and said the right things. You got played and I warned you. I've stood by you, came out here to help because I believed in you and in this place, and you think nothing of me."

"That's not true." But as Jeremy said the words he realized that, to a degree, Ryan was right.

He thought back to the men's group a couple weeks back and the discussion about the plank in the eye or, as one man put it, the beam that held him up. Jeremy had trusted what he imagined right would look like, not what it was—that kid who acted so sure, who had the charisma at eighteen to look you in the eye, shake your hand, and sell you the world—sell you drugs. He'd chosen the counterfeit over the genuine, again and again. He had missed what was going on right in front of him, because he was sure he knew better, sure he could see clearly, and to some degree, because he needed his perceptions to be true.

Jeremy stepped forward. "I was wrong. But it wasn't as much about you as it was about me . . . I wasn't sure, I'm still not, that I can do this. That we can do this."

"I can't do anything about that, can I? And don't use 'we.' It's insulting." Ryan looked around the kitchen. His gaze passed through the open door and into the dark coffee shop. "I closed up a few minutes after you left this morning. Once the police led you out—"

"Arrested me," Jeremy cut in, trying to lighten the mood.

Ryan continued as if nothing had interrupted him. "The tenor got pretty jazzed with gossip in here. You were on Instagram within seconds, but no one was buying anything. A pack of teenagers approached and hung around in the town square all morning, watching the place. No one came in. I don't know if they were curious or they were Brendon's customers, wondering if they were gonna get hauled in too. It wasn't good. I hope you don't mind I shut down."

"No. It sounds like it was the right thing to do. Maybe we should stay closed tomorrow."

"Up to you."

There was something in Ryan's tone that cued Jeremy. More was coming. The three words had the derisive cut of his *You're the boss*, but there was an added finality.

"I'm out." Ryan pushed off the counter.

"What?" Jeremy stepped forward again, then immediately stepped back. It felt aggressive.

"I'm out. I saw us building this place together, but you never did. It's time for me to move on."

"Please don't leave. I . . ." Jeremy stalled with the realization he had no right to ask, even beg Ryan to stay. What man would or could? "Are you leaving Winsome?"

Ryan crossed the kitchen toward him and slid his book off the desk. "I haven't got a clue what comes next. I only know it doesn't involve this place, or you." He then scanned the kitchen area as if searching for what was his and what more he needed to take.

"Give me a chance." Jeremy stretched out his hand.

Ryan chuffed and waggled his book, drawing Jeremy's eyes to the worn, bent paperback. "I'm no Candy." He looked around the kitchen. "Keep your own dream."

With that he pushed out the alley door and Jeremy stood alone.

Chapter 25

Alyssa flipped through television channels, seeing nothing.

Janet, just returned from the grocery store, had called from the kitchen as she entered the house. "Your dad has work stuff tonight, but Grandma called and would like to come for dinner to see you. Is that okay?"

"Sure," Alyssa had called back.

"Alyssa?" Janet then materialized at the family room door. Her face was soft, expression almost anxious.

Alyssa stared.

"Don't believe everything she says about me. If I was ever the person Grandma sees, I'm not anymore."

Saying nothing more, her mom had rolled off the doorjamb and returned to the kitchen.

Now Alyssa sat. Wave upon wave of emotion, new perceptions grasped but not fully understood, crashed over her until she wasn't sure what was real and what might have been the "intestinal soothing medications" the doctor prescribed.

She tried to sort through it and felt a hard nugget of guilt sitting at the bottom. She had fed the animosity between mother and daughter over the years, she couldn't deny it—not to herself, not now. She had played into her mom's rocky relationship with her grandma, finding safe harbor in her grandma's critical and exacting nature, relishing that it was directed at her mother and mirrored, even augmented, her own resentments.

But the last eighteen hours had changed that. They had changed everything. And it wasn't just the diagnosis, though that had been a shock. It was the fact that, stripped bare of every defense, curled into a hospital bed, scared and in excruciating pain, there was only one person she wanted near. She needed only one person not to leave, not to abandon her, but to stick close and endure every step with her. And her mom had done that—and more.

Alyssa clicked off the television, pushed off the couch, and padded into the kitchen. "What are you making?"

"I found a wonderful soup recipe while you were napping. Lots of root vegetables, all cooked in a bone broth. Very healing." She smiled. "And I hope tasty."

"Am I going to have to eat like this forever?" Alyssa's voice cracked.

Janet smiled. "Dr. Laghari said this is for a few days, but it's where we start, okay? One meal at a time."

Alyssa nodded and dropped onto the stool. "About Grandma . . . ?" She started it as a statement. It morphed to a question. Then she dropped it altogether.

Janet sighed and picked up the baton. "You don't need to worry about her, or me. We're fine and always will be . . . It's just . . . when you two get together, there's no winning for me." She waved a carrot at her daughter. "I'm not complaining. I'm glad you have her, but no matter what she says, please know I'm doing my best for her. Maybe that wasn't always the case. I've been pretty selfish in my time, but I'm trying now. Did you know I originally asked her to come live here, with me?"

Alyssa guffawed.

Janet raised a brow. "That was her reaction too. Laughed, then flat out refused. But I would have loved to take care of my mom."

Alyssa raised an answering brow.

Janet laughed, and the tension broke between them. "Okay . . . I would have endured it."

Within minutes the subject of their laughter arrived. Still in a little pain and a lot tired, Alyssa found herself pulling from the center, her usual spot between Mom and Grandma, and watching from the periphery. She noticed things she'd never seen before.

The same push and pull existed between them that existed between herself and her mom, only Janet played the daughter role. She tried to please her mom, yet failed. She tried to engage her, yet got rebuffed. Alyssa kept watching . . .

No. Not the same. Rather than watching an alive and present relationship unfold, it was like watching the skeleton of one that had changed, only one party hadn't realized that yet. Her grandmother was still playing by old rules. Alyssa recognized it because, she realized now, she had been doing the same for the past three weeks. Not only that, she also admitted that long ago she'd stopped trying to please, stopped trying to engage. She'd been playing her grandmother's role, the instigator, all while believing herself a victim.

Her grandmother's voice brought her back to the present.

"I'm sure you thought you were doing what was best, but you pushed that girl too hard." Grandma wiped the counters behind Janet, putting away things her mom was, in fact, still using.

"You're probably right. Hopefully she can heal now." Janet reclaimed her knife from the sink.

"I certainly hope so," Grandma clucked.

"I'm right here. I can hear you," Alyssa commented dryly. "And I'm fine, Grandma. I have celiac disease, and it just means a lifestyle change. A big one, but the doctor says I'll be fine."

"How'd you catch that?" Grandma asked Alyssa the question, but shot a look to her daughter.

The look's acidity made Alyssa cringe. "Again, not her fault, Grandma. I gave it to myself." She cycled through her head all that Dr. Laghari had said and synthesized it into bite-sized pieces for her grandmother. She left out the part of their conversation in which Alyssa's pain-tinged laughter had morphed to tears. "That's irony for you. Serves me right." She had refused to share anything more with Dr. Laghari—such as that her job at XGC centered around predicting such diseases—and certainly wasn't going to bring it up now.

"The bottom line, sort of, is that I didn't take care of myself, and my body started fighting itself—my small intestine to be exact. Did you know your small intestine is supposed to look like a putting green? Mine has all these cracks instead, like a cobblestone street."

"Alyssa, that's horrible!" Grandma exclaimed.

"But the point is, with proper diet, nutrition, and rest, she said the cracks can heal and get back to a smooth putting green again. I don't even need fancy meds, Grandma. I can be fine."

"Well . . . I can't imagine life around here can be restful. That's what you need right now."

Alyssa watched as her mom, without look or comment, turned back to her soup and stirred.

"Watch how much garlic you add, Janet. A friend of mine tells me it's very bad for one's stomach."

Without turning, Janet replied, "I'll be careful."

Soon the three sat at the kitchen table, and Alyssa couldn't avoid the center any longer. Janet set her bowl at the end of the rectangular table, positioned between her mom and her grandmother.

Alyssa glanced back and forth between the two women. They looked so much alike. Probably as alike as Alyssa and Janet. Three generations, Alyssa mused as she tried to follow the conversation between bites. Three generations playing the same games.

After an almost endless barrage of sideways comments and passive-aggressive insinuations, Alyssa wondered why her mom's head didn't fly off and how she'd never noticed the unequal dynamic before. Or perhaps it hadn't been unequal before. Perhaps her mom really had changed. But rather than engage, she poured herself another bowl of soup, and watched, and listened.

After Grandma left, Alyssa slumped at the kitchen island. "I need to help with the dishes, but she exhausted me."

"Not at all. Sit there and keep me company. No working for you tonight."

Janet cleared the table, rinsed the dishes, and began scrubbing her large soup pot.

Alyssa sat straight and finally asked the question she had pondered all night. "Did Grandma say you should stop painting?"

"Why would you think that?"

"I just wondered."

Her mom glanced back then focused on the pot again. "She never said to stop. She wouldn't do that. A declaration like that doesn't leave any wiggle room. She did say it was foolish, selfish, and something only a woman in my generation would ever consider."

Janet paused and her hands stilled, but Alyssa knew she was not waiting for her comment, she was just lost in the past.

Her mom turned on the water to rinse the pot. "My dad was second generation here and was the hardest-working man I ever knew. Grandma thought I was snubbing my nose at him by wanting to study then practice painting. It wasn't real work, it was even countercultural in her mind. He didn't think that—at least I never felt that. I'm sad you and Chase can't remember him. He was up every morning by four and worked until eight each night . . . Anyway, according to Grandma, first I was snubbing him, then after your dad and I married, I think she thought I was snubbing her and the choices she'd made. She definitely thought such silliness, as she called it, would keep me from being a good wife and mom." Janet turned to face her daughter. "And it did."

Alyssa quirked her head. That didn't make sense.

Janet leaned against the sink ledge and dried her hands on a towel. "She thought painting would keep me from being my best, and in the end, she was right. Only it was *not* painting that kept me from it."

She laid the towel on the counter and walked the two steps to the other side of the island. She pressed her hips against it, bringing her body closer to Alyssa. "There are things I need to say and things you need to hear, so bear with me . . .

"I'm sorry for the time when I took apart your picture for Mrs. Tuttle's art class. I'm sorry for when I barged in on your cookie making party and criticized the decorations. I'm sorry I redid your hair prom night when it already looked extraordinary. I'm sorry for all the times I told you to change, to stand up straight, to brush your hair, to study harder, to basically be more, do more . . . I don't know . . . to be everything I felt I wasn't. And I'm sorry about last week when I told you not to talk about XGC."

"How do you remember all that? Not last week, but the other stuff."

Janet let out a snuffly cough. "You'd be surprised how much I remember."

Alyssa swiped at her eyes. "There you go. What am I supposed to say now?"

"Nothing, but I think that's what drawing and painting did for me. It let me be me; and when I wasn't me I managed your business, everyone's business, in ways I never should have." She leaned even closer and spread her palms on the marble island. "And I'm sorry you're sick. Despite what you might think, I would do anything for you, take this on myself if I could. But since that's not possible, I will certainly apologize for any part I played in it."

"You didn't cause this. It's kind of what *autoimmune* means. My body is ticked off with me, not you."

Janet smiled. "Yes, but I read today that stress is a huge contributor to all autoimmune diseases, and I can't think of anyone who's caused you more stress than Tag Connelly and me."

"Good point." Alyssa softened her words with a smile. "I'm beginning to think he's a sociopath."

"Thank you for excluding me from that." Janet winked.

Alyssa wiggled a finger toward the back door, the one through which her grandmother had left a half hour before. "After that dinner, I'm surprised you don't have a few autoimmunes yourself. Has Grandma always been such a case?"

"Yes, but it's never directed at you. She is uniquely my case." Janet laughed. Then she frowned. "And I'm uniquely yours."

"What do you mean?"

"Mothers and daughters. It's a unique and complex relationship. You may never be able to see me in a new way. And I'm sorry for that."

Before Alyssa could reply, Janet swiped her hand through the air as if to erase her words. "I need to tell you something . . . Your dad wanted to be here to tell you, but Margery Williams took a turn for the worse and he's helping George and his kids with some financial stuff tonight. Anyway, I think you should know sooner rather than later." She stared at her daughter. "Your dad asked me to marry him. Again."

Chapter 26

Jeremy sank into the couch and let the devastation of the day wash over him. Becca was finally asleep after wondering why *The Giving Tree* had almost brought her dad to tears.

"The tree gave him everything, and he just took and took and took."

"They were together at the end, Daddy." She had taken his hand within her own and held it carefully, as if he were about to break.

That tipped him further over the edge.

He had swiped at his eyes with the back of his hand. "But it was only a stump, because he was so selfish. And even at the end, he didn't see what he'd done. He never saw it." He withdrew his hand from hers and pressed his fingertips into his eyes.

Becca's light tap had brought him back to the present. "Can we go to the park again tomorrow?"

"Of course we can. You need to sleep now." He had carried her to her room, despite her giggly protests that she was too big and too old to be carried, kissed her good night, flipped off her light, then flopped onto the couch where he now thought he'd stay—forever.

The day played over and over in memory, and its start didn't get any better with each replay. But after about a half hour of this fruitless exercise, Jeremy felt his mind drift beyond the moment Ryan walked out the coffee shop's alley door to the moment, not ten minutes later, that Krista and Becca banged on it.

Thinking it was Ryan, Jeremy had swung it open. "Thank you," he blurted before noticing his ex-wife.

"You're welcome?"

"Sorry. What—" He had stopped, unsure of what words should come next.

Krista stepped past him into the kitchen. "Did you get my texts? You never replied. I have an eight o'clock meeting at headquarters and my parents are still out of town. I hoped Becca could stay with you tonight."

Jeremy felt his breath release. Becca was exactly who he needed tonight.

"I'd love that."

Krista had set Becca's duffel bag on the stainless steel counter and looked around. The movement surprised Jeremy. She was the type to toss the bag, issue the command, then back out the door as fast as she came.

Instead, she had then turned and focused her attention on Jeremy. "What's wrong?"

"Why would something be wrong?"

"You look . . . It's not tired. It's deflated. Someone let all the air out of your tires."

Jeremy had forced out a laugh that sounded stilted and stiff to his own ears. He hoped it was good enough to fool Krista. "That's what a long day at a coffee shop will do to you."

Her eyes said she didn't believe him, but she nodded. "You sure this is okay?"

"Absolutely. In fact, I've got tomorrow morning off." He reached for Becca's hand. "We'll have a great time, Ladybug."

"You have tomorrow off?" Krista's voice took on that tone, almost ferret-like, digging for the truth.

"Things are smoothing out." He shrugged to give his lie life. "I'm not needed here *every* moment."

"That's . . . impressive. Okay. I'll call after my meeting."

He nodded. She left. And he turned to his daughter. "Do you want to go to the park? It's not quite dark yet, and I need a little fresh air. What do you say?"

Becca's ponytail bounced with her excitement.

So that's what they did. In the last light of the evening, they walked to the park. And rather than sit on the bench and watch her play, Jeremy felt a need, a compulsion, to be as close to his daughter as he could, for as long as he could.

He climbed the playscape with her, crossed the monkey bars behind her, sat halfway down the seesaw to counterbalance her much lighter weight, pumped higher on the swings than she could just to show her how high she could someday fly, and then, warning her not to follow him, he jumped off mid-flight to soar through the air and crash into the grass a full twenty feet away.

"Again, Daddy!" She had raced over and collapsed on his chest in the grass.

"Ugh . . ." He moaned. "I think I broke my ankle."

But he hadn't. It was a little sore, but after a few minutes of wiggling it, he could walk—and he did it again. Five times.

On the sixth soar, Becca disobeyed and attempted a jump. He watched as she flew forward, soaring what felt like forty feet through the air rather than his twenty. Time seemed to stop, and he wondered in a panic if she would ever land.

She did—and she collapsed facedown on the ground.

"Becca!" he yelled, dragging his feet to stop the swing. He couldn't jump. What if he landed on her?

He scrabbled through the gravel, then across the grass to reach her. He turned her over. Her face was red, but no breath came from her mouth. "Becca. Becca."

She gulped with a horrible noise, choking on the exhale. "That was awesome."

"Are you okay?" He sat her up and gently patted her back.

"It stung me," she exclaimed. "Let's do it again."

"No way." He hugged her close.

And that's when it happened . . . Holding her tight in the grass, he remembered. She had light brown hair. She smelled of lavender. He was tall.

They started as flashes. Sights. Smells. Sounds. No context. No story. And as much as he wanted to encourage them, to feed them and let them grow, they frightened him.

He picked Becca up, dusted off her knees, and the two of them walked back to Andante to pick up his car and head home. Only now, in the quiet of the living room, did the flashes return and stretch into memories.

Without thinking he slid his phone off the side table and tapped it to call the one person he wanted to talk to, the only person—well, second to Becca, now that she was asleep—he had wanted, and needed, to see all day. He smiled as he waited for her to answer. So many conflicting emotions were wrapped up in this too, he thought.

After the requisite preliminaries, he got to the point. "I missed you today."

"I am so sorry," Alyssa gasped. "I was in the ER last night. I only got released this afternoon."

"What?" He sat up straight. "Are you okay? I'm coming over. I can't come over. Becca's here. Do you need anything? What's wrong?"

Alyssa's light laughter calmed his nerves. "I'm fine. In fact, if you're home, I'll come to you."

She clicked off, and Jeremy looked around his small apartment—and realized he had work to do. He raced around cleaning until his buzzer rang.

Opening his front door, he saw the top of her head first, a high blond ponytail swinging with each step. She came into full view, wearing no makeup and dressed in jeans and an MIT sweatshirt.

"You?" He gestured to the shirt.

She nodded.

"Respect." He looked her over head to toe. "What happened? What got hurt?" Finding all parts functional and nothing encased in plaster, he reached for her. She smelled of roses and citrus, and he hugged her tighter.

If the hug surprised her, she didn't comment, nor did she step away. He felt swamped in gratitude for that.

"I got celiac disease . . . Well, not last night. I've had it, I guess. It just went nuts last night after our opulent dinner and sent me to the emergency room."

"I can't believe you came here. You shouldn't have." He ushered her inside.

"I'm fine and, oddly, I feel better than I have in months. Gluten is a trigger, and all those toast points, pasta, and gnocchi last night probably didn't help." She raised a hand. "I was already there anyway, so I guess that was the one last great meal before the end. And what a meal."

"That's not funny."

"It is, kind of."

He stalled in his kitchen. "Are you hungry? Thirsty? What can I get you? A banana?"

"I'm on soup and smoothies for the next few days . . . I'm good right now."

"Tea?"

She smiled as she turned from his short hallway into his living room. "Tea would be lovely."

While she settled into the same corner of the couch he had occupied moments before, Jeremy scurried around the kitchen making two cups of tea.

"Question for you," she called from the living room. "How on earth do you have my Smurfs?"

He laughed and carried in the cups. "How'd you know?"

She lifted Baker Smurf. A small black *A* was written on his left foot.

"Your mom let me borrow them. I was buying some books for Becca one day and I asked her about toys. As you can see, I don't have many yet. The next day she showed up at the coffee shop and handed me that box. To borrow only, I promise. She made that very clear."

"Good." Alyssa tucked her feet under her. "Because I love these little blue guys."

"Becca does too, but you can have them back if you need them." Jeremy winked and lifted off the couch.

She reached out and pulled his arm. "Sit back down. However much I may need a little comfort right now, I'm not taking toys from a seven-year-old." She then held her mug out to him.

He looked at it, clued in, and raised his for a toast. "Cheers. Thanks for coming tonight. I . . . You had a rougher day than I did, but mine was no picnic, and you're the one I wanted to talk to."

He felt his face flush. He couldn't believe he'd said that, but he also felt, after today, honesty was required—anywhere, everywhere, and especially now.

"I'm sorry I wasn't there today. I meant to be."

"I'd say you were busy with more important things . . . Tell me more."

Alyssa watched him and took a sip of tea without taking her eyes from him. "Honestly, my head's about to explode. I'd rather hear about your day, if that's okay."

"It was a disaster . . . Can we go back farther?"

Alyssa nodded.

Jeremy took a slow breath and felt peace with the exhale. "I mentioned it last night, but it's about today too . . . Remember how I said my parents died?"

Alyssa nodded again but said nothing. Her silent attention gave him the permission and the courage to continue. "They were killed in my dad's boss's prop plane when I was ten. My dad had an older sister, but I'd never met her, and when asked, she didn't want me . . . Anyway, I got to eighteen by being passed around a few foster homes—two good, one great. Not so bad really. But I never remembered anything about my parents until today."

Alyssa's head tilted in question.

"Nothing. It was like there was a line I couldn't cross no matter how hard I pushed . . . Until today." He circled his hands around the warm mug, drawing comfort from it. "I messed up today. It was a disaster all the way around. Then this evening I took Becca to the park and all these memories came flooding back. My mom had hair a little darker than yours." He gestured to Alyssa's hair. "She wore it long too. My dad . . ." He grinned. "He was tall."

Alyssa smiled. "I can imagine."

"I broke my wrist when I was probably five jumping off the swings. That came back today too . . . And my mom . . ." Jeremy felt his eyes burn, but he didn't care. "She carried me to the car. I even remember thinking I was way too cool for that, but secretly loving it at the same time. I did that to Becca tonight, carried her, and she acted just like I had. It was amazing. And my mom stayed with me until I fell asleep that night. Oddly, that came back too."

"Moms are important." Alyssa pushed out a small, sad, almost derisive laugh. "I'm only just now figuring that one out."

"I need to stop fighting Krista about the move, don't I?"

"What?" Alyssa refocused. "How'd you get there?" She looked toward the hallway as if imagining Becca sleeping in the room beyond. "Don't discount dads, Jeremy. You moved for her, opened Andante to be near her."

"Andante will close."

Alyssa inched closer to him. Her knees, feet tucked under her, nestled across his lap. "What else happened today?"

"The police came for Brendon today. Arrested him right in the shop. Then arrested me."

Alyssa stiffened.

"I'm not getting charged with anything. They just had questions, but in my panic I gather I was less than compliant at first. Customers filmed it all. Ryan said we were on Instagram before I even got loaded into the squad car. Heck, I'm sure the longer videos are on YouTube . . . Anyway, Brendon's been selling drugs out the alley door, and he stole that five grand we've been searching for." He paused. "But all that was after I practically accused Ryan of being a thief. So he's gone now too."

"Oh . . ." Alyssa gasped. "That's my fault. I'm so sorry."

"How is that your fault?" He rested his mug on her knee.

"Your credit card reader. That's it . . . You never 'lost' the money." Alyssa ticked her fingers into the air. "You had three accounts, set up either before or when you first bought the shop, but a fourth came online earlier this month and only received payments during your really high-traffic times. I didn't see it until yesterday . . . I didn't put it together fast enough. We spent all that time searching for an answer that was right there. Brendon set up the final account."

Jeremy sighed. "It still wasn't your fault. You mentioned four, and I didn't even know that was one too many. And even if you'd told me, I had my own running story line and could've landed right where I did. Ryan was furious—no, he felt betrayed, and he quit. I can't blame him."

"Don't give up, though. Please. It may all turn out in the end. Andante is a special place. You need it. Heck, Winsome needs it."

"I love that you said that." He smiled softly and toyed with her fingers now resting on his knee. Somehow batting that line between them had become, in so short a time, something incredibly special to him. "I lied to Krista tonight. I told her everything was smoothing out and I could take some time off to be with Becca over the next couple days."

"You can't?"

"No, that's just it, I can. I can because I'm not reopening the shop . . . It's over."

Chapter 27

Seth pushed at Andante's front door. It was locked. He cupped his hands against the window to peer in and saw Jeremy striding toward him.

The young man unlocked the door, opened it wide, and talked over his shoulder as he walked back to the counter and coffee machines. "Sorry. I'm not opening today."

"What? Why not?" Seth followed him in.

"You didn't hear about yesterday?"

"Well, yes. But I also heard you were released."

Jeremy perched against the counter. "This really does operate like a small town."

Seth nodded. He understood Jeremy's perspective. He'd only grasped how tight, insular, even invasive Winsome could feel when he was the subject of gossip himself. But there was another part to that, even then, a caring part that had carried him through. "Sometimes it does feel too small, but not today."

Jeremy lifted his head.

"I'm here for you if you need me."

"Thank you."

"And I'm going to ask a favor because I need you. Can I grab a box of coffee?" Seth looked around the quiet, dark shop. "Or is nothing up and running?"

"No. I can brew you one no problem. The Thursday group? No . . . Wait, I missed that. I completely forgot."

Seth shook his head. "A bunch of us weren't there either . . . Margery Williams passed away last night. I'm headed over to be with George and the kids."

Jeremy paused. "I heard she wasn't doing well, but not that." He moved quickly behind the counter. "Tell me what else I can do. Can I give you some muffins?" His hands flapped to his sides. "Good coffee, bad muffins, it's all I've got."

Seth smiled. "It's enough. Sure, give me a dozen muffins and a couple boxes of coffee." He reached for his wallet.

Jeremy opened his mouth to protest, but Seth shook his head and thrust his card forward. "Do something for George later. This is my gesture, with your help."

"Okay."

Minutes later Seth grabbed the paper bag with the coffee boxes in one hand and the bag with muffins in the other and headed to the bookstore. It wasn't open yet, but he knew Madeline, Claire, and Janet were all inside. They'd heard the news too early this morning and, as usual, gravitated together.

He tapped on the front door's glass window. Claire let him in. "Janet and Madeline are in the back."

He stepped through the office and into Janet's "studio." The little room always made him smile. "Hey, you two."

Madeline was perched on one of Janet's stools. Janet stood cleaning brushes, her eyes red with tears.

"Chris just left," Madeline said.

"Ah . . . Was he at the Williamses' last night?"

Janet snuffled with her nod. "He said she wasn't in any pain and that they were all there. All six of her kids . . . and . . ." She wiped her nose. "It was beautiful."

"That's a good thing."

"I know." She waved her hand as if trying to clear away sadness. "But she was a wonderful woman." Janet's tone suggested that wonderful women should defy the laws of nature and never die.

"She was." Seth couldn't stop a little laugh. His soon-to-be-wife-again really was dramatic. "I'm headed over there now. Do you want to come?"

Janet nodded. "Madeline?"

The younger woman shook her head. "I didn't know them well. The last thing anyone wants to do on a day like today is make small talk with an acquaintance."

Janet and Seth walked back out the front door and headed to his car, parked in front of Olive and Eve Designs.

Eve threw open the door and called out just as Janet opened Seth's passenger door. "Janet? Do you have a sec?"

Janet looked to Seth first. He gave her a tiny nod. There was time. "Sure. What's up?"

Eve pointed to the display windows. "Olive's on vacation for another two weeks. We decided to each take a full month this summer, but . . . It's horrible."

Janet faced the window and absorbed what Eve had put on display. Her mouth dropped open. The shop's three mannequins were dressed in green, toes to nose, with an odd accessory added to each. A black leather coat for one. A chunky brown necklace on another. And the most improbable white cashmere scarf gracing the third.

"I read that green was this summer's hot color."

"Maybe not on everything." Janet tilted her head.

When she snagged her lower lip between her teeth, Eve knew she was working not to laugh. "I said it was horrible. Can you help?"

Janet glanced back to Seth, who stood next to his car, eyes fixed with a mix of wonder and horror on the same sight. Eve thought he looked like he was trying not to laugh too. She slumped against the shop's doorframe. "I've been working on this since five this morning. Olive changes the windows every two weeks. She'll be furious if she finds out I let her last display sit almost a month."

Seth nodded. "It might have been the wiser choice."

Janet flapped a hand at him. "Stop it. Wait here . . . This will take five minutes."

She walked into the store and stopped. Eve followed her gaze as it skimmed across every shelf, rack, display, and detail. Without another word Janet darted around, grabbing a pair of white slim-fitting jeans, a fistful of gold necklaces, a multicolored silk blouse, blue capris, and a thin white belt.

She crossed back to the window. Eve stepped beside her.

Janet then dropped a pile at the base of each mannequin. "On this one, lose the pants, keep the blouse, and add these items . . . For this, keep the pants, but use this blouse and the necklaces." She stepped behind the final mannequin. "And this has to go completely. Use everything in this pile and nothing up there."

"Thank you." Eve pulled her into a hug. "And while you're here, can you give me Alyssa's cell number?"

Janet stepped back. "Alyssa? Why?"

"I hope to hire her."

"To work here?" Janet looked confused.

"No, to give us some ideas." Eve's confidence wavered. "Didn't I hear she was helping businesses? Lexi said she did some work for Mirabella that was invaluable. Andante too, I heard, not that it'll help him now. But Lexi called it a 'game changer.' We need one of those."

"What does she do?"

"I gather just what you did with the clothes, but with numbers. I can keep the books, but we need more than that. She makes the numbers make sense, tell a story, Lexi said, so you can run your business better. That's a silly analogy. I mean—"

"It's not. It's a perfectly good analogy." Janet stepped to the register and wrote Alyssa's number on the back of a sales card. "Call her. She'd probably love the business."

"Thanks." Eve beamed. "Have a great day."

Janet walked out the door and stopped in front of Seth. "Did you know our daughter is a 'game changer' and has been helping businesses like a one-woman consulting firm?"

Seth smiled. "Doesn't surprise me at all."

Chapter 28

A week can change everything . . .

Alyssa felt like a new person. After four days Janet let her off smoothies and soups, and she decided her new eating regime wouldn't be so bad after all—as long as it required chewing. Real food had never tasted so good. Neither had real care. It wasn't that her mom hovered for the week, it was that she was available without hovering. Something had changed, even Alyssa had to admit to that, though she couldn't articulate it. A fog, dark and heavy, had rested between them so long she didn't feel its pervasive weight until it lifted.

Not a single *Is that something you really want to do?* or an *Is that best?* or the real gem, *It's up to you*, with a raised brow and skeptical tone, was heard all week.

Part of it, she had to acknowledge, was that they hadn't talked about anything substantive or meaningful. They had laughed—and Alyssa had forgotten, or perhaps had never known, her mom's dry, sharp sense of humor and childlike enthusiasm.

"Drink this." Janet had slid a smoothie across the counter on day two.

Alyssa had lifted the glass to examine the brownish-green color within. "What's in it?"

Janet raised a challenging brow. Alyssa sipped and almost threw up. "That's disgusting. Are you trying to kill me?"

Janet howled. "I can't believe you drank it. I love that you did that! It's your favorite salad from Bistro North. The kale salmon with fennel . . . Here, pass it over."

Alyssa handed her the glass and washed her mouth out at the sink. "What are you doing?"

"Taking a sip."

"You can't do that. It's foul."

"You did. It's not funny if the joke's only on you."

With that Janet drank half the glass before gagging and bumping Alyssa away from the sink to wash out her own mouth.

The next afternoon Alyssa came home from Jasper's covered in grease. She had accidentally tipped an oil drainage pan onto herself. Janet was already in the laundry room vigorously scrubbing her own hands and arms.

"I shattered a glass bottle of ink all over myself." She snorted, taking in her daughter. "You'd better get in here. You look worse than I do."

The two of them stood side by side scrubbing themselves down with Goo Gone for a half hour. Both emerged pink, sore, and too hungry for soup that night.

"But tonight's your last night. Dr. Laghari said no solids for four days," Janet had groaned. "We can't give up now."

"One meal can't matter, Mom."

"But what if it does?" Janet pitched her voice low and earnest. The weight of the world, or at least Alyssa's gastrointestinal integrity, hung in the balance with this one last liquid dinner.

In the end they sat at the island together eating an entire recipe of sweet potato soup, from the pot.

And those were only two memories Alyssa now held close. There were two other hand scrubbings at the sink that turned into bubble fights as Janet washed off paint and Alyssa scrubbed at grease from Jasper's Garage; there was the afternoon they decided to eat only what Janet had in the garden and ended up with a ragu of tomatoes, zucchini, kale, yellow squash, and parsley—and nothing more. Then there were the two nights of movies, curled up in blankets, drinking tea, laughing at *Book Club* or crying with *Mrs. Miniver.*

But neither addressed the elephant in the room—the tensions, the misunderstandings, the chafing attitudes, or Janet and Seth's upcoming wedding. Or maybe, Alyssa thought, she had it wrong and the elephant was gone after all.

Part of her wanted to believe that was true, and to finally let it go, because this was the first time Alyssa felt side by side with her mom rather than two steps behind, unable to keep up. She no longer felt small, weak, lost, or even alone.

Janet found her at the bottom of the stairs staring up at her favorite painting. "You have always loved that."

"You never did. Why'd you and dad buy it?"

"Buy it? It was my honors project in college."

"You painted that?" Alyssa turned to her mom.

"You can have it if you'd like."

"Someday, yes, but . . . Come on, Mom . . . How could you never tell me that? Does Chase know?"

Janet tilted her head at Alyssa's question. "I doubt it. Why would I bring it up?"

"But . . . how did you just stop? You had real talent. You trained. It just feels wrong." She looked back to the painting. "Like a lie."

Janet laughed, a short rueful sound full of self-awareness, even self-reproach. "Of course it's not normal. Nothing about it was or is. I can't even tell you it was a different time, though in some ways it was; I can't tell you anything to explain it other than it was never an option for me." She faced Alyssa. "I had to fight for every step with my parents, and that got too hard. I got tired of fighting . . . Then I started fighting somewhere else." She reached up and tucked a strand of hair behind her daughter's ear.

Alyssa felt herself tip into the touch. "Dad?"

Janet shifted her gaze back to the painting. "Not your dad, at first. He didn't know how much painting meant to me. And to some degree that was what hurt the most after a while. But if I never shared with him how much it mattered, how was he to know?" She shrugged. "Of course I only came to that realization after we divorced."

"I had you on a pedestal, you know," Alyssa whispered.

Her mom nodded and ran her fingers through Alyssa's hair again, pulling a strand over her shoulder. "Toppling idols can be a messy business. If I'd been more honest with you, all of you, we might not have gotten to where we did."

Confirmation bias.

The term drifted to Alyssa's mind, and blaming her mom suddenly wasn't so easy, so cut-and-dried. She had seen what she wanted to see, maybe needed to see, and when it didn't suit her purpose she'd rejected it all and stormed away. Only to do the same thing again—only this time it landed her in the midst of a federal investigation.

Alyssa felt her stomach clench and brought herself back to the present. Standing at the bottom of the steps, staring at her favorite painting, she said, "You need an art show."

"What?"

"Jeremy has all that wall space at Andante. He needs to reach out to the community more, and you need to show your work. It's a win-win and I'm arranging it."

"No. You can't. I can't."

"Of course I can. You can too. We can plan it for the end of the summer. There's plenty of time and you've got plenty of pieces. You already have those tiny portraits by his front window."

"Because meddling Madeline gave them to him." Her mom's voice danced with laughter and something more, intrigue. "Do you really think we could?"

"Absolutely. Maybe that last weekend before Labor Day."

"Because you'll be gone after that."

Alyssa started in confusion. "I . . . I was thinking because we could hold it on a Friday night when the shops stay open late, and that stops Labor Day weekend, but you're right, that too."

"You don't have enough time. Let's spend your weeks getting you better so your next chapter in life is outstanding."

"Don't do that." Alyssa stepped back.

"What?"

"You always do that. You make my ideas sound like they're wrong or not enough or that something, anything, is more important. That A is better than B, because you thought it up, and they both completely preclude C. What if A and B and C all together are exactly what's right? What if helping you, doing this together, is what I need to get better?"

"You've lost me."

"Because you're not listening." Alyssa heard her own whine, and it frustrated her further. She couldn't explain what she had always felt. She took a breath to try again. "What if working for Jeremy and Lexi and Eve, and setting up an art show for you, finally connecting with you, is what I need in order to heal?"

"I just don't want— Eve Parker called you?"

"That's not the point."

"I'm sorry. You hadn't mentioned her."

"Again, stop saying you're sorry," Alyssa huffed.

Her mom stood silent.

Alyssa felt all her energy drain from her. What started only minutes before as an exhilarating idea exhausted her. "Yes, Eve called, and I've already started going through her data. They've got a lot of waste in that store and I think I can help. More than that, I'm still standing."

"I didn't mean it like that. I just didn't want you to spend your limited time on me."

Alyssa shook her head and walked up the stairs. "But somehow even though it's my time, it never feels like my choice."

AN HOUR LATER, DRESSED in her Jasper's Garage uniform shirt, Alyssa hit the stairs again. She looked around as she crossed from the hall into the kitchen, but couldn't find Janet. The house felt quiet and empty. She called a quick good-bye into the silence and headed out the door.

Within ten minutes Alyssa parked her bike behind Jasper's Garage and headed toward the small store through the service bay entrance. She hauled a box from the storage room on her way past and opened it with a box cutter.

"Jasper, how do you determine what to order for the shop?"

Jasper materialized from around the corner. "I order what sells. Same stuff always sells in here."

Alyssa shook her head and held up three bags of pork rinds. "No one eats these anymore, and this is the second box I've opened."

"I haven't redone the ordering in a while. You can shove the Fritos over to make more room." Jasper tucked his rag into his shirt pocket.

"But the Fritos sell. Tell you what, rather than me changing any more oil—"

Jasper chuckled.

"I'll pump gas, fill tires, and do all the easy normal stuff out that door." She pointed to the station's two islands. "But when no one is out there and you're back there"—she pointed to the service bay—"why don't I standardize all your ordering and inventory? Put it on a single system that will cue you as to what sells and what needs to be reordered."

"You can do that?"

She dropped the pork rinds back into the box. "It's about the only thing I can do." She grabbed her laptop out of her bag and opened it on the counter. A navy blue Porsche rolled up to the full-service pump. "As soon as I finish with this customer I'm going to wow you, Jasper."

He chuckled again, a full belly laugh this time, as she pushed through the door and headed to the Porsche.

Chapter 29

The next afternoon, Lexi was laughing at Alyssa too, except her laugh was high and clear and bright. "What are you on?"

"I have no idea." Alyssa flopped back in the booth. "Collagen and slow-stewed vegetables, I think, but I feel good, Lex, really good. I have all this energy."

"But?"

Alyssa stared at her best friend. "No but."

Lexi shook her head. "Not buying it. You have a touch of frantic about you too. Something's up."

Alyssa shrugged and snapped her laptop shut.

They had spent the last two hours going through Lexi's data as Alyssa gave her the final report and recommendations. What started with an assessment of every penny spent and every penny earned ended with the recommendation that, while the PR company had focused on downtown Chicago media, 80 percent of Mirabella's reservations and clientele came from the north and northwest suburbs. There was a lot more to do locally for a lot less money—including offer more chicken dishes and fewer organ meats.

"Tell you what. You can tell me everything while we walk to

the lake." Lexi stretched her back. "I can't thank you enough for all this, but I also can't think anymore. I need sunshine, and I've got a couple hours until I'm needed back here."

Alyssa slid from the booth and followed her friend out the restaurant's side door.

Ten minutes later, at a power-walk pace, they hit the beach. Every kid in town was there—laughing, playing, swimming, and chasing the waves. Lake Michigan looked like an ocean with its swells and deep blue.

Lexi pulled off her sandals, Alyssa her flip-flops, and they crossed the sand, heading for their favorite outcropping of rocks.

"You gonna talk now?"

Alyssa settled on her old favorite flat stone while Lex took the one next to her. Both looked out at the waves.

"I don't think I can stay two more months, Lex. Mom and I? We're good, then we're not, then— I don't get her and everything I do is wrong. I offered to help her hold an art show yesterday and she basically said it would make me sick."

"She cares about you."

"That's not care. She just didn't like the idea."

"I doubt that. But you're her first priority. Can't you understand that? She's doing her best, but she sees things differently than you." Lexi nudged Alyssa. "If you and I saw things the same way, I wouldn't have just paid you three thousand dollars. So there. Proof."

"That's not the same thing at all."

"Sure it is . . . Remember our fourth-grade art class?"

"How'd you get there? How do you even remember that class?"

"I remember that you hated it. You'd get so mad you'd crumple and pitch every sketch and painting. You were a pain the entire year, and that's when I figured out you don't like the unknown."

"That had nothing to do with the unknown. I hated art class

because *she* made it intolerable. She came to our end-of-year show and criticized every single piece."

Lexi pulled back. "That's not how it went down. You did that. *You* criticized every single piece. You hated that what you envisioned didn't translate to the page. It was a simple house, and you thought you had to have an architecture degree to draw it."

"No . . . I . . ." Alyssa cast back, but a few spotty memories confirmed rather than denied Lexi's interpretation.

"You two look alike, but you're different. Can't you imagine your mom might think differently than you? Show love differently than you? I'm not saying things didn't go wrong . . . I'm talking now. She's super artistic and comfortable in that creative space. You need answers. You need that security. She's a mom. She needs you to be well and whole. You don't have kids. You can't understand that. And all that doesn't mean she's wrong any more than it makes you right."

"But—"

"Give it a rest, Lys. People are far more complex than the boxes we put them in." Lexi chuckled. It was soft and low, and that made it more powerful than painful.

And so true, it didn't require comment. Maybe she, rather than her mom, was responsible for many of the frayed threads that stretched between them. Alyssa nudged Lexi back. "When'd you get so wise?"

"Are you kidding? That's a quality bachelor's degree in psychology working for you."

Alyssa laughed. "Glad I can put it to good use . . . My parents are remarrying, by the way."

"Are they?" Lexi dragged the question long and made it taste like delicious gossip. "I thought that might happen."

"You did?"

"Talk around town was they were dating again. And I never

believed they'd stopped loving each other when they divorced. Remember . . . I was around. A lot went sideways, but your parents were the real deal. That kinda love doesn't die."

Alyssa looped her arms around her friend. "I owe you a thank-you, by the way, and an apology."

"For insulting you?"

"No. Three years ago I acted badly, another instance, I know, and you stood by me. But in the midst of all that, I forgot what my mom meant to you. You reminded me at dinner the other night and I'm sorry." Lexi opened her mouth, but Alyssa cut her off in case she was about to protest. "No, she was. You just said a mom needs her kids to be well and whole, and I know she felt that way about you, and I took that away." Alyssa straightened and looked past Lexi to the water. "And you're right, I've been blaming her for a lot that's been wrong about me."

"Don't stop there."

Alyssa shrugged. "I don't know what else to say . . . Back then, I wasn't doing anything I liked or wanted or needed; and *I wasn't* anything I liked, wanted, or needed either. I blamed her, and it gave me a way out. Now I'm right back there—this time with an autoimmune disease I didn't find with my algorithms—don't you love that?—and a huge scandal at my feet. Blaming her doesn't feel so easy, or right, anymore." Alyssa twisted to face her friend. "So I'm sorry. I'm sorry I did that to you."

Lexi leaned over and hugged her. "You are a mess."

"Thank you." Alyssa hugged back. "I was jealous of you too," she whispered into Lexi's shoulder.

"What?" Her friend pulled away.

"In high school you two were closer than I could ever get. She was so easy on you and, I thought, way too tough on me."

"Because I *was* easy . . . Sure, she wanted me to be okay, but she had no expectations for me like she did for you. She had no responsibility for my successes, no blame for my failures, nothing truly invested in my future. You had to see that."

"When you put it that way." Alyssa scrunched her nose. "Don't act all wise. You didn't see all that fifteen years ago."

Lexi burst out laughing. "I didn't see it. I couldn't have articulated it. But I felt it. It just simply was."

"Stop by and see her sometime, will you?" Alyssa's comment stopped Lexi's laughter. "She misses you, Lex. She asks about you."

"I'd like that." Lexi kept an arm around her friend. "When's the wedding?"

Alyssa raised a questioning brow. "Tuesday, July fourteenth. They want it on their anniversary. Just a small ceremony and a lunch. No big deal. Why?"

Lexi grinned. "Because I know the perfect place to host it and I want to clear the calendar."

Alyssa laughed. "See? You're all excited, and I got miffed when I first heard about it. You are definitely the better daughter."

Lexi looped her arms around Alyssa again. "Oh, don't worry, you're helping me."

"I'd like that."

They sat in silence for a little while longer until Lexi checked her watch. "Back to Mirabella for me."

Alyssa arrived home a couple hours later after a few errands and a stop at Andante. Jeremy wasn't there. The shop sat dark and closed, again.

When she texted him about having a new and great idea, he answered.

Can't wait to hear it. I'm on the case with Becca and have so much to tell you. My place tonight?

It's a date.

Alyssa smiled as she pushed open the back door.

Janet stood in the kitchen unpacking food from two large paper bags.

"What's all this?"

"Lexi sent it over from Mirabella." Her mom lifted the containers one by one. "We've got a beet and grilled clementine salad; beef tenderloin with a balsamic glaze; grilled romaine Caesar salad, no parmesan in the dressing, it says right here, and no croutons; grilled broccolini with shallots and bacon, olive oil, no butter."

"She brought this over?"

"She sent a delivery guy. Here's the note." Janet stretched a thick linen card to her. A deep red *M* was inked in the center.

To Janet and Alyssa—Enjoy a night off. No gluten, no grains, no dairy, no guilt. All my love to you both, Lexi.

"She's such a good egg." Janet smiled.

"She misses you too." Alyssa popped a beet into her mouth.

Chapter 30

That morning Jeremy woke Becca at six o'clock. He couldn't wait any longer. They'd made all the muffins the day before, so he didn't need to get to work early, but he did want to open the shop. Alyssa was right the week before when she had said it wasn't over. It had taken him a few days to recognize it, but it wasn't. Not yet. And there was no honor in scuttling the ship. He at least wanted to let his dream sink with dignity, if he couldn't save it.

And the Fourth of July was in two days—he wanted Andante open.

"Sorry, Ladybug. We have to get going." Jeremy perched on the edge of his daughter's bed with a single hand on her hair.

Becca didn't complain. She simply blinked, yawned, nodded, and within a few minutes emerged from her room dressed in shorts, a striped T-shirt, and flip-flops.

"Come here, Bug." He tapped on a kitchen stool. Once she'd wiggled her way up, he ran a brush through her long hair. He felt the wonder of the simple yet profound motion. It was such a personal thing, brushing someone's hair, and he got to do that for his daughter—at least for now. When she moved, this connection, like so many others, would be lost.

And it was beautiful. He noted how her brown hair shone in

the light after he brushed through it. Reflected it even. It was darker than his or, in fact, anyone in his family. He smiled because he knew that now, for certain.

The memories hadn't stopped. Since that moment at the park last week, they flashed to him in waking moments and filled his dreams while sleeping. His mom was dark blonde almost to light brown, blue-eyed, and had one dimple when she smiled. And she had a laugh that had dissolved into a snort more often than not. His dad's hair was a light auburn with gray at the temples. Much like Jeremy's own. They watched football together, and his dad cycled. He wore that "kit," the brightly colored spandex you see on TV when you watch the Tour de France. And his mom ran in the mornings and on weekends. She used to meet his dad and him at his soccer games on Saturdays, glowing from her long run. And his dad always brought her a cream cheese bagel and a coffee to enjoy while she watched him play, and his dad coached . . .

"Mommy said we're going to look for a new house next week."

"In North Carolina?" The brush stilled in his hand.

His daughter twisted to face him. "I don't want to go . . . I'll work harder, I promise."

"Work harder?" He lowered himself to her eye level. "This has nothing to do with you. Mommy was offered a new job."

"She said I need a new school."

"Hey . . . If you move, yes, you'll get a new school, but that's not what this is about." He pulled her close.

"Yes it is, but I want to stay here. I like my school. Mrs. Guttierez says I'm the best in math class, and I was voted class captain for next year. And what about your shop? I wipe the tables and put the magazines straight. We made the muffins and now Ryan's gone. You need me."

"I always need you." He held her at arm's length to look her in the eyes. "You do a great job and I love that you help me out so much, but you can't worry about this, okay? We'll figure it out."

She nodded, and the tight expression in her face loosened. The sight almost broke his heart. She trusted him to "figure this out." He'd been in town only four months, known his daughter for four months, and she trusted him. As the wonder of the feeling swelled, it crinkled on the edges. Another, darker fear crowded over it. What if I can't do it? What if I let her down?

With that, he felt it. Clarity and a kick start to take his plans even further that day . . .

"Change in plans." Jeremy pulled Becca's hair into a ponytail, lifted her off the stool, and set her before him. "We're going to open the shop, sell as much coffee as we can just like we planned, but then we're going to close early and run some super-special errands. You in?"

"I'm in."

Upon hitting the store, Jeremy sent a quick email. Then he perched on his desk and left Ryan another voice mail—his sixteenth in nine days.

"I can't make this right, I know that. But I hope you'll let me apologize in person again and maybe someday forgive me . . . I'm sorry, Ryan. What I did . . . What I have done for a long time . . ." Jeremy took a deep breath. "I know I keep repeating myself, but please call me back, come to the shop, come back to work, anything . . . But I'm not pushing. Well, I am. Do it in your own time, when you're ready . . . I guess I just want to say I'm here. And I'm sorry, man. And if you want me to stop calling, I will, once you call and tell me that too. Okay, that's it. I'll call later."

He then gave Becca the signal to unlock the doors. While Becca wandered through the tables, clearing, wiping, or simply charming his customers, Jeremy worked the counter, all the while silently begging the old espresso machines to behave. No sunk shots today, he reminded them with each customer.

After all, the machines weren't going anywhere. Not only did he not have the money to repurchase the La Marzocco, he didn't want to. Georgia, it seemed, had understood what he had failed to grasp. That while the coffee was important, giving a people a home away from home, a warm place to gather, was more important. And right now, he felt those old machines were a vital part of getting it right. His daughter was too. All morning he'd watched as she worked with enthusiasm and chatted with everyone who walked in the door. His dream wasn't dead and he wasn't alone—and as long as those two things stayed true, he thought, he could fight.

When the lull finally hit at one o'clock, he called Becca over. "Go flip the sign."

She raced to the door and turned the sign to read *Closed. We'll see you tomorrow.* Then she sprinted back to her dad.

"Let's clear off your lunch, wipe down the tables, and get out of here. And grab your school reading list from your backpack too." At her quizzical expression, he pointed to the bag behind the counter. "Hurry up. Our first stop is the bookshop."

Hand in hand, they pushed open the door to the Printed Letter Bookshop.

Madeline, who was shelving books in Gardening, bent and addressed Becca first. "Good afternoon. How may I help you?"

Becca held up her list but said nothing.

Jeremy knew she was too embarrassed to speak. "Becca here has a summer reading list, and we hoped you could help us find a few."

"Of course I can. Would you like to come with me, Becca?"

Becca looked up at her dad.

"You go ahead. I bet Madeline knows all the books on your

list." He returned his focus to Madeline. "While you help her, do you mind if I talk to Claire a minute?"

"Not at all." Madeline pointed to the back. "She and Janet are in the office."

He walked back and knocked on the doorjamb. Janet and Claire sat crouched over a single computer.

"Good afternoon, ladies."

"Jeremy, what brings you here?" Janet rolled her chair away from Claire's.

"A book club." He looked between them. "I want to start a book club with your store. I was thinking . . ." He smiled at Janet. "Actually, your daughter did the thinking and advised me to start one, with the idea that if the bookshop was involved it could gain more traction and include more of the community."

He perched on the room's other desk. "We can pick the books together and run it once a month at Andante. I was thinking we could have neat posters announcing it, mention it to customers, maybe send emails if I can grow the coffee shop's email list . . . All that stuff and, on book club night, I'd offer free coffee, teas, and baked goods."

Janet looked to Claire, who nodded. "It's a smart idea. Count us in."

"What's your first book?" Claire asked.

"Ordinarily I'll go with whatever you all recommend. But first, for reasons of my own, I'd like to start with *Of Mice and Men*." He rushed on before either woman could protest. "I know the story has issues, but there are themes of understanding and the human experience in it that . . ." He dropped his hands to his sides. "Don't you think it could make for a good discussion?"

Janet and Claire shared a look. Claire gave her another nod and Janet turned to Jeremy. "Isolation, loneliness, and community."

"Who? Me?" He felt his collarbone heat.

The women laughed.

"The book. You can decide about you," Janet quipped.

"It's not far off," Jeremy conceded. "You should probably charge for that bit of therapy."

"Reading is therapy."

"It is . . . So you're game?"

Janet snagged a pen. "Give me the date and time, and I'll mock up a poster for you. And of course we'll give it the usual book club 15 percent discount."

"Excellent. I appreciate this. And what about July thirtieth, four weeks from now?"

"That's fast," Claire cautioned.

"If you don't think it'll be detrimental to the club, I'd like to move fast. It's time for me to get going."

"Then we'll make it work." Janet rolled her chair to her desk and started typing.

Jeremy smiled. Janet and Alyssa were alike, he thought. They both seemed to believe in him. "Thank you."

Movement caught Jeremy's eye and he turned away. Madeline and Becca had just dropped a stack of books on the customer service counter. "And speaking of that, I'd better go. My daughter's buying out your store."

Janet called after him, "I'll bring some posters by tomorrow."

"What did you two find?" Jeremy met his daughter at the store's bright green counter and lifted the first book off the stack.

Becca looked to Madeline.

Madeline shook her head. "You can do it . . . You tell your dad."

By the soft way she encouraged his daughter, Jeremy got the impression Madeline had picked up on Becca's consternation. And, while thankful, he lifted a hand to sift through the titles himself so as not to embarrass her.

But Becca picked up the book first. One by one, she sounded her way through each title. "*If You Give a Mouse a Cookie. Biscuit Goes Camping. Don't Let the Pigeon Drive the Bus. Frog and Toad: The Complete Collection.*"

Madeline smiled. "And I've put others aside for when you finish those, right?"

"Right." Becca grinned, then turned to her dad. "Frog and Toad wasn't on the list, but Madeline says it's her favorite."

"I'm a little like Toad." Madeline tapped the book. "Remember me when you get to the story about cookies and willpower, okay?"

"Okay." Becca nodded with more enthusiasm about reading than Jeremy had seen since discussions over school and moving, and everything else, began.

Books in hand, Jeremy and Becca hit the sidewalk again. "On to our next stop, Ladybug."

He led her across the square to the Sweet Shoppe and pushed open the door. The smell of sugar enveloped them, and Jeremy knew they would not leave without some yummy delight. Becca raced forward and reached the display case before the door's bell finished chiming.

"I'm coming" preceded a woman emerging from the back. She had shoulder-length dark hair and was probably only a few years older than he was. He had never met Jill Pennet before, but knew she owned the shop.

"I'm Jeremy Miller." He wagged a finger toward the door and across the square. "I bought the Daily Brew."

"Yes. I'm sorry I never got over to welcome you. I'm Jill." She reached across the counter.

Her hand felt small and cool within his own.

"It's my fault. I didn't reach out to anyone. I was so fixated on the shop." He looked down at her baked goods, then back to her. "I have a business proposition for you. Without duplicating what you sell here, I wondered if you'd be interested in creating some new things for Andante."

"Me provide your baked goods?"

"I'm using a mix."

"So I've heard." She smiled.

"I don't want to do that anymore. I need to do better and I thought since we should complement rather than compete, we could work together. If you're game for something new and different, I could sell your pastries, but the kind of stuff that won't cannibalize your sales here . . . And I hoped you'd even be willing to sell to me at a discount, or even wholesale."

"Wholesale?"

"It's a hard ask, but if we could share the profits, rather than me pay up front, it would really help me out. I'm struggling over there." She stared at him for so long he thought he was sunk. "It's okay if you're not interes—"

"I have a pistachio, tarragon, and thyme scone that will knock your socks off."

"Are you serious?"

"Yes." She grinned. "It's incredible."

"No. I mean about selling to me?"

"That too."

"Okay. I have one more favor to ask . . ."

Minutes later, after striking a deal he suspected was too good to be true, he and Becca hit the sidewalk again. Jeremy pulled out his phone to check his email. "Perfect timing."

"What, Daddy?"

He glanced at his daughter. Her face was covered in bright

yellow sunshine icing from a sugar cookie the size of her head. "I just got an email. Let's get the car from behind Andante and head to our final stop. We're going to school."

Becca threw him a hard look.

"Don't get grumpy . . . I'm not leaving you there. The home economics teacher emailed me that she's still clearing out her room and she's got some pillows for me. Don't you think some bright pillows will make Andante a happy place?"

Before Becca could answer, Jeremy's phone pinged and he swiped the screen to read a text.

I've got a great idea for you. Call me tonight.

"What, Daddy?" Becca repeated and pulled at his shirt hem.

"Just a text from a friend, Bug. Do you remember Alyssa? She took you to the park." He quickly texted her back that he couldn't wait, for the idea and to see her.

It's a date.

Her quick reply dialed his smile up a notch.

An hour later Jeremy parked his car again by Andante's alley door. He popped his trunk as Becca leapt from the back seat, and the two of them hauled out three large black trash bags. He looked toward the coffee shop's back door—and froze.

Becca did not. She launched herself forward. "Ryan!"

"Becca Boo!" Ryan swept the little girl high and held her aloft. His eyes remained fixed on Jeremy. "Can we talk?"

Chapter 31

The church was packed.

Margery Willliams, as far as Seth knew, had never been a demonstrative, loud, or particularly forceful woman. From all he'd heard she had been a sweet, behind-the-scenes soft light who brought a quiet joy every place she went.

When he had first met the Williamses, he suspected George's louder gregarious personality overshadowed his wife. But the years had taught him many things, including the fact that looks can be deceiving.

He reached for Janet's hand. She held tight and scanned the sanctuary again. Seth knew the last time she'd been inside this church was eight months before, for Maddie Carter's funeral, and it had left her bereft. He suspected her thoughts were cast that direction as well and hoped she'd be okay.

As usual, he was wrong.

"He's not coming. He doesn't get it, Seth."

"Who doesn't get what?" Seth followed her gaze, catching on that she was speaking of Jeremy.

He'd caught the younger man out running errands with his daughter the afternoon before. "I'm not planning on going to the funeral," he had said. "I'll be in the way. George doesn't know me. I'll express my condolences next time he comes into the shop."

"That's not good enough." Seth's tone had surprised them both. He softened it. "I can't tell you how much the men in our group have shown up for me in the past few years, and they'll be there for you. Tomorrow is part of that."

Jeremy had protested again, so Seth left him with one final thought. "You're either in or you're out, no matter how many times you make the meetings. Janet and I will save you a seat."

Janet squeezed his hand. "He doesn't understand that he needs us, all of us."

"Give him a few more minutes."

"I'm not sure how long I can hold out." She tucked closer. "Saving seats at a funeral is not cool."

He almost laughed out loud but caught himself just in time. Nevertheless, a hiccup escaped and that earned a quick hard glare from his soon-to-be wife.

As the organ began the first notes of "Be Thou My Vision," Jeremy slid next to Janet. Seth could feel her melt with relief and turn her focus forward.

Pastor Zach then stood and welcomed everyone. After a few words, he motioned to Bella Williams to begin the first reading.

As she read from Isaiah, Zach looked out into the congregation. In many ways he felt unworthy to officiate Margery's service. He had only met her twice, both times while visiting her at home after pain and weariness had slowed her speech and thinking. He recognized her peace, however, and it had been a beautiful gift—to him.

That's what humbled him now. Everyone in this place had known and loved her. Margery had lived in their midst for sixty-some years, and at the end, when he should have offered comfort and guidance to her, she had given them to him. Again Zach felt as if he were taking from his new congregation and not giving, not shepherding them.

As soon as the second reading ended, this one from Colossians, he stood for the Gospel reading and the homily. The family had chosen the Good Samaritan parable from Luke's Gospel, and he had prepared well. He'd stayed up late into the night making sure he hit all the right notes and could deliver each line with clarity and conviction.

He stepped forward and found his mind blank. He looked down at his notes and felt his fist crumple them without even recognizing that he willed the action. He closed his eyes for a beat and a prayer and then simply spoke without knowing where the next seven minutes would take them.

He talked of neighbors, friends, enemies—for there weren't many greater enemies than the Jewish people and the Samaritans in the first century. He talked of love, care, and sacrifice. He talked of Margery and the stories people had shared in the past week, the lives she touched and the legacy she left behind. He talked of what he saw within her children and the care that permeated their home. He talked of blessings. He talked of peace.

As he felt himself winding down, he glanced over to Father Luke, who sat fully vested to the right of the altar. He wasn't alone. The revelation was so clear and hit him so hard Zach looked around, fully expecting the entire congregation to have felt it. He had never experienced a placement or a town in which rectors, priests, and deacons from other parishes came to his church, planned events across denominations, or became good friends, but he had found that community and that home here. And for the first time since he'd arrived at Winsome Presbyterian, Zach paid peace more than lip service; he felt it sink deep within him.

As he stepped away from the lectern, Devon, Margery and George's fourth child, shook his hand and took his place.

Devon fidgeted with his notes. He didn't like being a step above everyone. He didn't like being the center of attention. Keep your head down, your mouth shut, blend in, and get by. Early life had taught him those lessons, and his seventeen years removed from them had only loosened their grip marginally. But it had loosened. And that was why he forced himself to volunteer today and stand up to speak. His mom would've been proud. He looked down at his dad. He looked proud too.

Devon cleared his throat. "I asked to talk to you today. No, it was more than that. I practically had to wrestle Michael for the honor." He paused to let the quiet laughter subside. "I wanted to share some really good things about my mom, but Pastor Zach got me moving a different direction, and those words don't feel so important anymore." He swiped at his eyes. "My mom was the gentlest soul, and it's true, she loved well. She was what she was, and there was no pretense about her. But a loving, gentle soul is made by and through fire. A loving, gentle soul doesn't get that way because life keeps it all safe and sheltered, up in a box on a shelf. Life isn't so kind. It's a gift from God and it's also a hard-fought choice. Most of you may be shocked to hear this, but Bella, Terrell, and I aren't our parents' natural-born children." A small laugh escaped throughout the church. It had been a running joke with his mom for years and everyone knew it.

"But what will shock you more is that my mom had a childhood a lot like Bella's, Terrell's, and mine before she and Dad saved us. She was adopted at nine, and some pretty sad and bad stuff happened before that day. She recognized us when she and Dad chose us. She went in eyes wide open."

Devon took a deep breath and gripped the sides of the lectern. He noticed how his dark fingers blanched with the pressure. "She and Dad chose us and remade us. And not just us. I expect Michael,

Candice, and Lee would say it rocked their worlds too. And stretching further, my parents have ten grandkids here today and three great-grandchildren, and all those lives are different too because of that choice. That one choice, and a million others after it, was the fire that was Mom. You saw the peace. We relied on the strength.

"I guess I just want to say, as we remember all the gentle, kind, and fun things about my mom, including the fact that she couldn't navigate her way down our driveway, I also want to call to mind her conviction and her endurance, because in defense of the downtrodden, the fallen, the hurt, or the marginalized—in defense of us—our mom was a fighter. We came to trust that and grew safe within her care.

"And Dad . . ." Devon looked down at his father and held eye contact for a beat. "He's made of the same good stuff. I love you, Dad." He then whispered, looking up, "I love you, Mom."

There wasn't a dry eye as the service ended with "Amazing Grace" and "Seek Ye First." Father Luke followed the family out of the nave, then outside the church, marveling over the beauty of the day and of a life well lived. He noticed Janet and Seth walking hand in hand, along with Claire, heading to the parking lot. He briefly looked around, wondering where Chris was, knowing he was somewhere there too. He also wondered if his little brother had proposed to Madeline yet, but pushed the thought away. Chris would have called.

Luke watched as Janet climbed into a car with Claire and left. Seth stood alone. Luke caught up with him and reached out. "Good to see you, Seth."

"I'm glad you're here . . ." Seth pumped his hand as he looked around the parking lot. There was something hesitant in Seth's look and tone that signaled to Luke that his friend was struggling. "They had quite a marriage."

Luke nodded. "Over sixty years, I hear. Margery and I spent some time together working on the gardens next to the church, so I got to know her pretty well, including her temper. Devon was right about his mom. When someone tried to deal shady with us a couple years ago, she dressed him down good. Everything said in there was certainly true."

Seth looked across the emptying parking lot as if pondering something about Margery, about George, about himself. "Janet is scared she'll mess things up." He looked back to Luke. "But I am too. I was so absorbed in my career, in what I was doing, I took her for granted. I stopped seeing my wife. How do I know I've changed enough? That I can be who she needs now?"

Luke said a quick prayer for guidance and then gave Seth his straight-up answer. "You'll never have certainty and you will mess up. We're human. It's what we do." He paused to let his words sink in. Seth stared at him. "But there is also grace, and you and Janet know about grace. So I suggest you pray. Every day. And you keep coming to that men's group and have the courage to share and talk. You've got good friends who have been there for you, and that doesn't change when things go well, as I hope they will for you two. In fact, I believe we need our friends, their support and grounding influence, more when things do go well. It's in those times pride can set us up for a good toppling. A man doesn't take his wife for granted in the trenches, only in the towers."

"That seems a little simple." Seth raised a brow.

Father Luke laughed. It was loud and it felt good. "Almost everything is. We just complicate it."

Chapter 32

Ryan had been back for two days and Jeremy was still smiling.

Not only that, within a single morning, the pillows had created a buzz. Jeremy felt it. He heard it. And in the few hours yesterday before he'd gone to Margery Williams's service, he'd witnessed it. New and different customers came in, probably called by friends. They walked in Andante's front door, looked around in surprise, and then stepped to the counter and ordered. They ordered drinks. They ordered Jill's pastries. They came back for refills. They lingered at tables. Even the two old espresso machines must have sensed something different and good was happening, because they only soured one shot in seven rather than their usual one in three.

"Can we talk?"

That's all Ryan had said in the alley two afternoons ago.

Jeremy had swallowed hard and bent to his daughter. "Bug, why don't you drag these bags into the shop and spread the pillows all around while Ryan and I talk. Anywhere you want."

Becca, without question, strong-armed the bags one by one toward the shop front.

"The middle school's home economics teacher gave me all her orphaned pillows." Jeremy flipped the light switch and gestured to Becca's retreating form. "It's a start."

Ryan's face revealed nothing.

"I'm sorry, man." Jeremy dropped his keys on his desk and turned back to face Ryan. Some things needed to be said face-to-face.

"You said that, about thirty times."

"It bears repeating. I'll keep saying it, and showing you too, if you'll come back to work here . . . Not for the work, that too, but because we started this together." Jeremy twisted back to the desk. "Wait . . . Can I read you something?" He picked up a copy of *Of Mice and Men*. He'd bought his own copy the day after Ryan left. "I marked something in here. It reminded me . . . of us."

He flipped through the pages until he found the dog-eared one, and read aloud. "'Guys like us, that work on ranches, are the loneliest guys in the world. They got no fambly. They don't belong no place . . . With us it ain't like that. We got a future. We got somebody to talk to.' I didn't get it, back in Seattle or even here after we moved, but I do now. You're as much 'fambly' as Becca is to me."

"One book and you see me in a whole new light?"

"No. But it was never about you. You could say, one huge mistake, after a ton of little ones, *plus* one book, and I see *myself* in a new light." He tapped the book against his palm. "And it didn't teach me anything new. Steinbeck simply gets it, like you said. He wrote what I felt but couldn't articulate, couldn't recognize . . . I've been alone a long time, Ryan. You know that. You said yourself my daughter couldn't pick me out of a lineup before we moved here, and even since then, you're easier with her, with everyone, than I am."

Jeremy set the book down and leaned against the desk again, bringing them eye to eye. "You saw the people where I only saw the place. Because for me, that was safest." When Ryan said nothing, he continued. "And I pushed you, I pushed here, and . . . it's going under. But I'm trying, man. For Becca, for you, if you'll come back, and for me. I figure it's worth fighting for as long as I can, but I can't do it alone. Besides, alone it doesn't have a whole lot of meaning to me anymore."

Ryan looked around as if taking in the room anew. He shifted his focus back to Jeremy. "I'll help."

"You will?" Jeremy popped up. "I mean, that's great. Thanks. Thanks for believing in me."

"I didn't say that." Ryan pulled his head back. "But you had no reason to believe in me a couple years ago either. You gave me a chance."

"Fair enough." Jeremy stretched out his hand. "We start there."

Ryan reached out quickly and his handshake was firm. Jeremy figured it wasn't such a bad start after all.

Now, two days later, they threw open Andante's door on a bright, clear Saturday Fourth of July morning and worked to caffeinate what felt like all of Winsome as the town gathered for its annual parade. Jeremy positioned himself behind the counter, and when he wasn't pulling shots at a record pace, he sought out Ryan working among the tables. Jeremy felt a compulsion to make sure he was still there. Something about Ryan's presence, Ryan's belief in his ability to change, felt as needed and as fundamental as Becca's trust.

Sure enough, Ryan was there every time he looked up—and working tirelessly situating customers, clearing tables, and even engaging in conversation when he had a chance.

Jeremy smiled. Both men were trying something new.

Chapter 33

Alyssa had waited seven months for the call, and when it finally came the Monday after the Fourth of July, it gave her less than three hours' warning.

"Ten o'clock? This morning ten o'clock?"

"2111 Roosevelt Road, Chicago. Agent Barnes will meet you at the front desk."

She was so stunned she couldn't think what to say next.

The person on the other end took her silence as acquiescence and ended the call. "Thank you, Ms. Harrison."

Alyssa tapped her lawyer's number in Palo Alto.

"I can't say good morning, Alyssa. Do you know what time it is out here?"

"It's not good here anyway. I just got the call. For this morning. Ten o'clock. Did you hear me? As in two and a half hours from now."

"Relax. That's not unusual. We talked about this." His voice came in a monotone across the line.

"'Anytime' does not mean less than three hours' notice."

He yawned. "Dress conservatively. Skip the coffee, please, and tell the truth."

"That's all you have to say? Aren't you going to send someone? Don't we need to prepare?"

"Of course I'm sending someone. Tracy Meyers will meet you in the lobby. She'll be there by 9:50 a.m. and she's up to speed. As I said, we've been waiting for this. And you are prepared. Tell the truth. It's simple."

"I'm glad I pay you so much."

"At present you don't pay me anything. Good-bye, Alyssa."

Alyssa smiled. The man barely had a pulse, kept conversations to a minimum—which she knew had saved her money—and refused to charge her interest on her past due bills. He also knew his stuff. If he said not to worry, she could trust that—to the minimal degree it was possible.

She tapped Jeremy's number next.

"Good morning. I can't wait for you to get here. Are you on your way? I can start your latte. And I think I'm getting used to the pillows. It's easy because they work. You should hear—"

"I'm not coming." She cut him off. "I just got The Call. Ten o'clock. This morning."

"Wow . . . Do you want me to come with you? Do you want me to drive you? What about your car? Take mine."

She smiled. First Jeremy's enthusiasm, then his instant concern, lifted her heart and relieved her fears. Sharing it—all of life, it felt like—lightened its burden. "I'll be fine. Jasper said my car would be ready this morning, and my lawyer is sending someone to meet me. I'll be okay . . . I'll let you know what happens."

"Call right after, will you? I mean . . ." He stalled, and she smiled.

She felt the same. The first reaction was to jump into the trenches together. The next was to pull back in fear they'd jumped too far, too fast, alone. "I will."

Alyssa stayed on the line, unwilling to hang up. Yet the seconds were ticking away. "I gotta go."

"Yeah, you do . . . You go. I'll be here."

He still didn't click off, so she did.

Four horrid early 2000s outfits later, she relented and raided her mom's closet. There was still so much they hadn't talked about—including borrowing clothes. She cast back to her refusal that first day and all the anguish and anger behind it. Talking with Lexi had given her relationship with her mom a new perspective, but it hadn't banished the distrust, the anger, and the frustration completely. In many ways, she admitted, her approach to her mom and their dynamic felt like the old clothes in her closet. Out of date. Out of fashion. But necessary. If she didn't wear them, what would she wear? Who would she be?

She pulled down one of her mom's blue skirts, then sifted through her blouses. There were so many bright ones, colorful ones. So different from her own closet. Alyssa favored more muted colors, solids, slim cuts, and no frills. Her mom, on the other hand, was no stranger to color, silk, scoops, and flounces. Alyssa wondered how she'd never noticed before.

She finally found a tapered and starched white blouse with wide bell sleeves—her mom's most conservative option—to pair with the blue skirt.

Then she called Jasper.

"I know you mentioned it might be ready today, but . . . is it?"

"She's good to go. Finished her up Friday, but you had the weekend off and I didn't want to bug you. You probably wanted it?"

"Not at all, but I need it this morning. Do you mind if I take the day off? I have an interview."

"I'll go fill her up for you."

"Thank you, Jasper."

Alyssa smoothed down the skirt, added a little more blush to her pale cheeks, and ordered an Uber. No way she could ride her bike today.

Jasper whistled as she climbed out of the Prius. "You look mighty fancy."

"It's an important interview," Alyssa dodged, unable and unwilling to explain further. "Thanks for getting it done for me. And . . . I don't know if my work covered repairs. I can still work here."

Jasper swiped a hand between them as if erasing a whiteboard. "You covered it . . . Your car is ready to go, and I suspect you might be too. You've done good work here. Better than good."

Without thinking, Alyssa stepped forward and hugged him. He seemed surprised, but delighted too, and after a hint of hesitation held her tight. Then he wiggled from her grasp. "You're gonna get all dirty. Off you go."

During the eighty-minute drive Alyssa found herself unable to look ahead. The unknown brought a knot and a surge of pain she hadn't experienced in almost two weeks. So she looked behind . . .

Last night Jeremy had again stepped onto his landing as soon as she buzzed his apartment from the lobby door. It felt as if he couldn't wait another second to see her. She felt the same. After all, she was the one looking up to see if he was there.

"Wait till you hear about my day," he called down.

She laughed. Something had shifted within him. She could see it from three floors below. The cloud of doom and gloom that had dogged him since Ryan's departure was gone.

He reached for her hand the second she stepped to the landing and pulled her close for a kiss. But just as she sank into his touch, his enthusiasm to share got the better of him and, from Alyssa's perspective, he pulled away too soon. "Come in. I have a surprise for you."

He led her into the kitchen and handed her a small cookie.

She stared at the cookie. She stared at him.

"Try it." He grinned. "Gluten free—grain free actually—sugar free, dairy free, and egg free. I guess those can be tough on celiacs too."

"Taste free?"

"Nope." He shook his head. "Trust me."

She took a bite. The small cookie melted in her mouth. Lemon and rosemary. It was sweet yet savory . . . It was delicious. She swiped another off his counter. "I haven't had anything sweet in forever."

Jeremy laughed. "Jill at the Sweet Shoppe made them for me, for you. I think she used palm oil and stevia and . . . She told me all the ingredients, but I can't remember. She's been working on those since Thursday and brought them in today."

"Are you selling them in the store?"

"Yes, and I sold ten." Jeremy pulled her close again. "Jill is as excited as I am . . . Thank you."

And—driving south on I94—that's where she paused, rewound the memory, and played it slow again. That kiss, Alyssa remembered with a sigh, had lasted a good deal longer.

Yet even that kiss couldn't overpower the fear that gripped her as soon as she made her final right turn. A massive fully glassed monstrosity of a building sat squarely in front of her. She had no idea an FBI field office could be so large and intimidating. She had no idea anything could.

She pulled into the parking lot marked for visitors and felt her anxiety grow. Only one other car was in the visitors lot. It felt as if the entire weight of the FBI tipped toward only her.

And as she walked toward the front door, only her heels clicked on the walkway.

She pulled open the large glass door and paused. The lobby

before her stretched three stories high. In the center was a large green space full of plants and surrounded by benches. A woman lifted off one of the benches the same moment a man strode through an open elevator door. Both headed straight for her.

He wore a blue suit. She wore green.

He reached her first. "Ms. Harrison. Mitchell Barnes. Please wear this and come with me." He handed her a badge.

The woman stepped forward and stretched out her hand. "Tracy Meyers, Perkins and Coie." She turned to the man. "I will be joining Ms. Harrison as counsel this morning."

Within minutes she and Tracy were ushered through security and sat on one side of a large conference room table facing three men.

Agent Barnes gestured between everyone seated. "Ms. Harrison, Ms. Meyers, this is Agent Campbell, Agent Martinez, and Special Agent Pullman."

The one called "special" was older than the other two. Perhaps denoting seniority? He almost reminded Alyssa of her dad, except his face wasn't as light. *He's seen things,* she thought.

"What's the difference?" she blurted, looking at the three men in turn. "I mean, aren't you all 'special'?"

The questions hung between them, and she felt heat bloom red across her cheeks.

Special Agent Pullman laughed. "As much as we'd all like to believe we're special, Ms. Harrison, I have the power to make arrests. These two do not."

"Oh . . . I see." She gulped. She should have kept her mouth shut.

Pullman spoke again. "Ms. Harrison, we've called you here today to find some answers."

"Yes. I'm ready." She glanced to Tracy, who nodded.

"You misunderstand me. We'd like you to do the finding." He

shuffled through a small stack of papers. "We are now at the point of looking into XGC's data, and a lot of the questions you posed in your final months mirror our own." He looked up at her. "What do you say to working together?"

"I thought you'd be done with all that. I thought you'd know, that you could tell me. I hoped—"

Tracy cleared her throat.

Alyssa pressed her lips shut.

"We're still in the early days . . . The movies always get that part wrong." He smiled as he slid papers, one by one, across the table. "None of this happens quickly. Cases this complex take years, not weeks or even months." He tapped one of the pages now set before her. "From where I sit, you knew nothing about what was going down. You ask in this email all the questions we're asking, and I've interviewed enough of your colleagues to understand how the company's silo structure and secrecy kept you from easy answers. But these?" He tapped different points on several more pages. "These prove to me you never got those answers and, more significantly, you never stopped searching for them."

He stood and leaned over the table to tap two more sheets of paper to her right. "In this email, you got downright belligerent." He tapped the last page on the far right. "And this email from Mr. Connelly to HR initiates the process to fire you."

"I was going to be fired?"

"Consider it a good thing, Ms. Harrison." Pullman sat again and stretched several more sheets of paper toward her.

She accepted them, and as she read her questions and concerns, the stress and the fear came back to her. It felt like a living thing crawling up her spine to fill her throat. This volley of emails was sent a year before XGC's doors closed. Tag had taken the company's trials live and had started notifying customers of looming health concerns. It prompted the company's first *Forbes* cover and *60 Minutes* interview. It was also when, in Alyssa's mind and according to her math, the hit rates and successes became statistically impossible.

These first exchanges raised questions no one wanted to hear. Everyone was overjoyed. Champagne flowed for four Fridays after that. Security tightened. And Tag, who'd always roamed the halls to "see and be seen," virtually disappeared. No one had direct access to him any longer.

A comprehensive assessment of the data. That's what she'd asked for. She didn't say something had gone terribly wrong. She saved that line for email number two. The first simply posed questions to her boss and asked for the raw data to run comparisons. She took it up a notch in her second email. She presented her previous trial scores and "hit rates" and raised concerns about the live trial's validity—and she sent that to the entire executive team. In her third email, she saw the graphs she had created and inserted to make her case in another format. No one had listened. Her final email in that first go-round ended with pleas for answers and continued demands for access to the raw data.

Alyssa's stomach burned and her head filled. Reliving her final year at XGC felt almost as horrid as her first run-through. She had forgotten how terse, then threatening, the replies to her emails had been. She was told she didn't have adequate clearance, there were security concerns, this wasn't the time to look back rather than forward. She was told she was counterproductive, damaging, even a risk to the company's well-being, mission, and culture. Then the replies stopped. Tag himself emerged one afternoon, found her alone in the south stairwell, and as they descended from the sixth floor to the fourth, reminded her, "Squeaky wheels don't get the grease here. They get replaced."

She set down the papers and laid her palm on them. "I never got the raw data. I don't know how I can help you."

"Now you have it . . . all of it. We want to reverse engineer everything that happened. We can do it ourselves, but you wrote most of the algorithms. You can save us time and the taxpayers a few dollars. As I said, cases like this take years. Maybe you could cut a couple of those down for us?"

"Why me? Sonia Keutz was our director, and there's Paul Morris or, better still, Arjun Chowdhury. He's brilliant."

"Yet you were the only fly in the ointment."

Tracy leaned forward. "What are you offering?"

Pullman looked at her, visually dismissed her, and locked eyes on Alyssa. "Nothing. We are offering you nothing, Ms. Harrison, but we are giving you the chance to help clean up this mess." He leaned back and waited.

"But—" Tracy opened her mouth again.

Alyssa cut her off. "Yes. Anything."

Tracy twisted toward her. "That is not how this works."

Alyssa wasn't listening. She was watching Special Agent Pullman with the complete knowledge that he had her measure. He saw through her to the core fact that, almost more than wanting to walk away and put XGC behind her, she wanted the data. She wanted answers.

"You're curious." He studied her.

"Beyond curious."

Pullman smiled and shifted his focus to Alyssa's lawyer. "Counselor? I think we're done here."

Tracy huffed as Alyssa stood up. "When can I start?"

Within minutes Agent Barnes and Tracy Meyers were batting legal issues back and forth at the end of the table before he guided her out of the building.

Within an hour Alyssa had been issued a temporary security badge and was sitting on a hard plastic chair in a small room on the third floor facing three monitors connected to two linked computers.

"What else do you need?" Pullman stood beside her.

"Nothing. Let me see what's here . . . I assume you've got the entire team's notes, algorithms, everything from the servers?"

"Everything."

Alyssa rolled her shoulders and set her hand on the keyboard. "Then I'm set."

He nodded and stepped to the door.

She twisted to face him. "Thank you."

He turned and studied her again. "You're welcome . . . Restrooms are down the hall, and there's a small kitchen past them on the right. You'll find coffee, water, some dreadful snacks. I'll have sandwiches delivered at noon, so plan on a break then."

"Could . . . could I have a salad instead?"

He raised a brow.

"Sorry. I just found out I have celiac disease." Alyssa's voice lifted, almost as if she were asking a question. It was the first time she'd used the word, called it out in public. It felt like a new identity and not as bad as she thought it would be.

"Salad it is, Ms. Harrison." Pullman chuckled. "Get to work."

Chapter 34

There was one person Jeremy wanted to walk through Andante's front door Monday morning—and it wasn't Alyssa. He knew she was headed to the FBI, and he checked his phone every five minutes, anxious to hear from her. No . . . He wanted to see George Williams. He wanted to show him the pillows. He wanted to tell him he was sorry about his wife. He wanted to ask him questions about his kids, his life, and the town. And his eagerness to do all those things surprised him. He wanted to learn from the man and, at some level, he admitted, he wanted to please him. He wanted George to walk into Andante, smile, and say, "Well done."

The approval of a parent . . . To have a parent near . . . To lose a parent . . .

He called across the shop. "Ryan?"

"Yes?"

Jeremy noted the wariness that lingered in Ryan's voice. He suspected Ryan was still working through how he felt about being back in Andante, and he couldn't blame him. The saying "forgive and forget" sounded a little too easy sometimes.

"Can you hold down the fort for a few?"

"Sure thing."

Jeremy pulled an espresso shot, turned it into an almond milk latte, and headed three doors down. He walked into the bookshop and, with Claire and Janet busy with customers, crossed to the side storage room he knew served as Madeline's law office. He tapped on her doorjamb.

She looked up and lifted out of her seat. "Hey, Jeremy. How can I help you? Did the police call you?"

"No. Nothing." He waved her back to sitting and sat across from her. Of the three women in the shop, she had been the most daunting. Although they were the same age, Madeline came from an entirely different world. She was educated, polished, and she spoke quickly with a no-nonsense manner that had intimidated him. Yet when he'd called the shop from the Winsome Police Station two weeks before, she had come without question or hesitation.

He slid the latte her direction and cleared his throat. "I wanted to ask you about something else."

She raised the cup in thanks and nodded for him to continue.

He rushed over his words, not sure how to frame things or what details mattered, but by the end he thought he'd covered the salient points: Quick marriage. Quicker divorce. Becca's birth. His move to Winsome. Krista's plan to move to North Carolina.

At some point in the telling, Madeline had set down the latte and started typing.

"No, don't take notes. I don't want to take up your time. I just want to know if there's anything I can do."

Madeline's fingers stilled for a moment. "I think better this way." She typed on and started talking. "The move can't be imminent. Your ex-wife has to provide you with written notice before leaving the state. So until that happens, perhaps she's just dreaming."

"But Becca said they were heading there to look at houses this week. When I asked Krista, she denied it, but that doesn't mean they aren't going."

"Looking for a house isn't moving. Don't let that worry you. Not until she gives you official written notice. How are parenting rights allocated?"

Jeremy shook his head and leaned forward, resting his forearms on Madeline's desk. "I'm not sure that applies to us. I didn't have a lawyer when we divorced. I just signed the papers she sent to me and mailed them back to her. Becca wasn't even born yet."

"Is your divorce sited in Illinois or Washington?" At his shrug, Madeline typed up a storm before looking at him again. "Are you named on your daughter's birth certificate?"

"Yes." That question he could answer.

"Good. Now . . ." Madeline sat back and picked up her latte again. "Walk me through this . . . How does it work when you want to see your daughter?"

"I call and drive to pick her up if Krista lets me."

"There are no set times?"

Jeremy shook his head.

"I need to do a little research into this, including getting eyes on that divorce agreement. I'd also like a copy of Becca's birth certificate." Madeline leaned forward. "At the most basic level, your ex-wife can't move your daughter out of the state without your permission. You are Becca's father. If Krista persists, I suspect our first step will be to file an injunction against her to keep her in Illinois until we work out your parenting rights, if you have none delineated."

"How do we do that?"

"I file a petition with the court and we schedule a hearing. Two hearings. The first will request Krista stay in Illinois, and that can come fast. The second could take months. That one will determine parenting rights."

Jeremy pushed forward. "But say I get weekends and Tuesdays

or something; she can't leave after that, can she? What will it matter if I have rights if Becca's halfway across the country?"

Madeline's eyes softened. "Let's take this one step at a time."

One step at a time. Jeremy sat back and thought about all those "one steps" he'd made over the past several months, and how few of them turned out to be good ones. "I don't want to lose her." He pressed his lips tight. "She's a pretty incredible kid."

"I would agree with that." Madeline smiled.

Jeremy stood. "Okay. I'll get you the papers and . . . What do you charge for this kind of help? For the Brendon stuff too, you never told me."

Madeline smiled again. "Why don't we worry about all that later too?"

Jeremy opened his mouth to protest. To accept such help, such generosity, was hard. It stuck in his throat and made him feel weak. But, quick on the heels of that thought, he reminded himself he had no money—and Janet knew it. And if Janet knew it, he suspected there were no secrets from Madeline either.

"Thank you. I will pay you . . . I will."

"I trust you and I'm not worried, Jeremy."

He waved good-bye to Janet and Claire on his way back through the bookstore and returned to his coffee shop. Everything inside him felt jumbled. But as much as he wanted to sit in the back office to settle, he needed to make one more stop.

Ryan stood at the register talking to a young woman, coffee already in hand.

Jeremy tapped him on the shoulder. "I'm sorry to leave again, but I need to go talk to Krista."

Ryan glanced at him. "You okay?"

"I hope so. I'll be back to close up."

Ryan nodded and Jeremy heard him resume his conversation. A

laugh reached into the office space as Jeremy grabbed his keys and headed out the alley door.

As he drove the half hour to Park Ridge, one thought filled his mind. He had, perhaps, poked a sleeping bear. He wasn't sure if he would change what he had done, but he wondered if he should have warned Krista first. She hated surprises and she fought when backed into a corner.

And Madeline could be wrong, he thought. He'd never read his divorce papers. Maybe they were different. Maybe Krista could do whatever she wanted. Maybe she didn't need to present him with her move in writing. And if he made her mad . . . he might as well have purchased the two one-way tickets to North Carolina himself.

Krista answered the door dressed in jeans and a white T-shirt. "What are you doing here? Becca's not with you until Thursday."

"I need to talk to you."

Something in his voice must have cued her, because she narrowed her eyes and stepped outside. Her gray-blue eyes always took on a stormy tone when she got annoyed, and they morphed to steel gray now. And she always stepped outside when a fight was about to go down. She never wanted her parents to hear a note of conflict.

"What's going on, Jeremy?" She asked the question with slow, crisp diction.

He tried to warm to the subject. "I really don't want you to move."

She sighed and slumped as if weighed down by some force he couldn't see. "Look around, Jeremy . . . Becca and I live with my parents. When I left you and she was young, it was the right thing. I was a mess. I was twenty-one, a college dropout with no job and no money. But I'm twenty-eight now. I've worked hard. And I never thought I'd still be here. That this would be my life. Don't you get that?"

"Then move out. Stay in the Chicago area, but move out of here."

"It's not that simple."

"North Carolina is?"

"Yes." She sputtered out the word. Laden with derision, it fell between them. She pointed back to the house. Red brick with black shutters, it stood sturdy like a two-story fortress behind her. "My dad's so proud of me he cracked open a bottle of champagne. My mom almost cried . . . It's a good job, Jeremy, a really good job."

"There will be others." At her questioning look, he clarified. "Other good jobs. Better jobs."

"Not in front of me right now . . . I'm not trying to hurt you, but this is happening."

"I talked to a lawyer today." He blurted the words.

"You did what?" Krista stilled. Almost. Jeremy noticed her jaw working right beneath her earlobe.

"I did it to help. To ask if you could legally take Becca away or what I could do to keep you from moving, because I want to be in Becca's life. I want regular times to see her, not have to call and get her whenever it's convenient. A father doesn't do that. You said it yourself. I need to show up and I want to. When I get back on my feet, I'll pay for some of what she needs. School. Extra tutors. Books. Whatever she needs . . ." His words drifted away.

"You shouldn't have done that."

"I had to. I don't want to be cut out, Krista. Knowing what you know about me, about my parents, how can you think, especially now, that I could live like that again?"

Krista opened her mouth just as Becca ran out the door behind her mom.

"Daddy, I saw your car." She launched past Krista. He lifted her up and hugged her tight. Something between them had changed that day at the park two weeks ago. And it only got better the Thursday before as they ran all around town forming the book club, arranging the pastries, and stuffing Andante with pillows. But the real highlight was welcoming Ryan back that afternoon. It had been Becca's idea to put candles in a blueberry muffin and make Ryan's return a celebration. In fact, she'd made that entire day a celebration, his new beginning, and he couldn't go back. She was a part of everything right in his life.

"Daddy's not staying." Krista laid her hand on Becca's back.

"You can't?" Becca leaned away, her face inches from his.

Jeremy slid on his best smile, kissed her cheek, and set her down. "Not today, Bug. I just came to say hi."

"Hi."

"Hi to you too." He kissed the top of her head.

"You head inside, Becca, and I'll be right in to finish the cookies."

Becca happily slapped her flip-flops up the few stairs as Krista turned back to Jeremy. "Call off the lawyer, Jeremy, please."

"I can't do that, Krista. I've recently learned there are a few things worth fighting for. Becca's one of them."

Krista shook her head. In many ways it was the saddest, slowest motion Jeremy could imagine.

"Fine." She sighed. "I guess we're doing this."

Without another word she turned around, stepped inside the house, and shut the door.

Chapter 35

"You asked to see me?" Special Agent Pullman rolled a chair next to Alyssa's. She glanced over at him. Over the past five days she'd lost her fear of the man and had even come to regard him as more friend than foe.

"I'm done. I found everything you need." She pointed to the left monitor. "Tag created code E435, and everyone with that code attached to their data was added after a clean data set was run through our algorithms. Back it up further, and the code was added to every individual who answered yes to questions 12, 84, and 119 on the patient questionnaire and showed polymorphisms of a few different genes, and did not have ANA, antinuclear antibodies, in their blood. That last test had to be negative."

"Why negative?" Pullman pushed up his reading glasses.

"Because if a patient had those antibodies, there was a good chance their doctor had already had a discussion with them, and that could get messy. Not only would Tag not want patients to claim he'd told them nothing new, but if he missed the diagnosis, say the doctor had already talked about hypothyroidism and Tag cited lupus, then red flags would be raised about XGC's work. The true algorithms could pinpoint a patient's area of vulnerability, but

Tag was going off script. He was basically throwing darts and hoping to land on a chronic disease that sounded feasible."

Alyssa leaned forward and ran her finger down the second screen's far right edge. "These are your E435s. Customers who had genetic markers, polymorphisms, without antibodies. And since they were the ones most likely to have something in their family history, but nothing themselves yet, these people gave Tag a warm lead-in. Most were probably already a little worried, and their diagnoses named and confirmed their fears. Confirmation bias. They were less likely to question XGC's results."

Pullman sat back and pulled off his glasses. "Good work. Can you document this?"

"Already did. I tracked every step and outlined it for you. I even labeled all the files. You'll have no trouble tracing what I did. I even designed a clean parallel program that walks you through it."

"Very thorough."

"Keeps me out of jail?" Alyssa quipped and rolled her chair back a few inches to better see Pullman's expression. She hoped for a smile, a laugh, something to let her know everything was okay. She got nothing—which oddly made her feel she had little left to lose. "I also found that the rumors were true."

"What rumors?"

"You gave me access to everything . . . I had to dig around a little."

The corner of his mouth finally lifted. "How long?"

Alyssa studied him and conceded she'd pulled nothing over on him. She even suspected his question was more a test than a query, so she opted for honesty. "I finished this morning and have been poking around all day. But you knew that, didn't you?"

Pullman's expression revealed nothing.

She looked down at her hands. She found she was twisting them together, and stilled them against her knees. "He really sold all those names to pharmaceutical companies abroad. I hoped that was just a rumor."

"That's how much of this began. We got solid evidence from a company that purchased XGC's first set of customer data. I'm still trying to discover if he shopped it domestically. We haven't found any communications yet."

"Then he didn't. Tag was completely OCD; he personally tracked everything. I mean everything down to the numbers of ink cartridges used per department. Honestly, this E435 was hard to find, but it never needed to be there either. Tag created the code because he wanted it, not because he needed it." She waited a beat. "Can I ask you something else?"

"I get the feeling this is a more personal request."

"It is." She pulled the keyboard toward herself and brought up another spreadsheet before tilting the screen in Pullman's direction. "Winsome has statistically more participants in XGC data sets, far above the national average."

"We noticed that. Almost everyone in management had support from their hometowns. Interestingly, yours was the highest. Mr. Connelly's was the lowest."

"I heard my mom practically got all Winsome to sign up. But Tag should've had good numbers too. He's from Bettendorf, Iowa. Another town with good Midwest loyalty."

"Mr. Connelly grew up in LA."

"That was a lie too?" Alyssa dropped back in her seat. "Was nothing he said real?"

"I haven't found anything yet . . . But back to your question."

"Someone from Winsome was coded E435. She was told she was headed toward early onset Alzheimer's."

"Still not a question."

"Can I talk to her?"

"No." The word was short, direct, and it brooked no argument. Pullman slid a cloth from his coat pocket and wiped at his glasses. "We're on dangerous ground, Ms. Harrison. One XGC client committed suicide in March, and that means a charge of reckless homicide is on the table. Right now we must make sure our information is accurate and handled properly. This is confidential medical information and it has already been abused." He set his glasses back on his nose and peered over them. "Furthermore, beyond myriad legal issues, these are people's very lives."

Alyssa couldn't breathe. All her refutations, rationales, and her insistence in every interview that all could be made well, played before her. She had consoled herself, justified herself, with the fact that "these are future predictions, not diagnostic." Confirmation bias struck again. She believed only what she chose to see and had seen only what she needed to believe.

"Ms. Harrison? . . . Do you understand?"

Alyssa shook her head trying to clear away her guilt, which was tipping to panic with each shallow breath. "I didn't know . . . No one reported that. I've been searching the internet every day, and it's nowhere. No one said that happened."

"It isn't something we've made public."

Alyssa felt her body go hot. She rolled her chair inches away, as if distance could help.

"Do you understand, Ms. Harrison? I need to hear you say you will not approach this woman. I also need to remind you that you signed a confidentiality agreement the day you arrived here. It covers all information pertaining to this case. All of it."

"Yes . . . I . . . Of course." She popped out of her chair. "Do you need me? I . . . I need to go." She scanned the room for the way out. She had forgotten where it was. "Do I need to come back next week? I'm done. I . . . I don't know what else I can tell you."

Pullman stood. "We're fine. Thank you. I'll have the team look this over on Monday, and we'll reach out if we have further questions." He stepped beside her and pulled her chair closer. "You've gone pale. Why don't you sit down again? I didn't mean to shock you, I simply want you to understand the severity of this."

Alyssa could not sit. She needed out. "I do, and I'm fine. I didn't know, but I'm fine, really, I just need to go . . . Thank you." She picked up her bag and stepped to the door. She spun around. "You're not going to arrest me anymore, are you?"

"I may have more questions for you, but no, I doubt I'll arrest you." Pullman gave a half smile.

Alyssa fled the building.

ALYSSA SAT IN HER car outside the Sweet Shoppe. She shouldn't be there. She should go straight home. She watched Jill Pennet inside wiping her counters; she watched customers come and go; and no matter how many times she told herself to drive away, she remained right where she was.

After another fifteen minutes, she got out of her car and pushed open the door.

The bell chimed, and savory smells hit Alyssa first. They reminded her of Jeremy. The Sweet Shoppe didn't carry the savory baked goods Jill provided for Andante.

Jill emerged from the back room wiping her hands on her apron. "I'm sorry if I kept you waiting."

Alyssa shook her head. Jill was about ten years older than she was. She didn't know her personally, but she'd always known of her. Jill's picture had still hung outside their high school gym during Alyssa's years. High School All-American in field hockey. 1995.

"Not at all. I . . ." Alyssa stalled. She hadn't thought this through. She hadn't thought anything through. "I wanted to buy—" She looked to the display cases filled with sugary delights, none of which she could eat. "Lemon and rosemary," she blurted. "You made grain-free lemon and rosemary cookies for Andante. I wanted to buy a dozen."

Jill grinned. "I am so glad those are selling. It took me days to get that recipe right." She gestured out her front windows and across the town square. "But I sell nothing here that I make for Andante. It keeps us from competing. We hope."

"Oh . . ." Alyssa twisted to look out the window as well. After a moment she turned back to Jill. "But you're okay, right? You're okay?"

Something flashed in Jill's eyes. Alyssa felt herself tip backward, as if physically pulling herself from a metaphorical ledge. "That came out wrong. I'm sorry. I mean your business. Andante isn't taking too much of your business?"

Jill studied her before answering. "Not at all."

"Good." Alyssa looked down at the display case. She couldn't look at Jill any longer.

"In fact, I think it's improved it. People see the little sign over there and then remember to come over here. I've sold more out of this display case this week than I can remember in a long while, and I've got ten birthday cake orders to fill. Usually this time of year brings in about five per week."

"That's good." Alyssa felt her breath hitch. "That's really good."

Jill's eyes softened. "It's okay if you turn around and hightail it over to Andante for your cookies. I won't be hurt. They are mine, after all."

"Yes. Yes . . . I'll do that." Alyssa spun and pushed her way out the door.

Chapter 36

Maybe it would all be okay.

Jeremy tried to convince himself of this as he drove to Park Ridge to take Becca back to Krista. Becca listened to her favorite music in the back seat, and he cycled through the last few days. Everything had gone smoothly—better than smooth. The tide was turning and maybe, just maybe, it would all work out.

When he'd picked up Becca yesterday for their daddy-daughter night, Krista said nothing about their conversation, nor had she brought up the move. And Becca confirmed they hadn't gone to North Carolina either.

Krista had been warmer yesterday too, asking if he wanted an extra night with Becca. She asked how the shop was going and what he thought of her Instagram posts. He didn't have an answer for the last one. He'd stopped checking Instagram after his arrest video had gone viral. But he checked when he got home, and her new posts astounded him. Over the past several days she had posted microblogs about their parenting, their cooperation, and their mutual respect. So now—between the posts and her attitude yesterday—he'd allowed a glimmer of hope to grow.

And if that wasn't enough, Andante's day-to-day trend was heading in the right direction. Granted, the percentages remained far less than ideal, but that could change, trends could grow. They could go viral too. Janet thought so—at least that's what she said when she hung the book club poster in his front window two days ago. Eight customers had already signed up. And all that happened on the same day that Madeline called and left the message that the Winsome Police had reported to her that, while he might be needed for details later, he was in the clear. They even returned his financial records.

Yes, Jeremy thought, it was all good.

He sighed as he kicked his assessment of life up a notch. It was humming along much better than merely "good." Alyssa was in it.

When she had called the night before to say she was headed to his place, he'd been so excited he put Becca to bed early, just to have more time with Alyssa and learn about her four days at the FBI. Once again he dashed through his small apartment, making sure it looked as good as possible.

Becca, of course, popped out of bed ten minutes later with an "I'm not tired," ruining his romantic plans just as Alyssa crossed the threshold.

So while Jeremy popped popcorn, Becca showed Alyssa how to make Smurf houses. He watched with wonder as Alyssa crawled around the floor with his daughter, and suspected that's what love looked like—felt like too.

Two hours later they all settled onto his couch, popcorn long gone and his entire floor covered with book houses, and he listened as Alyssa read *Sylvester and the Magic Pebble* to them both.

Becca finally yawned so long and loud Jeremy hoisted her into his arms. "Bed, little one."

"You can keep that if you want." Becca pointed down to the book still resting on Alyssa's lap.

"Why would you give this to me?" she asked. "It's your book."

"You said at the park that you liked it. That's why I asked you to read it."

"I do like it." Alyssa gripped the book to her chest. "Thank you. If I borrow it, I promise to return it."

Becca nodded and Jeremy carried her to bed.

Anticipating a long evening with Alyssa, Jeremy returned to find her standing at the front door. "You're leaving?"

She nodded. "I have to be back at the FBI by seven tomorrow. If I wait longer, traffic builds." She held the book close. "You have a very intuitive daughter."

"How so?"

She shrugged. "I needed this. There's something so wonderful about the moment Sylvester gets reunited with his parents. It's the way it should be, right?" Alyssa's face dropped. "I'm sorry. That was thoughtless."

He wrapped his arms around her waist and pulled her close. The book rested between them. "Don't be. I love that story, and yes, it should be like that. If I lost that with Becca it would break me."

"That's just it . . . I can't get there, and I'm the one holding back from it. It's like fog I can't see through. There is so much I can't let go of and . . ." She shook her head. "I'm being silly. Thinking I'll find answers in a children's book."

"There is nothing silly about that. I think Madeline L'Engle's *Wrinkle in Time* series saved me in middle school. There was this sense Meg carried that she didn't belong—until she found out where she did. Kids' books are powerful things." Jeremy dropped a light kiss on her lips.

"See you tomorrow night? I should be done by then—with the FBI, I mean." She'd smiled at him, her lips still inches from his own.

Alyssa had made it clear in their texts she couldn't tell him what she was doing, so he didn't ask. It was enough to have her confide that much to him. "By the look in your eyes, I sense it's gone well. I'm happy for you. Plan on tomorrow." Then he really kissed her, just as he'd planned since the moment she'd called hours before.

The bubble of that sweet memory burst as he now turned into Krista's driveway. She sat, arms wrapped around her knees, on the house's front cement steps.

He put the car in park and got out. "What's wrong?"

"Something has to be wrong?" she called too brightly.

He stood by his open car door. "You sit out here when you need to tell me something in person and you don't want your parents to hear."

Krista snorted as she stood, brushed off her jeans, and approached his car. "And you ask why I need to move."

Becca climbed out of the back seat and looked between them.

"Hey, sweetheart." Krista looped an arm around her daughter and pulled her close. "Can I talk to Daddy alone a minute?"

Becca nodded, looked between them again, and shuffled inside.

Jeremy watched her go. He recognized the sliding flip-flop *thwap* of the night Becca had arrived quiet, stressed, and uncommunicative at his apartment. It felt like a lifetime ago. "This isn't good for her, Krista. This isn't how we should be acting. I'm not saying don't move. Just not so far away." He waved his hand between them. "We shouldn't be at odds with each other, not in front of her. Not at all."

Krista motioned toward the house's front stairs. "I need to talk with you. Come sit. Please."

This is new, Jeremy thought. He was dictated to or yelled at, but talked with? He led the way to the steps and sat down.

Krista dropped next to him as she slid a white envelope from her back pocket.

"This isn't easy, and before you react, I want you to hear me out." She paused a beat, then handed him the envelope.

"What's this?" He slid his finger along the envelope's seam.

She stayed his hand. "It's the results of a paternity test. I had my pediatrician rush it because I thought you'd want proof."

"Is this a joke?" He pushed the envelope back toward her.

"I'm sorry. I never meant to hurt you or tell you like this or . . . You're not Becca's father." Krista shook her head and tucked her hands between her knees. "I'm terribly sorry, Jeremy. You don't deserve this. But you have to understand, I was so scared back then, and I really messed up."

"What the—" He popped up and spun around, stopping himself just before the last word flew. Becca had left the door open behind the screen. He suspected she was close by.

Krista looked behind her, noted it, got up, and shut it. She turned to face Jeremy again. "I know. I know I should have told you, and if you'll calm down, I will." She stepped down the two stairs and met him on the sidewalk. "I met him the spring before us, and I thought . . . It doesn't matter. He dumped me and he graduated. I never meant for us to be more than a fun summer, but . . ."

Krista stalled so long Jeremy filled in the next sentence. "You found out you were pregnant."

"Yes."

Jeremy felt hot, like every nerve ending was on fire. He glared down at her. "Before or after?"

"Before or after we got married?" Krista stared up at him.

"Before or after we slept together."

Krista's silence gave him his answer.

He paced to his car, then circled back. Noting the door again, he kept his voice low. "That night—you were so determined. What a fool I was . . . You played me just right, didn't you?"

Krista reached out to him. He stepped back and her hand fell. "I didn't mean to, I promise. I was scared. I wasn't thinking straight."

"Don't even—you were thinking straight . . . Does he know? What was his name again? This was David, right?"

"It doesn't—" Something in his expression stopped her, because she stopped talking. She bit her lip as if trying to decide which road to take. Jeremy waited.

"Yes, it was David, and yes, he knows. I called him and I told him, and it didn't change a thing. He didn't want either of us. In fact, he told me never to contact him again, no matter what happened."

"Cue Jeremy."

"It wasn't like that. It wasn't like how you're making it sound, and I thought we could work." Krista reached out again, but stopped just before contact. Her hand stayed suspended inches from his arm.

"For like, what? Five minutes?"

"That's not fair."

"Are you kidding me? Fair?" His voice pitched high. He noted a front living room curtain move. He crossed the strip of grass between the front walk and the driveway.

Krista followed. "I never meant to hurt you."

"Does Becca know?" He ground out the question so soft Krista leaned closer.

"No." The answer came out short and emphatic. Her hand clamped on his forearm. "Please. Don't tell her. You said yourself all this isn't good for her."

"You needed her DNA for the test. You needed my DNA." He shrugged away from her grasp.

"It was a swab to the inside of her cheek. She thought it was normal checkup stuff, and I took a hair from your sweatshirt she wore home last time . . . Look, I didn't expect any of this to come up. I never thought you'd follow us. You were in Seattle and—"

"*Her*, Krista, not you . . . I followed *her*." He towered over her. "And now this is my fault?"

"I'm not saying that. I'm saying I messed up. I'm trying to tell you I'm sorry."

"Why now?" Jeremy leaned against his car, suddenly weary beyond belief. "I need to hear you say it . . . That you're telling me now for you, not for me, and certainly not for Becca. You're telling me now because you want to move and I'm in the way. Like seven years ago, my role here is over."

"No."

"Be straight with me, for once, Krista. If it didn't help you get what you want, we wouldn't be having this conversation—ever—because I tried. Remember that?"

Krista took a step back.

Jeremy straightened. "Becca was a month early, and when I came to visit I asked. I asked if she was mine and you got all teary and indignant, yelling about the birth certificate. You made me feel guilty and you made me pay. You didn't talk to me for weeks, refused to send me pictures, cut me off for almost a year because I'd questioned you."

"It looks really bad, I know, and I'm sorry. But we were married and that made you her dad. You are her dad. So I wasn't lying. I was, but it was also true—I mean, I didn't think it through."

Jeremy closed his eyes. This was not going anywhere good. As with most conversations with Krista, it would wind like spaghetti until he ended in the wrong about something. And at some level, despite the birth certificate and her teary indignation back then, and her petulant assurances afterward, he'd wondered. He'd always wondered. A sliver of doubt in the back corner of his mind.

But now doubt became fact, and that changed everything.

Jeremy opened his car door.

Krista lunged forward, clasping the top of the driver's door. "You never told me you were doing this, Jeremy. You never said you were going to show up here and sink all your money into a coffee shop. If you had, I—maybe I would've said something earlier. But I'm saying something now because it's getting too complicated. It's a mess and it's going to get worse. You hired a lawyer, Jeremy . . . This is horrible and I'm sorry, but I'm trying to make things right." She let go of the door and stepped back. "Please believe me."

"Nothing about this is right, Krista. Nothing." He dropped into his car.

She grabbed the door again to keep it open. "Can we talk later? Please?"

He held up a hand, palm out, fingers splayed. He couldn't talk anymore. He couldn't listen anymore. And he didn't trust himself with a reply. He stared at her hand until she let go of the door. Then he shut it and drove away.

Chapter 37

Alyssa took a deep breath, her heart still lodged just south of her throat, and pushed open the back door of her home.

"Alyssa?" Janet called from the living room. "Come on in. Grandma's here . . . How was today?"

Alyssa stalled and looked around the kitchen for an excuse to linger. She couldn't face them.

"I'll be right in. I'm just getting some water." She rifled through her bag. No Tums. She'd thrown them out after Dr. Laghari had told her to stop taking them.

Two glasses later, she was waterlogged and out of time.

"What's wrong?" Her grandmother straightened on the living room love seat as she rounded the corner.

"Why would you ask that? Nothing."

"You look super pale," her mom chimed in. "Are you feeling okay? Has all this been too much?"

"I'm fine. It was a long day." Alyssa shrugged away their concern and stepped up the stairs.

"Don't go. Come sit," Janet called to her. "Come tell us. You were so excited this morning."

Alyssa looked back, then up the stairs again. Escape felt so close.

She looked at the painting at the top of the stairs. Her fictional dreams of escaping into that starry night seemed so foolish in the harsh light of today. Safety took a more narrow form—a childhood bedroom, decorated in white, blue, and yellow, with enough pillows to lose herself within.

"Alyssa?" her grandmother prompted.

She turned, crossed into the living room, and perched on the sofa next to her mom's chair. "There's nothing to tell. I finished my work and they don't need me anymore. I figured out what they wanted to know and it's over."

"You don't seem happy."

"I'm not happy. It was horrible. What XGC did, what I helped to do, ruined lives, and nothing I did this week is going to change that."

"Of course it will. They'll let people know if they were lied to, and you said it yourself, it was all predictive, way-in-the-future kind of stuff."

Alyssa turned on her mom with a ferocity she couldn't point at herself. "That's a cop-out. You don't think that if you were told you were going to get early onset Alzheimer's—that's before sixty-five, Mom—you'd panic. You're only a few years from that now, which means any day you'll start forgetting, and wondering, and worrying. You don't think you'd be scared to death, so terrified you might do something stupid and irrevocable? You're about to forget them, Mom, your family, your new granddaughter, and everything else that was ever good in your life. But not your family—they won't forget you. They'll still have to pay for your care, expensive care, maybe for years. Don't you think that would terrify you now, not down the road in some nebulous future? Right now."

"Stop." Janet lifted off the cushion with a hand outstretched. "Stop it. What's gotten into you?" She glanced to her own mom before looking back to her daughter. “I’m sorry I said that, but please stop. I wasn’t saying it wasn’t serious, but I hardly think—”

“That someone wouldn’t die over this?” Alyssa blanched. She shifted her words. “Couldn’t die?”

“What?”

Alyssa’s head filled with fuzz. She had said too much, but she couldn’t remember what she was not allowed to say. She pointed to her mom and her grandma. “Nothing. I didn’t say anything and you didn’t hear anything. Do you understand? Neither of you.”

Her grandmother lifted from the love seat and sat next to her. She reached for Alyssa’s hand. Her knuckles were swollen. They looked tender. Yet she held Alyssa’s tight without saying a word.

Alyssa felt the panic and rage pull like tide away from the shore. She whispered to her grandmother, “I’m sorry. I’m sorry I said all that.”

“Seems it needed to get out of you.”

She looked at her grandmother, then across to her mom again, who sat silent and still. “Don’t repeat what I said. To anyone, okay? I could be in real trouble.” She swiped at her eyes. “Listen to me . . . Worrying about real trouble for me.”

“Don’t think like that, sweetheart.” Grandma tucked her close.

After a few seconds, Alyssa pushed to stand. “I’m going to go upstairs.”

She reached the bottom step when her mom called after her.

“Oh . . . Eve Parker stopped by the shop this afternoon. She submitted your name for the Chamber of Commerce position. I know you don’t plan to stay here and I told her that, but she was so pleased with all the work you did for her. She said she couldn’t help herself.”

Alyssa didn’t turn or acknowledge her mom. She simply wanted to reach the top of the stairs.

"Alyssa?" Janet prompted her again.

She paused and looked back. "I'm leaving next week. With the money Lexi paid me, I can go."

"You're leaving? Just like that?" Janet's face fell.

"What do you want from me? Yes. I'm leaving." Alyssa continued up the stairs.

"Respect!" her mom yelled. "A lot more respect than that."

Alyssa turned. Her mom stood in the center of the room, eyes blazing.

"I've had enough. You don't get to come home like a spoiled child, dump all over me for almost two months, scream at me about my mental demise because you now understand the severity of what happened at XGC, apologize to my mother but not to me, then walk up those stairs with an 'I'm taking my ball and going home' attitude. Well, this is your home. And run away again if you want, but think long and hard about what you're leaving behind."

Janet stiff-arm pointed to the front door. "A friend of mine took the time to come over here to thank you for what you did for her and was thrilled to have done something she thought was nice for you. You need a job, and she thought that would be a perfect one for you. I didn't put her up to it. I didn't ask her to get involved. She did that all on her own because she cares. You tell me how many people in Palo Alto did that for you, did what Jasper did for you. I'm not saying it can't happen, but I am saying your attitude and your behavior are unacceptable. Your life wasn't so bad here, and it isn't so bad right now. Yes, be sad about what went down at XGC and do your best to help clean it up, and while you're doing that, grow up and be a little thankful. Respectful too. Never come in here and dump on me like that again."

Alyssa's focus drifted to the sofa's side table. A cluster of family photos rested there. Happy times of Christmases, vacations, and birthdays. There was one of Lexi, her dad, and herself at the Fourth of July parade when she was about ten.

Alyssa stared at the picture. Lexi had always been at Alyssa's house, with Alyssa's family, even bullying Alyssa's younger brother as much as she herself had—and she'd been there because Alyssa's family was safe and her home was a good place to be. And even when Alyssa had felt a sliver of green over Lexi's warm reception in her own home, she'd also held a little nugget of pride that this was her family and her home.

Alyssa closed her eyes, desperate to "come home" as her mom had just said, but she had no idea how to do that.

"Coming back was a mistake," she whispered before she raced up the stairs.

"Alyssa," her mom called after her.

"Janet," her grandmother barked. "Let the girl alone. You've done enough."

Yes, Mom, Alyssa thought as she reached the upstairs hallway, let the girl alone.

Chapter 38

Years ago Winsome's town council voted to string lights in the trees lining Main Street during the holiday season. The twinkling trees created such a winter wonderland, town traffic increased a whopping 39 percent. Of course it wasn't just the lights. It was December, and the year's fourth quarter always brought more folks to town and more sales to the shops.

Then seven years ago the Chamber of Commerce's executive director suggested turning the lights back on during the summer. Now every night from Memorial Weekend to Labor Day weekend, Winsome glowed like a storybook. Last summer an artist had made somewhat of a name for herself photographing the site—the image graced the cover of *Midwest Living*.

In the wake of the publicity and the magazine cover, shops began to stay open late and offer special sales and giveaways. Couples strolled through town holding hands; families rode their bikes in after dinner for ice cream; kids chased each other around the fountain. Friday evenings turned into the town's own weekly meet and greet, and the boosted sales numbers sent every store owner home happy and tired at 10:00 p.m.

Worn by late afternoon events, Janet dreaded returning to the Printed Letter for the late shift.

Madeline's pestering didn't help. "You don't look good. Where's that thousand-watt smile I love? Did something happen? Come on, spill."

Janet knew she meant well, and most of the time she loved Madeline's direct and inquisitive manner. It mirrored her own. But tonight she felt bruised and tender and back at the very beginning. She wasn't even sure what her "beginning" was anymore, other than it felt very low.

Her reprieve from Madeline's barrage came when Seth walked in the door and invited her for a stroll.

"You look tired. Is everything okay?" He leaned against the customer service counter.

"That's exactly what every woman wants to hear," she snapped back.

"Take her away, please," Madeline called with a laugh. "See what I'm dealing with in here?"

As they walked to an empty bench near the fountain, Seth asked, "What happened today?"

Janet pulled her hand from his and crossed the final two steps to an empty bench facing the fountain. She looked around to make sure no one stood too close. "Why does everyone think something happened?"

Seth raised both brows. "It feels obvious."

Janet plopped onto the bench. "If you must know, I think we should call off the wedding."

"What? We are four days away." Seth dropped next to her.

"It's not right, at least not right now, if that makes sense. We're a mess. Our family is a mess, and we're not coming back together. You want us to be perfect, and we're not. We never will be, because

I'm not perfect, and I can't go back to what I was, but I . . . I don't know how to do this anymore." She bit her lip against the tears.

"How to do what?"

"Any of this. All of it." She pressed her fingers to her eyes. "How to do us. I'm messing everything up. I thought I wouldn't do that anymore," she whispered.

"Janet, where is this coming from?" Seth twisted to fully face her.

"From me, because it's right. It's what we need to do."

Seth narrowed his eyes and studied her. He was silent for so long and stared so hard she wiggled under his assessment. He finally spoke. His words were soft, but not gentle. They struck just above a whisper. "You have got to figure this out."

"That's what I'm trying to do." Her voice arced high in defense.

"Then take it up with your daughter." His pitch rose too. "Or if the problem isn't her, go talk to your mom, because it's one of them, and I'm tired of it."

"What?" Janet sat straight.

"She dumps on you—pick either 'she' you want—and you dump on me. I get that you're safe for them, so they launch on you, and I like that I'm safe for you. But I'm not your punching bag. How can you not see this? What was it this time? Her apartment? Or pick the other. Her stomach? Her job? Her FBI work?"

Janet stilled. She felt as if threads were unraveling before her eyes, straightening, untangling, clarifying. "Yes."

"Well, she needs to figure it out. You both do. And no, she's not moving in with me, so don't ask again. I gave that mattress away last week and I'm not buying another. Neither are you." He stood and faced her. "This has gone on long enough. Let me know when you either come to your senses or you've canceled our appointment with Pastor Zach. And you'd better let Lexi know. She's put a lot of work into next Tuesday."

With that, Seth walked away.

Janet sat and stared after him.

Ryan lifted a hand in greeting but, noticing Seth's tight expression, lowered it as quickly. Seth was striding across the street, head down, aiming for his car. Ryan was sure he hadn't seen him and felt grateful he hadn't—just by raising his hand he suspected he had intruded on a private and unpleasant moment.

He glanced back to the bench where Seth had been sitting with his ex-wife, the blonde who worked at the bookshop. Her expression was nothing like his. He was thunder. She was thunderstruck.

And both reminded him of Jeremy. He had sported Janet's amazed, slightly befuddled look for almost a week—until today, when he darkened into Seth's.

Ryan looked back to the counter. Jeremy stood talking with a customer. He was saying all the right words, but his expression still looked grim. It had been that way since he'd come back from dropping Becca off at Krista's with a piece of paper crumpled in his fist and the news that he wasn't Becca's dad.

"You are her dad." Ryan had shoved the paper back into Jeremy's hands. "No matter what that says, you're the one around. What do you think makes a dad, anyway? Not that paper."

"The court won't see it that way."

"Forget the court!" Ryan had yelled—not because he was angry, but because he was afraid. He knew what it felt like to lose everything, and his friend had come close too many times. "Forget Krista. They don't matter here. Becca's is the only opinion that matters, and to her, you are Dad."

That had gotten a near smile from Jeremy, for only a second. Within the next beat, defeat draped over him again like a curtain. Krista's constant calling didn't help. At least ten times Ryan saw Jeremy click Decline when her ringtone sounded. The fact that

Becca's picture was the one that flashed when it rang probably made it all the more painful. Jeremy had finally turned the ringer off and thrown the phone into his desk drawer.

Ryan had also overheard him talking to Madeline this afternoon at the shop's side counter. Although he didn't hear the whole conversation, the body language conveyed enough—as did the few words he caught.

"I'm very sorry, Jeremy. If there's anything I can do, let me know . . . Is there anything you want to do?"

"Nothing," he'd said to her. "Nothing at all."

"Are you open tonight?" An older man paused in front of Ryan.

Ryan realized he was blocking the door and stepped aside. "Yes. I was watching everyone in the square, sorry. Please come in."

George Williams nodded to the young man and headed toward the counter. Color caught in his periphery. Something was different . . .

Ah . . . He stopped. He smiled. He savored the sight. The pillows.

He'd have to tell— George stalled. She wasn't waiting at home. She wasn't putzing in the kitchen or searching for her readers, which were invariably resting on top of her head. She wasn't calling the kids and gently pestering them for a visit or the latest news. How long would sharing something with Margery be his first reaction? His first desire? He breathed deep and, for the first time in too long, felt true pleasure and peace in the action. Probably until my last breath, he thought.

It had been one week since Margery's service, and this was his first time out and about. Everything felt new and raw—exposed to the air and too blistered to heal. It wasn't as if Margery had been able to accompany him to the coffee shop for months before her death, but the fact that she never would again, and that she wasn't home for him to tell her who he saw, who he talked to, and what was going on, felt foreign and wrong. He didn't like this new world he woke up to every morning. He also wondered if he'd ever get used to its silence. But he did like remembering her. Small moments were beginning to come back to him through the pain, and he cherished each one.

Not that, with the kids around, he had many opportunities for those silent savorings. They chattered constantly. But the noise felt different now. As much as he loved them, their comments and musings never reached that corner of his heart he'd reserved over sixty-five years ago for Margery alone.

Three of the kids had gone home. They had work, and their kids had either jobs and babies or, if they were younger, sports camps and internships. Three still remained. Michael, Devon, and Bella hovered. He imagined them right now, sitting around his kitchen table checking their watches and discussing how long they should leave him alone, who was going to come look for him when darkness descended, and what kind, bolstering, and consoling words they'd say when they found him.

He couldn't blame them. He even appreciated their efforts. After all, they were grieving too, and to fake such chipperness took energy. They loved him; they wanted to protect him. But *protect me from what?* he asked himself. *Life?*

Because that's what this was. At eighty-one, this was life.

"George, it's good to see you." Jeremy nodded to him as he reached the front of the line.

George pointed out into the shop. He felt, then saw, his own hand shake. That was new too. *Perhaps sleep will help*, he consoled himself. He had gotten little in the last few weeks. That too was hard alone. "I like the pillows."

Jeremy smiled, but it wasn't the happy smile of victory or the smooth smile of peace George expected. Andante was busy tonight.

The young man should be pleased. But there was something empty about his expression and his smile that, oddly, mirrored George's own loss.

"Everyone else does too . . . What can I get for you?"

"Tea. Do you have a nice chamomile tea?" George infused a little spark into his voice.

"I do." Jeremy turned to scoop the tiny yellow flowers into a small silk pouch, then twisted back to talk to George while he worked. "Your wife's service was beautiful, by the way."

George nodded. "She would have loved it, especially Devon getting up to talk. He's the quietest of the bunch, believe it or not. I almost had a stroke when he walked up to that lectern. No one told me." He patted his chest. "I did mention to them later that it was not the best time for surprises."

"Oh . . ." Jeremy placed a white china mug on the counter between them.

George laughed. "It was a good surprise though, and yes, it was a beautiful service."

Jeremy looked behind him with such a questioning glance George turned too. No one was there. He turned back to the young man.

"Can I ask you a question?"

"Of course."

Jeremy leaned toward him. "What Devon said?" The question was so soft, almost a whisper, that George had to lean closer to hear him. "That you chose him and his siblings . . . Is it enough? To be chosen?"

George straightened. He knew nothing about Jeremy, his situation, or what was behind his question. But he knew exactly what to say. Margery had said it to him just about twenty years ago. "Sometimes that's all a kid has, and yes, it is enough. It is more than enough, I promise you."

Jeremy swallowed. His Adam's apple rose and fell as if dropped hard.

George wasn't sure if his comment was reassuring or upsetting.

"Thank you." Jeremy slid the mug closer to George.

As George reached for his wallet, Jeremy waved it away. His eyes shone and his mouth worked to form words. "Tea is on the house tonight."

George didn't protest. Instead he quickly lifted the cup in thanks and turned away.

No man wanted another to see him cry.

Chapter 39

Jeremy wiped his hands on a pristine white towel. He'd gotten the idea from Liam, and even though coffee grounds turned his towels brown almost as quickly as he pulled them from the drawer, he found a battle cry in each fresh towel. He understood now why Liam used them. Sure, they looked good, but they also felt like a call to do his best.

Ryan joined him behind the counter.

He saw that call within Ryan too, and wondered how he hadn't noticed it before. Without being asked, Ryan had not only picked up the slack left from Brendon's departure, but had taken ownership for certain parts of the business and pushed them ahead too. He actively talked up the book club every chance he got and had signed up another twenty customers.

Jeremy shook his head. None of this within Ryan was new. Jeremy had simply discounted it. No, that wasn't right. He'd been wary of it, even envious. To know what you want, to push for connection . . .

"Can you close tonight?" Jeremy tapped Ryan on the shoulder. "I've been in and out all day, but I need to go talk to Krista."

"I'm fine here, but are you okay? It's late. Don't you want to take a breather? Let her bomb settle for a few days?"

"I thought I did. I'd like to never see her again." Jeremy looked across the shop to where George sat with his cup of tea. "But time isn't on my side. I've got too much to lose."

"Sure. Go."

Before he knew it, Jeremy pulled into Krista's driveway. It stunned him how a dark and silent half-hour drive could fly by without one noticing a moment of it. He hadn't turned on the radio, Spotify, or anything. Not because his thoughts were loud, but because he was beyond thought—too tired, too worn, and too overwhelmed. And he had no idea what he was going to say now that he'd arrived.

Krista answered the door. She said nothing. She simply stepped outside under the lantern mounted above the front door and shut the door behind her.

He turned and dropped onto the steps.

"I called you. Several times." She lowered herself next to him.

He resisted the urge to scoot away to create more than a few inches of space between them. "Don't you get I don't want to talk to you? I don't want to look at you, hear your voice. I—I can't even process what you've done." He gripped his hair and pulled at the ends.

"Then what are you doing here?"

"Because this isn't about you, or me. I don't have the luxury of walking away." He shook his head as if imagining another scenario, one in which he could walk away. "On some level, right now, I wish I could. God forgive me. But what you did, Krista? From the moment we met everything was a lie, and you doubled down, again and again."

"I'm sorry—"

"No." He leaned back, creating that space he wanted, and held a hand up to her. "I get to finish." He bounced up, needing more distance and needing to move. The pressure built like the foaming wands on the espresso machines. It needed escape, even if only in paced circles. "What you did was inexcusable and we'll deal with that later, but . . . I have an aunt. Somewhere. And after my parents died, she didn't want me. She didn't choose me, Krista. She walked away, and I carry that every day of my life. That's what you're doing to Becca. You lay this 'truth' of yours on me to push me away, to force me to make that same choice and walk away. And you? You get to play innocent victim or savior, whichever you want. You get to be the parent who stayed." He stopped and thrust his pointer finger her direction. "It was rotten, wrong, and I . . . I almost hate you for it. And do you know what that feels like? Despite everything that's gone down between us I have never hated you." He curled the finger into his fist and smashed it into his chest. "I don't want to feel this way."

"How can I—" Krista stood.

Jeremy stiffened and held out his hand again, whether to silence her or keep her from coming closer, he wasn't sure. "I'm not walking away. I won't do that to my daughter. And I'll fight you if you try to take her from me. I may not be able to do anything in the courts, but I *can* fight you. I can keep showing up and poking holes in every lie you dish out . . . This isn't about you anymore, do you hear me? It should've stopped being about you the minute she was born, but it stops now. So no matter what you do, that little girl in there"—he pointed behind Krista to the house—"will know I chose her, I love her, and I will fight for her. Do you hear me?"

"I do." Krista nodded. "And I won't lie. Not anymore." At his snide chuff, she wilted. "I deserve that, but it's true. And I know you have no reason to believe me, but I am sorry, Jeremy. Really I am."

Jeremy didn't move a muscle.

"It hasn't been easy for me. I'm not trying to let myself off the hook, but I never meant it to go on like this. It took on a life of its own and I didn't know—" Something in his eyes stopped her. She watched him a beat before continuing in a softer, more conciliatory tone. "And Becca's been horrid since you dropped her off. I don't think she heard anything, but all this tension . . . She blew up this afternoon in Target over a toy she wanted. A stupid toy for a baby. She's seven." Krista flopped her hands to her sides. "I feel like we're coming undone."

"Because we are. And of course she's freaking out. She absorbs all this, and how do you think it's going to come out? Over coffee and a scone?"

"I don't need sarcasm, Jeremy. That's not helpful."

"I'm not here to be helpful to you, Krista." He again looked up to the house. "I want to see her."

"She's asleep." Krista raised her chin to meet his eyes. Jeremy watched as something almost vulnerable flashed through her eyes, and she backed up immediately. "Of course, of course you can see her. Go on up."

He didn't ask or comment on the change. He stepped past her, opened the front door, and paused. Krista's parents had never warmed to him, and he wasn't sure he wanted to confront, greet, or chat with them now. What lies had Krista told them? And for his part, he *had* married their daughter within a month of meeting her and had only met them on his one short and tense visit to Park Ridge weeks after Becca was born. Despite everything Krista had done, he hadn't left the best impression either.

Krista gestured inside. "They're not here. Becca exhausted them too. They went to a movie."

Jeremy walked up the stairs. He hadn't been in the house in almost seven years, and even then it was only for that single dinner, with Becca sleeping in a bassinet next to the dining room table.

He paused on the stairs. The walls were lined with pictures. Krista's parents' wedding picture. Family Christmas photos with a young Krista smiling with pigtails . . . with braces . . . with vertical hair-sprayed bangs. Pictures of Krista morphed to pictures of Becca. Jeremy paused to search her face in light of his new understanding. Hints were there, perhaps, in the eyes and in the mouth. But not enough to be sure. She looked very much like Krista. Sure, Becca's hair was darker and she was taller—but Jeremy always appropriated those attributes. Perhaps Krista had a "type," he thought, and he was more like David than he ever wanted to know. He took the final four stairs in two quick strides.

Krista followed him and gestured to a cracked door on his right. He pushed it open and looked around the room, lit by a single night-light and glowing pink. He remembered when Krista posted a three-week Instagram series on the room's transformation right before he moved to Winsome. She'd gotten a bonus at work and wrote that she was using it to make her daughter's room "a sanctuary for creativity and fun." She then posted short videos of painting the room, stenciling the flowers around the windows, and even arranging all the pillows and toys.

"Hey, Bug." Jeremy perched on the edge of Becca's twin bed. She was lying on her back, arms splayed out, buried beneath pillows and her giraffe named Mr. Tall. He shifted the mass of pink and yellow, then brushed Becca's hair from across her face. She didn't move. Only kids sleep with such abandon and trust, he thought. Watching her, he hoped she could and would sleep like that her whole life.

"Ladybug?"

"Daddy?" Her eyelids fluttered. "Why are you here?"

"I was in the neighborhood and thought I'd stop by for one of your super-powered hugs."

Without another word, his daughter popped up and hugged him tight.

"I love you, my Ladybug. I want you to know that."

"Mmm . . . hmm . . ." Becca wiggled, and Jeremy reluctantly let her go. She flopped back into the pillows.

"You sleep now."

She curled onto her side.

He walked out of the room and pulled the door shut save a couple inches. Krista waited for him in the hallway. "Do you want to come downstairs? We can talk some more."

Jeremy shook his head. "Not tonight. What I said when I arrived still stands, Krista. You and I . . ." He motioned two fingers between them. "This is no 'conscious uncoupling,' this is no 'respectful and mutual parenting,' and I won't pretend with you any longer. We'll talk someday, but not now."

"When?" she called after him as he reached the downstairs hallway.

"Someday."

Chapter 40

Alyssa heard the front door open. By the light of the corner street-lamp she saw her mom step onto the porch. Janet paused in the dark, and Alyssa wondered if her mom could see her tucked into the porch swing.

"I'm here," she said.

Janet turned to face her daughter. "I saw your car out back, but you didn't come inside."

"I wasn't ready to come in, and it's nice out here . . . I went to Mirabella."

"How is Lexi?" Janet crossed the porch and perched in the chair next to the swing. Alyssa shrugged away the feeling of loss. It was mingled with regret and tinged with responsibility. She knew, if given the choice, her mom would have sat beside her.

"She was too busy to talk. I didn't want to anyway. I just wanted to be . . ."

"Someplace safe?" Janet interjected.

"Something like that." Alyssa pushed her foot against the porch floorboards and set the swing into motion.

"What happened today? It's more than what you said."

Alyssa looked at her mom.

"It felt personal," she added.

Alyssa stayed silent.

Janet talked on, unfazed. "I blew up at your dad tonight. I called off the wedding."

"You didn't." Alyssa shot straight up.

"I did. Then I went to his apartment and we talked some more and it's back on. But do you know what he said when I called it off?"

Alyssa shook her head again.

"He told me to 'figure it out' and to stop using him as a safety net. Then he asked who'd flipped out on me, you or Grandma. Those were his two choices. All these years . . ." Janet laughed, a short, sad sound. "Part of me is annoyed he never let me in on it before, and part of me is stunned he figured out what I never could. But maybe I was too close to see. And I probably would have attacked him for even suggesting it."

She sat back and Alyssa noted her head tilt up to the porch ceiling.

"I've spent the past five months trying to make amends, ask for forgiveness, and experience all that grace, joy, and good stuff I know exists. You weren't around last February, but I hit rock bottom—which was a new low because I thought I'd hit rock bottom the night your dad left . . . Anyway, as I said, I've spent the past five months imagining a new way to live, but never once did I take a step back to recognize I would, despite my best intentions, keep making mistakes—daily—nor did I examine what ran, like an underground river, beneath certain situations and certain relationships. Currents that needed to change."

Janet leaned forward and dropped her focal point to Alyssa. "They change tonight." She let the sentence settle between them before continuing. "And while I hope you'll stick around and get to know me, and let us change this dynamic between us, you're an adult. You should move to where you want, work where you choose, and know you will always be welcome here. You will always be loved here. You are my daughter, and despite how you have ever felt, I was always on your side. Most of the time I had no idea how to best show you, but that doesn't mean it wasn't true. However . . ."

She paused, and Alyssa felt herself lean forward in anticipation.

"No blaming me for your choices any longer. They are yours. You get to own them. So if you stay, stay. If you leave, run toward something. Don't run away convincing yourself I drove you to it. And if you want to talk, I'll ask you once again . . . What happened today?"

"I can't . . . I can't talk about it."

"Okay, then." Janet stood and stepped toward her. Alyssa detected the notes of jasmine and lily she'd caught in her mom's studio that day. She breathed deeper and felt herself unfurl with the promise of sunlight, hope, and summer—everything Janet's perfume held within it.

Her mom kissed her forehead. "I love you, sweetheart. Good night."

The porch's wooden planks creaked as Janet stepped toward the door. The screen screeched slightly at her pull. Time was running out . . .

"I tried to rationalize it away, convince myself that what XGC did wasn't as bad as, say, what Theranos did, but I was wrong. Maybe it was even worse. And I'm responsible for that. I was part of that. And look at me—a celiac who spent her career working predictive analytics against autoimmunes and didn't catch her own. And I'll be okay. But after what I did, some people will never be. Never."

Janet nodded. "There are more things in heaven and earth, Horatio, than are dreamt of in your philosophy."

"What?" She asked the question softly, wanting an answer more than an argument.

"A little Shakespeare for you . . . You always say numbers tell a story, but it's not a whole story, sweetheart. We're more complex than that. You may not have been a celiac three years ago when you handed in your own lab tests. And in the end, here, maybe you did find what you were looking for all along. You can't see the whole picture or even how scenes, strivings, events, moments, desires . . . They all overlay one another. As for others, I don't know. My heart breaks that anyone was hurt by this, but you can't know their whole stories either. To take that on, to take that blame, is a hubris beyond anything imagined."

Alyssa felt her lips part and pressed them together. "How did I ever think I understood you? I have no idea what you mean there."

"The point is, you do what you can, and the rest, you must now let it go."

"How? I can't make it better. To do what I can is tiny, insignificant. It's too big. And even how I got there . . . You were right. I blamed you and I ran. Then, even after I left and how I left, you supported me. You got practically the whole town to sign up with XGC. I liked that, by the way. I never called and thanked you, but I knew it was you who did that for me. It was promoted all around the company. I was so proud—and look what happened. All those people. Some here in Winsome. I'm responsible for their pain."

Janet crossed back to the swing and sat on the end. Her weight sent it into a slight sway. "That's too much. You must see that."

Alyssa shifted her gaze from her mom. "I don't know how to forgive myself. I don't know how to stop fighting and pushing and kicking. It's all I do, but it's not me. It feels horrible and it's exhausting. I just want to be myself again. My real self again."

The words sat between them. Alyssa didn't even know what they meant so much as what they might feel like if they became true. She also knew where she'd read them. *Sylvester and the Magic Pebble.*

"And who is that?" Her mom leaned over and lifted a strand of hair from across her forehead and tucked it behind her ear.

"Someone who doesn't feel anxious and angry all the time. Someone who doesn't mess up everything she touches. Someone who doesn't pick fights when she doesn't even want to. Someone who can do good things . . . Someone who feels joy. Someone who can stay."

Janet laughed. "Oh, sweetheart, you aren't that first person and you can be and are the second. You've been through a lot, and you don't mess up all the time, and we've both picked plenty of unnecessary fights, but that can change too. And you *do* 'good things,' as you call them. And . . ." Her mom stalled so long Alyssa shifted to see her better. "Give yourself a little grace. That's where you need to start. Recognize you didn't single-handedly create the problems at XGC—that's your hurt pride talking, and I get that—but you need to let it go. Trust the FBI to see it through." Janet shifted closer to her daughter. "Come home and stay. Because despite all the bad, it feels right for you too. There's been good these past weeks."

She offered the words with an upward lilt, as if unsure of their reception.

Alyssa soaked them in.

"It was never the perfect plan because I wanted it; it was the perfect plan because you wanted it. And despite any misgivings, you sure stepped into it. Ask Lexi, Jeremy, or Eve . . . Ask me . . ." Janet tipped back against the swing's wood slats. "And of course you'll still mess up. I certainly learned that tonight. We all do."

Alyssa sputtered out a laugh. "That's supposed to make me feel better?"

"It should." Janet reached an arm around her and pulled her close. "Recognizing that is the most freeing thing in the world."

Alyssa snuggled closer to her mom and felt it.

The fight was over.

Chapter 41

The next morning, Alyssa found her mom making coffee in the kitchen and her grandmother sitting stern and silent at the island.

"What's going on?" She looked between them.

"Grandma came to check on you, and she thinks your father and I are rushing this wedding."

"I didn't say that," Grandma barked.

Janet pressed her lips shut and filled the coffee maker's glass carafe with water.

Alyssa manufactured a laugh to cut the tension. "It's not like they weren't married for almost thirty years, Grandma. I doubt they'll have many surprises."

If she expected that to smooth ruffled feathers or warm the kitchen's interior frost, she was wrong. Her grandmother stared at her, and her mom worked the coffee maker with such focus one might think it brand-new rather than ten years old.

"Why don't you share your thoughts?" Grandma lifted her chin to Alyssa.

Janet's eyes flashed to her, and a torrent of conversations, some years old and some days old, rushed at Alyssa. Calls to Grandma to complain about her mom, heedless as to whether the charges were true; feeding the discord between her mom and grandmother because it kept the focus off her; her comment only weeks ago at her dinner with Grandma that Mom had manipulated Dad again—she always gets her way.

But that was before, Alyssa thought, before she listened. Before she understood. It didn't matter. She had said those very words.

"I was wrong." She placed her hands on the island in front of her and spoke only to her grandmother. "I said I thought Mom was manipulating the situation." She glanced to her mom. "But that was when I had a vested interest in believing that. If I could point the finger at her, I didn't have to look at me."

"Now don't go blaming yourself, dear. That's not what we're talking about here." Grandma reached over and covered Alyssa's hand with her own.

"But we are."

Alyssa slid her hand out from under her grandmother's and walked over to her mom. She hugged her from behind, facing her grandmother over Janet's shoulder. "And I say it's going to be a gorgeous wedding, just what they deserve, and Lexi and I are going to finish planning it."

Janet spun. "It's going to be small and it's all set."

"You've got Pastor Zach coming to the living room and a booth at Mirabella. I don't think so."

Janet stared at her. Her expression tender, eyes glistening. Alyssa nodded. She understood. The currents were changing.

Grandma cut across the moment. "That's all it should be. Anything more would be inappropriate. This is a second wedding, to the same person. We don't celebrate indiscretions."

A shocked "Grandma" and a "Mom" issued simultaneously from Alyssa and Janet.

Alyssa looked at her mom, who stepped away and turned back to her coffee making.

"Grandma, we are celebrating a marriage. And I hope you'll come ready to have a good time, because it's going to be beautiful . . . Excuse me, I've got to go call Lexi."

As she walked out of the room, she heard her grandmother huff. "Fine. Have it your way. You always do."

Alyssa glanced back. Her mom's eyes were fixed on her own. Her face beamed.

Neither replied to Grandma.

ALYSSA WATCHED LEXI POUR champagne into a dozen flute glasses as she crossed Mirabella's dining room. "I'm sorry you're working and not enjoying this."

"Are you kidding me? I'm having a blast." She slid the flutes to Liam one by one. He poured fresh peach puree into each, transforming them into his famous Bellinis. "To see your parents so happy. This is the least I could do."

"We actually pulled it off." Alyssa twisted to look out into the restaurant. She now saw what they'd been too tired to recognize at 3:00 a.m. What they thought veered toward kitschy and simple, homemade and underwhelming, looked beyond lovely—and felt like the first "good thing" Alyssa had done in a very long time.

Mirabella glowed with white linens, tablecloths, small mixed bouquets on each table, and lights, strung between the chandeliers, so tiny they looked like fairies had dropped dust on the festivities. Those had been Jeremy's idea. He'd purchased the lights for Andante but had never strung them. And the storm that had dumped rain all Monday shifted south around sunrise and left them to celebrate under clear blue skies. Bright light shot through the windows, and the stained-glass red borders created a warm ruby cast dancing with the gold across the black-and-white tiled floor.

Alyssa shifted her attention from the scene to her mom. Janet outshone it all. Resplendent in a lavender linen dress, she stood laughing near the buffet table with one arm tucked tightly within Seth's.

Lexi tapped Alyssa's back. "That's Rich Farin over there. He's on the town council. Go talk to him."

"Down, girl." Alyssa spun back to her with a grin. "He already talked to me. He said he opened my application as soon as it hit his in-box yesterday morning. Then he forwarded it to the entire council."

"And?" Lexi pressed.

"My interview, which he called a 'mere formality,' is on Friday. It seems you and Eve hold real sway in this town."

"That was all you; we simply shared the work you did. Jeremy did too." Lexi passed her a glass and lifted one for herself. "Congratulations, Miss Executive Director of the Chamber of Commerce."

"Not yet."

"Fine." Lexi lifted the glass an inch higher. "Then to my best friend who has finally come home." She sipped her champagne to end the toast before Alyssa could protest again. "And to seal the deal, I've got a lead on an apartment for you. A studio just opened in my building."

"I don't need it. Dad is letting me take over his lease."

"That's wonderful, and convenient. That's just a building away from Jeremy." She lifted her chin and gazed over Alyssa's head. "Are you pleased with your new neighbor?"

Alyssa felt Jeremy's touch on her back as he joined her at the bar.

"More than pleased." He leaned closer. "I'm sorry to do this, but I need to get Becca out of here. She's getting super squirmy and I think we're at her end."

Alyssa turned and found Becca looking forlorn and fidgety in a booth. "She's acted like a dream all morning. Take her."

"Thank you." He dropped a kiss on Alyssa's lips. "Meet me at the park later? I thought we'd go home, change, then go run all the energy out of her."

Alyssa checked her watch. "They leave for the airport in a few minutes. After I help clean up, I—"

"The staff, Liam, and I will clean up," Lexi cut in. She then shifted her attention to Jeremy. "She'll be there in twenty."

"Okay then." Alyssa nodded to Lexi, then to Jeremy. "Since I'm on the clock now, I should go check on the happy couple and get them moving."

One last kiss and Jeremy walked one direction while Alyssa headed the opposite.

She caught her mom's eye halfway across the room. Janet's face lit a notch brighter as she stepped away from Seth and met Alyssa in the middle. She pulled her daughter into a hug. "This is the most beautiful gift you could've given us."

"It wasn't just me." Alyssa squeezed her tight.

"I don't mean the reception. I mean forgiving me, staying, being here today, and standing beside me at church this morning. Everything." Janet's gaze drifted to the corner. Alyssa followed and landed on her grandmother, who sat in a booth talking with Jasper, a sour expression on her face. "Especially for your generosity."

"I'm sorry she hasn't been kind. I thought she'd warm up by now. She loves Dad."

"She thinks I've gotten off too easy." Janet glanced to Seth before refocusing on Alyssa. "Maybe I have . . . I'm sure I have."

"You haven't." Alyssa shook her head. "And I'm sorry for my part in that, Mom. All of it."

Chapter 42

Jeremy slid into the leather booth across from his daughter. "What do you say we head to the park?"

He laughed as Becca shot from the booth and dashed across the restaurant. "Come on, Daddy," she called from the other side.

"I'm coming."

Within seconds he was outside standing behind Chris and his brother Luke. Neither noticed his arrival.

"No, I don't want to hear it." Luke had his hand up in his brother's face. "That's not how proposals work. She should be the first, then she can tell me. How can you not know this?"

"Ugh . . . You *are* good at this stuff," Chris replied.

Grasping the topic, Jeremy opted not to interrupt, and instead bent to clasp his daughter's hand and whispered, "Let's go, Bug."

As he opened his car door for Becca, he saw Chris climb into his truck and leave his brother standing on the curb. "Do you need a ride?" he called.

"Thank you, no. I'm walking today. It's only a couple miles, and it's about the only time I get to slow down and savor life. And today deserves a little savoring."

Jeremy watched Father Luke set off down the road. Twenty minutes later, after a quick stop at his apartment to change, he noted Luke still on his walk, now passing the edge of the park.

He raised his hand in a wave and received an answering one as Becca pulled him to the swings.

"Come on, Dad."

Within minutes, he soared. Becca, on the swing next to him, was only a little lower in her arc. She watched his every move and had already become an expert at leaning back on the downswing and pumping her legs hard on the up.

"That's kind of high. Slow down a touch," he called. "And wait until after I land."

Two more pumps with his legs and he soared through the air to land at least twenty feet from the swings. He let his weight and momentum roll him into the wood chips. "It's a new record."

Becca leaned forward as her swing came through its final arc. He could see the concentration on his daughter's face and wondered if, perhaps, this wasn't their best game. Too late now, he thought, as she flew through the air.

He stood in her path and caught her as she reached the ground. The two of them crashed together with Becca resting safely on top of him. She was roaring with laughter.

Her joy inspired his. He scooped her up and swung her around in a circle. Becca's legs flew behind her, making them laugh even more.

"Again?" she called as soon as her feet touched the ground.

"Can't. I'm too dizzy. We gotta take a break, Bug." Jeremy stretched his back. "Besides, Alyssa's here. Monkey bars?"

Her reply was to race to the monkey bars, waving to Alyssa on her way.

"I'd say you're getting all the energy out."

"Trying to." He covered the distance between them in three

long, slightly skewed strides. Then he wrapped his arms around her and pulled her close. As he bent to kiss her, he wondered if he'd ever tire of these first moments, seeing her with the anticipation of talking to her, kissing her, being with her.

Just as Alyssa lifted on her toes, an incongruence caught his attention. He straightened and looked toward town.

She dropped back to her heels. "Jeremy?"

He looked down at her. "Sorry. I thought I just saw Krista standing over there. That woman walking away."

Alyssa turned. "Are you sure?"

"No, but . . ." He gave a slight shrug. "Doesn't matter. Where were we?"

Becca perched by Andante's front door. Just behind, actually. She didn't want to greet people. She wanted to count them.

Her dad, standing next to Ryan, clapped his hands from the counter area. That was the signal. She darted away from the door, skirted around the adults milling about, and tucked close to her dad. He laid a hand on her shoulder. She lifted her chin and stretched taller. This was a big night.

"Thank you all for coming to our first Literature and Lattes book club event." His voice rose above the din and everyone quieted. Two ladies near the fireplace didn't, and Becca felt her mouth purse like Mrs. Gutierrez when she would "tsk" the boys at the back table during reading.

But maybe her dad didn't hear. He kept talking. "We will pass around another round of cookies and coffees, and if you'd like tea, please come let us know. We'll begin in about five minutes."

Becca pulled at his arm and waited until he bent close. "There are forty-four people here."

"No way." His eyes lit, and Becca thought her chest was going to swell right out of her rib cage. Her dad gripped her shoulder the way he did to Ryan when he was saying something super important.

She straightened. "I filled the cookie tray again. Will you pass it around? Be sure to put more napkins on the edge."

Becca ran behind the counter and disappeared into the kitchen.

"She's excited." Behind Jeremy, Alyssa settled a last white china mug of coffee onto another tray and lifted it.

"I'm glad one of us is. I might throw up."

Alyssa set the tray down and reached for his hand across the counter. "Why? This is a far better turnout than we expected."

"That's why. It's like tasting the best coffee in the world, then discovering an embargo on the beans. This is it—what I've been after before I even knew what it looked like. But it'll be gone in a month. So unless the community comes out and drinks coffee by the gallon and cookies by the dozen, I'm sunk. One night can't change that." He looked at her, really looked at her, and realized she was biting her lip against a smile. "Are you laughing right now?"

"Yes." She gestured past him. "What do you think is happening here? This *is* coffee by the gallon and cookies by the dozen. And what's more 'community,' and enduring, than a good book club? Look around, Jeremy."

He took a deep breath. It rattled every nerve on its way past his lungs to his stomach. But the exhale, as he swept the shop, came out slow and smoothed his frayed edges. "Thank you."

"You're welcome." She squeezed his hand again. "And you are trending in the right direction. Only one more day in July, but the numbers are looking good. Really good."

"Are you just saying that to make me feel better?"

"Numbers don't lie," she quipped as she leaned across the counter and kissed his cheek. Then she picked up the coffee tray and wove her way through the tables.

Jeremy leaned against the counter. Alyssa was right. This was what community looked like. He noted David Drummond; George Williams and his son Devon; Madeline, Claire, *and* Janet—who'd only landed from Italy that afternoon; Seth, standing over near Mike and a few other men from their group; Jill Pennet, who had supplied all the cookies free of charge for tonight; Eve Parker and Olive—whatever her last name was—and more.

"You ready?" He turned to Ryan, who was striding past him and had been working like a whirling dervish since six that morning.

Ryan stopped as if yanked by a rope. "You should lead. There are a lot of people here, far more than we thought. And it's your shop."

"No." Jeremy suppressed a chuckle. Ryan was more nervous than he was—and somehow he found that calming. He put a firm hand on Ryan's shoulder. "You've got this. This is your book, always has been. We'll take turns leading in the future, or maybe we'll bring in guest authors." Jeremy felt his eyes widen. He wasn't used to such positive thinking and hadn't even realized he'd dreamed up plans, with the full expectation that Andante would be open to see them through. He shook his head to bring himself and his expectations back to reality. "We have no idea about tomorrow, but tonight, you got this."

Ryan nodded and nodded and nodded until Jeremy squeezed his shoulder tighter. "Breathe and go."

Ryan circled the counter, concentrating on his steps. *No idea about tomorrow.* Jeremy's statement struck deep. It used to bother him, that not knowing, and it had led him to some pretty dark places. Then he'd found understanding. He'd found Jeremy, who believed in him; he found work he loved; and just when he needed it, he found Winsome. He'd never told Jeremy that. The first day he'd plopped on that ugly brown couch in the coffee shop's corner, it hadn't been the shop that was perfect; it was the town. He had begun to feel untethered in Seattle; it was too big, moved too fast. But Winsome? Just like Steinbeck wrote, it was "fambly."

He stopped in front of the ordering counter and raised his hand to silence the shop. "Hi, everyone, I'm Ryan. I work here with Jeremy, and I'll lead the discussion tonight as we've chosen my favorite book. I know some themes within it . . ."

Alyssa stood at the back of the room, the empty tray dangling from her hand. Her mom, after offering her chair to an older woman, came to stand beside her.

Alyssa gestured to Ryan. "He's killing it. I had no idea Ryan could be so engaging."

"About books," Janet whispered, eyes still trained on Ryan. "He comes into the shop constantly to chat with us. He is an incredibly well-read young man; English literature major, I gather."

Alyssa turned to her in surprise.

"He'd be a good teacher," Janet offered.

"I don't doubt it." Alyssa returned her focus to Ryan, who was now giving a brief synopsis of Steinbeck's major themes within *Of Mice and Men*. Friendship . . . Isolation . . . Justice . . . Community . . . She tilted her head toward her mom. "Just don't suggest it yet."

Janet stifled a quiet laugh. "I'll wait until Jeremy's got this place humming before I meddle . . . Speaking of meddling, your dad and I want to celebrate your new job with dinner. When can you come to the house?"

"Name the night and I'll be there. Just not next Tuesday. I have my first Chamber of Commerce meeting that night. You should be there."

Janet shook her head. "That's Claire's and Madeline's job. I'm just a salesperson and the resident artist."

"Speaking of which, I've worked out the details with Jeremy. We're thinking the first two weeks in October for your show here."

"What?" Janet's voice arced high and a few heads turned. Ryan glanced their way.

Alyssa mouthed a quick "Sorry" before facing her mom again. Janet's face revealed more surprise than displeasure, and that was all Alyssa needed to see. "We'll talk about it later; it's going to be wonderful." She wagged a finger out into the room. "I need to refill coffees. I see empty cups."

Alyssa pushed off the wall and circled the crowd to collect abandoned mugs. As she approached the counter to gather empties resting there, she noted someone standing outside peeking in at the front window's edge. Alyssa gestured for her to come inside but was rebuffed with a head shake and a wave. Just passing by, Alyssa assumed, as she carried the cups toward the kitchen.

Krista watched the blonde walk around the side counter to the back of the shop. She recognized her from the park a couple weeks earlier. She had been coming across from the far end as Krista turned away from watching Becca and Jeremy on the swings. Krista hadn't been spying; she'd been curious. Jeremy's vehemence about staying in Becca's life had shifted something in her. Love like that was alluring, and even though it hadn't been directed toward her, it had left her restless and resolute. Restless enough to check out Winsome and resolute enough to go to headquarters and ask for the social media job she wanted.

The blonde paused at Jeremy, who stood near the kitchen door, and whispered something in his ear. Whatever it was made him laugh. His eyes widened before curving into those half-moons she remembered whenever he chuckled. Then he kissed the woman, quick and sure. If the kiss didn't shock the blonde, it shocked Krista.

She stepped back from the glass and turned toward the front door. She stalled. The book group was in full swing with Ryan fielding questions. Everyone was engaged. Everyone was paying attention. Everyone would turn to the door the minute she approached.

Perhaps now wasn't the best time to tell Jeremy she wasn't moving after all.

Don't miss these other stories from Katherine Reay!

"Katherine Reay is a remarkable author who has created her own sub-genre, wrapping classic fiction around contemporary stories. Her writing is flawless and smooth, her storytelling meaningful and poignant."

—Debbie Macomber, #1 *New York Times* bestselling author

Thomas Nelson
Since 1798

Available in print, e-book, and audio!

An Excerpt from *Dear Mr. Knightley*

April 2

Dear Sir,

It has been a year since I turned down your generous offer. Father John warned me at the time that I was making a terrible mistake, but I wouldn't listen. He felt that by dismissing that opportunity I was injuring not only myself, but all the foster children helped by your foundation.

I hope any perceived ingratitude on my part didn't harm anyone else's dreams. I wasn't ungrateful; I just wanted to leave Grace House. A group home is a difficult place to live, and I'd been there for eight years. And even though I knew graduate school meant more education and better job prospects, it also meant living at Grace House another two years. At the time I couldn't face that prospect.

My heart has always been in my books and writing, but I couldn't risk losing a paying job to pursue a dream. Now I'm ready to try. Not because I failed, but because this degree gives me the chance to link my passion with my livelihood.

Please let me know if the grant is still available. I will understand if you have selected another candidate.

Sincerely,
Samantha Moore

April 7

Dear Ms. Moore,

The grant for full tuition to the master's program at Northwestern University's Medill School of Journalism remains available. At the strong recommendation of Father John, and due to the confidence he has in you, the director of the Dover Foundation has agreed to give you this second chance. There is, however, one stipulation. The director wants to receive personal progress letters from you as reassurance that this decision was the right one. You may write to him as you would to a journal, letting him know how your studies are going. He has opened a post office box for this purpose so you won't feel the added pressure of an immediate connection to him or to the foundation. Additionally, he will not write back, but asks that you write to him regularly about "things that matter."

He recognizes that this is an unusual requirement, but the foundation needs to know that its resources are being used in the best way possible. Given your sudden change of heart, he feels it is not too much to ask. To make this easier for you, he will also remain anonymous. You may write to him at this address under the name George Knightley.

Sincerely,
Laura Temper
Personal Assistant to Mr. G. Knightley

April 12

Dear Mr. Knightley,

Thank you so much for giving me this opportunity. I submitted my application to Medill this morning. I had to use a couple papers on Dickens and Austen in place of the journalism samples requested. While that may count against me, I felt the rest of my application was strong.

If you will allow, I want to honor Father John's trust and yours by explaining my "sudden change of heart," as Ms. Temper described it. When I graduated college last spring, I had two opportunities: your grant to fund graduate school or a job at Ernst & Young. In my eagerness to leave Grace House and conquer the world, I chose the job. Six weeks ago I was fired. At the exit meeting my boss claimed I was "unengaged," especially with regard to peer and client interactions. I did good work there, Mr. Knightley. Good solid work. But "relating" in the workplace is important too, I gather. That's where I failed.

I'm guessing from your literary choice of pseudonym that you are very likely acquainted with another admirable character from fiction—Elizabeth Bennet, Jane Austen's complex and enchanting heroine. At Ernst & Young I tried to project Lizzy's boldness and spirit, but clearly she had a confidence and charm that was more than I could sustain on a daily basis. So now here I am, back at Grace House, taking advantage of the state's willingness to provide a home for me till I'm twenty-five if I stay in school.

Nevertheless, Father John still doubts me and couldn't resist a lecture this morning. I tried to listen, but my eyes wandered around his office: photographs of all the children who have passed through Grace House cover every space that isn't taken up with books. He loves murder mysteries: Agatha Christie, James Patterson, Alex

Powell, P. D. James, Patricia Cornwell . . . I've read most of them. The first day we met, right before I turned fifteen, he challenged me to stretch beyond the classics.

"Are you listening, Sam?" Father John finally noticed my wandering eyes. "The Medill program is straight up your alley. You're a great reader and writer."

"'I deserve neither such praise nor such censure. I am not a great reader, and I have pleasure in many things.'" Elizabeth Bennet has a useful reply for every situation.

Father John gave a small smile, and I flinched. "What if I can't do this?" I asked. "Maybe it's a mistake."

He sat back in his chair and took a slow breath. Eyebrows down, mouth in a line.

"Then turn this down—again—and find another job. Pound the pavement quickly, though. I can give you a couple weeks here to get on your feet, then my hands are tied." He leaned forward. "Sam, I'll always help you. But after this, if you're not in school, Grace House is closed to you. This foundation helps a lot of kids here, and I won't jeopardize that support because you can't commit. So decide right now."

A tear rolled down my cheek. Father John never gets charged up, but I deserved it. I should only be grateful to you both, and here I was questioning your help. But help is hard, Mr. Knightley—even when I desperately need it. Every foster placement of my childhood was intended to help me; every new social worker tried to help my case; when I was sent back home at twelve, the judge meant to help my life too . . . I'm so tired of help.

"I'm sorry, Father John, you're right. I want this grant and I asked for it again. I must seem so ungrateful to you, to be questioning again."

"You don't, Sam, and I can understand wanting to stand alone.

Even in the best of times and circumstances, it's hard to accept help—"

In the end, Father John believed my commitment. I hope you do too. Here is our agreement: you will pay for graduate school, and I will write you letters that give an honest accounting of my life and school—and you will never write back. That simple, right?

Thank you for that, Mr. Knightley—your anonymity. Honesty is easier when you have no face and no real name. And honesty, for me, is very easy on paper.

I also want to assure you that while I may not relate well to people in the real world, I shine in school. It's paper-based. I will do your grant justice, Mr. Knightley. I'll shine at Medill.

I know I've said more than was necessary in this letter, but I need you to know who I am. We need to have an honest beginning, even if it's less impressive than Lizzy Bennet's.

Sincerely,
Samantha Moore

April 21

Dear Mr. Knightley,

Each and every moment things change. For the most part, I loathe it. Change never works in my favor—as evidenced by so many foster placements, a holdup at a Chicago White Hen, getting fired from Ernst & Young, and so many other changes in my life I'd like to forget. But I needed one more—a change of my own making—so I pursued your grant again.

But it's not of my own making, is it?

Father John told me this morning that he was the one who proposed journalism for me—it was not an original requirement for your grant. I wouldn't have chosen it myself. My professor at Roosevelt College said I produced some of the best work on Austen, Dickens, and the Brontes he'd ever read. I'm *good* at fiction, Mr. Knightley. And I don't think it's right that Father John took away my choice. I'm twenty-three years old; I should be the author of the changes in my life.

I went to Father John and explained all this. I feel he has arbitrarily forced me into journalism—a field I don't know and don't write. "You need to undo that," I pleaded. "They'll listen to you."

Father John closed his eyes. One might think he'd fallen asleep, but I knew better. He was praying. He does that—a lot.

Minutes passed. He opened his eyes and zeroed in on me. Sometimes I feel his eyes are tired, but not at that moment. They were piercing and direct. I knew his answer before he opened his mouth.

"Sam, I won't . . . but you can. Write the foundation's director and ask." Father John stared into my eyes, measuring his words. "Don't lie. Don't tell them I've changed my mind. I have not. I am wholly against a change in program."

"How can you say that?" My own shrill voice surprised me.

"I've known you for eight years, Sam. I've watched you grow, I've watched you succeed, and I've watched you retreat. I want the best for you, and with every fiber of my being, I am convinced that 'the best' is not more fiction, but finding your way around in the real world and its people."

I opened my mouth to protest, but he held up his hand. "Consider carefully. If the foundation is unwilling to alter your grant, you may accept or you may walk away. You always have a choice."

"That's not fair."

Father John's eyes clouded. "My dear, what in your life has ever come close to fair? That's not how this life works." He leaned forward and stretched his hands out across the desk. "I'm sorry, Sam. If I could protect you from any more pain, I would. But I can only pray and do the very best God calls me to do. If I'm wrong about this, I hope that someday you will forgive me."

"'My temper would perhaps be called resentful.—My good opinion once lost is lost forever.'" When Elizabeth Bennet doesn't come through, one can always count on Mr. Darcy to provide the right response. I shook my head and, quoting no one, said, "I won't forgive you, Father John. I don't forgive." And I walked out.

I don't care if that was ungenerous, Mr. Knightley. He overstepped, and he's wrong. So now I'm asking you: Will you let me decide?

Sincerely,
Samantha Moore

The story continues in *Dear Mr. Knightley*
by Katherine Reay.

Acknowledgments

I had so much fun with this story. I have never returned to a town before, but after inventing Winsome in *The Printed Letter Bookshop*, I was eager to return and meet old friends again. And while many of these thanks I will deliver in person, it's also important to note them here.

Elizabeth, I'm forever grateful for your insight into this story. Your suggestions and encouragement helped push me when I wasn't sure which way to go. Thank you to Mason, Matthew, Elizabeth, and Mary Margaret—you are beyond gracious and incredibly generous! And Coffee Man, you keep me going! Thank you!

Endless gratitude goes to my agent, Claudia Cross, and to Amanda Bostic, Jocelyn Bailey, LB Norton, and Jodi Hughes for . . . well, everything; Kristen Andrews and HCCP's design team; Paul Fisher, Kerri Potts, Matt Bray, Marcee Wardell, and Margaret Kercher for all your marketing support; and the sales team for championing my stories.

Last, but never least . . . Thank *you*. Thank you to the readers, bloggers, reviewers, and now friends who generously read my stories, trust me with their hearts and time, and share me with their friends! Thank you for joining me here and reaching out to me on social media.

Discussion Questions

1. Alyssa's friend Lexi states, "Things are only as small as you make them." Would you agree? Would the converse be true too, that things are only as large as you make them?
2. Alyssa talks about "confirmation bias," seeing what she expects to see regardless of an objective reality. Do you believe she is right, that we can perceive situations and people as we want to see them rather than how they are?
3. The author stresses the concept of "home" throughout *Of Literature and Lattes.* What are different meanings of "home" each character seeks? How do you define "home?"
4. Perspective is an important theme in *Of Literature and Lattes.* How does Alyssa's perspective change? Janet's? Jeremy's? Krista's? How much does each misjudge in the beginning? How clearly does each see things in the end?
5. Early in the story, Alyssa states—and later Jeremy thinks the same thought—that people can't change. Do you agree or disagree? Do you feel if either Alyssa or Jeremy were asked at the end of the story, they would change their answers?
6. *Of Mice and Men* plays a crucial role in Jeremy's journey. What are some of your thoughts on Steinbeck's themes in the novel

of loneliness, community, marginalization, and connection with *Of Literature and Lattes*?

7. Lexi states, "People are far more complex than the boxes we put them in." Comment on the boxes Alyssa puts Janet in and Jeremy puts Ryan in. How did their perceptions blind them?
8. Early in the novel, Alyssa comments that mother and daughter relationships are complex. She then admits after her time in the hospital that Janet was the only one she wanted near. Did her feelings toward her mom change, or was she more aware of what was always there?
9. How complex or simple are mother-daughter relationships?
10. Janet declares to Jeremy that "Reading is therapy." Would you consider that true? What novels have been therapeutic for you?
11. What made Ryan return to Andante?
12. Why did Alyssa go to the Sweet Shoppe, despite being told by the FBI not to contact Jill? Could you stay away?
13. Would you like to visit Winsome again?

About the Author

Katherine Reay is a national bestselling and award-winning author who has enjoyed a lifelong affair with books. She publishes both fiction and nonfiction, and her writing can also be found in magazines and blogs. Katherine holds a BA and MS from Northwestern University. She currently writes full-time and lives outside Chicago, Illinois, with her husband and three children.

KatherineReay.com
Instagram: katherinereay
Facebook: katherinereaybooks
Twitter: @Katherine_Reay